"Something the matter, Lily?" Sean asked.

"Oh, no," she replied. "I'm just surprised, that's all." Head cocked to the side, she studied him.

"Surprised? About what?"

"I'm surprised you're here." Her mouth curved upward.

"I warned you I'd be joining you."

Throwing caution to the wind, he let his eyes roam slowly over her, lingering. She'd have to be blind not to see the hunger in them.

Which she clearly wasn't. She retreated a step. He followed, his longer legs closing the distance, until his body almost brushed hers.

Lily's cool composure was unraveling, no matter how hard she tried to pretend otherwise. The signs were all there, in the fine trembling of her limbs, in the flush that stole over her porcelain smooth cheeks. Fierce satisfaction filled Sean at her involuntary reaction.

He dipped his head until his lips hovered, a soft whisper away. . . .

NIGHT SWIMMING

LAURA MOORE

IVY BOOKS • NEW YORK

An Ivy Book
Published by The Random House Ballantine Publishing Group
Copyright © 2003 by Amey B. Larmore

www.ballantinebooks.com

ISBN 0-8041-2004-8

Manufactured in the United States of America

First Edition: May 2003

OPM   10   9   8   7   6   5   4   3   2   1

For N. and J.
With All My Love

ACKNOWLEDGMENTS

I owe heartfelt thanks to Joanne Delaney, Research Interpreter, Florida Keys National Marine Sanctuary, and to Mike Johnson, Fisheries Biologist, National Marine Fisheries Services. Joanne allowed me to question her about coral reef habitats for hours on end, providing me with clear and articulate answers, all given with endless patience and good humor. Coral Beach is a fictitious town, but Mike Johnson offered invaluable suggestions about locations along Florida's Atlantic coast where I might create a coral world.

For those who know and love the magic of the sea, Joanne Delaney and Mike Johnson are your true champions. Any errors and oversights about this fascinating realm are mine.

I would also like to thank Rebecca Abrams and Nathan Benn for their many useful pointers regarding photography and photo processing.

Greek mythology has three graces. I'm blessed with four. Four wonderful women: Joanie, Denise, Susie, and Jennifer, who, through their unwavering support and encouragement, have taught me much about friendship.

PROLOGUE

"Quit it!" Lily hissed, jerking backward.

"No! You quit it! *I'm* leading. You're the girl, you're supposed to follow." *Ha, what a joke,* thought Sean. Lily Banyon wasn't a girl, she was an alien—a pale, blond-haired, freaky-eyed alien monster.

Lily glared down at him. Her light blue eyes glittered with contempt. "This is so dumb. Why should you get to lead just because you're a boy? You don't know anything. You're doing it all wrong . . . as usual."

Lily was, without a doubt, the biggest pain that ever lived. Arriving on this planet within weeks of his own birth (her mother claimed Lily'd been born in a hospital, like most kids, but Sean would never fall for that one), all she did, day in and day out, was contradict and correct him, Big Miss Know-It-All. *Like now,* he thought, telling him he didn't know how to lead her in the stupid fox-trot. Sean lifted his head to glare back at her, and got a prime view of her snot-filled, snooty nose. *Gross me out.*

She was still trying to lead. Sean jerked hard, hoping he could throw her off balance, have her land on her butt in front of everyone. Even though that was like thinking you could fell a giant sequoia simply by tugging on its branches. He felt a surge of triumph as her feet stumbled forward in his direction, finally following his.

Victory was fleeting. Lily stopped cold, her abrupt halt causing his feet to tangle with hers. Their bodies smacked, and then ricocheted.

Jeesh! Holding her hand was bad enough—even with the protective layer of Lily's white cotton gloves. Sean didn't want to touch any more of her than that. He lurched backward, tripping over her monster-size feet in his hurried recoil.

"Ow!" Lily's squeal made his ears ring. "You stepped on me! Oh, wait! Let me guess. This is one of your new moves! Though if you think this is dancing, you're stupider than I thought." She curled her lip, flashing metal. "But that's probably not possible."

Lily actually believed she'd invented sarcasm. "Just shut up and dance," Sean hissed, tugging on her hands once more, willing the dumb song to end so that he could go back to his seat on the opposite side of the school gym—as far away from Lily Banyon as possible.

"No, *you* shut up."

God, Lily hated him, the little runt. Why did Deadly Dudley, the dance teacher, always stick Sean McDermott with her? Why should she have to dance with a twerp who was more than a foot shorter than she was? So what if he was the tallest of the sixth-grade boys? If she was going to have to dance with a midget, at least give her a less obnoxious one. Anybody. She *hated* Sean McDermott. Hated him. Loathed, detested, *abhorred*—Lily had looked that last one up in the dictionary, needing a richer vocabulary for the list of grievances that grew each time she saw him, which was practically always, thanks to their mothers.

Her mom and his were best friends. They did everything together—shopped, gossiped—everything. The friendship stretched way back to when they were kids, actually further than that, all the way back to their grandmothers. The older ladies still talked on the phone every morning and were the best bridge players in Coral Beach, trouncing other grannies on a weekly basis. Their mothers and grandmothers took it for granted that Lily and Sean would get along like peanut butter and jelly.

Grown-ups were so lame.

Lily could feel their eyes on them, Sean's mom's and her own mom's. Typical of their totally clueless state, they'd volunteered as chaperons for these lousy social dancing lessons. Lily didn't need to glance over to know they were watching her and Sean's "progress" on the floor, nudging each other with their tanned elbows and giggling behind cupped hands over how cute Sean looked (with Mrs. McDermott loyally adding that Lily looked quite nice, too, which her mother would ignore as a polite but blatant untruth) and wasn't this a good idea to insist their kids take dancing lessons, such an invaluable tool for later on in life. Cripes.

Hadn't they figured out yet that she and Sean couldn't stand each other? Had hated each other forever? Lily wouldn't be surprised if they'd exchanged squinty-eyed glares from their strollers.

And here she was, dancing with the enemy. Lily scowled, noting how Sean's dark hair was brushed neatly, perfectly, his part straight as an arrow. Even his curls were neat. She knew that when people looked at them together, they shook their heads in pity. Next to cute, perfect Sean McDermott, Lily resembled an ugly stork. Unlike ducklings, storks stayed ugly. The angry frustration, which seemed permanently lodged at the core of Lily's being, welled, rising to the surface.

If Sean stomped on her foot one more time, she'd make him really sorry.

Pushed up against the walls of the gymnasium, where the social dancing lessons took place Tuesdays and Thursdays for eight consecutive weeks, was a single line of gun gray, metallic folding chairs. Everyone who wasn't out on the gym floor was supposed to be sitting properly, knees together, back straight, the girls' white cotton–gloved hands folded primly in their laps.

That's what they were supposed to be doing, but this year's batch of sixth graders was the unruliest yet. Such was the considered opinion of the dancing teacher, Miss Clarissa Dudley, who'd been teaching Coral Beach's youngsters the ins and outs of the box-step for the past twenty-five years. Today's class wasn't even half over, and, already, Clarissa longed to be back home in her pink, air-conditioned cottage with the bedroom's lights dimmed, a cool cloth placed over her throbbing temples.

An outraged scream erupted, shattering the strains of Frank Sinatra's "Red Roses for a Blue Lady." Clarissa's permed head swiveled back and forth along the line of folding chairs, searching out the offender. The guilty party, however, wasn't to be found in the seated group, squirming with boredom though it was. The disruption came from the far end of the dance floor.

Dear Heaven! It was Lily Banyon and Sean McDermott, practically duking it out.

Her pumps clacked urgently as she scurried across the

heavily shellacked floor. But Clarissa Dudley's legs were made to cha-cha, not to run the twenty-yard dash. By the time she reached them, Sean's and Lily's mothers were already separating the two brawlers.

"Lily, Lily, would you please stop making a spectacle of yourself!" Her mother's voice echoed shrilly. "Why can't you ever behave like a young lady? And for Pete's sake, put your shoulders back. You're all hunched over!"

At Kaye Harrison's words, the gym fell as silent as a tomb. Even Frank Sinatra stopped his warbling. All of Coral Beach's sixth grade stared, riveted with morbid fascination while Lily's mother continued scolding her daughter.

Everyone except Sean. He dropped his head, suddenly engrossed in studying the faint scuff marks on his brown suede Hush Puppies. He didn't want to gawk as Lily's face went beet red with humiliation. He didn't want to see her lips quiver or her shoulders shake with suppressed tears.

Kaye Harrison's blistering tirade continued, echoing throughout the gym, and Sean's guts twisted in shame. It was one thing for him to detest Lily, quite another to witness her own mother lashing out at her—in public, too. It was moments such as this, when Kaye let fly her painful barbs, that Sean felt almost sorry for Lily. Perhaps, just perhaps, she didn't deserve everything she got.

It was a mystery why Kaye constantly harped at Lily. Perhaps Kaye couldn't help herself, sort of like picking at a mosquito bite until it oozed blood. Most of the time, Sean liked Kaye. Who, besides Lily, wouldn't? Kaye was a fairy princess, *I Dream of Jeannie,* and Miss America all rolled into one. Kaye was sunshine and smiles—until her eyes lit on Lily.

Things would be much easier if everyone—Kaye especially—accepted the simple truth: Lily was an alien. It wasn't fair to blame her for something she couldn't help, a cosmic goof-up. If Sean realized that, so should her mom. Yet Kaye acted as though it was entirely Lily's fault that she wasn't pretty and cute, like her.

Fat chance of that. Forget graceful, too. Sean knew from personal experience that Lily didn't have a coordinated bone in her body. Dancing with her was like dancing with a deranged and very angry polar bear.

Though it killed Sean to admit it, what Lily did have was brains. Not that brainpower did her any good at home. Kaye Harrison went ballistic each time she got a whiff of one of Lily's science experiments wafting up from the basement. Never once had Sean heard Kaye brag about the straight A's her daughter pulled off; she seemed to think it no big deal that Lily had been placed in accelerated math, and was currently whizzing through freshman algebra.

But it was a big deal. Lily was so smart, there were times when Sean wondered if his own brain were made of lead. But that thought, along with any trace of empathy for Lily's unhappy home life, vanished in a blinding flash of pain.

Wrenching free of her mother's restraining grip, Lily had landed a swift, wickedly hard kick to his shinbone.

While Kaye shrieked, Sean clutched his throbbing shin, hopping like a drunken cricket. Lily's face bobbed before him. It was lit by a smile of fierce satisfaction. Teeth gritted, Sean vowed that someday, someday soon, he'd get even with Lily Banyon.

CHAPTER ONE

It was a long hallway. Sean's secretary caught him at the top of the marble steps, in front of the town hall's double doors. Evelyn Roemer was firmly convinced Sean's responsibilities were far too pressing to wait until he was seated behind his desk. She walked abreast of him, talking a mile a minute as they passed the Florida and U.S. flags, the framed photographs of previous mayors, and old, oversized and slightly yellowed maps detailing Coral Beach and the surrounding county.

"I printed out your upcoming schedule, Sean. You've got two meetings this morning. The first is with the reps from the waste management union. The sanitation workers' contract is up for negotiation. I highlighted in yellow the major trouble spots in your copy of the contract. Your next appointment's at ten, with Chief Reynolds and the CPCB, the Concerned Parents of Coral Beach. The parent organization wants the police department to explore new safety initiatives for next spring's senior prom. Roadblocks, compulsory handing over of car keys, etc. The folder's label is highlighted in blue—just think blue for police. That'll bring you to eleven A.M., just enough time to get to the airport for your flight to

Atlanta. Your speech is in a folder on your desk. The label's highlighted in . . . ," Evelyn paused.

"Orange?" Sean hazarded a guess. Evelyn's color theories were something of a mystery.

His secretary shook her head. "No, pink," she corrected. "I got a new batch of pink highlighters yesterday. The old ones just weren't doing the job."

Evelyn Roemer had a real thing for highlighting. A few might even call it an obsession. Whatever it was, though, it was difficult to ignore. Someone, at some point, started a rumor that Evelyn had invested heavily in whatever company manufactured those thick, fluorescent markers. As rumors went, this one was just plausible enough to be accepted as Gospel.

As she walked, Evelyn's index finger, its nail lacquered a bright fuchsia, tapped loudly against the sheet of paper. "Where was I?" she muttered under her breath. "Oh, right." And lungs replenished, she dove back into her rapid-fire monologue. "You come back from the mayors' convention in Atlanta on the first flight Thursday, which should get you back in the office by ten. The press will be ready and waiting. Then, at eleven-thirty, there's a brown-bag lunch with the Department of Transportation. Should be a long one. Matt Jacobs wants to go over anticipated traffic reroutes due to upcoming construction. How the town will handle the extra traffic once the season starts is beyond me, but that's your headache. The fun really begins at two-thirty. The high school's holding a school-wide forum on civics this month. You, Sean, you lucky thing," she chirruped brightly, "are delivering the keynote speech. You're to speak for twenty minutes on what made you decide to dedicate yourself to public service. Questions and answers to follow—"

Here Evelyn was forced to pause once more. This time because the two of them had reached the door to the office suite they shared. Of solid oak, the door had "Mayor Sean C. McDermott" neatly stenciled in gold paint on its panel. Sean turned its brass knob, then held it open so Evelyn could precede him. He grinned down at her. "And good morning to you, Evelyn. That's an extremely becoming shade of yellow."

In fashion as well as highlighters, Sean's secretary went for eye-popping. Although she often favored electric blue to offset hair dyed somewhere between a vivid scarlet and a delicate rose, today her couture color of choice was lemon yellow: tight yellow pants stretched over her pencil-stick legs, her shirt a matching hue, emblazoned with larger than life daisies.

"Thank you, Sean," she replied, smoothing the vibrant daisies over her hips. "Now, tell the truth, did you hear a word I just said?"

" 'Course not," Sean replied amiably. "You know politicians can't multitask. Let me sit down, then I'll give you my undivided attention." Sean followed Evelyn through her own office to the adjacent, slightly larger one, shrugging out of his jacket as he walked. He draped it over the back of his leather office chair, unbuttoned the top button of his shirt, and gave the knot on his tie a hard yank, feeling immensely better when it gave.

"All set now? Oxygen flowing properly? Oh, silly me, of course not, you haven't had your morning shot. Coming right up," Evelyn said, already moving toward Sean's cherished espresso machine.

"Could you make it a double, Evelyn? Who knows when I'll get a fix as good as yours over the next two days?"

"Flattery will get you reelected," Evelyn quipped.

From day one of Sean's term as mayor, they had established a standard routine in which he played the role of the bumbling politician, she the impatient secretary. It made for a casual mood in the office—something both of them appreciated when the phones were ringing off their hooks and the fax machines churning out reams of paper, irate citizens demanding that Sean right whatever recent outrage had befallen them.

"Here you go," she said, as she set a small, white porcelain cup in front of him. "Double shot for you, green tea for me." Evelyn had recently gone on an antitoxin kick. *Probably decided to restrict substance abuse to her hair only,* Sean thought, lifting his cup to hide his grin.

Evelyn sat down in the chair facing Sean's desk. She took a sip of tea, grimaced, and set it aside.

"Ready?" she asked, as she picked up her notepad and pen.

"Mmm, yes." Quickly, he downed half the espresso in his cup. "Absolutely. Please, Evelyn, don't keep me waiting; the suspense is more than I can bear. What thrills await me after I extol the virtues of public duty with this year's teenagers?"

"Who, if you bore them to tears for too long, will get their revenge by voting you out of office at the next election."

Sean grinned, remembering how deadly some of the "special" speakers had been back in high school. "I promise I won't go a second over the allotted time."

"Good, because after that, you've got the coral reef advisory committee."

"What?" he asked in astonishment.

Evelyn pretended to consult her notepad. "Four P.M.: coral reef advisory committee," she informed him with a wide, pink lipsticked smile.

"You mean Dave found a scientist willing to take over for Lesnesky?" Dave Cullen was the commissioner of Coral Beach's Department of Parks and Recreation and Sean's closest friend in and out of town hall. "When did this happen?"

"Late yesterday afternoon."

"That's fantastic," he said. "I was beginning to lose hope. Who'd he find? Someone from around here?"

Evelyn shook her head. "It's not a local team—no one was interested in taking on a project that was so close to completion." She made a moue of disgust. "Dave had to telephone his way up the East Coast until he finally wrangled a *yes*. Took him several hundred miles . . ."

Sean's eyebrows rose. "That far, huh? So who was willing to come to Coral Beach's rescue?" He reached for his cup of espresso, bringing it to his lips.

"The Marine Center in Massachusetts."

Sean replaced the cup, espresso untouched. "Did you say the Marine Center in Massachusetts? The one in Gloucester, Massachusetts?" he asked carefully.

This time Evelyn did check her notes. She gave a firm nod, saying, "Yes, that's the one, Gloucester, Mass. Dave was positively ecstatic—"

"Who are they sending?"

"The head of the department himself—name's George Hunt. He's apparently some big muckamuck. And guess what else: The Marine Center's offered to do the study *pro bono*. That's two big pluses on our side."

Sean hadn't realized he'd been holding his breath until he sank back against the padded leather of his chair, expelling it with a whoosh of relief. "This is terrific news. And the Marine Center's willing to waive its fee?"

"That's right. An excellent PR move. All we have to do is supply the accommodations, research boat, and lab."

"You'll see to it?"

Evelyn nodded. "Dave gave them my number. I don't know how many are coming with Dr. Hunt—I'm assuming he won't be working alone."

George Hunt could bring as big a team with him as he liked, Sean thought. Lily Banyon wouldn't be doing the grunt work of an assistant; she was a senior researcher at the Marine Center. And besides, hadn't May Ellen told him Lily would be in the Bahamas over the next month? *No,* he thought, his muscles relaxing one by one. Lily Banyon wouldn't be coming back.

"Evelyn, can you contact the university and have them send us a copy of the report Lesnesky was preparing? I'm sure Dr. Hunt will need to refer to it."

"I'll ring them at nine, when the university opens."

"Good. And make sure they understand we need it soon. We're not on an academic schedule here—not with this development company breathing down my neck. I assume you've already notified the other committee members we'll be meeting on Thursday?"

"Yes, I called them. Everyone will be there." She paused, then added, "Pete Ferrucci, too."

"Well, no meeting would be the same without him," he replied easily.

"That's for sure. I wonder what he'll come up with this time."

"Your guess is as good as mine. Ferrucci's low enough to try anything. But I'm going to see to it that this reef gets a thorough and proper study, no matter how much Ferrucci protests."

Evelyn cocked her head, regarding him shrewdly. "And what if the team finds no evidence that the reef is endangered?" she quizzed.

"Then, and only then, will I consider the development project more seriously. The reps are full of promises for this development and what it will do for the town. But I refuse to be steamrolled into anything."

"Good for you." She gave an approving nod. "Though not everyone is going to love you for taking this position. Especially with all the fuss Ferrucci's been making about your emptying the town's coffers in the name of preservation. Once word spreads about this development proposal, and all the money and jobs it will bring . . ."

"Hey, if these developers can guarantee the construction won't damage the coastal area and won't have a negative impact on the reef system, I'm all for enriching our town. But not if it means trashing the environment." Sean glanced quickly at his watch. Damn, he had only ten minutes until his meeting with the waste management union.

Evelyn too, checked her watch. She stood, her eyes traveling down her page of notes. "Oh, one last thing, Sean. I'm afraid the town will have to negotiate a deal with Mr. Ferrucci so we can lodge Dr. Hunt and his team. With the season gearing up, there aren't many vacancies right now—none that our budget can afford, that is."

"That's all right." Sean grinned. "Having Hunt finish the study constitutes a major victory for us; we can be generous to Ferrucci. By the way, Evelyn, if I don't have time before I leave for the airport—call Dave and give him my thanks. Tell him I owe him big-time for getting Dr. Hunt."

CHAPTER TWO

Two constants distinguished Tuesday mornings at the Marine Center where Lily worked as a marine biologist: the weekly staff meeting and the massive consumption of doughnuts. Her boss, Simone Devaux, the director of the center, claimed she'd instituted the doughnut ritual as an inexpensive and surefire way of keeping some twenty-odd scientists dazed and happy—or, at the very least, with mouths too full to argue with her.

There'd been more than enough doughnuts to go around this morning. A number of the center's staff were absent, on assignment in the field. The unconsumed Krispy Kremes rose from the plastic plates set in the middle of the row of tables like mountains of temptation. Lily had just succumbed to the persistent cry of a powdered cruller calling out, *Eat me*. It now lay on a napkin by her legal pad, a healthy bite taken out of it.

As Lily munched, she listened with half an ear to the easy rhythms of Simone's Caribbean accent. Her boss was outlining an upcoming project that the center and NASA were embarking on early next year. Lily already knew the details of the joint venture. George Hunt, who was the Marine Center's supernova as well as the head of

Lily's department, had talked of little else these past six months.

Taking another bite of the cruller, Lily picked up her pen. From the pen's nib, a giant tsunami wave emerged, rushing across the paper toward a Disney World–like castle. Lily was adding the finishing touches—the foam of the wave's crest, the pennants flying from the castle's turrets—her mouth busy with powdered sugar and saturated fat, when Simone said, "One last item of business before we go. George received a call from Florida yesterday. We've been asked to finish a reef study down there."

Lily's pen stilled. She frowned at the castle.

"George?" Simone said. Her lilting voice pitched, so the name became an invitation.

George Hunt was sitting beside Lily. He cleared his throat. "That's right. They're looking for someone with an in-depth knowledge of Florida's reef ecology. The scientist the town originally hired for the study fell seriously ill. The project's been left only three-quarters complete."

"What would we be dealing with?" Simone asked.

"It's an Atlantic patch reef, a sizeable one, too," George replied. "But as the reef is situated so far north of the Keys, it's been pretty much neglected by the scientific community. The guy I talked to, who's with the Parks Department, told me no one's done a systematic assessment of this reef system in over a decade. I said we'd be happy to step in and finish the job for them; it shouldn't take longer than a few weeks."

"Thanks, George. Any volunteers?"

Stubborn silence greeted Simone.

The reaction was hardly surprising, Lily thought, as she glanced around the table at her colleagues' closed expressions. Everyone here was swamped with work. She tucked a stray lock of her blonde hair behind her ear and lowered her head, avoiding Simone's almond-eyed stare as it swept around the joined tables. Despite the fact that Lily knew she was safe—she was heading to Lucaya next week to start the second phase of a study on reef regeneration—she felt safer still with her eyes fixed on her pad. Since hearing the words, *Florida*, *patch reef*, and *north of the Keys*, a peculiar uneasiness had crept over her. Perhaps that was why the heavy wool fisherman's sweater she'd donned this morning, though appropriate for the damp autumn bite of this gray, Massachusetts' morning, now prickled unpleasantly against her skin. Needing a distraction, Lily resumed her doodling, the wave on her page growing higher and more menacing with each stroke.

"Come on, guys." Simone's voice held a rare note of impatience. "George has already accepted the job on the center's behalf. I'm surprised at you—you all know how important it is to get the center's name out whenever the opportunity arises. And we haven't done any work down in Florida in quite some time. Now, who's going to step up to the plate?"

George, who'd been watching the natural disaster on Lily's paper take shape, leaned closer to whisper out of the corner of his mouth, "Hope Snow White can grab her surfboard in time. She'll catch a wicked ride."

Lily gave a snort of amusement, the sound loud in a room full of obstinate silence. Quickly, she tried to muffle it, shoving the last of her doughnut into her mouth.

The weight of Simone's gaze landed on them nonetheless. "Where'd you say this reef was, George?" she asked.

George looked up from Lily's drawing. "Sorry, guess I forgot to mention that." He opened the folder in front of him. "Hey, kiddo," he said, nudging her elbow with his own. "How about this for karma? The reef's located off Coral Beach."

Lily's head jerked, as if someone had just slipped a noose around her neck.

Peter Sloane, another senior researcher in Lily's department, was seated directly opposite her. Through the lens of his horn-rimmed glasses, Peter's eyes met hers. He smiled, a broad smile of relief. "Coral Beach?" he repeated a shade more loudly than necessary. "Isn't that where you grew up, Lily?"

Instantly, Lily became the focal point of twenty eyes. But it was only Simone's gaze that caused her throat to close around the half-swallowed doughnut.

"There we go!" Simone pronounced happily. "A perfect match."

It would be a long time before she heeded the lure of a Krispy Kreme doughnut again. Lily's throat still ached from the violence of her coughing, from trying to expel powdered sugar from her windpipe. She took a tentative sip of the hot tea George had brewed for her, watching him and Simone warily over the mug's brim.

The three of them were alone in Simone's book-lined office. Simone was seated behind her desk, looking slender and elegant as she relaxed against the black webbing of her ergonomically correct chair. Elbows propped on the armrests, she regarded Lily with the patience of a sphinx.

"Feeling better now?" she asked. "I was worried we might have to try a Heimlich maneuver on you."

"Yes. Thanks." Lily rested her mug on her blue jean–covered thigh. She cleared her throat and looked at her boss, who just happened to be her closest friend. "Please Simone, can't you get someone else?" Inwardly she winced at the pleading note that had crept into her voice.

Lily prided herself on her professionalism, her can-do attitude. It was these qualities that had helped her rise through the ranks of the still very much male-dominated field of marine biology. She was a respected scientist. Her work appeared in key journals, her presence was requested at colloquia and conferences throughout the country and abroad. Whining was as foreign to her as a panic attack. She wouldn't succumb to either.

She took a deep, steadying breath and began again. "Everyone, everything's set to go for Lucaya . . ."

Simone's tightly curled brown hair brushed against the back of her chair as she shook her head. "Sorry, Lily. The Bahamas study won't be affected if you delay it a few weeks. And Coral Beach needs the reef assessment completed as soon as possible. Isn't that right, George?"

George had eschewed a chair, preferring to sit with a hip propped on the corner edge of Simone's desk. With his bent leg swinging lazily, he looked every inch the marine adventurer. Jacques Cousteau meets Indiana Jones.

"Yeah," he nodded. "I'd fly down and do the study myself, Lily, but these next few weeks are going to be a killer. Fund-raisers up and down the coast for the NASA project," he explained with an aggrieved sigh. "But truth be told, kiddo, you're the best person for the job. You know those waters better than me—better than anyone at the center. You're exactly what the committee's looking for. And what could be finer than Coral Beach's

native daughter coming to its aid in its hour of need?"
He crossed his arms over his broad chest and gave her a
warm smile.

At George's smile, Lily knew she'd been right to be
wary. George Hunt could charm at will with his dashing
good looks. She'd seen him use that cajoling smile at
fund-raisers, seen him reduce CEOs to sentimental mush
puddles. Very *generous* sentimental mush puddles, which,
by the evening's end, had written gratifyingly big checks.
The man was a genius. But Lily was made of sterner
stuff.

Listening to Hunt's smooth delivery had sparked an
idea. Lily leaned forward, almost overturning her tea in
her eagerness. Impatiently, she set the cup aside.

"Don't you see, Simone, George? That's exactly why
someone else should go. Florida's *such* a territorial place.
If word gets out that I'm a local, I might be accused of
partiality. Which could cause real problems. For the sake
of the center's reputation, I think it would be better if
you gave the project to someone else." That last bit was
an especially nice touch, selfless and altruistic.

Amusement lit Simone's exotic features. She clapped her
hands, applauding, her silver bangles clinking musically.

Lily scowled. *Damn.* She should have known Simone
would be too smart to fall for it.

"Come on, Lily. You've handled studies and committees like this one before. Moreover, you're an acknowledged expert in your field. No one on this advisory panel
will be able to argue that."

"That's right. Nothing to worry about, kiddo," George
chimed in reassuringly.

"By the way, when was the last time you went back for
a visit, Lily?" Simone asked.

"Oh, I don't know." She tried for a casual shrug. "Ten years, maybe."

"Ten years?" Simone parroted, astonished.

"You know how it is with work." At her boss's look of blank incomprehension, Lily added defensively, "My mother's newest husband lives in Palm Beach, my half brothers have moved away, too. So the only family I have left in Coral Beach is my grandmother."

"And that would be the delightful Mrs. Farrady?"

Lily blinked at George. "Oh, yes, that's right. I forgot I introduced you to her after your lecture on the Galapagos when she was in Boston."

"Ten years," Simone repeated. She was shaking her dark head in disbelief. "My God, Mother would drag me home by the ear if I dropped out of sight for more than two weeks."

"My family's not quite as close-knit as yours, Simone." Indeed, Lily often marveled at her friend's vibrant, loving, and supportive parents. Simone's father was a geologist, a professor at MIT, her mother an art dealer, born and raised in Martinique. Lily had been invited to dinner at their home in Boston's Back Bay several times over the past years. Long, marathon affairs, with wooden platters piled high with spicy food, torches and candles illuminating the brownstone terrace where they sat. While the Devaux and their guests ate, the conversation would turn to plate tectonics, global warming, and marine ecology. Heady stuff. The debates often lasted far into the night, ending only when the candles sputtered and died.

A far cry from the stilted atmosphere at Lily's childhood home. If plates were ever mentioned, they were the ones on sale at Bloomingdale's. Or how important it was to align one's fork and knife just so on a china plate. Which, to a younger Lily, had been more than ample reason to turn deaf and dumb. After hurriedly gobbling her food, Lily would quickly mumble an "Excuse me," and make her escape—either to race downstairs to her chemistry lab in the basement, or upstairs to the sanctuary of her bedroom and her biology books.

The sound of Simone's voice broke into her thoughts.

"There's no such thing as a perfect family, Lily." Simone's exotic eyes studied her intently. "Let me guess," she said in a voice as gentle as her smile. "You were the quintessential science nerd. The proverbial square peg."

"Yes." Lily managed a light, unconcerned laugh. "And hideously ugly to boot."

George's laughter joined hers. His blue seaman's eyes swept over her. Arms crossed, he leaned back as though in judgment, then gave her a real smile, one filled with frank, masculine appreciation. "Well, Dr. Banyon, I think it's time to show the folks back home the woman you've become."

Lily felt heat stain her cheeks.

Simone leaned forward in her chair and poked George in the side. "Quit it, Hunt. Or I'll turn into a jealous shrew, and then Lily will be *really* embarrassed."

George grabbed Simone's hand and pressed his lips to her palm. "Never fear, love. Lily knows I, uh, admire her brains even more than her beauty. Right, kiddo?"

Lily rolled her eyes. "Especially when you want to sweet-talk me, George."

"Ah, but I'm only doing it with your best interests at heart. Simone's right. You can't ignore family, Lily. Or your roots. This assignment is a wonderful chance to make up for lost time, and in the bargain do some valuable research on your hometown's reef system. And you'll be making a lovely old girl so very happy."

"Just how long did you and my grandmother talk for, George?" she asked suspiciously.

George merely grinned.

Lily looked at him and Simone. The stint in Coral Beach wouldn't last long. She'd be able to visit Granny May and then leave, with her suddenly troubled conscience clear. Resigned, Lily sighed. "Okay, I'll do it."

George's whoop of triumph startled a laugh out of both women. With a wide smile, he raised his mug, as if toasting Lily. "Knew we could count on you, Dr. Banyon."

Simone leaned back in her chair. She, too, smiled. "Thanks, Lily. As soon as you're done in Coral Beach, we'll get you to Lucaya without delay. I promise. Now," she continued briskly, "we've got a lot to do before you leave Thursday morning. Let's get cracking."

CHAPTER THREE

Forty-eight hours later, Lily was thirty thousand feet in the air, heading toward Miami far too quickly for her peace of mind. The airplane was packed, full of snowbirds getting an early jump on the season. Karen Masur, the photographer who'd been assigned to work with Lily, was sitting in the adjacent seat. She was flipping through an airline magazine as she listened to music on her Walkman. With the plane filled to capacity, Lily's other assistant, John Granger, had been assigned a seat at the very rear of the plane, by the toilets. A more fitting location for him, Lily couldn't imagine.

Karen had recently been promoted from volunteer to staff photographer. While Karen's lack of field experience was a potential drawback, Lily knew that at least Karen was a talented photographer, keen to learn, and willing to work. Lily far preferred dealing with a novice to putting up with a first-class jerk. That was the nicest way to describe John Granger.

When Simone had informed her that she would be giving Lily John Granger as a research assistant, Lily had blurted, "Simone, that's not giving, that's *foisting*."

"Lily, I'm sorry, really I am." For the first time that

morning, Simone had looked distinctly uncomfortable. "I wish I could send Craig with you, but he's developed a middle-ear infection. He can't dive until the doctor gives his A-OK. Besides, it'll be more useful if, as soon as Craig's ear heals, he heads to Lucaya and begins the prep for your reef regeneration study."

"We understand your, uh—" George had paused to clear his throat. "—reluctance to take John with you, Lily. But you've done a great job training the other graduate students. Look at how far Craig has come."

"Craig actually wants to use his brains," was her heated reply. "Whereas the only thing John wants to exercise is in his pe—"

"John's been significantly more restrained ever since your little conversation with him, Lily—for which we're all extremely grateful," Simone interrupted. "You know the data collecting will go much faster if you've got help, and when he chooses to, John does decent work. It's only right to give him the opportunity."

"And you've already proved how adept you are at dealing with a 'personality' like Granger," George added.

Though George was managing to keep a straight face, Lily could see the effort was hard-won. "Very funny, George. Maybe *your* next assistant will be an opportunistic ass grabber." She gave a sunny smile at his appalled expression.

Simone had coughed loudly, the sound awfully close to a strangled laugh. "I promise you I'll talk with John before the three of you leave on Thursday. Now, I know you have a ton of stuff to do. I'll get Rachel to make copies of everything we've received on the coral reef advisory committee. And George will contact the guy from the Parks Department, let him know you're coming. Have a great time, Lily, and don't forget to send us postcards."

And that was that. The only good thing about having to organize a project virtually overnight—creating and ticking off checklists for the equipment needed for the study, then packing it and all the diving gear for express shipment to Coral Beach—was that Lily had been too busy to think about just where she was headed.

She still hadn't so much as glanced at the file Simone's secretary, Rachel, had handed her. She was stalling. But now, with two more hours of flight time ahead of them, the manila folder was screaming for her attention from the depths of her leather shoulder bag. For the umpteenth time Lily wished this were all some bad dream from which she'd awaken and find herself safe and sound in a rented cottage on the outskirts of Lucaya.

Reluctantly, Lily bent forward and withdrew the folder from her bag. She opened the folder to the first page and stiffened with a gasp.

"Hey, Lily, what's the matter?" Karen asked, shifting in her seat.

Lily didn't reply, could only stare, horrified, at the topmost name on the sheet. Shuddering, she squeezed her eyes shut.

"Hey," Karen said again. "Are you okay?"

Lily opened her eyes, but seconds passed before she could focus properly. Dazedly she noted that Karen had pulled her earphones down. They hung around her neck, along with her assorted collection of silver chains and pooka shells.

Karen shook her forearm lightly. "Should I call the

flight attendant? *Lily*," she said, fingers squeezing more urgently, "come on, speak to me; you're freaking me out." At that, she stretched upward, her index finger aiming for the little rectangular button that would summon the flight attendant.

Before she could press it, Lily stirred. "I'm all right, Karen. Really." Her voice was the weak croak of a dying frog.

"You sure? To tell you the truth, you look, well, kind of green."

"It must be the turbulence," Lily mumbled. She shut her eyes again, refusing to look down at the paper clenched between her fingers. From her side of the armrest, she felt as well as heard Karen's snort of disbelief.

"Yeah, right. There's been hardly a bump since takeoff. But maybe it's because you've been reading—that sometimes makes people really queasy."

Truer words had never been spoken. "Yes, that must be it." She swallowed. "But I'm feeling better now."

"Oh," she said, then added, "Glad to hear it." Resettling the earphones over her head, she went back to her magazine.

A pathetic hope consumed Lily. It was possible she'd been hallucinating, the delusions brought on by her imminent return to Coral Beach. Screwing up her courage, she peeked at the printed list of committee members one more time.

No, fate was definitely not smiling upon her. There it was, Sean McDermott, mayor.

And he was heading the advisory panel.

Mayor. How and when had that happened? Why hadn't anyone mentioned it to her? True, her mother had hit the social jackpot with husband number four and was now living in Palm Beach, spending her days at the tennis club, her evenings at whatever charity ball was written on her social calendar. But that didn't mean her mother was out of the loop. She and Dana McDermott, Sean's mother, still called each other daily; Kaye would definitely know that Sean was mayor of Coral Beach.

But Lily communicated with her mother as little as possible, never asking questions or volunteering any information, rarely venturing beyond monosyllabic responses. Lily's calls were made strictly from a sense of duty, to let her mother know where she could be reached in case of emergency. Given the brevity of their long-distance conversations, it would have been difficult for Kaye Alcott to introduce that particularly newsworthy bit of information.

But what about the rest of her family? Her half brothers, Ned and Mike, lived outside Orlando. They'd always idolized Sean. And Granny May was, as ever, best friends with Sean's own grandmother. They certainly might have mentioned something, at least in passing.

In spite of the fact that Lily had turned her back on her hometown, the news that Sean was mayor made her feel vastly out of touch, disoriented. She could hardly have been more shocked if she'd learned that Sean had been elected president of the United States. Actually, that'd be preferable, far easier to swallow. Because then he wouldn't be chairing the committee to which she was supposed to report.

With sudden longing, Lily looked at the long red handle of the emergency exit.

If only they provided parachutes on these flights.

* * *

Sean pressed the power button on his cell phone the instant the airline steward informed the passengers that it was safe once more to operate their cell phones. It rang immediately.

"McDermott," he answered.

"Sean, it's me." Though tinny, Evelyn's voice conveyed an extra urgency this morning. "Where have you been?"

"Circling. There was a storm front we had to bypass, then every plane in the region wanted to land simultaneously. Sky traffic's become as bad as Route One. What's up, Evelyn?"

"It's a zoo here, been like this the entire morning. The press meeting's canceled, of course . . . which is about the best news I can give you right now."

"That bad, huh?"

"Yes. For starters, there was a head-on collision on the western curve approaching the bridge into town. The car that sustained the most damage had a mother and three kids in it. They're alive, but one of the children was pinned for about an hour. Rescue workers had to saw through the metal to get him out."

"*Jesus.* Which hospital?" Sean fished a pen from the inside pocket of his suit.

"Saint Francis. Family's name is Ritter, mother is Sue, children are Tabitha, Hank, and Jake. Hank's the one who was trapped." Evelyn paused so Sean could scribble down the information, then continued. "Sean, both Pete Ferrucci and Jack Gehring were interviewed live on the community TV station this morning. Topic of the day is how you vetoed the plan to widen the bridge."

"That proposal was nothing more than a scam to line Jack Gehring's pockets," Sean replied. Gehring ran the largest construction company in the county. He had amassed a fortune in contracts by underbidding the competition, to the point where practically every major building project had Gehring's name on it. "Ferrucci and Gehring are just making noise," he reassured his secretary. "The police department hired safety experts to look at the Bellemer Bridge proposal. Their conclusion was that widening the bridge would only encourage people to drive faster. Besides, Evelyn, you said the accident happened at the curve approaching the bridge."

"I don't think Ferrucci, Gehring, or any of their cronies care about petty details like that. They're having a field day."

He cursed silently. "Well, I'll deal with the town council members after I've visited the hospital."

"No, sorry, Sean, you'll have to deal with the waste management services first," Evelyn informed him. "This morning at eight, the head of the union announced a general strike. Effective immediately."

"What? We went over the contract with a magnifying glass. Every item was okayed."

"That was then, this is now."

Exasperated, Sean rubbed his face with his hand, and then spoke directly into the mouthpiece. "Call the union rep; tell him I'll be there as soon as I can."

He was still talking as he exited the plane.

CHAPTER FOUR

Today was one of those days when all of Evelyn Roemer's organizational efforts were blown to smithereens. Sean's carefully planned schedule was transformed into a mad dash, with him racing from one disaster to the next. The only truly good news came early, when he visited St. Francis Hospital. Hank Ritter, the little boy who'd been trapped beneath crumpled metal in the car crash, was miraculously unharmed. The doctors were keeping him overnight at the hospital for routine observation only. When the nurse on duty ushered Sean into Hank's room, he was sitting up in bed, slurping chocolate pudding and watching a cartoon program on Nickelodeon. Sean got a casual, "Hi," and a, "Yeah, I'm okay," from him before he switched his attention back to the TV show. Sean left Hank's room considerably lighter of heart.

Mrs. Ritter and her other two children had been exceptionally lucky, too. The kids suffered a few bruises and Mrs. Ritter was sporting an egg-size lump on her left temple. The police had already interviewed both Mrs. Ritter and the other driver, and made a preliminary examination of the crash site. From the angle of the crash, it looked as if both drivers had taken the curve too wide, making a collision unavoidable.

There was also a strong suspicion that Mrs. Ritter had been driving one-handed—sheer, reckless folly. When the police examined the wrecked car, they discovered her cell phone still on, lying underneath the accelerator. They'd confirmed that the automobile lacked any type of hands-free device designed for cell phones.

After Sean had checked on the rest of the Ritter family, he arranged to meet with the police chief and the head of the Department of Transportation to see what additional measures could be taken to improve safety on the bridge. From the hospital, he then hightailed it over to the other end of town, where the Sanitation Department's office was located. It took an hour and a half of heated wrangling over workmen's comp and pension benefits—issues Sean and the union's spokesman had previously agreed upon—before he was able to walk away with the promise that the town's garbage men would return to work and stay there until the town board could vote on the proposed changes.

Sean had never stared into as many blank-eyed faces before. Throughout the high school civics talk, he felt as if he were speaking to the kids in a foreign language, one they had no intention of learning. Scrambling for a way to reach his audience, he ad-libbed, tossing out anecdotes about his own years at Coral Beach High. He confessed that as a teenager his decision to run for student government had been little more than a wily excuse to approach the best-looking girls. But what ultimately hooked his interest in student government was the startling discovery that the kids at school, all so different—

jocks, nerds, preppies, and brains—could unite behind a common cause.

During his senior year, when he'd been president of the student council, Coral Beach High raised seven thousand dollars to aid Florida's hurricane victims. Wouldn't that be something to feel good about? Sean asked his teenage audience.

The response he received was as rousing as a herd of cows chewing their cud. Except this group was blowing big pink bubbles with their gum.

The question and answer period, too, turned out to be a joke. The teens' main preoccupations: his salary and whether he got driven around town in a chauffeured limo. When they learned he was willing to work for peanuts and that he drove an eight-year-old convertible, he might as well have stamped a big fat *L* on his forehead. He was weak-kneed with relief when at last the principal mounted the auditorium steps and thanked Sean for his electrifying speech.

While Sean was politically seasoned enough to put the morning's snafus behind him, and not worry overmuch that the apathetic bunch he'd just talked to represented America's future voters, it was the high school principal's long-winded enthusiasm, telling Sean how much of an inspiration he was for these kids, that truly set Sean's teeth on edge. And made him even later for the final meeting of the day, the coral reef advisory panel.

Sean's office suite was empty when he returned, Evelyn doubtless waiting in the conference room with the other committee members. The aqua blue folder that contained all the relevant information Evelyn had compiled was on the middle of his desk where he wouldn't miss it.

He grabbed it and strode down the hall, the folder open in his hands. His eyes skimmed the list, double-checking everyone's name.

The vibrant Day-Glo orange of the highlighter Evelyn had selected was as shocking as the name she'd used it on.

Dr. Lily Banyon, Center for Marine Studies, Gloucester.

So fitting, so ironic, it was just what Lily herself would have done: try her damnedest to knock him flat on his ass. The jolt caused by reading Lily's name with George Hunt's name neatly crossed out in thin, red marker, sent Sean tripping over the threshold, entering the conference room with the exaggerated clumsiness of a clown entertaining the spectators beneath the big tent.

He recovered just before he careened into a chair. He stood, gripping the chair's wooden frame for support. His mind reeled as he searched the faces in the conference room. The wave of relief that flooded him when he realized Lily wasn't there would at any other moment have been laughable. Someone spoke, asking if he was okay, a reasonable question given his bizarre entrance. Sean managed to pull himself together and reply before turning away. He'd spotted Evelyn at the other end of the room.

Thanks to Evelyn's excellent shorthand, she'd been designated the committee's secretary, responsible for recording the minutes. True to form, she was all set to go, the rectangular yellow legal pad tucked under her arm, her bony fingers wrapped around an assortment of pens, Day-Glo orange among them. Sean scowled.

"Hi," Evelyn said. "I just called in an order for cookies and coffee, a double espresso for you. You look like you're in serious need of one," she clucked. "It should be here any minute now. Almost everyone's here," she added, looking around. "Except for—"

Sean's hand wrapped around her elbow, and he pulled her further away from the nearest cluster of committee members. "What's going on, Evelyn?" he demanded in a low hiss.

Startled, Evelyn looked up at him with a bewildered expression. "Excuse me?"

"What in hell is Lily Banyon doing on this committee?"

His secretary responded with a mutinous thrust of her chin. "If you're looking for a verbal punching bag, Sean, go pick on someone your own size."

"What?"

"You heard me." Evelyn glared at him with righteous indignation, as though she'd just discovered he'd robbed the senior pension fund.

Jaw clamped tight, he counted silently to ten, then enunciated carefully, "Evelyn, could you please tell me what happened to George Hunt?"

"How should I know?" she snapped. "Why the fuss, anyway? Dr. Banyon's from the same institute—Dave was all excited when he got the news. He's right over there," Evelyn informed Sean. "Go yell at *him* if this Dr. Banyon is such a problem."

Sean's gaze found his friend trapped in a corner with one of Coral Beach's more "vocal" citizens. There'd be no escape for Dave until the meeting came to order, and Sean was hardly in the mood to be patient with the likes of Mrs. Cannady.

Evelyn gave a knowing smile when Sean remained at

her side. "In case you're interested, Dave thinks we got a great deal. By all accounts, Dr. Banyon is a real star."

Sean shut his eyes briefly and shook his head in denial, in despair. "Evelyn, believe me, you don't want Lily Banyon anywhere near this committee."

Then she was there, as if by saying her name aloud he'd conjured her. The air changed, an arctic crackle in Florida's sultry heat. The small hairs on the back of his neck prickled in awareness, his skin suddenly stretched tight.

Evelyn, too, must have sensed the shift in atmosphere. She craned her head to peer around him. He watched her expression transform from annoyed to surprised to awed.

"Oh, my," she breathed.

"She's here?" he asked unnecessarily, refusing to look. Resisting temptation.

"I'm assuming it must be her; I pretty much know everyone else in the room." There was a short silence as she inspected the newcomer thoroughly. "My heavens, I didn't realize scientists came like this. She's simply . . . magnificent."

"There's not one thing that's simple about Lily Banyon."

Evelyn's eyes were still focused on the other end of the room. "*Hmm,* I think I see what you mean." A smile played over her lips. "How utterly refreshing and fascinating—you'll have your work cut out for you. Come, Mayor McDermott, duty calls."

"I don't need to meet her. I already know her. Too well."

Evelyn made a *tsk*ing sound. "My, my, don't we sound like we've missed our afternoon nap?" she murmured as she brushed by him, assuming the role of Coral Beach's welcome wagon, fully equipped with bells, whistles, and highlighters.

His secretary had abandoned him for the enemy. How much worse could things get? A clause should be inserted into their contracts prohibiting secretaries from treating their bosses as though they were three-year-olds. Had there been dirt instead of mocha-colored industrial carpeting underfoot, he'd have kicked it. It wasn't anyone's business but his if he refused to rush over and blurt, *Hey, Lily, long time no see! So, tell me, what've you been up to since Rome, when you slammed the door in my face so hard you almost broke my nose for the second time?*

He was the mayor. He could do as he liked. And what he most wanted, right after making Lily Banyon disappear from his life as suddenly as she'd reappeared, was an armed guard. Then maybe he could confront her and walk away in one piece.

Reluctantly, Sean turned and looked.

Three seconds was all he permitted himself. Lily Banyon wasn't going to catch him staring like some hormone-crazed adolescent. Three seconds was more than enough, though. Lily's image burned, a brilliant flame behind his retinas.

She looked good. No, make that great, incredible . . . yes, *magnificent*. She'd chopped off her hair, about a foot and a half of it. Her wheat-blond locks fell in a casual, tousled style, framing her face, accentuating those startling, ice-crystal blue eyes.

She looked even better than he remembered, a memory hot enough to make him lie awake at night, aching.

Evelyn Roemer's pink head was tilted back in animated conversation with Lily. From the angle of his secretary's chin, Sean realized Lily must be wearing high heels, so she'd stand nearly as tall as him. That fact alone put fifty points on her side of the scoreboard. She must have known beforehand he'd be at the meeting.

But Sean wasn't going to let her win.

Not this time. She'd won the last round, back in Rome, when the wooden door to her room in the slightly cheesy *pensione* nearly flattened him.

It certainly hadn't been Sean's idea to visit her. Her mother, Kaye, had called long distance, pleading that he look Lily up, take her out to dinner. Lily was traveling with her college roommate, and Kaye was certain she'd be out of her depth in Italy. To add to Kaye's worries, neither girl spoke a word of Italian—whereas Sean had spent the entire year in Rome, studying political science at the university, which made him practically a native. Surely he could take the daughter of his mother's best friend out for a bowl of pasta, some Chianti? Kaye would sleep so much better knowing Lily was with Sean, and not some louche foreigner—Italian men had such ideas! And she was sure Lily would be thrilled to see a friendly, familiar face.

Surprised at Kaye's belated display of maternal instincts, Sean relented, promising he'd get in touch with Lily. Besides, he knew his own mother would never forgive him if he refused such a simple request. As he made his way down the narrow streets to the *pensione* opposite the Pantheon, where Lily and her roommate were staying, Sean steadfastly refused to acknowledge any other reason for agreeing to take Lily out. It had been three years since they'd left for college; not once had she come home to visit. But Sean still couldn't look at a blonde without comparing her to Lily.

He'd mounted the four flights of narrow, winding stairs, the sound of his steps muffled by red, threadbare carpet. At number seventeen, he'd stopped and stood, giving his racing heart a chance to quiet before he knocked. *Calm down,* he'd instructed himself. *It's only Lily.*

His knock echoed loudly in the empty hall. Through the door he heard the sound of approaching footsteps. Then it opened and there she was. She stood with her mouth agape. Her eyes, like beacons of light in the obscurity of the drab hallway, blinked at him with astonishment. "What are you doing here?" The question ended on a squeak. As if annoyed with the sound, she shut her mouth with an audible snap.

Was it possible Kaye hadn't bothered to tell Lily he'd be coming?

"I heard you were spending a few days in Rome." Sean realized he was staring like a dolt, but couldn't help himself. It rattled him, seeing Lily again. A barrage of emotions and impressions mixed and churned inside him: how good she looked, different somehow, more self-confident than in high school, how maybe this time they might get along for more than 3.5 seconds. He became aware of a happy buzz of anticipation zinging through him. He was already picturing the two of them at a really nice trattoria. They'd be sitting at an intimate corner table. A waiter would come and take their order and Sean would impress her with his flawless Italian, his casual sophistication, his *sprezzatura*. By the time the waiter had served them their dessert and espresso, she'd be smiling at him across the soft candlelight. He'd reach out and take her hand. . . .

Then Lily spoke again and Sean's neat fantasy evaporated like a puff of smoke.

"But how did you know I was here?" she'd asked, with what he'd conceitedly assumed was genuine confusion—that is, until a guy their age appeared. Standing just behind Lily, he had stared back at Sean through the aperture of the open door with a knowing smirk upon his face.

And suddenly Sean understood.

Lily wasn't frowning from confusion. She was annoyed. Annoyed because he'd barged in on her and Lover Boy.

Lily didn't give a damn about him. At the realization, his jumbled thoughts at seeing her again, all those newborn hopes inside him, faded to black.

His brain must have shorted after that. Suave, sophisticated guy that he was, Sean had blurted out, "Hey, this wasn't my idea. I only came because Kaye begged me to—"

Stupendously dumb. He knew better, had known since he was eight years old. If you wanted to push Lily Banyon into the red zone, all it took was a whispered, "Kaye."

The door to her hotel room had come at his face faster than a bullet train. He guessed he should be grateful she hadn't been using a more lethal weapon, like the volleyball she'd smashed in his face during gym class back in eleventh grade. Even so, he'd been forced to jump back or have the number seventeen imprinted on his forehead.

Their last skirmish, the one back in Rome, he'd definitely lost. He'd stood outside her room like a fool, banging on the door, Lover Boy's laughter his only reply. Finally, the *pensione*'s night clerk had appeared, insisting he leave *la bella americana* in peace. He'd gone away, humiliated and oddly deflated.

It was past time he evened the score, maybe got a few points up on her. He walked over to his place, the center of a U-shaped configuration of tables, and set his papers down, pretending to consult them. Instead, he inspected Lily covertly, hoping to detect a weakness, some tiny chink in her armor.

Damn her for being more beautiful than ever, he thought. A single glance and he began wanting things he knew were impossible. Sean tore his gaze away, and became aware for the first time that Lily hadn't come to the meeting alone. On her right was a young woman who bore an alarming resemblance to the teenagers he'd spent the afternoon with at Coral Beach High. Dozens upon dozens of cornrows covered her head, the thin braids ending in brilliantly colored beads. At the moment, she was nodding in reply to some remark of Evelyn's, making her braids sway and jangle.

The man next to the young woman was a different story altogether. He had that ultra-groomed look, as if he spent way too much time in front of a mirror. *And it doesn't look like he uses the hours to practice his smile,* Sean thought, disliking the sneer on the guy's face. Sean pushed aside his less-than-favorable impression of Lily's two companions. What he thought of them hardly mattered, not when it was Lily's own presence that bore all the signs of a catastrophe in the making.

The time had come, Sean determined, to face the woman of his nightmares, of his dreams.

CHAPTER FIVE

The tension had been building inside her since that awful airborne moment when Lily read Sean's name. Now that she was standing in the conference room, it was almost more than she could bear. Like live wires, her nerves sparked with dangerous intensity.

She'd spotted Sean instantly, of course, despite the fact that his back was turned. His dark head topped most of the room's occupants. When he remained on the other side of the room, deep in conversation with a little old lady, Lily let out a sigh of relief. His attention elsewhere, all she had to contend with was the sight of his broad shoulders, how well they filled his olive green jacket, with the short, sun-kissed curls of his brown hair just skimming the jacket's collar. That alone was disconcerting enough. Quickly, Lily averted her eyes.

About fifteen other people were gathered in the conference room. Since joining the research department at the Marine Center, Lily had participated in many such meetings and committees. She knew there'd be representatives from the planning board, the town council, the Department of Parks and Recreation, as well as anyone else keen on exercising his or her democratic right to hold forth in a public setting. The thing about these meetings, there was always someone with an agenda, sometimes an obvious one, other times so deeply hidden that trying to unearth it required the cunning of an archaeologist at an excavation site—you had to know where to dig. What Lily found disheartening was the monotony of the root causes that motivated so many people—money, power, or often a nasty cocktail of the two.

Despite her general aversion to committees and panels, Lily still found one aspect of them entertaining. She loved playing the game of *Guess Who*. As with marine biology, it involved determining category and type of species. On dry land, the challenge translated into matching faces to titles—she'd picked out the parks and recreation rep in a mere five seconds: mid to late twenties, well-worn but pressed khakis, white polo shirt with an embroidered insignia over the left breast. Behind the gold wire rim glasses, his face had that open, all-American expression. He was one of the few people opting for mineral water rather than the catered coffee, which had just been wheeled in on a linen-covered tea wagon.

Lily moved on to a more challenging level: the suits. One was particularly eye-catching. A shiny, bluish-gray double-breasted jacket with matching trousers, the look was completed by a pair of glossy tasseled loafers. The man inside the suit was as slick as the clothes he wore. His heavily pomaded hair was the inky black of shoe polish, his carefully trimmed goatee the same improbable shade. Lily put him somewhere in his fifties and watched, fascinated, as he worked the room. In constant motion, he would target a group, slap backs with hearty enthusiasm, and then veer off again. If she hadn't known better, she'd have thought *he* was mayor.

Lily's species cataloging came to an abrupt end when, spritelike, the old lady who'd been talking with Sean materialized in front of her. Decked out in a blinding lime green pantsuit, she thrust a thin hand toward Lily. "Dr. Banyon, welcome. I'm Evelyn Roemer, Mayor McDermott's secretary."

"Hello." Lily shook the proffered hand, careful not to squeeze too hard. Ms. Roemer looked fragile enough to fly away in a strong breeze.

Standing next to Lily, Karen exclaimed, "Wow! I love your hair color. Did you get that done around here?"

Evelyn Roemer fingered a cluster of spring tight curls that were a delicate shade of . . . raspberry. "Why thank you, dearie," she replied with a gratified smile. "No, I have this special formula I mix myself. That way I know it'll come out just right." Her bright gaze shifted back to Lily. "Did you have any trouble finding the condominium, Dr. Banyon?"

"Oh, no. No trouble at all."

"We certainly do appreciate your willingness to take over Dr. Lesnesky's work. We were left in something of a bind when he fell ill."

"The Marine Center's primary goal is to further awareness and understanding of our oceans' ecosystems," Lily recited dutifully. She had a vision of her boss, Simone, applauding Lily's diplomatic effort on the center's behalf. . . . *Boy, Simone is going to owe me big-time.*

Lily had just finished introducing Karen and John to Evelyn Roemer when Sean approached the group.

"Ahh, Mayor McDermott," Evelyn Roemer said cheerfully, when Lily fell abruptly silent. "I was just chatting with Dr. Banyon and her assistants. Karen, John, allow me to introduce you to Sean McDermott, Coral

Beach's mayor. Mayor McDermott, this is Karen Masur and John Granger. Karen's an underwater photographer, and John will be assisting Dr. Banyon with her research." Evelyn paused as Sean shook their hands. "Of course, you and Dr. Banyon need no introduction. I understand you are already acquainted."

As one, Lily and Sean ignored Evelyn's remark.

"Evelyn," Sean said. "Let's get the panel members seated and call the meeting to order. Now that Dr. Banyon and her assistants are here, I think we should begin without further delay."

His secretary nodded briskly. "Certainly, Mr. Mayor." She turned to John Granger. "John, you look like a strapping young man. Would you mind moving a few chairs for me, perhaps the ones over in the corner? I'd like to put them on either side of Dr. Banyon's place, so the panel can meet the three of you together. Come along, Karen, we'll get some refreshments. I doubt you've had time to eat, what with all your traveling."

Sean watched Lily turn as if to follow them. Clearly she wished to avoid him. While Sean wasn't terribly eager to chat about the good old days, Lily's patent reluctance to speak to him had the predictably perverse effect of his being determined to do so.

"So, your Lungness, I see you've finally decided to come up for air." The nickname was a relic from their swim team days, and had popped out unintentionally. Still, it had the desired result: Lily stopped in her tracks.

She turned and faced him. "I assume this is one of your attempts at wit. As usual, though, you've fallen way short of the mark. I have no idea what you're referring to, nor do I particularly care. However, if you call me that again, I'll walk right out that door."

"What? Your Lungness?" he repeated, all innocence, ignoring the fact that his behavior was childish, unprofessional, too.

How could she stand there looking so coolly collected, as if seeing him again meant absolutely nothing to her? *Because, you idiot,* an inner voice mocked, *that's exactly what you are to Lily. Nothing.*

Lily's nails gouged the palms of her hands. From the gleam in Sean's hazel eyes, she knew he remembered how much she'd detested being called Her Lungness. Years ago, someone on their swim team had dreamed up the moniker because Lily was able to swim underwater for the entire length of the fifty-meter pool in one breath, then turn around for the return trip before surfacing. But Lily had always thought the name stuck, especially with the guys on the team, not on account of her incredible lung capacity, but because by the time she was fourteen, her bra size was already a 36C.

The recollection of those awkward adolescent days had Lily's shoulders rounding—as they had in the past. It was a futile attempt to make everything about her smaller, more conventional.

The gleam in Sean's eyes intensified, and Lily read it for what it was: satisfaction. She jerked her spine to regal stiffness. "Knock it off, McDermott," she hissed.

It was silly to have worried, Sean thought, relaxing. He could handle the return of Lily Banyon, no problem. He only had to keep pushing the right buttons.

"Sorry. I was only trying to jar your memory a bit. After all, it's been so long since you were home. I suppose you've been too busy saving the oceans all these years to come back and visit your family."

His comment stung, but Lily refused to justify her actions to Sean McDermott, of all people. "That's right, I have. Why don't you get this meeting started, *Mayor.*" Lily spat the word softly. She spun on her heels and strode away to where John was rearranging chairs under Evelyn Roemer's vigilant command.

And Sean was treated to a knockout view of her long, shapely legs. Legs made impossibly longer thanks to her strappy, three-inch-heeled sandals. His gaze traveled upward and stalled. He swallowed in an effort to dislodge the quartzlike lump lodged in his windpipe, created by the sight of Lily's enticingly rounded buttocks wrapped in a snug, cream-colored skirt whose hemline ended miles short of her knees.

Lily had come a long way in the dress department. In the old days, she invariably opted for shapeless, baggy clothes that offered no hint of the body underneath, using them and her long, thick, blond hair as a protective shield. In the cold war between them, Sean always thought of it as Lily's very own iron curtain.

How in the world was he going to lead this blasted meeting with the image of Dr. Lily Banyon's high-octane body burning up his brain cells? And if—rather make that *when*—he blew it, he knew exactly who'd be the first one laughing her bright blond head off.

Lily was sure the wild hammering of her pulse was from righteous fury. She didn't care if Sean had become a devastatingly attractive male, his face all strong planes, his body six feet of elegant muscle. So what if his olive green jacket and his azure blue shirt enhanced the whirl of green and brown in his hazel eyes, making them deep and oddly compelling?

She was immune.

Besides, he'd always looked good. There'd never been an ungainly moment in Sean McDermott's development, his body always athletic and beautifully proportioned. In addition, the countless hours of training demanded by Hal Storey, their swim coach, had sculpted Sean's adolescent body to the point where seeing him in his racing Speedo could cause a female heart palpitations. She could recall vividly how the girls on their swim team used to park themselves on the bleachers and ogle Sean, as he stood perched on the starting block before a race. Breathless sighs would sound when Sean's body dropped down into his racing start, his fingers gripping the edge of the slanted platform, the muscles in his body tensing in anticipation. Their breathless sighs were transformed into gasps of appreciation as the official's gun sounded and Sean's body shot forward, rocketlike, his trajectory a smooth arc over, then into, the water. A weird, brief moment of silence followed, an expectant hush, and then Sean was surfacing, already halfway down the length of the pool, slicing through the water, the effortlessness of his stroke testimony to his young body's incredible power. Excited cheers erupted, accompanying the cadence of his stroke.

Sean was as handsome as ever. No, more so. Lily resisted thinking about how *much* more—how his body had matured, his shoulders even broader. How his mouth, how his face—with skin scraped daily by the blade of a razor—offered such an intriguing and inviting contrast of curved smoothness and the rough hint of light brown stubble. How his voice was lower, deeper. And rich with dislike for her.

But Lily wasn't going to think about Sean. Once this

meeting was over, she'd make sure she steered clear of Mayor McDermott. *Out of sight, out of mind . . .* a cliché she'd repeated to herself for ten long years.

CHAPTER SIX

As committee chair, Sean opened the meeting. For the benefit of the new research team, he introduced the other panel members, then gave a brief summary of the town's decision to conduct a reef study.

"Like many seaside communities in Florida, Coral Beach has become increasingly concerned with the health of its coral reefs. When it came to my attention that the most recent study of our reef system was made over a decade ago, I urged the town to initiate a new one that would determine if there has been significant deterioration, and if so, what steps should be taken to protect this vital ecosystem. Our study was begun by Dr. Abe Lesnesky, a marine biologist at the University of Miami. Sadly, Dr. Lesnesky was diagnosed with cancer and was forced to abandon his work here. It is, of course, essential that this key study not remain incomplete, inconclusive—"

"Excuse me, Mayor McDermott. If I may interject here?" It was the glad-hander, the flashy older man who'd been assiduously working the room. Lily remembered his name. It was Pete Ferrucci. He was apparently chairman of something or other.

Ferrucci rose to his feet, one hand buttoning his double-breasted suit. "Mayor McDermott, if you please, I'd like it duly noted that not *all* the members of this committee agree on this point. Dr. Lesnesky's study was essentially complete. None of his tests revealed the presence of anything harmful to humans or to marine life in the water. Nor were there any other signs that our reef was diseased. *None whatsoever,*" he repeated, glancing around the room to make sure everyone had heard. "Personally, as a tax paying member of this community, I remain unconvinced the town's dollars are being spent wisely in continuing this study, especially when so many other projects deserve funding, yet remain on hold. For example, it troubles me deeply that an accident occurred this very morning on the Bellemer Bridge. A bridge that many council members, myself included, have argued is unsafe and have repeatedly petitioned the town to widen."

"Thank you." Sean inclined his head. "Your input has been duly noted, Mr. Ferrucci, but as you may recall, the coral reef advisory panel outvoted you," he said, his tone dry. "The decision was made to finish the present study, and allay any lingering concerns about the reef's present condition."

"Yes, but at what cost to our town? Why continue a study like this when we already have more than sufficient data? Why throw money away needlessly? Shouldn't we be using that money to improve our town in ways that *matter*? What's more important, really? The Bellemer Bridge—"

"May I remind you, Mr. Ferrucci," Sean interrupted smoothly, "that this is a meeting for the coral reef study?

I will, of course, be delighted to debate the issue of the Bellemer Bridge with you at the next town council meeting. It's been scheduled for tomorrow, at six o'clock, I believe. Is that right, Ms. Roemer?"

His secretary nodded, without bothering to look up from the pad she was filling with her rapid shorthand.

"Before I return to the topic at hand, that is, the coral reef study," Sean stressed deliberately, inviting muffled laughter, "I should mention the following, in the hopes it will ease certain members' fears about exceeding the dollar amount we've allocated for the reef project. The Marine Center has generously offered to waive its fees and finish the reef study at no additional cost to the town."

An audible murmur of approval swept the room. One thing was clear, Lily thought—noting the ease with which Sean conducted the meeting—her childhood nemesis had evolved into the quintessential politician. Though it irked her to admit it, he was good. He presented a thoroughly convincing image of a caring, concerned politician . . . an extremely savvy politician. Right now, the other committee members—with the exception of Pete Ferrucci—all had big smiles on their faces, thrilled with Mayor McDermott's announcement that the town wouldn't have to spend a penny to continue the reef study.

If Lily hadn't spent the first eighteen years of her life watching Sean McDermott con the world with his charm, she, too, might have bought his smoothly delivered words—but she had. And because of her work as a marine biologist, Lily was doubly skeptical; years observing politicians use environmental issues to suit their own agenda had left her distrustful.

The issues surrounding the coral reef were a capsule

version of an increasingly familiar story heard the world over—not just in tropical seaside communities.

A spectacular, natural environment became a town's golden goose, attracting people from near and far. Soon, tourist-oriented businesses sprang up, first and second homes were built, jobs created, all dependent upon the natural beauty of the surroundings. But inevitably the day came when the environment could no longer support the overwhelming toll humans placed on it. What had started out as a wondrous golden goose began to look more like a mangy chicken.

Yet even then, people refused to relinquish their vision of endless profit, wanting nothing more than to continue living their fairy-tale dreams.

Coral Beach's golden goose was its spectacular beaches, its numerous water activities, and its offshore reef. Lily knew that if the town's coral reef was unhealthy, chances were that all the rest—beaches, water sports—would eventually be affected, too.

But who in Coral Beach would willingly sacrifice something to care for the reef's vital ecosystem, and who instead would choose to exploit the area until it was too sick to save? Would Sean McDermott be the one to take a stand and conserve this natural environment? A secret corner of her heart wished to believe it so.

The words *Marine Center* floated past, and Lily dragged her attention back to the meeting.

Sean was nodding in reply to the comment. "Certainly," he said. "But why don't we let Dr. Banyon and her assistants answer that—"

"Sorry to cut in again, Mr. Mayor," Pete Ferrucci apologized with a self-deprecating chuckle. "I confess to being a bit dismayed by the last-minute switch in scientists. Initially, we were informed that the head scientist from the Marine Center would be Dr. George Hunt. Naturally, I looked him up, checked him out, and was pleased to see he had the right experience for the job. Now, suddenly, we've got ourselves a brand-new scientist. Could you tell us, Mr. Mayor, why the committee members weren't advised such a change had taken place?"

A muscle jumped above Sean's lean jaw. "I apologize that my staff and I were unable to alert the committee sooner."

Ferrucci wasn't listening. He'd fixed his attention on Lily, Karen, and John. He had a flat, dark stare. Typical of most predators, he picked the most vulnerable member of the research team first.

"Ms. Masur, would you mind sharing your credentials with us, along with your area of expertise in marine biology?"

Karen glanced around the room full of strangers, and blanched. "Uh, I'm the photographer." Karen's brown eyes widened when the committee members continued to look at her, waiting expectantly. "I take pictures," she managed.

"Oh." Ferrucci's smile shifted, turning into a smirk. "I see. And do you have a degree in marine biology?"

"Um, no, I don't."

"Environmental science, perhaps?"

Karen shook her head.

"How about a degree in photography?"

"I took a leave from college," Karen's admission was delivered in a near whisper as bright splotches of embarrassment spread across her cheeks.

Ferrucci's smile grew wide. "Mr. Mayor, I'd like it duly

noted in the minutes that the scientific team the Town of Coral Beach has contracted to replace Dr. Lesnesky has less than stellar—"

All right. Enough was enough. Lily would be damned if she'd allow anyone to make disparaging remarks about her team.

"Excuse me for interrupting," she said as she stood up. All eyes turned to her. "Mr. Ferrucci, members of the committee, let me assure you of Karen Masur's abilities as a photographer. Her work at the Marine Center—one of the most highly regarded institutes in the country— has been consistently excellent. Let me stress how vital her role as photographer is. As you doubtless know, the principal aim of a reef study is to document its physical state and record any signs of deterioration. To accomplish this, we scientists utilize a variety of tools to provide us with visual evidence. Even with advances in computer technology, photography remains an *essential* tool for recording the health of the coral, and for documenting different types of species—plant and fish alike. I have full confidence that Ms. Masur will do a superb job with this study."

Ferrucci's mouth opened, a big gaping hole ringed by black facial hair. Lily looked away. "Now, so we don't waste any more of the committee's time discussing my team's credentials, let me simply add that although Mr. Granger is still working on his doctoral dissertation, he's already written a number of articles on coral reef ecology. I'm sure Mr. Granger would be delighted to circulate copies of them among you, and would be equally happy to talk about the work he's been doing on his dissertation."

She turned to John, who was paying far closer attention now that he was the focus of discussion. "John, why don't you tell the committee a little bit about yourself?"

Lily suppressed a smile as John eagerly launched into a detailed description of his dissertation topic. *Take that, Ferrucci,* she thought as she relaxed against the back of her chair, unfazed by the waves of hostility emanating from him.

It was a good ten minutes before John finished explaining why his Ph.D. dissertation was destined to be hailed as a groundbreaking work of scientific research. The final syllable of John's last sentence still hung in the air when Ferrucci sprang from his seat, like a jack-in-the-box with a broken lid.

"And you, Dr. Banyon?" he challenged, thrusting his chin forward aggressively. "Ms. Roemer was kind enough to provide us a few details. I see here that you boast a Ph.D. from Brown University." His drawl implied Lily might as well have received her degree from one of those correspondence schools that advertise on the inside of matchbooks. "And it says here you hold a senior research position at the Marine Center. Very impressive. Nevertheless, despite these accomplishments, I doubt your scientific background truly meets the needs of this study."

Before Lily could react, Sean was speaking, leaving her to sit in stunned disbelief as his reply registered.

"Which merely shows how wrong a person can be. In this case, that person would be you, Mr. Ferrucci." Cool amusement laced Sean's voice. A few discreet chuckles disguised as coughs circled the room. "Dr. Banyon is acknowledged throughout the world as an expert in coral reef ecology. Her work has taken her to such far-flung sites as the Seychelles and the Galapagos. Of particular importance to us, however, and a fact most people in this room are unaware of, is that Dr. Banyon also happens to be a native of Coral Beach. Her knowledge of these waters is extensive. Indeed, an entire chapter of a book she coauthored on environmental pollution and its effects on marine ecosystems is devoted to the Florida Keys"— Sean paused to clear his throat and his lips curved in a small smile—"As you might already suspect, I could easily continue listing Dr. Banyon's many scientific accomplishments. Fascinating as they are, I'll refrain. . . . I know you'd like to get home before midnight." Sean's smile became a grin as laughter swept the room. "Suffice it to say, *any* community would be thrilled to have Dr. Banyon lead its study. And we should count ourselves lucky that Dr. Banyon is willing to accommodate her busy schedule to suit our own. She was to begin the second phase of a project in the Bahamas. . . ."

A growing sense of unreality had spread through Lily as Sean fired off highlights of her professional career. When he mentioned her work in the Bahamas, her disorientation was complete. How in the world did he know about her next planned tour of duty?

Recitation complete, Sean paused to look directly at her. Lily's gaze skittered away, afraid of what he might see there. His unexpected defense left her confused, uncertain. Never in a million years would Lily have pictured Sean as her valiant defender. Then again, Lily reflected, Sean's role as mayor and as a driving force behind the reef study practically forced him to adopt this stance—at least publicly.

She knew only too well how he felt about her privately. Sean spoke again. "With Dr. Banyon's professional commitments as numerous as they are, she and her team will doubtless begin their research as soon as possible. I suggest we reconvene in three weeks, by which time Dr. Banyon should be able to give us some further data."

Someone dutifully made a motion to adjourn. Around the room, hasty seconds and thirds were pronounced in favor of the motion. The committee disbanded rapidly.

Thank heaven that's over, Lily thought. She had three weeks, then, before she'd have to deal with Sean Mc-Dermott again. She stood, muscles stiff from too many hours spent sitting in planes, automobiles, and over-air-conditioned meeting rooms.

"Uh, Lily?" Karen said.

She looked up from the pile of papers that she was shoving into her shoulder bag. "Yes?"

"I just wanted to say thanks." Karen's cheeks continued to sport those telltale stains of embarrassment.

"Nothing to thank me for," she replied mildly.

"Uh-huh," Karen insisted, setting her braids swinging. "You stood up for me, even though I'm just starting out. I know you would have preferred having someone like Ethan down here." Ethan Ford often worked as Lily's photographer. He was one of the center's best, a veteran. But Ethan was currently on leave, his wife having just given birth to their first child.

"Having Ethan here would have been nice," Lily admitted with a casual shrug. "It's always easier to work with people who are old hands, familiar with the ropes and with the way I like things done. But that's what this project is all about—at least for you: getting experience in the field. So that next time you'll be better able to handle someone like Ferrucci. Besides, what I told the committee was the truth. You are a great photographer."

"You think?"

"I never exaggerate someone's professional skills. So," she continued briskly, as Karen was looking a shade perkier, "here's what you're going to do to justify my confidence: You're going to do a first-rate job photographing every inch of this coral reef, everything from plankton to sea turtles. Then you're going to take those spectacular slides and shove them down Pete Ferrucci's throat. Got it?"

"Excellent advice, Karen. I'd take it if I were you," Evelyn Roemer said. She had once again materialized at Lily's side. "Dr. Banyon clearly knows her way around small-town politics—big city, too, I'd imagine."

"Yes," Lily acknowledged. "I've run into 'Pete Ferruccis' before."

"You were great, Lily. Mayor McDermott, too," Karen gushed enthusiastically. "Together you left Ferrucci without a leg to stand on. It was awesome, the way Mayor McDermott rattled off all that stuff you'd done. He blew everyone away. I could tell they were super-impressed by him . . . uh, I mean by what you'd done career-wise."

Lily sighed inwardly. Yet another wonderstruck fan of Sean McDermott. He'd always had that effect on women. Time to let Karen in on what politicians' staff spent their time doing. "I'm sure we have Ms. Roemer to thank for that polished recitation."

Evelyn Roemer's lips curled in a smile worthy of the Mona Lisa. "You mean did I prep him?" she asked, the cryptic smile still playing about her lips. "No, that's not Sean's style. He's too quick on his feet to need his lines spoon-fed. To tell you the truth, I myself am mystified how he managed to pull that one off. You see, Dr. Banyon, until half an hour ago, Sean didn't even know you were on this advisory panel."

CHAPTER SEVEN

Lily wanted a drink. Actually, anything would do if it succeeded in banishing Sean McDermott from her mind. Evelyn Roemer certainly knew how to drop a bombshell. Before Lily could ask who, what, when, or why, she had hustled Karen off with the promise of a guided tour of Coral Beach and its brand new organic market where Karen could stock up on food. It turned out that both women shared a passion for bean curd. Lily had forgotten Karen was a vegan and Simone had been far too smart to remind her.

John Granger had vanished, something for which he had a true talent. Maybe he'd been scared Evelyn Roemer might boss him into more furniture rearranging. Lily wasn't about to spend time searching for him. He had a key; he'd find his way back to the condo. She grabbed her bag and headed toward the exit, keeping her eyes down, avoiding eye contact, lest anyone try to start a conversation.

Lily vaguely recalled a restaurant with a bar, located on Palmetto, near Division . . . or was it Main? Who knew what the place was like now, but after a day like today's, Lily wasn't feeling particularly choosy.

"Dr. Banyon, just a minute please."

Lily glanced at the hand detaining her. "Yes, Mr. Ferrucci?" she inquired, resisting the urge to shrug him off. A few years ago, in Jamaica, she'd made friends with a Rastafarian blackbelt named Louis, who'd taught her a truly neat trick that would have Pete Ferrucci on his knees and howling in about three seconds flat.

Ferrucci misinterpreted the reason for her smile. "I'm glad you didn't take anything I said during the meeting personally, Dr. Banyon. As I'm sure you realize, this is an incredibly delicate issue for our community. As chairman of the Board of Commerce, I feel obliged to represent the . . . how shall I put it? The business side of any debate."

And in so doing hack my research team's reputation to shreds.

"I understand perfectly, Mr. Ferrucci."

"Fine, fine," he replied with a joviality that grated. "You know, I hadn't realized you were a local until Sean mentioned it." He paused, his brow furrowing. "Banyon, Banyon . . . funny, I moved here years ago, but that's not a name I recognize."

Ferrucci probably had the *Who's Who* of Coral Beach memorized, *a* to *z*. Lily clenched her molars, knowing what was coming. "My grandmother is May Ellen Farrady."

It would have been pointless to conceal his astonishment. "You don't say! Why, that means you must be Kaye's daughter."

"That's right, Mr. Ferrucci."

"A marvelous woman, simply delightful. I met her a few times before she moved to Palm Beach. Your grandmother, too." Lily felt him scrutinizing her even more closely. "I, uh, should have seen the resemblance before."

Was he joking? "I take after my father's side of the family," Lily informed him curtly. "He left town twenty-eight years ago, so unless you've visited Oslo recently, I doubt you'd have met him." She turned back toward the door. "I'm sorry to cut our conversation short, but it's been a long day and I'm hungry and tired."

"Of course. I won't keep you. If you're looking for a nice restaurant with a relaxing atmosphere, let me recommend the Blue Dolphin, at the corner of Palmetto and Main. It's quite popular, but if you tell the maître d' I sent you, you'll get a table immediately. The Dolphin's recently come under new management." He preened with self-importance.

Well, she could scratch that place from her list. Better to try the opposite side of town.

"Nothing would give me greater pleasure than to invite you as my personal guest to the Dolphin," he continued. "Unfortunately, however, I have a previous commitment this evening. A rain check, perhaps?" The smile Ferrucci gave her was unctuous.

"You're too kind," she returned with an equally false one.

"Before I forget, Dr. Banyon, I wanted to tell you that if there's anything, anything at all that you need, don't hesitate to buzz the management office."

Lily regarded Ferrucci blankly.

"Oh, that's right!" He laughed. "You haven't lived here in quite some time. The apartments you and your assistants are staying in? I own the condominium complex."

"The apartments we're using belong to you?"

"I feel it's my civic duty to offer space to the town," he said modestly.

And make a neat bundle on the side. "Isn't that convenient?" she murmured. *Now I'll know who to call for the exterminator.* "If you'll excuse me, I'm going to duck into the ladies' room and wash off the travel dust." Lily seized the convenient pretext, although in reality, it was contact with Pete Ferrucci that left her feeling decidedly unclean.

Locating the restroom a few doors down the hallway, Lily lingered unnecessarily, until she was positive the other panel members would be long departed. With a certain sheepishness, she opened the door.

And froze as Ferrucci's loud, carrying voice reached her.

"So, McDermott, you got this study up and running again. We all know the reef's in fine shape, but it'll be nice to have these scientists confirm it for us. I couldn't be happier about it, really."

Sean answered. But although Lily strained to hear, his words remained frustratingly inaudible.

Ferrucci spoke again. "About this development proposal. The architects have drafted some preliminary plans based on the engineering reports. I think it'd be a good idea to walk around the marina with them, get a feel for what they have in mind. How about we do lunch? I'll call your office and set a date with Evelyn."

Lily closed the door softly. She didn't need to listen any more. Overwhelmed with sudden weariness, she laid her forehead against the door.

"So what's got you in such a piss-poor mood?" Dave Cullen asked. "I thought the meeting went pretty well." He had his elbows propped on the Rusted Keel's scarred and pitted bar, one hand wrapped around an ice-cold beer. He took a long pull, swallowed, and added, "After all, the good guys came out on top today."

Seated next to him, Sean acknowledged his friend's comment with a tired shrug. He supposed Dave was right. But that did little to dislodge the sinking feeling in the pit of his stomach that with Lily Banyon on the scene, things would go to hell in a handbasket awful quick. Too tired to explain the hows and whys, Sean concentrated on his whiskey, savoring its smoky peat-flavored bite.

Unperturbed by Sean's silence, Dave nursed his beer, the fingers of his free hand drumming an accompaniment to one of the bar's perennial favorites, Otis Redding's, "Dock of the Bay," which someone had selected from the jukebox's list. The Rusted Keel was Sean and Dave's preferred after-hours hangout, one of the few remaining places in Coral Beach the tourists hadn't taken over, most likely because from the outside the bar looked like a run-down bait-and-tackle shop. Stepping inside, one's second impression wasn't much better.

Though there were a few tables covered in ancient red-and-white checked plastic, no one in town came to the Keel for its spiffy decor. Most of the regulars avoided the tables, preferring to congregate around the pool table in the back, or to while away the hours throwing darts at the dartboard with unerring, unnerving accuracy. For those more vegetatively inclined, the battered TV above the bar where Sean and Dave were sitting was tuned to ESPN twenty-four–seven. And, of course, there was the jukebox, which hadn't been updated since Don McLean's "American Pie." Five songs for a buck.

But the finest thing about the Rusted Keel was its clientele. Not a single person in the place besides Sean and

Dave had a political bone in his body. After a hard day fighting the good fight, there was nothing so relaxing as the sweet scent of beer, salted peanuts, and political indifference. Sean had never once been approached by someone wanting to know how to obtain a building permit for a two-car garage, nor been badgered about why he'd voted for or against such and such a proposal. And while every now and again a disgruntled fisherman or boat captain shot Dave a hostile look, the tacit rule at the Rusted Keel was that while bitching about the Marlins' or the Dolphins' miserable season was acceptable behavior, griping to locally elected officials who only wanted to throw back a couple of beers in peace was not.

But Sean's drink of choice this evening was whiskey rather than Rolling Rock, and he was staring moodily at the dust motes, which told Dave he hadn't yet shaken off his mayoral responsibilities.

"Come on, Sean, quit worrying," he said. "You knew after the panel voted to continue the study that Ferrucci would be in attack mode. Ever since you beat him in the mayoral election he's wanted to kick your butt. He's not going to let an opportunity pass him by, especially not on this issue." He pushed a red plastic bowl toward his friend. "Here, have a peanut, it'll make you feel better."

Always nice to see words of wisdom penetrate, Dave thought, as Sean reached and scooped out a handful of the salted nuts. "So, what'd you think of the bodacious Dr. Banyon?" he asked while Sean munched. "Liked her photographer, too. Very sparkly."

"Forget it," Sean replied. The peanuts had apparently revived him. "Banyon's trouble with a capital *T*. Her assistants probably are, too," Sean added between mouthfuls. "Should've told me you were planning on contacting the Marine Center. I'd have warned you to avoid Lily at all costs."

"Sorry, bud." Dave shrugged his shoulders. "I only learned yesterday that there had been a change of plans, that we'd be getting Banyon in place of Hunt. I couldn't exactly call back and say, 'Thanks, but no thanks.' Not that I would have anyway." He paused for a swallow of beer. "From that nifty recitation you gave earlier, you obviously don't need me to tell you she's one of the best. You read her latest book?"

"I've glanced at it," Sean muttered into his glass.

Dave looked at him out of the corner of his eyes. "Pretty thorough glancing," he said mildly. "Banyon's got a great track record. Not afraid to tackle tough issues or tough opponents. With someone like her on the panel, we'll be sitting in clover."

"Don't be fooled by Lily. As you'll discover, the experience is much closer to lying in a field of poison ivy."

Dave grinned. Dr. Lily Banyon did indeed look like the kind of woman who'd leave a mark on a man. He glanced at Sean, wondering. McDermott was behaving a bit peculiarly. Moody, tense, and edgy. Not Sean's usual MO, that was for sure. "Come on, Sean," he said. "Banyon can't be as bad as you imagine. After all, she jumped in and saved her photographer when Ferrucci was going for the jugular. Pretty damned courageous, if you ask me."

Sean scowled but remained silent.

"Did you see how big Karen Masur's eyes grew when Ferrucci was tearing into her, all for the greater good of Coral Beach? I thought she was going to faint. Ferrucci did too. Swear to God, his teeth must've grown four inches. Noticed it when he flashed his signature smile." Dave gave a mock shudder. "His smile disappeared damned fast, once Banyon leaped into the fray; so you see, that proves Banyon's got the right instincts."

"What that really proves is that Ferrucci's got a big mouth." Sean gave a small grin, suddenly looking more like his usual self. "Maybe I should write Pete a thank-you note for being such an ass."

Dave laughed. "Be bighearted, send him a fruit basket while you're at it. So, how far back do you and the doctor go?" he asked casually.

Sean swirled the amber liquid at the bottom of his glass. "Pre-diaper. Lily's hated me from the womb. And probably will—right up to the grave."

Dave whistled softly. "Is this possible?" he asked in an awed tone of voice. "You mean to say there's a woman alive who won't canvass the entire district for you on election eve?"

"Stuff it, Dave," Sean replied without heat. "When we were kids, Lily had a notebook where she listed all the reasons why I was the scum of the universe. Didn't take her long to run out of pages and move on to volume two. One of her favorite pastimes was to quote passages to me. I still remember a few of them." He drained his whiskey and signaled to Charlie for another round.

Dave shifted in his stool and studied Sean's closed expression. "That's it." His grin spread slowly. "You got a thing for the beautiful scientist."

"Yeah." Sean's shrug downplayed Dave's discovery. "But like I said, Lily's detested me forever. I doubt her attitude has changed much." And after the way he'd behaved toward her earlier, at the reef meeting, it was practically guaranteed Lily wouldn't be entertaining any warm, fuzzy feelings about him. Probably thought he was a bigger jerk than ever.

"So how long have you been suffering the effects of unrequited, uh, you know . . ."

Sean tilted his head, his look measuring. "Would you believe eighth grade?" He smiled and waited.

"You're kidding!"

Sean solemnly shook his head. "I kid you not."

"Eighth grade," Dave mused aloud. "What'd she do?"

"Took off her sweater in Ms. Geller's English class," Sean replied with a sorry laugh.

"She took off her sweater?" Dave echoed, his expression mystified. Understanding dawned as he recalled what he'd been like at age thirteen, a hormone-crazed adolescent. "Oh, yeah, right." He nodded sagely as he brought his beer to his lips.

"I was a goner from that day on," Sean said. "Didn't matter where I was. One look at Lily, and my mind and body went haywire. The worst of it was, I never quite figured out how to shake the Lily Effect. The next four years in high school were absolute torture."

"Oh, man," Dave said with an appalled laugh as he clapped a hand to Sean's shoulder in a show of fraternal commiseration. "I'm sorry. That's a hell of a tough break."

They leaned back in their stools while Charlie set new drinks before them.

"Thanks, Charlie," Sean said, going for his wallet.

Dave stopped him with a wave of his hand. "No, let me. When I have a story this sad, you buy the rounds."

"Thanks." Sean managed a rueful smile. His hand reached back to knead the kinks in his neck. "Yeah, it's a mess," he conceded. "On top of being Lily's public enemy number one, I've got Ferrucci trying to shove these development people down my throat—when he isn't attacking me on community TV."

"Don't waste your time worrying about Ferrucci's machinations, Sean. It's Lily Banyon you should be devoting your, uh, energies to. You're not a lust-struck teenager anymore. Why don't you spend some time with her, let her get to know the real you?" Dave ignored Sean's decidedly unenthusiastic grunt. "Hey! I've got it! You can tag along on the research boat as an observer."

"A monumentally bad idea, Dave," Sean said flatly.

"Why not? It's perfect. You ran on an environmental platform; this shows how committed you are to monitoring the reef's health. You don't need to go often—otherwise our friend Ferrucci will cry foul—just enough to dazzle her with that McDermott charm. So, how about it?"

Sean shook his head. "No dice, not in a million years. I don't want to be anywhere near her."

Dave wasn't cruel enough to tell Sean he was lying like a rug.

A brief silence ensued as they nursed their drinks, absorbed in thought. At the corner of the bar, a conversation rose in decibel, becoming animated.

"Yo, Frank, take a look at what just walked in! Is it Christmas already? 'Cause that sure is a pretty package."

"You got that right. . . . Wouldn't mind unwrapping her bows."

Instinctively, Sean cast a glance over his shoulder and groaned in despair. The scene from *Casablanca* played in his mind . . . *Of all the gin joints in all the towns in all the world, she had to walk into mine.*

This could not be happening. This was his turf, his town, his bar. She had no right to trespass.

Okay, so this wasn't *Casablanca*. This wasn't Rick's Café. Sam's fingers weren't summoning the haunting melody, "As Time Goes By," from the ivories of an old, upright piano. There weren't any ceiling fans with long propeller-like blades slicing through thick clouds of cigarette smoke, nor were the voices that could be heard an exotic mélange of foreign languages and accents.

But those differences were superficial, of no consequence. The only thing that really mattered was that Sean understood exactly how Bogie felt when his eyes lit on Ingrid Bergman. That terrible mix of bitterness, longing, and fury eating away at him.

He groaned again.

At the sound, the two men sitting at the corner of the bar broke off their conversation, eyeing Sean curiously. Just as quickly, they dismissed him and returned to their avid inspection.

"Must be lost or confused. Palm Beach is twenty-five miles north."

"Let's be friendly and give her directions. How 'bout that, Ray?"

"You frigging nuts? The only directions I'm giving her are to the slip where my houseboat's moored." He elbowed his companion. "Stop drooling, Frank. She's coming this way."

Because of the Keel's gloomy interior, Lily didn't notice that he and Dave were at the bar until she was almost upon them. The second she did, her step faltered. She was doubtless debating whether to spin 180 degrees and march right out again.

He should have known Lily would tough it out. After

that initial hesitation, she *strolled*—it was the only word Sean could find that adequately described the confident sway of her hips—to the bar.

Once there, her gaze flit over Sean and Dave with total disinterest, the kind of look one reserved for strangers—with whom one had no intention of ever becoming acquainted.

"Tequila and lime, please," she ordered quietly when Charlie approached.

"Coming right up," Charlie said with a nod. He set a shot glass and a tequila bottle in front of her. Disappearing through the swinging door that led to the kitchen, he returned shortly with a white porcelain saucer, lime quarters neatly arranged in a radiating pattern.

Sean's eyebrows rose. Lily was getting the royal treatment; most of the Rusted Keel's patrons considered themselves lucky if they got their limes tossed into a plastic red Solo cup.

Charlie poured a shotful. The bar fell eerily silent as Lily leaned forward. Holding the lime bracketed between index finger and thumb, she bit into its flesh, her teeth flashing white in the subdued lighting. She lifted the shot glass to her lips. With a quick backward toss, she downed its contents. Her eyes closed.

Watching her, Sean imagined the fiery yellow liquor racing down her throat, setting her aglow from within. Involuntarily, his eyes traveled the sinuous contour of her profile and down the length of her neck. And descended further still.

Gone was the short jacket she'd been wearing earlier. The top two buttons of her blouse were undone. The blouse, made of some kind of shimmery material, shifted bluish purple in the half light.

Shadows and mysteries. The glimpse of Lily's milky white skin exposed by the shirt's plunging vee filled him with wanderlust, a need to explore until all her secrets were revealed. He moved restlessly on his stool.

A solid thud of glass against wood resounded in the near-silent bar. Then Lily was laying a ten-dollar bill on the bar and heading toward the door. In the wake of her departure, male speculation frothed in bloated bubbles.

Sean was already on his feet. He tossed a large tip on the bar. "Thanks again, Charlie. See you later, Dave."

"See you," Dave echoed. With a glimmer of a smile, he nodded in the direction of the parking lot. "Catching a ride?"

"That's the idea."

"Good luck."

"Thanks. I'll need it."

Sean had slipped his jacket off the back of the stool and was shrugging into it when one of the men seated at the corner spoke.

"Hey, McDermott, what's your opinion? Silicone for sure, huh?"

Sean paused to glance their way. Ray and Frank were partners in a small sport-fishing business. He knew them vaguely. Now he wished he didn't. He shook his head in contempt. "Think I'd tell you, Ray?"

Ray's eyes narrowed. "Like you actually know, McDermott. You claiming you've handled the goods, Mayor?" His tone matched the sneer on his face. "If so, the lady sure don't seem to remember." He poked Frank with his elbow. "Looked right through him, didn't she, Frank?"

"Like a pane of glass."

Sean ignored their snorts of laughter. "Let me give you

some friendly advice," he said mildly. "I'd be real careful not to let the lady catch you staring at her like that."

Ray pulled a comical face, pretending to look scared, then laughed even harder.

Sean smiled in return. Yet when Ray opened his mouth to speak, he cut him off. "But if *I'm* the one who catches you gawking, if I hear you talking about her that way again—" he paused, and his smile turned dangerous, "—your sorry carcasses will be feeding the fish."

CHAPTER EIGHT

How would you know, McDermott? The question taunted Sean as he left the Rusted Keel.

How did he know Lily Banyon's breasts were 100 percent warm, pliant flesh and not synthetic balloons?

That was easy. Because she'd had them since she was thirteen years old.

You claiming you've handled the goods, Mayor?

Never had the pleasure.

Correction. There was that one fleeting moment. But that memory, along with so many others, was Sean's personal Pandora's box. In his surprise over her return, he'd dropped his guard. And the box had opened a crack. With fierce resolve, Sean slammed its lid shut as forcefully as he wrenched open the door to Lily's metallic blue subcompact.

The engine of her car idling, Lily had been waiting an eternity for a break in the rush hour traffic. Too busy scanning the cars roaring past in either direction, she hadn't seen Sean crossing the length of the parking lot, aiming straight for her.

When the passenger door flew open, Lily's head whipped around in alarm. "What the—" Alarm turned to outrage when she saw who it was. "What the hell do you think you're doing?" she demanded.

"Hitching a ride. It's Thursday, Lily. You haven't forgotten what happens on Thursday nights, have you?" Sean smiled.

Thursday. Since time immemorial, Granny May cohosted a barbecue Thursday evenings with Sean's grandmother, Anne Prentiss, inviting six other biddies. Afterward, the women all settled down for an evening of bridge and gin fizzes.

"No. No way!" Appalled, she shook her head violently. The prospect of being the focus of an interrogation by eight inquisitive matrons was so unnerving that Lily forgot about shoving Sean out of the car.

"Yup. You may not care about May Ellen's feelings, but I do. I'm not going to let you break her heart when she learns that you're here in town and haven't bothered to see her."

"I was planning to visit her in the morning—"

"Not good enough. Drive, Lily." Sean gave her a mocking smile and asked, "Or do you need directions?"

Without thinking, Lily flipped him the bird and hit the accelerator hard. The car burned rubber out of the parking lot as Lily cut into the heavy traffic. Behind her came the outraged blare of car horns, beside her echoed the ring of Sean's laughter.

She shot him a venomous look. He was leaning back against the passenger seat, for all appearances having the time of his life.

"Know what's nice about you, Lily?" he said, laughter still threading his voice.

"I can't imagine," she snapped.

"You never change."

"Neither do you. You're as obnoxious as ever."

"That's me. Ran on the obnoxious ticket," he agreed complacently. "Landslide victory."

She was driving like a maniac, switching lanes as though she were in a chase scene in a cops and robbers film. Throughout, Sean remained aggravatingly relaxed. His fingers threaded behind his neck, he merely observed in a bored drawl, "By the way, we have speed limits in Coral Beach."

"Tough. I can't get to May Ellen's fast enough, if it means I get to be rid of you."

He sighed. "There you go, breaking my heart. I was hoping we'd have time to reminisce. No? Then I'll take the opportunity now to lay the ground rules out for you, Lily."

"You lay ground rules for me?" she scoffed. "I don't think so."

Sean continued as if she hadn't spoken. "See, Lily, this reef study means a great deal to me."

Recalling the snippet of conversation she'd overheard between Sean and Pete Ferrucci had Lily's knuckles turning white against the rim of the steering wheel. "Indeed? Oh, I understand. Of course, it means a great deal to you *politically*." She stressed the word. "So much has changed here." She nodded at the scenery speeding past. "New houses, new construction . . ." As her voice trailed off, she cast a quick glance at Sean and saw that his jaw was clamped tight.

"Yeah, that's right," he replied, his voice now altered, too, edged with anger. "You guessed it, Lily. The study means a lot to me politically. So forget any burning desire you might have to cross me."

She felt her own temper flare. "I'm a scientist, not a

politician. The only thing I plan is to report my findings to the advisory panel. . . . I'll do my work like I always do. Objectively. It'll be up to *you* to twist the results to suit your purposes. And I do wonder where your political interest lies."

"You're smart. I'm sure you'll figure it out."

"Oh, I have a pretty good idea already." Lily only hoped Sean interpreted the heavy disappointment in her voice as sarcasm. "Traffic's certainly heavier than it used to be. Big boom in business recently?"

"Economy's better than ever."

"How nice for you. Lot of new developments planned for the area?" Lily threw the question out recklessly.

"Slow down, Ace, or you'll miss the turn," was his only reply.

Damn and damn again, he was right. Lily braked hard.

They exited the heavily traveled highway, turning onto a smaller county road. They were heading north now, nearing one of Coral Beach's oldest residential neighborhoods, Laguna, where Lily's grandmother—and Sean's too—lived. Many of the houses in Laguna had winding paths leading from their backyards down to private beaches of pinkish-white, pristine sand.

It was a neighborhood of gently meandering streets, neat lawns, groomed flowerbeds, and well-maintained homes. Late-model Cadillacs, shiny as the day they were bought, were displayed in the driveways.

They arrived at May Ellen Farrady's Spanish Mediterranean ranch in what was doubtless record time. Across the street was a line of neatly parked cars, seven of them. Granny May's guests were already assembled. A dozen butterflies took flight in Lily's stomach.

Lily pulled into her grandmother's U-shaped driveway,

giving the steering wheel a hard yank. She'd hoped the jolting turn might rap Sean's elbow against the window, but she was clean out of luck today.

Just remember to breathe, she told herself as she turned off the car's engine. It wasn't such a big deal to be walking into her grandmother's home for the first time in ten years. But, God, she wished she could be doing this without Sean McDermott's sharp gaze watching her every move.

The thought of him observing her had Lily pausing, her hand on the car door latch. "I can't help but wonder, McDermott. Even if I were to try to fix this study, how do you think you'd be able to tell?"

Sean shook his head, his expression one of grave disappointment. "Not as quick as you used to be, Lily. Preparations for the season aren't in full swing yet; there's lots of open time in my schedule. I've decided to keep you company, go on some of your dives."

Her laugh of amusement filled the car. "Oh, please! Do you have any idea how many dives we'll be making to collect our samples? I estimate close to twenty-five. Sometimes we'll be diving twice in one day. Naturally, Mayor McDermott, you're welcome to join my team and me on as many expeditions as you wish. But I'm truly intrigued. . . . What could you hope to discover or, rather, *uncover*? After all, you wouldn't know the difference between a fire sponge and a fire hydrant."

"True. But I know *you*, Lily, only too well. And I know exactly how you feel about me. So if anything about your work on the reef strikes me as remotely—pardon the expression—fishy, I'll nail you publicly."

Shock had Lily's mouth hanging open. "What?" she gasped.

"You heard me. You fool with this project, and I will smear a big, black, messy mark on that twenty-four carat reputation of yours."

The nerve of him. How dare he imply that she might try and manipulate a scientific study. "Now it's your turn to listen, Mr. Mayor. I don't give a damn about your political ambitions, or your plans for Coral Beach," she hissed. "They mean nothing to me. The only thing I care about is the condition of this town's reef. You managed to get one thing right, though. I do have a good reputation. It's excellent actually. Say one thing to defame it, and I will sink your political career faster than the *Titanic*." Incensed, Lily shoved the car door open and scrambled out. Sean's opened in tandem.

His words carried over the sound of doors slamming, one after the other. "I always think it's great to clear the air like this. Must admit, I'm looking forward to these next few weeks. Diving with a world-renowned scientist. Hey, maybe I'll even drop by the lab; we could do an experiment together, just for old times' sake. Wouldn't that be fun, Lily?"

Lily glared at his smiling face. Her most fervent wish was that they might already be in the water. So she could drown him.

As if he could read her mind, Sean shook his head. "Shame on you, Lily," he cheerfully mocked. "Now, let's see a big, happy smile for your Granny May."

CHAPTER NINE

Sean's longer gait allowed him to reach May Ellen's front door just ahead of her. He pressed a finger to the doorbell, and then stepped back, standing directly behind her, his solid presence barring escape.

Had Sean perhaps caught her wiping damp palms against her skirt as they walked up the neatly edged, brick-laid path and recognized her gesture as the onslaught of nerves? Had he guessed at the emotions warring inside her? How part of her was filled with eagerness to see her grandmother, how an equally strong force longed to flee rather than revisit one of the settings of childhood past?

Lily's tension mounted as they waited, neither speaking, while from the inside of the house the muted sound of footsteps grew louder. The wooden door opened to reveal Granny May framed by the foyer's golden light. She stared up at Lily with eyes that grew ever wider and shimmery bright with emotion.

"Lily? Is that you, Lily?" She breathed at last. "My heavens! This is wonderful, simply wonderful!"

The anxiety that churned inside of Lily sputtered and

died. Her lips parted in a tremulous smile. "Hello, Granny May," she said, her voice gone husky with emotion.

Without turning her head, without taking her eyes off Lily, May Ellen called urgently, "Anne, Anne, come quickly! You'll never guess whom your handsome grandson has brought." With a radiant smile, she held out her arms in invitation.

For a fraction of a second, Lily hesitated before taking that decisive step across the threshold, back into the fold of her family. In her preoccupation, she nearly forgot Sean's presence behind her. The not-so-subtle nudge to the middle of her spine was a shocking reminder. Lily barely muffled her startled gasp as she stumbled into her grandmother's warm embrace.

Holding Lily's hand, Granny May led her into the living room, where the rest of the bridge party had gathered. Like May Ellen, the other women wore what Lily still remembered as their Thursday night outfits: madras skirts and pastel cardigans, their fake lizard handbags propped against the legs of their armchairs.

Her arrival was greeted by an excited chorus of, "Oh, how wonderful to see you, dear!" and "Aren't you just thrilled, May Ellen?" and "Isn't Lily looking sophisticated; I'd never have recognized her," and "Why, she's nearly as tall as you, Sean!" Lily could do nothing but smile and nod weakly. Thankfully, Mrs. Prentiss, Sean's grandmother, came to her rescue.

"The barbecued shrimp is ready, ladies, and Alicia's brought her famous chicken-and-pineapple salad. Sean, dear, May Ellen looks in need of a gin fizz." She turned to Lily. "What can Sean get you, Lily?"

"A whiskey neat, please, Mrs. Prentiss. But I'll—"

"No, no, you sit with May Ellen," Sean's grandmother replied. "And I insist you call me Anne—Sean's been addressing your grandmother as 'May' for *years* now. I'm so happy to see you home, my dear. This is a real occasion, isn't it, May?"

"It certainly is," May Ellen replied, patting the hand she still gripped.

Once they were alone, May Ellen turned to her. "Come sit and tell me what wonderful miracle has brought you home."

Lily patiently answered May's barrage of questions, explaining how she'd been asked to finish the coral reef study and that she'd arrived in town only today, but would be staying for a number of weeks. She would have had to be blindfolded to miss the light that flared in her grandmother's eyes when she learned that the job would require a prolonged stay.

"Oh, how perfect!" her grandmother exclaimed. "We'll get to spend time together."

Seeing her grandmother's poignant happiness, Lily was assailed by a wave of remorse. She became acutely conscious of how infrequently she'd made time for her grandmother recently.

Lily knew she had a stubborn streak a mile wide. It had been years since she'd left for college. The hurt and bitterness she'd harbored toward her mother had faded to a dull ache. Yet long after the pain had dwindled, Lily had continued her self-imposed exile. While she had excuses aplenty to justify her actions, right now, they struck Lily as merely petty and selfish.

Seated across from her grandmother, Lily forced herself to face the consequence of her long-standing feud with her mother. What had her aloofness actually accomplished except to hurt others in her family by denying them the chance to share her life?

A deep sense of regret settled over Lily. *Simone had
been right,* she thought. She couldn't ignore her roots, her
family, anymore. It was time she made up for the past.

Sean deliberately loitered on the patio with his grandmother and the other septuagenarians before going to
the kitchen to pour May Ellen and Lily's drinks. He
wanted to give them a bit of privacy. *As for me,* Sean
thought—drawing deep drafts of the scented, heavy
Florida night air into his lungs—*I need to pull myself
together.*

Because it was happening already: the Lily Effect was
at work on his brain.

Why in God's name had he told her he'd be accompanying her and the team on some dives, when that was the
last thing he wanted to do . . . especially if he intended to
maintain his sanity?

Unfortunately, as dumb as he was feeling, Sean had the
answer to that one. It pained him to realize that he was
still as hung up on Lily as ever—and just as susceptible to
her disdain.

It had taken her, what, two hours since she waltzed
back into Coral Beach to accuse him of crooked politics?

Did Lily have any idea of the high-wire act he was attempting by trying to get the reef accurately documented
and assessed before he took a public stance on the marina development? No, of course not. Sean might have
filled her in, if she hadn't made it clear she assumed his
sole motivation was political gain.

Stung, he'd retaliated in kind, implying that Lily might

stoop so low as to manipulate the reef study—even though Sean knew the sun would set in the east before Lily Banyon committed an act of professional dishonesty. Her integrity had always been one of the things he admired most about her. That Lily actually fell for his bogus threat merely showed how profound her distrust, her dislike of him was.

At the Rusted Keel, Dave had urged him to seize the opportunity to go on the research boat and work on charming Lily.

Yeah, thought Sean acidly, as he carried the cocktails toward the living room. He and Lily were off to their usual great start.

Both women looked up when Sean entered, a gin fizz and two whiskeys nestled in his hands. Only May Ellen greeted him with a smile.

Already beset with remorse toward her grandmother, Lily's sense of composure deserted her entirely when Sean joined them. How, especially after their last conversation, could she still react to him like this? It would have been a soothing balm to her pride if she could blame the immediate surroundings for making Sean appear so striking, so breath-stealingly handsome.

May Ellen's living room had always reminded Lily of a movie set for a film entitled *Jungle Fever.* The room's decor was dominated by zebra and jaguar printed throw pillows nestled against the sofas and chairs, and ceiling-high palms which rose in wide, leafy arcs from their celadon green planters. The side tables were cluttered with bric-a-brac, family pictures, and lamps sporting heavily fringed shades. Against this visual cacophony, Sean stood out, all austere masculine beauty.

Unfortunately for Lily's nervous system, he'd looked

just as good in the Rusted Keel's musty gloom. And downright devastating sitting two feet from her in the tiny rental car.

Sean placed May Ellen's gin fizz on the nearest side table. "Why thank you, Sean. I only wish I'd known Lily was coming, I'd have chilled some champagne."

"And ruin the tradition of Thursday night gin fizzes?" Sean teased with a smile. He circled the mahogany coffee table to where Lily sat.

He stopped and waited.

Slowly, her blond head tilted upward until her eyes met his. Enormous and wide, they looked like a winter sea, tossed with mystery. For the thousandth time, Sean wished he could ignore his feelings for this beautiful, intelligent, and damnably frustrating woman. That he could forget a lifetime of desire. Tamping down on the need to kiss Lily senseless, he pressed the whiskey into her hand instead.

Frustration came out as a low growl of warning. "Here. Try drinking it a little slower than you drive, or I'll get a police escort to follow you to the condo."

Icy sparks flew from her incredible eyes. Sean welcomed them. It helped that he could rile her, gave him the fleeting illusion that he had some defense against this cursed attraction. As an added touch, he laughed, taunting softly, "Careful there, Dr. Banyon, your temper's showing."

Lily's hand tightened around the glass, but before she could reply with a cutting comment of her own, May Ellen asked, "What was that you said, Sean?"

"Nothing very interesting, May Ellen," Lily said flatly.

"*Humph!* I don't believe that." May Ellen leveled a bright blue gaze at Sean, who'd crossed the room to stand with a shoulder propped against the archway that connected the living room and the dining room. "It seems to me there's a lot of *very* interesting things you've been keeping to yourself these days, Sean McDermott. Such as the fact that my granddaughter will be working here—"

"It's only for a few weeks—"

"I didn't know she was coming—" Lily and Sean answered simultaneously.

"Well, I forgive you," May said magnanimously. "Because this was the nicest surprise I've ever had. And I know what a relief this must be for you, Sean, and the advisory committee, to have Lily working on the reef study. She's the best," she boasted with grandmaternal pride.

A moment of charged silence followed. Lily's face burned, flames fed by the dual embarrassment of her grandmother's outlandish praise and Sean's reticence. Yet just when she was sure he would damn her by refusing to respond, Sean surprised her. Again.

"You're absolutely right, May Ellen. Lily is the best. I'm thrilled she's heading the study. The other members of the panel will be, too, once they see the quality of her work."

May Ellen beamed with delight. "Now, isn't that a nice thing to say, Lily?"

Lily managed a feeble nod and downed a healthy gulp of whiskey. She hoped it might clear her head. It didn't help. She was still dizzy, not from spirits but from Sean's quicksilver temperament. At the reef meeting Sean had defended her from Ferrucci's criticisms. But when they'd been alone in the car, Sean had not only doubted her professional integrity, he'd threatened to ruin her reputation.

Now he'd changed his tune again, singing Lily's praises to her grandmother. . . . Oh, of course. That was it. Sean cared deeply for May Ellen. That's why he was willing to pretend so very convincingly.

It was an excellent performance, indeed a brilliant one. Listening to Sean, Lily's heart ached. His words of praise were perversely cruel, far more painful than any slight, for no matter how desperately Lily wished it otherwise, there was one thing she was sure would never change: Sean's true feelings for her.

Lost in thought, Lily didn't register May's voice until she heard her say, "I've had the most wonderful idea: I'm going to throw a party in Lily's honor. A homecoming celebration. Won't that be splendid, Sean? Lily?"

From across the room, Sean pinned Lily with an enigmatic gaze and lifted his glass in mock salute. "Just wonderful, May."

CHAPTER TEN

Pete Ferrucci shook his head in disgust. "I tell you, John, the system's really going down the tubes, that's for sure. My brother-in-law teaches at the local community college. He once sat me down and explained to me about women in academia and the sciences. This whole affirmative action thing? All it really means is that women get promoted 'cause they're banging the chairman of the department."

"Only too true, Mr. Ferrucci," John Granger said in wholehearted agreement. His graduate program in marine biology had several women pursuing their Ph.Ds. They always seemed to receive funding, research grants, teaching fellowships, you name it. The male professors in the department didn't vote to award those plum fellowships and grants to the women because they were better than him at bio; the chicks were just better at fellatio.

People on the outside of the university system rarely understood these things. Pete Ferrucci was a refreshing exception. And a good guy, to boot. John had been flattered when Ferrucci caught up to him in the town hall parking lot and invited him to drop by his restaurant, the Blue Dolphin, later in the evening for a drink.

John had been worried he'd be bored crazy in this one-horse town. But things were looking up. The Blue Dolphin's staff was treating Ferrucci and him like royalty. Ferrucci had a good thing going here; the Dolphin was a real classy establishment. Expensive. Hell, the menu didn't even come with a price list. And there were some purely dynamite-looking babes dressing up the place. One of them, over by the bar, was wearing a tube top and a shimmery gold micromini. She'd been exchanging glances with him in the long mirror behind the bar. Then, just to make sure he got the message, she'd walked past their table on the way to the powder room and brushed his arm with her naked thigh. If Ferrucci hadn't been pouring Dom Perignon like it was soda pop, he'd have gotten up and followed her for some vertical drilling against the bathroom stall.

No, pussy could wait—especially since it was guaranteed he'd score some tonight. Ferrucci was talking, and John was too smart to offend the owner of the hottest spot in town.

"Your boss strikes me as exactly that type of woman."

"Banyon?" John tried to remember what they'd been talking about. The champagne was really good. He was getting a bit tanked. "You think?"

"Yeah." Ferrucci grimaced in distaste. "A walking, talking superbitch."

"Oh, right. Damn straight." He knew just what a frigid bitch Banyon could be. And he was also damn sure everyone at the center still laughed about it. Still laughed at *him*.

It had happened in late August. A group of the center's scientists and assistants were up in Maine, working on a study that hopefully would shed some light on the inexplicable surge in the local lobster population. New to the team, John hadn't yet understood about Lily Banyon: she was cold as ice inside that purely dynamite body. So, for a week he followed her around, bumping against her accidentally on purpose, and feeding her some of his best lines—damned confident he was making progress. Those cool glances had really turned him on.

One afternoon, she'd been bending over a box, packing up samples to take back to the lab.

Hey, what was a guy supposed to do when presented with an ass like that? Of course he'd copped a feel. Big fucking deal.

His hand hadn't even left that sweet cheek when Banyon nailed him with some kind of Bruce Lee martial arts move. She'd twisted out of his grasp, kicking with her leg as she spun. Somehow she managed to plant it right in his midsection. Next thing John knew, he was toppling over the *Drifter*'s port side, and landing with a splash in the chilly Maine waters.

The bitch. Thank God it was August and a heat wave.

He'd surfaced, spluttering, and swam as best he could in his sodden shirt, jeans, and sneakers over to the ladder.

Banyon was waiting for him. John had a choice, she told him. He could climb up the ladder and cut the crap permanently, leaving her and the other women on the team alone. Or he could stay there. The water might be just cold enough to act as an anesthetic. She would dive in and bring one of the lobster traps to the surface. Since he'd been asking all week, she'd happily handle his you-know-what for him. And stuff it in the lobster trap. It'd be a yummy little appetizer for those big, hungry lobsters.

An angry flush crept up the sides of John's neck as he

remembered how everyone onboard the research boat had overheard Banyon. He drank thirstily. Yeah, super-bitch was an excellent description for Lily.

"Yeah, your boss is easy to figure out," Ferrucci said. "I had her number in seconds. Now that she's where she wants to be professionally, she's determined to keep any man who might overshadow her from getting promoted. Take yourself, John." He lifted his champagne flute, tilting it toward John in a salutary gesture. "Why, after the advisory meeting I went straight to my computer and looked up your site on the Internet. My God, a guy with a mind like yours, with the number of articles you've written, let me tell you, I was shocked. . . . It's an outrage." The base of his glass clinked against the tabletop as though in emphasis.

From across the table, Pete Ferrucci regarded John Granger calculatingly. For the past half hour, he'd been plying him with champagne and praise. He probably could have skipped the bubbly and stuck to the articles he'd downloaded from Granger's Web site. It hadn't even been necessary to read the crap. A few key sentences and Granger had ballooned with pride. Now to prick his ego before the jerk became too shit-faced to understand a thing.

"It's an outrage, a real outrage," he repeated heavily. "You've got this prodigious body of research, yet you're nothing but an assistant at the Marine Center—on paper, no better than that ditzy photographer, Karen Masur."

Oh, yeah, a direct hit, he thought with satisfaction when Granger's face darkened with resentment.

"I know," John replied bitterly. "I can't believe it, either. Karen's the center's charity case. Her photos are okay, I guess, but from the way everyone raves about them, you'd think the Cousteau Society was pounding on her door. They have to justify putting her on the payroll somehow."

"Should've guessed. Is the director of the Marine Center a woman, too?"

"Oh, yeah." John's lip curled in disdain. "The place is a hotbed for bleeding heart liberals. Simone Devaux's what they like best, an affirmative action two-fer. She's black." He paused, and then added, "Get it, black? Woman? Two-for-one?"

Ferrucci shook his head, his expression one of total sympathy. "Man, what you are up against. So Banyon has a lot of influence with the director?"

"Gets *whatever* she wants on a gold platter. The rest of us are treated like peons." She treated him like a peon, that was enough.

"Well, she's going to find out things work a little differently here in Florida, John." Ferrucci's expression hardened. "I think it's time for someone else on her team to get a share of the glory."

"What do you mean?"

"I've made a lot of friends in this state, John. There's a real concern about what might happen to this area if the advisory panel recommends a ton of restrictions on the reef and the coastal area. Now, I can tell you're not one of those doom and gloom environmentalists, and what I say won't offend you. Conservationists and their asinine committees are destroying Florida. That's the unvarnished truth. I'm damned tired of environmentalists caring more about some stinking manatee than a guy's right to take his powerboat out where he wants, fish where he wants . . . do what he damn well pleases 'cause he's paying whopping taxes for that very privilege."

"Well." John cleared his throat.

Ferrucci raised his hand and smiled. "Don't get me wrong, John. I know *some* places should be protected. I'm not arguing with that. But Coral Beach? Who do they think they're fooling? There's not even that much to see down there."

"Atlantic reefs are different—"

Ferrucci raised a hand, cutting Granger off. The last thing he wanted was a lecture from this jerk. "Know what, John? Sitting here, talking to you, getting to know and really like you, I've been doing a slow burn." He reached for the bottle and topped off Granger's glass. " 'Cause I can predict exactly what's gonna happen: Banyon's sharp. She'll pick that brain of yours, work you like a dog, then take all the credit when she presents the research team's findings."

"Well, yeah. But she is the head—"

"The bottom line, John, is that we'll both get screwed. You're not going to get the recognition you deserve. And Banyon's going to do the same as the rest of these conservation freaks are doing around Florida. Turn the reef into a protected zone, with restrictions up the wazoo. But then I got this idea." Ferrucci paused to lean forward, then continued eagerly, "What if I got you together with a few of my friends? You could listen to what they have to say. Who knows, maybe we could work something out that might help you career-wise. These people, they've got connections all over. And I really want to help you, John."

"Weren't they the most beautiful babies?" Anne McDermott said. Her fingers traced the edges of the old photographs that crammed the pages of the bulging family album.

"Yes, indeed," May Ellen agreed with a wistful sigh. She was seated beside Anne on the sofa with the photo album resting over both their laps. "Oh, look at this one, Anne! Lily's got that pink polka-dotted sun hat on, the one we picked up on our cruise. Remember how it always slipped forward when she walked? She's fallen into the hole Sean dug."

"She was wearing that same expression when I joined the three of you. I suppose she and Sean were butting heads. . . ,"

"A couple of times," May conceded. "Old habits die hard, you know. I just hope we're doing the right thing."

Anne laid a reassuring hand over her friend's. "Don't fret, May Ellen. I'm certain it's going to work out this time; I can feel it in my bones."

"Are you sure that's not the new arthritis prescription Lloyd wrote for you?"

"No, dear, this feels much better. Purely right."

"But Anne, what if Lily's as stubborn as ever? Or Sean for that matter? He seemed very severe tonight. Hardly spoke a word to her."

"Shocks of this magnitude tend to do that to McDermott men. My Henry was just the same," Anne replied, smiling at the memory. "True, Sean can be hardheaded. And remember, May, he adores you. That makes him feel very protective." She turned to the next page of the photo album and gazed fondly at the blur of faded colors that showed Lily and Sean at age six, hunched over the handlebars of their bikes as they tore down the street. Racing each other, as usual. "I don't doubt our two grandchildren will both go down fighting," she said.

"But in terms of sheer stubbornness, they're mere amateurs compared to us. Just stick to the plan, dear, and we'll wear them down."

CHAPTER ELEVEN

Other people had their sleep troubled by nightmares, by anxiety dreams of parading stark naked in a packed football stadium, or in front of the boss's hysterical wife. Sean's dreams were far more disturbing. . . . They were of Lily.

Even asleep, a part of Sean's brain maintained a wary vigil, alert to her presence. So when in the landscape of his dreams, Ray's snide voice echoed, demanding to know if Sean had ever *handled the goods*, his muscles tensed in expectation. Once again, Lily would haunt his rest.

A scene appeared and Sean was back in tenth grade, in Mr. Sneel's zoology class.

Sean knew this dream, and knew, too, how wretchedly faithful it was to that day in March, right down to the tiniest detail. Even the lighting was right, the rows of fluorescent tubes flickering over Mr. Sneel's bald head as he stood at the front of the class and patted the lid of a large white Styrofoam cooler.

A malevolent grin split his shiny face as he announced the little surprise he had in store for the class. He was giving them a pop test—a frog dissection, which would count for a fifth of the semester's grade. Sneel would assign partners, one to perform the dissection, the other responsible for taking notes.

With sick fascination, Sean watched him remove the cooler's lid. Sneel's hand delved into it, then withdrew. Between his fingers, he dangled a squishy sealed plastic bag with a greenish, blackish blob trapped inside. At the sight, the class went quiet as the grave.

Sneel picked up the cooler and carried it around the room. With each formaldehyde-pickled frog he plunked down, he rattled off two students' names.

Sean moaned in his sleep, dreading what was coming.

Sneel stopped and crooked his finger toward the other end of the lab. "Miss Banyon, if you please? I'd like you to take notes while Mr. McDermott dissects the specimen. Oh, and don't even think about taking the scalpel away from him, Miss Banyon." His lips thinned in a smile. "I'll be watching."

The dream's pace shifted, fast-forwarding, and Sean was standing hunched over the lab station, staring at the frog on the metal tray. Legs splayed, it lay waiting to be sliced open with the kind of precision one saw Friday nights, sitting around a table at Benihana.

Sean began sweating. Not because of the test, but because Lily was right next to him. She hadn't stood this close in years, certainly not since eighth grade. Sean had seen to that, by doing his damnedest to avoid being anywhere near her. It was the only way to control his body's treacherous response.

He picked up the scalpel. And Lily sidled up to him. His indrawn breath captured the warm scent of her skin. Her long hair, which she brushed impatiently over her shoulder, was as fragrant as crisp green apples.

Sweat popped out on his forehead, while his body

temperature became an inferno of teenage lust. Unable to endure the torment, he gritted his teeth. "Back off, would you? Your breath stinks worse than formaldehyde," Sean heard his sixteen-year-old self saying, "Give me some room here, or I'll hurl all over you."

Lily was as frustratingly obstinate in his dreams as in real life.

Did she listen to him?

No, she pressed *closer*, peering over his shoulder, driving him crazy. Sean couldn't stop his hands from shaking—couldn't cut a straight line to save his life.

But then the miraculous occurred. Sean got to feel the goods.

In her distraction, Lily had unwittingly positioned herself so her left breast rubbed the rigid muscle of his arm. It was exquisite, the sublime softness that was Lily. The contact electrifying, his whole body jerked—hand and blade with it, plowing through frog guts and organs. Sean let loose a string of curses.

Then, as though needing visual confirmation of her worst fears, she practically flattened herself against him, craning her neck to inspect the green flesh beneath his knife.

Sean was past caring about the frog, the dissection, the test, anything. *He'd touched Lily's breast.*

All he craved was more of that earth-shattering sensation. He pivoted and faced her. His hand hovered, his fingers opening instinctively.

The dissecting knife fell with a metallic clatter as it hit the linoleum floor.

Lily's gasp of horrified disbelief echoed throughout the lab. Shock made her eyes enormous. She was staring at the frog. What was left of it. In ragged pieces, it looked like it had suffered a particularly nasty encounter with a lawn mower.

"My God, you botched the dissection completely!" Lily's wail replayed with stereophonic clarity. "I told you to be careful! You ruined it on purpose . . . because, because you hate me!" she cried.

Sean's mind screamed at the gross injustice of Lily's accusation. *Hate her?* She was practically all he ever thought about!

"I *was* trying, damn it all!" came his outraged reply. "But how was I supposed to see the friggin' frog when you were sticking your boobs in my face?"

Loud laughter erupted around the room. They were suddenly the center of a horseshoe configuration, the entire class abandoning their stations to become avid spectators. They were pointing at him as they laughed. Sean glanced down. To his horror, his right hand still hovered guiltily close to Lily's breast.

It dropped like a ten-pound weight as Lily leaped back to the other side of their lab station. Around them, the laughter redoubled.

The dream wouldn't release Sean until Lily had her revenge. And Lily Banyon always gave as good as she got. It happened now, just as it had in tenth grade.

Before Sean could duck, dodge, or hit the deck, Lily had hurtled a green, gut-filled bomb through the air. It found its target, smack dab in the middle of his chest.

Then Lily was running from the lab, but not before he'd seen her face awash with tears. He was left, covered in green goo and sick with the knowledge that he'd never get another chance to be near her again.

With a start, Sean sat up, fighting bed sheets tangled like thick ropes around his naked limbs. He looked wildly about the darkened room. With a shudder he dropped his head into the cradle of his hands and wearily closed his eyes.

As quickly, Lily materialized again. No longer age sixteen, but as she was now. Random images teased him. Of how she'd appeared earlier at the reef meeting, then later, at May Ellen's. They showed Lily, a woman grown, and a hundred times more dangerous.

Sean straightened with a curse and swung his legs over the side of the bed without bothering to glance at his watch. He could forget sleep. He knew there was only one remedy for what plagued him.

A cold shower.

A cold shower to numb his body. Supplemented by hours of predawn work to barricade his mind. He hoped it would be enough to keep Lily at bay.

"You're up early," Karen observed with a squint and a yawn as she padded her way to the galley-style, walk-in kitchen. "Did you use the pool?" she asked with a glance at Lily's wet hair.

It was common knowledge at the Marine Center that Lily was a swimming fanatic.

"Not likely," Lily scoffed. "Three strokes and I'd be doing a flip turn. I've been in Turkish baths that were bigger."

"So how far did you go?"

"Half an hour out, then I turned back."

"Must have been tempting to swim a bit farther and check on the reef regeneration project in the Bahamas," Karen said with a grin, which morphed into a second yawn.

Lily laughed and shook her head. "I restrained myself."

She drank the last of her freshly squeezed orange juice and watched as Karen opened the refrigerator to stare blankly into its interior. "There's sliced fruit in a bowl if you want some."

"Oh. Yeah." Karen rubbed her face sleepily. "Thanks." She bent, half her body disappearing into the maw of the refrigerator. With a backward shuffle, she withdrew, one arm wrapped around the plastic bowl containing sliced melon, kiwi, and orange. A package of whole-grain organic bread dangled from her fingers. "Want some toast?"

"No, thanks. I ate enough fruit to keep me going for a while. Anyway, I have to go pound on John's door."

"Ugh," Karen said as she dropped two slices into the toaster. "I'd pound hard if I were you. He didn't get back until about three-thirty last night. These walls must be insulated with tissue paper," she added around a mouthful of melon.

"He'd better answer the door. We've got to haul the gear and the equipment over to the *Tangiers*. I want to get an early start." If they left early enough, Sean McDermott might very well miss the boat. Lily hadn't forgotten his threat to keep tabs on her. He'd have to lose a little sleep to do so.

Lily rose from her stool at the breakfast bar and turned to face the living room. The apartment's ultramodern look had been radically altered. The place now resembled a FedEx warehouse, boxes aligned in rows. Box-filled or empty, the only thing Lily liked about the apartment was the view.

On the far side of the living room there was a wall of ceiling to floor windows, which looked over a crescent-shaped bay. The bay demarcated Coral Beach's northern-most point. From the fifteenth floor, the palm trees and fine ivory sand were graceful sweeps of a painter's brush, curling around and embracing the limitless expanse of sparkling blue sea.

The sight of all that glorious, shifting blue filled Lily with impatience. She longed to be reimmersed in that watery vastness. She turned to Karen. "Can you be ready in twenty minutes?"

"You bet."

"Time to wake Sleeping Beauty, then."

It took longer than twenty minutes to rouse a bloodshot-eyed John Granger. Her research assistant had obviously found some worthwhile entertainment in Coral Beach. Deciding to take pity on John, Lily left him at the condo, his sole task to stand guard over the boxes in the condo's parking lot. It was easier to drive the equipment over with Karen than badger a hungover John Granger. And Lily didn't want her mood spoiled this early in the morning—not on day one.

Today they'd begin diving, exploring the reef. It was the most exciting day of all, when one's impressions were freshest, when the exotic colors and shapes of the coral reef and its extraordinary inhabitants jumped and waved, a welcoming parade of brilliant-colored flags and shapes buffeted by the current. As always, Lily couldn't wait to lose herself in the magic of the spectacle.

Still, a sense of unease dogged her, setting her on edge.

Would Sean McDermott actually come and dive with them? And what if he did? This was her domain. She was the scientist and this was her project. She'd be cool, calm, and collected.

The only problem with that scenario was, Lily seemed to have forgotten how to be cool, calm, or collected when Sean McDermott was near.

CHAPTER TWELVE

It was early, even for the marina types. As Sean walked along the maze of wooden planking to where the *Tangiers* was moored, his footsteps thudded in steady rhythm to the accompaniment of short, metallic *pings* of halyards banging against sailboats' masts, the low, drawn-out screech of hulls rubbing against fenders as the waves slapped them. Against the soft pinkish gray of the morning sky, the *Tangiers*'s lights glowed like a golden beacon.

Owen Rafern, the captain hired by the Parks Department to ferry Lily and her team to the reef for the duration of the study, was at the stern of the *Tangiers*.

He called out as Sean approached. "Mornin', Sean. Dave left a message saying you might be joining the expedition." Owen Rafern's nostrils flared and he sniffed the air. "That bacon and egg on a bagel I smell?"

"Direct from Norma's." Sean tossed Owen a brown paper bag. Norma Jean's was a diner that dished up cholesterol and sold cold six packs to go. It was a favorite of the harbor crowd. Rafern's girth attested to his steadfast devotion. "A welcoming present, Owen. Hope you don't mind my tagging along."

"Not if you bring these, I don't," Owen replied grinning as he extracted the tinfoil-wrapped bagel and crumpled the paper bag into a ball.

Sean swung his large, nylon duffel bag, which held his scuba gear, onto the deck, then passed his air tank to Owen, who grabbed it with one hand.

"Dr. Banyon and her team show up yet?"

Owen nodded vigorously, his jaw working fried egg and bacon. A jerk of Owen's thumb had Sean noticing the boxes stacked against the pilothouse. Next to them, two air tanks and two bulging gear bags completed the picture.

"Should be back any second now," Owen managed at last. "Banyon seemed in a hurry to weigh anchor."

"I bet," Sean murmured dryly. He had figured Lily would try and ditch him.

"Fair amount of equipment they've got," Owen remarked. "I'll be interested to hear what this Dr. Banyon thinks about the reef." Owen scratched his grizzled jaw reflectively and continued, "Don't know whether I care to have any restrictions put on the reef, though. Seems like lately, everywhere you turn there are more dang rules and regulations." He slanted a look at Sean. "What's your stance on the issue, Mr. Mayor?"

Sean glanced at the sky. "Little early for politics, Owen. Besides, I do believe the experts have arrived."

Owen looked past Sean. "Yep," he confirmed to the sound of car doors slamming. "Got a guy with them this time. Must be one of those women's libbers, letting Banyon and the girl carry those boxes by themselves."

"That must be it," Sean agreed blandly and jumped onto the trawler's deck as the others approached. It was a preemptive move on Sean's part. It'd be damned hard for Lily to convince Owen to cast off and leave him stranded on the dock if he were already on board the *Tangiers*.

Sean was there, waiting, as she'd more than half expected. The apprehension that had plagued Lily vanished in a rush of excitement, the thrill of anticipation.

It made her realize how intimidated she'd been by Sean yesterday, by the sense of power, of easy command he exuded. But today things would be different. This was her world. The sea, its underwater cities and exotic citizens her familiars.

Sean was the trespasser.

He was standing on the deck next to Owen, his legs slightly apart, arms crossed. From this distance it was hard to read his expression. His body language, however, said it all: If she wanted to do battle, here was a strong, implacable rival.

Lily leaped onto the fiberglass deck, then swayed easily, her body following the rocking pitch of the trawler as John and Karen boarded, too. She was dressed in what she jokingly referred to as her "field attire": ancient canvas tennis shoes with holes big enough for her toes to peek through and wiggle in the Florida morning air; cutoffs and a faded cotton T-shirt that were equally old and disreputable. A floppy canvas fishing hat covering her short blond hair completed the look. She was a walking fashion disaster and loved it—usually. Seeing Sean, she abruptly wished her ensemble looked a little less like a composite of Salvation Army rejects.

He, too, was wearing shorts, navy surfer shorts, and a gray T-shirt. The casual attire suited him as well as the elegant jacket and tie he'd had on yesterday. Better, she amended with a glance at his bare legs. They were as muscled as ever, tan with golden hair softening the sculpted lines of his calves, the corded muscles of his quads. Thank God she was wearing her mirrored sunglasses. They hid the direction her eyes had taken.

Since overhearing Ferrucci talking to Sean, Lily's instincts screamed that she should be wary of Sean. He certainly must have ulterior motives for wanting to supervise her study so closely. Now, however, she had another reason to be on her guard: her frightening vulnerability whenever she came face-to-face with him.

Sean fixed his gaze on the distorted mini-image of himself in Lily's sunglasses. Otherwise it'd be too easy to spend the rest of the morning salivating over her mile-long legs. In a state that teemed with sunburned, over-tanned bodies, Lily's fair skin gleamed like the finest marble.

"Great hat," he heard himself say. A truly brilliant opener, but anything was better than, *Hey, Lily, I realize you hate my guts, but would you be willing to let me drag you below deck, lay you on top of the cabin's table, and trail my tongue over your legs for the rest of the morning?*

"Thanks. It does the job," Lily said. She would not be so ridiculous as to worry about how unflattering the dratted hat was simply because Sean had remarked on it. They were on a research boat, for Pete's sake.

She turned to the trawler's captain. "We're all set now, Owen. Let's take her out to the site. John, stow your dive gear over there, next to ours. Then if you'd give Owen a hand with the lines? Karen, you can check that the tanks are secured properly."

"I'll help get the lines with John, Owen," Sean offered.

Lily wasn't the only one in authority here. "John, do you want to take the fore or aft?"

"Aft," John replied, choosing the shortest distance from where he stood. He walked away, gear bag and tank in hand, his gait careful, as though he were walking on egg shells.

"Oh, brother," Karen exclaimed, watching John's snail-like progress. The beads on her braids clicked as she shook her head. "He's going to feel like crap when he gets underwater," she predicted. Then she, too, moved off to ready the *Tangiers*, leaving Sean and Lily alone.

"Something the matter, Lily?" Sean asked. "You seem a trifle annoyed."

She recovered quickly. "Oh, no," she replied. "I'm just surprised, that's all." Head cocked to the side, she studied him.

"Surprised? About what?"

"I'm surprised you're here." Her mouth curved upward.

"I warned you I'd be joining you." He ignored the heat that spread inside him at the sight of her smile.

"That's just it." Her smile grew wider. "A politician who keeps his word—what a remarkable aberration in the species."

"How could I have forgotten that keen wit of yours?" he marveled. "Yeah, I'm full of surprises. Might want to remember that." Then, throwing caution to the wind, he let his eyes roam slowly over her, lingering. She'd have to be blind not to see the hunger in them.

Which she clearly wasn't. She retreated a step. He followed, his longer legs closing the distance, until his body almost brushed hers.

That cool composure of Lily's was unraveling, no matter how hard she struggled to pretend otherwise. The signs were there, in the fine trembling of her limbs, in the flush that stole over her porcelain smooth cheeks. Fierce satisfaction filled Sean at her involuntary reaction.

He dipped his head until his lips hovered, a soft whisper away. "Lily?"

"Yes?" There was a husky catch to her voice.

Sean's fingers reached up and traced the rosy bloom on her cheek. Was it the sweet flush of desire that made her skin so soft? he wondered, his eyes and fingers memorizing every detail, every sensation. God, he'd die for a taste of her. But Sean denied himself the pleasure. He raised his head, putting distance between himself and his greatest temptation, and forced himself to lower his hand.

At the loss of contact, Lily's head jerked, as if coming out of a trance.

Sean stepped back before she could flay him alive. "You're looking a little pink, Lily. I've got some zinc oxide in my bag. I'd be happy to put some on you. Especially on those hard to reach places." He gave her a casual smile and pulled his sunglasses from the breast pocket of his T-shirt, ignoring the violent thudding of his heart against the cotton fabric. His hands shook, too, racked with tremors of need. Somehow, he managed to settle his shades across the slightly crooked bridge of his nose, before shoving them deep into his pocket, out of sight.

Damn Sean and his effect on me, Lily swore silently. He had only to bestow the paltriest of caresses and she nearly swooned. Even more galling was the fact that she was equally helpless before Sean's verbal taunts. The thought of Sean's hands, slick with lotion, gliding over her body in long, sweeping caresses had her pulse racing.

Lily's voice was filled with contempt—never mind that it was self-directed—as she spoke. "You know, you and John Granger should get to know each other. You could compare notes on really great pickup lines. By the way, Sean, your nose? Does it trouble you still? I hope so."

"Hi, Mayor McDermott. Guess what? Lily's assigned me as your dive buddy."

"Hey, Karen. The name's Sean," he replied, opening his eyes to smile up at her. "That's great. Have a seat." He moved sideways along the red Naugahyde-covered bench to allow Karen some room. "Beautiful morning, isn't it?"

"Sure is." Karen dropped down beside him.

After Sean and Lily's flare-up, they'd both retreated to opposite ends of the boat, as far from each other as they could get without jumping overboard. Sean had helped John Granger cast off the moorings and then had staked his territory here, by the bench that ran along the front of the pilothouse. It offered a stunning view of the sun-dappled ocean, but even better, it made it impossible to track Lily's doings.

He'd spent minutes staring up at the sky, counting the gulls overhead, willing his body to relax—steadfastly ignoring the erection caused by one almost-kiss with Lily Banyon.

To ensure no one else noticed his condition, he'd pulled on the lower half of his wet suit. The upper half, the torso with its long neoprene arms, lay doubled over his outstretched legs. As a result, he was broiling hot and his bare chest was beaded with sweat, but it was worth it. He was in control once more.

The *Tangiers* had left the marina, navigating the narrow, bottleneck channel of the Intracoastal Waterway. Once on the open sea, Owen had set the *Tangiers* on a northeast course. Sean had heard Lily ask Owen to drop anchor a few hundred yards from the northernmost tip of the reef. By Sean's estimate, they had about fifteen more minutes until they reached the spot where Lily intended to begin diving.

His eyes drifted shut, lulled into laziness by the feel of morning sun mixed with the cooling mist of ocean spray against his bare torso and the steady throb of the trawler's powerful engines.

Next to him, he felt Karen shift, and opened his eyes a fraction. She'd stripped down to her bathing suit, a lime green and orange tankini. Her wet suit was folded over her arm.

She must have noticed he was more alert, for she spoke. "Can't wait to get out to the reef. It's perfect weather for a dive: calm, good light conditions."

"Will you be taking photographs today?" he asked.

"I never dive without my Sea&Sea." Karen grinned. "I'll probably shoot at least two rolls of film today, maybe more." She broke off to stick her feet into the legs of her wet suit. Then, lifting her hips off the bench, she gave a series of hard tugs, pulling until it covered her lower body. With a happy sigh, she leaned back, adopting Sean's relaxed posture and continued. "Besides, you can never bank on the weather, and Lily's not one for wasting time. I want to do a great job here. I promised Lily I'd photograph every nook and cranny of this reef."

"She a good person to work with?" Sean tried to keep his tone casual.

"The best. Every assistant at the center tries to get assigned to her."

"Why's that?" he asked, shifting so he sat a little straighter.

Karen was silent a moment, then spoke slowly, as though choosing her words. "Well, I guess she's kind of inspirational. She works incredibly hard and is totally committed to what she's doing. When a person's got that sort of energy, it rubs off. You really learn stuff on her team. Craig Stevens—he's a research assistant who's worked with Lily a lot—told me that when he dives with her, it's as if his eyes are extra sharp, 'cause he's looking at a reef the way she does."

"What do you mean by that?"

"Lily's dived all over the world. She's studied so many reefs that she has this incredible sense of what should be there, and what shouldn't. Reef ecosystems are kind of like cities or countries—they have certain populations. If a reef's biodiversity is out of whack, she picks up on it right away, then starts looking for the reason why—" Karen stopped abruptly. "Sorry," she said with an abashed expression. "I get carried away. I probably don't explain it very well. It's complex—"

"Don't apologize, you explained that as clearly as the previous scientist we had working for the town. You've obviously learned a lot working at the center."

"Thanks." Karen grinned. "It's pretty cool stuff. I'm not quite sure what I want to do with my life, if I'll ever go back to school, but the center's an incredible place. And working with Lily is a huge break for me, even though this project is pretty minor—" She clapped a hand over her mouth, then smiled awkwardly. "Gosh, I didn't mean that your reef study isn't important or anything."

"Don't worry about it, Karen, I know what you meant," Sean said with a smile. "Although what happens to the reef *is* a big deal for a lot of people here. So do the most thorough cataloging you can. I'll try not to stick my ugly mug in the way of your lens this morning."

"Better not." Karen laughed. "I'd have trouble explaining to Lily why I was photographing guys instead of coral."

"Uh, where is she by the way?" It was imperative he maintain a safe distance from Lily. If they butted heads again, he might do something he'd truly regret. Like kiss her senseless.

"She's in the loo, suiting up."

"What? She's getting on her wet suit down there?" He knew she had on her swimsuit; its outline had been visible through her ancient T-shirt. He'd nearly gone blind trying to see more of her through that tantalizingly threadbare shirt.

"Yeah."

"Tight space." He pictured the tiny toilet below. There was hardly room to turn around. It'd be like trying to change in a coffin.

"Precautionary measure. She's had some, uh, problems in the past with guys," Karen explained in a voice filled with disgust.

Sean coughed. "Go do your boss a favor," he suggested. "Tell her Owen's got seven kids and eight grandchildren."

"*Owen's* not the problem."

Sean's head whipped around and searched her expression. Had she somehow guessed?

"No, not you, Sean." Karen giggled. "You're not that type of guy."

Sean's eyebrows rose. He shifted on the bench, uncertain how to take Karen's pronouncement.

She didn't appear to notice. She leaned closer, lowering her voice to a conspiratorial whisper. "It's John. He can be a real butthead."

Sean exhaled in relief. "That right?" came the automatic reply. Then Karen's words penetrated. Unbidden, his mind conjured an image of John Granger spying on Lily, a lascivious leer on his face. Sean found himself as enraged as he had been listening to Ray's and Frank's moronic comments at the Rusted Keel.

"Where's Granger?" John Granger had just taken a fast trip to the top of Sean's shit list. If he was anywhere near Lily—

"Don't worry," Karen replied. "John's dead to the world, using the stern ropes as a pillow." She rolled her eyes. "That's probably why Lily decided you and I should be dive buddies. So she could make sure he's okay on the dive." She shook her head, tucking a few braids behind her ear. "You'd think he'd wise up, especially after the lobster threat."

"Lobster threat?"

"John tried to put the moves on Lily. She came real close to castrating him with a Maine lobster. I was there, helping one of the other photographers. Man, some of those suckers were big." With a grin, she spread her arms to indicate the size.

"I guess it's a good thing for him lobsters in Florida don't have those big claws."

"Oh, Lily's smart," Karen said breezily. "She'll figure out how to keep John in line. Personally, I'd love to see her go at him with a sea urchin. There are some species here that have *superlong* spines."

"Ouch." Sean crossed his legs protectively. "A little bloodthirsty, aren't you?"

Karen patted his neoprene-covered knee comfortingly. "Relax, Sean. Coral Beach lucked out when they got Lily Banyon—and me. John's not so bad, either, just needs a shock to his system. The fear of having his favorite tool turned into a pincushion might be just the ticket," she added, grinning gleefully. She stood, and a flash of gold winked back at Sean from her belly button.

Wow, Sean thought, dazedly counting two more rings, one on either side of her tanned navel. Who'd have thought such intelligence—or such killer instincts—lay beneath that mass of cornrows and brightly colored beads? Karen was a hell of an impressive young woman. Maybe Dave should get to know her . . . after Sean had warned him about her enthusiasm for supplying the world with eunuchs.

Around them, the steady rumble of the *Tangiers*'s diesel engines quieted and died. The boat slowed, gliding on momentum alone. Footsteps sounded, voices, too. "Wake up, John. You've got to get off the ropes so we can drop anchor."

Silence, then, "Okay, okay, I'm up," came the grumbled reply.

"Good. Go help Owen, then suit up. I'll unpack the equipment."

Karen turned to Sean, her eyes bright. "Come on, Sean. This is where the fun starts."

"Lead on, partner."

CHAPTER THIRTEEN

Their equipment lay clustered in a neat circle by the *Tangiers's* stern. Lily was doing a final check to make sure nothing was missing.

Karen was on her knees, fiddling with her cameras, lenses, and strobe attachments, in what Lily had come to recognize was a standard last-minute ritual for many photographers. Specially designed test tubes topped with red rubber stoppers were packed in a carrying case next to John's bare feet. He also had his mesh bag, with his underwater notebook for sketching and note taking tucked away inside. A sudden noise made Lily glance up from the deck. John's hand was curled into a fist while he stifled a loud yawn.

Oh Lord, thought Lily with annoyed dismay. She was more than half-convinced that the minute John jumped in the water, he'd swim straight for the nearest brain coral where he'd curl up for his second nap of the morning.

With an exasperated shake of her head, she bent down and retrieved the secchi disk. "Ready, John?" she asked, her voice carefully neutral.

"Yeah, hold on a sec." John kneeled and began digging through the pile of equipment by his bare feet. With a mutter of disgust, he gave up the search and walked over to one of the cardboard boxes by the pilothouse. He pulled out a notebook and pen. "Right, go ahead," John said.

"You got some nice toys here, Dr. Banyon," Owen said. He and Sean had finished positioning the red-and-white dive flags and had joined them.

Sean came to stand beside her. He was wearing his wet suit. The fit as snug as body armor, it accentuated the strength of his broad shoulders, his long muscled legs.

Her mouth abruptly dry, Lily swallowed.

"What's that thing?" Sean asked, with a nod toward the metal disk Lily held.

"This? It's called a secchi disk," she replied, grateful for the distraction. "It's your basic no-frills instrument—we have a lot of them at the center."

"So does town hall." Sean grinned. "We've only recently entered the computer age."

Lily looked up in surprise. Sean's grin became a smile and she realized she'd never seen his eyes crinkle like that, with easy charm. Warmth seeped through her and she lowered her head, examining the black metal disk as if it were an object of profound interest.

"So what's it for?" he asked.

"We use the disk to take readings of water clarity, our first step in data collecting. Here," she said, "I'll demonstrate how it works." She walked over to the *Tangiers*'s railing. Sean and Owen followed, coming to stand on either side of her.

"See this string?" Lily lifted the thin rope that was tied to the disk. "It's premeasured. All I do is lower the disk into the water, and let it sink until I can't see it anymore."

Lily leaned over the rail. As the men peered over the railing, the disk hit the water with a splash.

The string slid through Lily's fingers as she played it out. "Bottom reading, John," she called over her shoulder. "Five meters."

"Got it." Standing off to the side, John scribbled in the notebook, snapped it shut, and then dropped it back into the cardboard box.

Lily began hauling the disk up, coiling the rope as she went.

"So what's a bottom reading mean?" Owen asked.

"Today I could see the disk all the way down to the ocean floor—as you know, Owen, we're not in deep water—so I got a bottom reading at a depth of five meters."

"That's good, right?" Owen said.

"Yes. Water clarity is vital because it allows the sun to penetrate. Corals need sunlight to feed and grow. Murky water blocks the sun. That's—"

"Bad," Sean interjected with a slight grin.

Lily inclined her head. "You must have been doing a lot of background reading."

"Only enough to pass the course." Sean's reply had Owen chuckling. Lily smiled and arched a brow.

"Yet another underachiever turned politician," she murmured dryly.

Owen's chuckle became a bark of laughter. "Oh, no, Dr. Banyon, Sean's different. He works real hard for this town. Full of plans. This town's changed a lot since he took office."

But has it changed for better or worse? Lily bit her tongue to keep from asking, but in any case, Owen's attention had shifted to the rest of the equipment on the deck.

"And what's with this other stuff here?" he asked with a sweeping gesture.

"Like the secchi disk, it's pretty much standard issue, I'm afraid, but essential nonetheless. These," she said, kneeling and pointing to the slates in the gear bags, "are our underwater notebooks. We use them to note the different species, sketch reef formations, et cetera." She reached out and picked up a container with a colored flag attached to it. "This is a sediment trap. It measures the amount of sediment that settles in an area over a given period of time. The cylinders and test tubes in the case here are for core and water samples." Lily sat back on her heels. "Once we've finished taking readings and collecting samples, we'll plug the numbers and stats into a specially designed computer program. The program organizes all the information and numbers, and creates a 3-D map with visual overlays of the reef. All the different species of coral are recorded, as well as the condition of the reef as a whole. We can track where the areas of disease are, and whether other corals are threatened."

"So today you'll be starting with the area closest to shore?" Sean asked.

"Yes, with zone one," Lily replied with a nod. "With this type of reef—a patch reef—I like to move in progression from one zone to the next. Patch reefs grow in strips or patches. Coral Beach has three that run parallel to each other, the last in the deepest water. Because of the different depths where they're located, each zone has a distinct form dictated by the types of coral which can thrive there, and the kind of reef dwellers, plant and animal alike, which inhabit it."

"That's a hell of a lot of territory to cover," Owen remarked.

"The bigger the better, Owen." Lily smiled. "But we have ways to cover the whole reef system as efficiently and thoroughly as possible."

"Such as?" Sean asked.

"One way is to divide the whole of the patch reef into transects."

"Transects?" Sean repeated with interest. "Dr. Lesnesky never used that term in his presentations."

Lily shrugged. "That's not terribly surprising. Everyone has his or her own favorite methodology. I prefer doing transect dives because they allow for the most complete sampling. At the end of a study, I know I've covered a segment of each zone at the same latitude."

Owen was scratching his chin. "Think I lost you there, Dr. Banyon," he admitted ruefully.

Lily gave an inward sigh. *Okay,* she thought. How could she explain this better? She looked around the deck and grabbed her mesh bag. "This might help make it clearer, Owen," she said, pulling out her underwater slate. "Imagine these are your three reef zones." Quickly she sketched three bands running parallel to one another, then made an *X* on the bottom edge of the slate. "This is us right here, at the northern section of zone one. On our next dive, we'll do zone two, at the same latitude." Lily made another *X* directly above the first. "With a reef this size, it should take approximately twenty to twenty-five dives to collect samples from the whole area."

Sean looked at Lily's slate and envisioned a sweep of neatly regimented *X* marks covering it. It was startling—and a little disturbing—to realize that he'd learned more about scientific procedure in the past few minutes aboard the *Tangiers* than he had during months of listening to Lesnesky's convoluted jargon.

Dr. Lily Banyon was damned impressive.

Sean was fully aware that this reef study wasn't one of Lily's pet projects, that she wouldn't receive any kudos for it. Yet she was approaching the job with total dedication and an enthusiasm that was palpable.

"Looks like this is going to be a truly educational experience, Owen," he observed mildly.

In the midst of slipping her slate back into her goody bag, Lily stilled. While she'd been explaining about the reef and how she planned to conduct the study, Sean had appeared truly interested. What if he'd actually been mocking her and her irrepressible enthusiasm for her work?

Suspicious, she glanced at his face.

No, Sean's expression was open, his gaze equally so. And when he smiled, something tight eased inside her. Lily's own lips curved in shy response.

She discovered she was eager to call a truce in their private battle of wills. After all, unless you were in a James Bond film, it was hard to fight underwater. And Lily desperately wanted to dive in, cool off her overheated body, and refocus her wayward thoughts.

Because smiling or not, Sean McDermott was looming far too large in her mind.

Lily inspected the group, her eyes alert as she scrutinized every article of diving gear until she was satisfied.

Head bowed, Sean was busy adjusting the weight belt slung about his slim hips, checking the release to ensure it opened quickly in the event of an emergency.

Lily's gaze traveled up, to Sean's buoyancy control device. The bulky vest camouflaged him, hid the impossible perfection of his body. For that, she was absurdly grateful. Sean's mask rested on the crown of his head. The mouthpiece of his snorkel grazed his cheek, swinging backward as Sean lifted his head. Hazel eyes met hers, and Lily felt their intensity penetrate to the very core of her being.

Warmth unfurled inside her, spreading, and Lily suddenly felt as if she'd been transported back in time . . . back to when she was seventeen, discovering for the first time Sean's dangerous allure. And how much she wanted him.

Renewed longing tore at her.

The *click* of Sean's weight belt snapping shut saved her. It brought her back from the land of memories to the deck of the *Tangiers*.

Her bare feet gripped the fiberglass deck as the boat rolled over a wave. She needed to be underwater, she realized with a trace of panic, where she could clear her mind of everything except the job at hand, where she could be free of Sean's terrifying power.

She coughed, hoping to rid her throat of any betraying huskiness. "Tanks on, everyone. It's show time. Karen, you and Sean go first. I'll pass your cameras down to you. John and I will follow. Owen, if you could hand us our equipment?"

"Sure thing, Dr. Banyon."

"That's it, then. Remember: Check your gauges frequently and stay in sight. Let's do it; let's dive."

Lily loved water. Loved the feel of it over her, against her, surrounding her. Lulling, sliding, breaking, crashing, it could be rough or gentle, salinated or fresh. Immersed in it, Lily was transformed. Rid of all terrestrial awkwardness.

Water was her true element.

As a girl, Lily had excelled at swimming underwater

farther and longer than anyone on her swim team not simply because of her extraordinary lung capacity, but because she had lived for those special moments of suspended silence. Following the contoured depths of the pool, water slipping past, Lily had longed to remain in its embrace. Because during those moments, the incredible happened: Lily became an entirely new creature, her need for air secondary. A magical moment in a magical substance.

The reef was before them.

They swam in alignment, Lily and Karen center, Sean and John on either end. Her previous irritation with John Granger, her conflicting emotions toward Sean were forgotten. Lily opened herself to the ocean's mysteries and infinite beauty, embraced them.

Her fins kicked in a steady rhythm, propelling her over the patches of sea grass, which, like a wavy carpet, led to the first outcroppings of coral reef. Behind the tempered glass of her scuba mask, Lily's eyes tracked the marine life flitting past.

All around, fish zigzagged and darted, largely indifferent to her and the others' presence. Without conscious thought, Lily retrieved her slate from her mesh bag and began cataloging, in rapid shorthand, the schools of grunts, snappers, parrotfish, and butterfly fish, which flashed and flickered against the aquamarine blue of the sea. Their hues a shimmery wealth of silvers, greenish blues, deep lemons, and vibrant purples, the fish streamed by, their destination the same as the humans'—the extraordinary living sculpture of coral.

Rays of sunlight penetrated in slanted bands, lighting the shapes and spectral colors of the reef. Its low-lying form stretched before her, beckoning like an exotic city.

Lily, as ever, was its avid, indefatigable tourist. Sleek as a seal in her black wet suit, she went to work.

She was more than magnificent.

Seeing Lily in the sea had Sean regretting his impetuous decision to accompany her and her team. He should have stayed on land, never beheld this other side to her. Already too beautiful above water, beneath it, Lily's body glided with sinuous elegance, tempting him. His fingers longed to reach out, grab her, and pull her against him. Below water, pressure increased. And with it, so did Sean's unruly, unwelcome desire.

He didn't want to need her.

The profound silence beneath the ocean's surface heightened Sean's awareness. Eerily crystalline images floated before his mask—all of her. Lily, suspended over a large, treelike coral with branches flat and wide, motioning to Karen, then pointing carefully so Karen could photograph whatever creature was hiding by its base. Lily then swam away, to exchange a flurry of hand signals with John as he filled test tubes and tucked them securely into their case. Sean watched them pull out gauges and compare readings, making the thumbs-up sign after they'd jotted them onto their slates. He saw Lily place a sediment trap, record its location in her notebook, and move on, only to stop, look, and signal to Karen once more.

Nothing seemed to escape her notice. When she hovered over a coral that resembled an overgrown cabbage, Sean found himself swimming nearer. And then he spotted it: the minuscule red crab nestled in a tiny shell, waving its claws energetically.

Lily, so competent, so capable . . . that didn't surprise

him. No, it was her spontaneous smile of joy when she came upon a sea feather, a species even Sean recognized. A delicate shade of maroon, it undulated like a dancer dressed in lace. Her smile didn't fade away when her mask turned toward him and she beckoned, her glowing smile inviting Sean to share in the wonder of this world. An incredible smile that made him dizzy with a euphoria of the deep. With a euphoria of Lily.

Sean breathed slowly, in and out, the mix of oxygen and nitrogen in his tank replaced with a far more potent mixture. With every breath, awareness and desire invaded, overwhelming his defenses.

His eyes fixed on Lily, Sean succumbed.

CHAPTER FOURTEEN

There were certain calls Pete Ferrucci placed from public pay phones only. Not a foolproof system, but the risk of tracing or tapping these conversations was greatly diminished. Years of delicate business dealings had demonstrated the usefulness of pay phones and of watertight, ready-made alibis.

A voice answered on the second ring.

"Hi, it's me." Pete Ferrucci didn't need to identify himself.

"You talked to him yet?"

"No, he's out of the office. That pink gargoyle of a secretary won't tell me where he's gone or when he'll return. She'll doubtless continue giving me the run-around right up to the six o'clock meeting."

"Got to put the pressure on him. Some influential people will be deeply disappointed if this doesn't pan out." The condescension in Jack Gehring's voice was clear as a bell despite the faint crackle of the connection.

"I'm working on it," he replied, annoyed. Who did Gehring think he was? "Like I've already told you, the way to win is to beat him at his own game." And that would happen as soon as the scientists gave the coral reef a clean bill of health. Ferrucci would then push the committee to vote against any restrictions—either on the reef or on the parcel of coastal land he and his associates had purchased. Then there'd be nothing to stop the town from voting in favor of the marina development.

"So what's this about a new team of scientists? That was an even longer article than the one about the bridge crash."

Like a kid in a candy store, Gehring had his eye on the Bellemer Bridge. Every conversation they had, Gehring brought up the topic. He'd even convinced himself that getting the bridge widened was the way to get the town thinking "big," as in a bigger marina. Gehring was a fool. Ferrucci, however, saw no point in enlightening him about the bridge or his limited intelligence. Gehring and his bridge would come in handy eventually. And with Gehring fixated on his own plans, he wouldn't see that Ferrucci had already grabbed the big, fat pot of gold with both hands.

"Yeah, well, the Courier's a liberal rag; what do you expect?" Ferrucci said. "But I've got an idea about how to keep the bridge accident on page one for some time."

"That reporter made this research team sound like hot shit. Not a good thing."

"Got that under control, too." Ferrucci ground his molars. He was getting tired of Gehring's constant whining. "I invited one of them for drinks at my place the night before."

"Yeah? Which one, Banyon?"

"No, not her." Banyon had the stiff righteousness of a true believer; she'd blow the whistle on him before he'd even finished his proposition. "There's a guy with her.

He's her assistant. We're in luck. He's got a chip on his shoulder the size of Mount Everest."

"Is that big enough to get the tests to come out squeaky clean?"

"I made my first pitch the other night. I'm real optimistic he'll see things our way."

Gehring gave a noncommittal grunt. "Damned inconvenient of you-know-who to fall ill," he observed. "This whole thing would be over and a certain somebody a hell of a lot closer to being a one-term wonder if he'd finished the study."

The idea of McDermott winning a bid for reelection had the vein on the side of Ferrucci's temple throbbing violently. "No way is there going to be a reelection party," he spat. "I have too much invested in this town. I'm bringing in someone I've done business with before, a stringer for the tabloids."

"What good'll that do? Everyone knows the guy's pure as fucking Galahad."

"Maybe, maybe not. Turns out the head scientist grew up here. Their families are close."

There was a pause as Jack Gehring digested this bit of information. "Conflict of interest, huh? That enough to use?"

"Not by itself. But my gut says there's something between them. I'll let my guy do some sniffing around, see if my hunch is on the money."

"Still, you'll meet with him, the assistant?"

"I'm pretty sure we'll be running into each other." He'd instructed the Blue Dolphin's bartender that John Granger should be welcomed like he was Donald Trump, Bon Jovi, and Dan Marino rolled into one. The girls who received drinks on the house because they were built like the *Playboy* bunny-of-the-month had been "encouraged" to be extra friendly to Granger, as well.

"Good, that'll please our associates. Let's talk again real soon."

"Right." Pete Ferrucci hung up the receiver, stepped out of the Amoco station's phone booth, slid behind the wheel of his black Mercedes, and drove back to town.

The four of them had changed into dry clothes. The postdive atmosphere mellow and relaxed, they sat around the fore deck, enjoying the cool spray off the boat's bow.

John was shirtless, working on his tan as he sprawled on the sunlit deck. A few feet away, Karen sat cross-legged, surrounded by her camera gear, carefully wiping each piece of equipment with a soft cloth before returning it to her camera case. Lily had opted for the shade of the Naugahyde bench. She was transcribing her notes on the reef into a spiral-bound notebook. Next to her, Sean was taking advantage of Lily's absorption to study her profile, mesmerized by the sight of her worrying her lip as she wrote.

Not wanting to interrupt her work, Sean waited until she'd finished writing and closed her notebook. In a voice that was carefully casual, he asked, "So what's your opinion of the reef? Did this section look okay?"

Lily shot him an assessing glance, and Sean knew she was thinking of their conversation in the car, of his "political" interest in the study.

"It was only the first dive, but yes, I'd say this section looked healthy," Lily said. "When we get the analyses back from the lab we'll have a much better picture. But there was lots of coral down there, which is always great to see."

Out of habit, Sean had half expected that Lily would tell him to back off. Her reply had him smiling. Encouraged, he shifted, angling his body to face her. "There were a number of things down there I was curious about. You think you could tell me what they were?"

His question had Lily arching her brow. "I'll give it my best shot," she said dryly.

He grinned. "Right, dumb question." Sean paused. "Of course, we could make it harder, a little more of a challenge. Care to play *Name that Coral*, Dr. Banyon? The fewer clues you need to identify it, the more points you score."

"Sounds like fun. Can I join in?" Karen asked, looking up from the lens she held in her lap. "What about you, John? Want to match your wits against us?"

"Buzz off, Masur," John growled sleepily before rolling over onto his stomach, his face turned away from them.

"So, Lily, want to play?" Sean asked. The words ignited a flare of need inside him.

Lily's head turned, her face now tantalizingly near. And the rest of the world melted away. His gaze dropped to her mouth. He thought about what he'd like to do to those lush lips. Head angled, Sean leaned forward . . . and Karen spoke.

Instead of stealing a kiss from Lily, he nearly brained himself against the pilothouse. In the time it took to gather his scrambled wits and hazard a glance at her, she'd gone and tugged the brim of her fishing hat down low, shielding her eyes. . . . *Ahh, shit*.

"Go ahead, Sean, ask away," Karen urged again.

He took a deep breath, trying to think of something besides Lily's mouth. "Right . . . how about this: wide branches—"

"Elkhorn coral," Lily and Karen pronounced simultaneously.

Sean shook his head with equal parts amusement and awe. "Two points apiece," he decided. "Obviously I'll have to make these questions a lot tougher."

The quiz show continued, the three of them laughing as Sean's clues grew increasingly far-fetched. Karen was doing a pretty good job, whooping with pleasure whenever she scored a point. But Lily won the contest when Karen drew a blank at the final round. Sean's clue: *pink spaghetti.*

"Beats me," Karen said with a frown.

"Up to you, Dr. Banyon," Sean nodded, his eyebrow quirked in challenge.

"That would be a sea anemone."

At Lily's response, Karen dropped her head in her hands and groaned theatrically. Smiling, Lily continued, "Technically though, your question wasn't really fair. Anemones don't fall into the same category as coral," she explained.

"Doesn't matter," Karen said, with a shake of her braids. "You won. *Darn it!* I should have gotten that."

"Hey, you did really well, Karen. I was just lucky. There were a number of sea anemones, which caught my eye. And besides, soft coral doesn't grow like 'pink spaghetti' in zone one." As Lily spoke, she took off her hat to rake her fingers through her hair.

Sean wondered if she had any idea how her hair looked when she made it all tousled like that, as if she'd just gotten out of bed. He doubted it. Which only made her unconscious ability to seduce that much more lethal.

She was looking at him with a bemused expression. "Pink spaghetti," she repeated, her tone marveling. "I can only say it's a good thing you don't spend your life cataloging species. I shudder to think how you'd describe a sea worm."

"And what's a sea worm look like, Lily?"

She was silent a moment. Then, with a small smile playing over her mouth, she said, "Let's just say a guy would recognize one instantly."

While Karen rocked with great snorting guffaws, Lily merely smiled and batted her eyelashes innocently. Sean felt his grin stretch wide across his face.

Hot damn! Lily Banyon was actually flirting with him.

Sean was still wearing a grin when the *Tangiers* entered the marina.

"Yoo-hoo! Ahoy there, Sean. Ahoy!" The voice calling was high-pitched, feminine, and very eager.

Sean looked up. His scuba gear was laid out on the trawler's deck. He straightened reluctantly, and the rubber hose he was using to rinse his equipment splashed onto his bare feet. He winced, not from the ice-cold water spraying his skin, but from the sight of Stacy Malloy clicking her way toward him. Though her advance was somewhat hampered, her steps perforce carefully measured so her heels wouldn't sink between the gaps of the dock's planking, Stacy nevertheless positively bubbled with enthusiasm as she approached. Sean sent a prayer heavenward that he could get rid of her fast.

"Who's that?" John asked.

"Who's who?" Lily replied distractedly. She and Karen

were packing equipment into boxes, sorting what would be needed at the lab from what could remain aboard the *Tangiers*, to be stowed away under lock and key.

"The babe who's clinging to McDermott like he's her lifeline," John replied.

Lily's head jerked like a puppet on a string. She stared. Who, indeed, was that? Whoever it was, she was wearing white jeans that weren't simply tight; they seemed laminated onto her curvaceous lower body. *The woman obviously has a thing for clothes two sizes too small,* Lily thought, eyeing the tiny red halter top. It was stretched to the max. A heavy sigh and it would split.

"Man, she sure is friendly. Some guys get all the luck."

For once, John wasn't exaggerating a woman's enthusiasm.

It was silly to feel such a sharp pang of disappointment. This was Sean. Women routinely stood in line, waiting their turn to throw themselves at him. Now it was this woman's chance.

Why should Lily care if the mystery woman's hair had dark gold streaks, its thick mass pulled into a high ponytail? So what if Sean's taste in women hadn't evolved past cheerleader look-alikes?

Who cared? Not Lily. The only reason her insides ached with such an awful hollow emptiness was because she hadn't eaten anything since dawn.

Lily resumed packing the box, but blindly. Her eyes were riveted on the couple.

Karen studied the woman, too. She gave a loud snort, then said, "You're so bent, John. Anyone with eyes can tell Sean's not interested."

"Yeah, right, Einstein. McDermott clearly hates her.

Speaking of which, don't you think he's a little old for you?"

"What are you talking about?"

"About the mega crush you have on him."

"Get real, Granger."

"And you're about as obvious as that chick over there." He jerked his thumb in the direction of Sean and the woman. "I heard you earlier: 'Oh, Sean, you're such a great dive buddy. Let's do it again sometime,' " he simpered exaggeratedly.

Karen's face reddened with embarrassment. "God, you're such a troll. No wonder you can't get a date."

"Shows how much you know, Masur." John laughed. "Though with your looks, I'm not surprised. You wouldn't know a date if it bit you."

With an inarticulate cry, Karen jumped up from where she'd been helping with the boxes and flew at John. She shoved him—hard.

Unprepared, he stumbled, landing on his rear with a loud thud and even louder curse as the backward momentum of his fall sent him crashing into the empty scuba tanks. They toppled, one after another, like bowling pins as the discordant clanging of metal resounded.

The noise had the woman turning her head. The better to observe the mayhem, she lifted oversized sunglasses, until they perched on top of her streaked blond head.

Lily reeled with the shock of recognition—as stunned as if one of the scuba tanks had bashed her in the head.

That was Stacy Malloy clinging like a limpet to Sean.

Funny how nothing ever changed.

Sean and Stacy. Why, it was just like old times.

* * *

The artfully applied makeup couldn't hide the crow's-feet that fanned the corners of Stacy Malloy's eyes or the deep brackets that framed her mouth—lines Stacy could have avoided for at least a few more years if she hadn't cut quite so many classes in favor of lying prone on the beach, broiling her body for hours on end.

Lily knew it was petty of her to feel smug; the only reason she herself avoided the pitfalls of the sun-equals-crocodile-skin equation was because of her father's fair Scandinavian genes. Lily didn't tan. She blistered.

That John was transfixed by Stacy's teensy-weensy, red Lycra halter top came as no surprise. But Lily would have thought that Sean, ten years down the road, would be a bit more discerning . . . but then again, she'd never been able to figure out what Sean found appealing in Stacy Malloy.

Stacy had exchanged her earlier, limpetlike characteristics for those of a vine—a clinging vine at the height of summer. Sean looked quite content to be her stake.

"It's so nice to see you again, Lily." Stacy's heavily mascara-ed eyes flicked over Lily, taking in her ragtag clothes. "You don't look any different."

"You haven't changed at all, either," she replied coolly. One whiff of testosterone and Stacy was on the prowl.

"Thanks. It's incredible how some of the girls from high school have let themselves go. Their bodies gone to pot, dressing any old how." Her toned shoulders shimmied with obvious pride that she was still pouring herself into a size four, as she squeezed Sean's arm for what had to be the eighth time in as many minutes.

Yes, Stacy was the same as ever, crow's-feet notwithstanding, Lily decided. She was convinced that if Stacy could only figure out how, she'd defy the laws of physics and crawl into Sean's lap right now.

Sean listened impatiently while Stacy discoursed on her favorite topic, counting off an entire legion of women who'd supposedly lost their figures. Unfortunately, he couldn't wander off, out of earshot. Stacy was clamped tight. It would take a force of nature to loosen her hold. *Even that might not do the trick,* he thought, his imagination conjuring a cartoon sketch of Stacy flying through the air, hurricane winds buffeting her about, her hands latched tight about his torn-off arm.

Sean coughed, muffling his laughter, and Lily's eyes fixed on him with a cool glare. *For Christ's sake,* she didn't truly think he was amused by Stacy's catty remarks?

"Stacy, I think Owen would appreciate it if we cleared the *Tangiers's* decks so he can scrub them down. I'll get back to you about this matter first thing tomorrow." Maybe now Stacy would let go. Wrong. He winced as her fingers tightened determinedly.

"But Sean," Stacy said, the pout in her voice matching the one on her cherry red lips, "I really need your input on a few matters. I promise it won't take long."

Lily thought she might be ill, right then and there. Stacy had been waiting for Sean's "input" for as long as Lily had been paying attention to these things—probably far longer, as Lily had been admittedly slow on the uptake in terms of sexual awakening.

Stacy mistook Lily's revolted expression for rapt fascination. "You see, I'm the Junior League's new president," she explained brightly. "We're sponsoring the very first fund-raiser for Sean's reelection campaign. As you can imagine, it's an enormous job, with hundreds of details. I want everything perfect for Sean's big night. He'll be giving a speech, and afterward there'll be dancing, bathtubs of champagne, and balloons everywhere. That reminds me—we have to choose the colors. You'll have to come, too, Lily. If you're still here."

Stacy named the date.

Lily smiled. Her first genuine smile since she'd laid eyes on Stacy Malloy. "Gosh, it sounds like a great event. Unfortunately, our study will be finished by then and I'll already be in the Bahamas."

"What a shame," Stacy replied with blatant insincerity. "Now, whatever was I talking about? Oh, yes! You're a hard man to pin down, Sean McDermott," she accused. "So I'm kidnapping you for lunch. We'll be able to talk without interruption."

Not in this lifetime, you're not, Sean retorted silently. "Sorry, Stacy," he said, shaking his head. "The reef committee's arranged for Lily to use one of the college labs. I'm going along to make sure it's adequate for her needs—"

Lily raised her hand. "No, no, Sean, that's okay. We can handle things from here. The lab's mainly a storage cum work space. Once we've collected enough samples, we'll be sending them back to the center. Our labs there can run far more sophisticated analyses."

"Nevertheless, I'd—"

"I'd hate for your reelection party to be anything less than a resounding success for you—and the Junior League. Really. You stay and talk with Stacy; we'll head over to the lab and get organized. If we need any little thing, though, I promise we'll be in touch with your secretary. No doubt you'll still be *busy* with Stacy." Which was fine by Lily— Stacy Malloy could have Sean for as long as she wanted.

She forced herself to smile at Stacy. "Lovely seeing you again, Stacy." She turned to Sean. The angry cast to his jaw filled Lily with bitter satisfaction. *He didn't like having his plans foiled,* she thought. *What a shame.* " 'Bye, Sean."

Chapter Fifteen

Sean had foreseen how it would be with Lily back in Coral Beach. His life would quickly become fucked up beyond all recognition. But, while he was long accustomed to having Lily destroy his peace of mind, he was going to do everything he could to protect his heart.

What really got him, though, was that he was partly to blame. He'd let himself fall under her spell.

This morning, aboard the *Tangiers*, Sean had encountered a whole new Lily Banyon, a Lily who was self-assured, patient, committed, caring.

A Lily Sean liked. Really liked.

How could he not be beguiled by a woman this entrancing, mesmerizing? Hell, Lily had even talked to him, for once had treated him as something other than a pariah.

And when she'd batted those beautiful eyes of hers, she'd turned him into a mush puddle of goofy hope.

It hurt to realize that he'd been fooled by an illusion, that he'd been gullible enough to believe things might be different between them. Lily'd set him up, and he'd swum right into her sucker trap. *Dumbass.*

Then she had happily abandoned him to the merciless clutches of Stacy Malloy, the lowest trick of all.

Despite being free once more, at safe remove from Stacy's tired and stale ploys, Sean was still fuming. Unfortunately, he wasn't the only one: Stacy was well and truly pissed that he'd sent her packing only a minute after Lily, with a jaunty wave from the driver's seat, pulled out of the parking lot and sped off. Which meant that the next time he ran into Stacy, she'd be even more determined to get him alone. *Damn,* he detested this side of politics. Fund-raisers were hell on earth. And a sad comment about politics that election campaigns—even for small-town elections—required that the candidate go begging for obscene amounts of money.

Sean rarely closed his office door, but today he didn't want to deal with anyone, not even Evelyn. A knock sounded. He cursed softly. He should have known he wouldn't be allowed the luxury of licking his wounds in peace.

"Come in." He picked up his pen and bent his head, staring blindly at the speech he'd written at four o'clock this morning on controlled growth in communities.

There was a slight creak of hinges as the door opened. Footsteps signaled Evelyn's approach. Although Sean kept his eyes trained on the text before him, he could feel the weight of Evelyn's careful scrutiny.

"I've brought you the folders on the Bellemer Bridge and the engineer's report."

"Thanks." He didn't look up.

"Ferrucci's been trying to reach you all morning. Wants to arrange a lunch with these developers. What do I say when he calls again?"

"I'm not here. He can wait until the six o'clock meeting to begin his wheeling and dealing."

"All right. You had some other calls, too. Your mother telephoned, ship to shore. She said that she and Mrs. Alcott are heading back to port. Both send their love. Your grandmother called. Mrs. Farrady apparently needs some furniture moved for her party, asked if you'd be willing to lend your back—her words, not mine," Evelyn informed him, a smile in her voice. "And she wants to know when you can come to dinner. Here are the others; no messages, just to return the calls . . . Ms. Malloy was particularly insistent." Evelyn deposited the pink rectangles of paper just inside his line of vision. Stacy's name was topmost.

Sean ignored the pink stack.

"Besides Ferrucci and Ms. Malloy, there was one other eager caller today. Mr. Feldron, the high school principal. He's dying to have you come back for another talk."

"No."

"It's not until next week," Evelyn said, adding, "It's for their career day." As if that might make a difference.

"No."

"Sean," Evelyn's voice was patient, "it's not a bad idea to have Coral Beach's parents know how much you care about their children. This is what's known in politics as an *opportunity*: excellent publicity, upstanding cause."

"Evelyn," he said, laying his pen down with exaggerated care. "There is no way that you are going to make me go back and talk to those kids again. Do you understand? No way."

"But Sean—"

"Forget it. I'm not doing it. I wouldn't ask my worst—" he broke off. "Wait a sec." An idea occurred to him, too beautiful by half. Forget opportunity—this was a gift from the gods, and a smart man used it to his advantage. And Lily would absolutely hate it. "This is for the school's career day?"

"That's right. You only have to—"

"All Feldron wants is someone to talk about his or her job?"

"Why yes, Sean, that's generally what one does for a career talk," Evelyn replied, shaking her head with exasperation.

The black cloud hanging over Sean lifted, sucked into the building's vast ventilation system. A wicked smile spread over his face. He leaned back in his chair, his fingers drumming lightly against the wood of his desk as he considered the possible pitfalls.

There were none that he could see.

"Get Feldron on the phone for me, would you please, Evelyn? While unfortunately I won't be able to participate in the career day program, I have someone in mind who'd be absolutely perfect."

Evelyn regarded him in silence. "And that would be?"

"One of Coral Beach High's very own." Sean smiled. "The return of the native."

"This could be interesting," Evelyn murmured. "And who is going to inform Dr. Banyon of her good fortune?"

"I believe I'll let you make that call."

"Why, gee, thanks, Mr. Mayor." Evelyn's tone was dry. "And in the event your star speaker displays the same enthusiasm you yourself have shown?"

He gave her a sunny smile. "Ah, Evelyn, that's when you pull out those thumb screws you always carry in your pantsuit pockets. Tighten them at will. I'll call Feldron and make his day."

* * *

Later that afternoon, Lily returned to the apartment. When her call of "Hello" received no response, she cocked her head and heard the faint sound of running water. Dropping her bag by the door, she walked into the kitchen and put the kettle on to boil, then went over to the table in the living room and booted up her laptop. She was entering the day's notes and temperature readings in her reef log when Karen came into the room.

Freshly scrubbed and in purple sweats, she plopped down onto the sofa. "Hi, how was the lab?"

Lily looked up from the screen. "Fine. We didn't do much today, just got things set up and labeled samples from the site."

"Did John come back with you?"

"Yes, but I think he said he was going out again later."

"Oh. Do you think I should go talk to him, apologize?" she asked.

Lily took off her black-framed reading glasses to stare at Karen. "Whatever for? Apologize, I mean."

"Because I acted like such an idiot on the boat. John gets me so mad. I should have come up with something really clever to say instead of losing it and pushing him like that. Now he probably hates me," she concluded with an unhappy sigh. "I've been trying to figure out what to do. Perhaps if I were nicer to him—you think that would work, Lily?" Karen looked at her with an earnest expression.

"Uh . . ." At an utter loss, Lily extended the syllable for as long as she could. But before she could fabricate an appropriately sage response, Karen spoke.

"Then there's Sean," she said, veering abruptly to a new topic. "He's so cute, totally ripped."

It was lucky the chair Lily was sitting in had arms, otherwise she would have fallen out of it. She gripped them tightly while Karen continued blithely.

"And such a good guy, which is pretty unusual when you think about it. Most men who look like he does don't bother being decent. And really, drool-worthy only goes so far in a guy. Sean was even nice to Stacy what's-her-name . . . and you could just see he was dying to get away from her."

Actually, Lily hadn't seen any such thing.

"But like I said, Sean's decent. Why can't John be? His tongue was practically to his knees when he was staring at her. And she's so *old*."

Stacy was a year younger than Sean and Lily.

"And John, telling me *I* shouldn't have a crush on Sean 'cause he's too old. Boy, John should practice what he preaches—that Stacy could be his mother!" she finished indignantly.

"Uh, probably not," Lily said, appalled to find herself defending Stacy Malloy. Still, there were certain biological realities. . . .

"Thing is, I *was* kind of checking Sean out—not because I have a crush on him or anything—but because he's so charismatic. It's funny, though, Lily. I looked and looked, even framed him the way I would if I were photographing him." She put her hands together and made a squared U. "But it wasn't until he angled his head just slightly that I figured out what makes him so appealing." She smiled. "You know what it is?"

The enormity of the question staggered her. "No, what?" she replied, and immediately regretted opening her mouth.

"It's his nose," Karen pronounced, triumphant. "He's

got this little, funny bump on the bridge, right here." She pointed with her finger. "I think it must have got broken at some point. Totally makes his face. Wild, isn't it?" Perhaps taking Lily's stunned silence for indifference, she shrugged. "I guess you don't notice his looks, 'cause you know him already. Too bad Sean's so much older, though I'm not sure he's really my type anyway—I'm not that into politics. But if I were you, Lily, I'd go for it. For sure, Sean would rather go out with you than someone like Stacy. Well, I'm gonna knock on John's door, see if he wants to grab a bite to eat. Maybe if I offer to treat . . ."

Karen was *so* wrong.

The thought repeated, complete with a high school stress on the *so*. It played unendingly, mercilessly, like a loop of tape in Lily's head as she stared blankly at her computer screen.

With a tired groan, she exited the reef program, then stood and walked over to the large windows.

The sun was sinking into the sea. Fifteen stories below, the beach glowed dusky golds and pinks. Yet the sight of it, like Karen's innocent chatter, evoked painful memories and served as a harsh reminder: Sean had never wanted to be with her.

The memories were of a night Lily wished only to forget. But coming back home, seeing Sean, and then Stacy, made Lily achingly aware that although years had elapsed, an important part of her still lodged there, unable to let go of the past.

The setting hadn't been far from the strip of beach Lily gazed upon now. There'd been a beach party one Saturday night during high school. A crowd of kids was sitting sprawled around a blazing bonfire. Music blared from a boom box, accompanied by laughter and the loud popping of burning driftwood. The fire's flames glowed bright, illuminating the stand of black palm trees with their arched fronds rustling in the night breeze.

Sean and his friends arrived later than Lily's and when he dropped down directly across the fire from her, it was obvious he hadn't noticed her. At seventeen, Lily was keenly aware of what Sean thought of her, knew he'd never intentionally sit where he might have to see her, look at her. She was too ugly, too much of a big-boobed nerd for someone like Sean McDermott.

Perhaps that's why she chanced it. Because tonight was safe. Sean was truly unaware of her presence.

Through the shifting screen of fire Lily watched him. Sean sat cross-legged, his blue-jeaned knees slightly upraised, his arms locked loosely about them. His chest was bare, and the reddish-gold cast of the dancing flames transformed his skin to dark, sculpted bronze. Lily's eyes lingered and lingered, tracing the restless shift of muscles, the quiver of warm flesh, as her heart beat harder and harder.

Sean's looks and his easy, careless charm made him incredibly popular, eternally so. He was never alone. This night, it was Stacy Malloy next to him. Though younger, Stacy was accomplished beyond her years at flirting—boys the one subject she considered worth studying. Stacy had planted herself next to Sean, leaning against him as she teased and chattered.

Lily watched the slight grin on Sean's face widen with every ridiculous, provocative idiocy Stacy uttered, saw how close Stacy pressed when she whispered into his ear, retreating only a hair's breadth while she waited for his reaction, a practiced smile of promise on her face. All obliging, Sean threw back his head and laughed, his eyes closed, blind to the stars shining down on him.

That night, so many years ago, Lily couldn't fully comprehend why the vision of Sean sitting and laughing, all golden and carefree, was such an intensely powerful one, why it made her throat tighten, made her heart run wild.

The reckless race of her heart pounded in counterpoint to the concert of night sounds: the crackle of the fire's hungry flames, the cymbal-like crash of surf pounding sand, the trill of laughter and animated chatter of the other kids.

Over all those sounds, Sean must have heard the fierce beating of her heart. His head lowered and across the bright orange flames, his gaze collided with hers, and held.

Through the frenzied dance of fire they stared and stared. Time suspended. In the capricious light, Lily fancied something new in his face, an expression she'd never seen before, and couldn't easily define. Intense longing for Sean made her burn as hot as fire itself, made her breasts ache with sudden heaviness.

Impossibly, her heart raced faster still, so fast, a wave of dizziness swept over her. Faint, Lily struggled for breath, closing her eyes.

But when she opened them again, whatever it was she believed she'd discovered in Sean's face was gone, as if it never were.

Like a dumb statue, she watched Sean grab Stacy's hand, surge to his feet, and lead her, laughing, into the shadowed stand of palms. She sat, devastation shattering her heart.

The following Monday, in gym class, they were playing volleyball. One of Sean's teammates had nudged him in the ribs and loudly inquired, "Hey, McDermott, you get lucky with Stacy?"

Sean's cocky grin had been his only answer. But that had been more than enough for Lily, listening from the other side of the volleyball net.

A volatile mix of fury, jealousy, and despair erupted inside her. She would show him, she'd raged inwardly, scooping up the volleyball. Her plan, to send it flying directly at Sean's head—knowing full well, of course, that she would miss. Except for swimming, she was a horrific failure at sports. She was the butt of jokes when it was her turn to serve, kick, or shoot. Lily knew she'd miss, but she'd succeed in wiping that stupid, conceited grin off his face.

She'd tossed the ball in the air and hammered it, putting all her strength, all her fury behind the serve. Off to the side of the court, someone yelled, "Watch out, McDermott!"

Sean had pivoted and, for some reason, looked straight at her. The movement brought him directly into the path of the white leather missile. It nailed him, a perfect strike, a bull's eye, or rather a bull's nose, seeing that it practically flattened Sean's.

Naturally, everyone believed Lily had actually *intended* to break his nose.

She hadn't thought Sean capable of despising her more. But she was wrong.

The violence of her act had horrified her. Yet every time she screwed up the courage to speak to Sean and apologize, he had walked away. Finally she understood: He would never forgive her. So Lily buried every feeling born that night at the beach beneath numbing layers of ice. And their silent war resumed.

Soon, everything was back to the way it had always been.

Not even leaving Coral Beach had changed things between them, Lily reminded herself sadly.

The memory of Sean's seemingly magical apparition at her *pensione* in Rome still made her cringe with embarrassment. She'd been flustered, speechless with wonder at his presence, her heart giddy at the idea of Sean tracking her down. Her naiveté laughable—Chris Jenkins, her college roommate's boyfriend, certainly found it so. Actually, he'd thought it hilarious when he overheard Sean bluntly informing Lily that the only reason he was there was because Kaye had *begged* him. Chris spent the rest of their week in Rome talking about "the poor slob from Florida who was wandering around the city with a broken heart."

From the mileage Chris got out of that remark, Lily knew he'd guessed who the "poor slob" really was: not Sean, but a miserable girl with long blond hair.

Oh, God, Lily thought, turning her back to the window and walking away. She was still that same pathetic, love-struck girl. Because despite a history of hurt, Lily had never met anyone who could make her heart pound, make her breathless with yearning like Sean.

If only Karen weren't so very wrong.

CHAPTER SIXTEEN

"Jesus, Sean, you trying to give me a heart attack?"

"What?" Sean managed a grin between gasps of air. "You going soft on me, Dave?"

"Up yours, McDermott," Dave growled, shooting him a baleful look. "I hope I live long enough to see you feel this shitty."

Sean laughed. With a yank, he pulled his goggles off and tossed them onto the pool deck, jacked his arms overhead, and let his body sink until his head was completely submerged. The water felt delicious against his heated skin. He resurfaced, shaking his head like a dog, making water spray in an arc, then reached up and grasped the lower rung of the starting block.

Dave's chest was still heaving like overworked bellows. "Christ almighty, this is supposed to be a *workout*, McDermott. Do you mind telling me what's got you swimming like a man possessed?"

From the far end of the pool came the ringing baritone of their coach, a voice almost as big as the man who owned it. "Yo, Sean, Dave," Hal Storey called. "What's with the lounging? You finished that last set already?"

"That's right," Sean yelled back. Next to him, Dave

cursed. "Cullen's raring to go, Hal," he added. "Thinks you're giving us way too much rest on our intervals." He grabbed his goggles and put them back on.

"Well, he'll like this next set, then. It's a killer. Be right over, Dave."

Dave groaned loudly. "Since when did you become such a sadist, McDermott?"

Since Lily Banyon rolled back into town. The answer trumpeted inside Sean's brain. "You should be thanking me, Dave, rather than griping. After all, I'm what's keeping you from hauling a spare tire around your middle, what's allowing you to chug down that third brew at the Keel."

"Funny, though, ain't it? How this newfound concern of yours to whip my butt into shape just happens to coincide with the arrival of a certain marine biologist?" It was Dave's turn to grin. "Yeah," he continued with a nod, "I think Lily Banyon might have something to do with this new boot camp mentality of yours, Sean."

"Lily Banyon? Did I hear you say Lily Banyon?" Hal Storey towered over them, his stopwatch dangling from his neck, a clipboard with one of his infamously grueling workouts tucked underneath his arm.

"You know Lily Banyon?" Dave asked, tilting his head back.

"Sure do," Hal replied. "Heard a rumor she was back in town, part of that reef study you two set up. Boy, I'd love to see my little water Lily again."

"Little? She was *never* little, Hal," Sean corrected before he could stop himself. "She joined when, at thirteen? She was the tallest kid for years."

Damn it, Sean couldn't believe this was happening.

The pool was one of the few places he should be able to forget Lily's existence. Here he was talking about her.

"I didn't know you'd coached Lily, Hal," Dave said.

Dave had only moved to Coral Beach four years ago, when the Parks and Recreation Department hired him. Sean couldn't fathom Dave's sudden interest in Hal's coaching career, unless it was to torture him by getting Hal to reminisce about his "little water Lily," which Sean had a sinking premonition was precisely what was going to happen.

"You bet I did," Hal said. "I started out here coaching the age group swimmers. Lily joined the team pretty late for an age grouper. But she was an absolute natural in the water. Within two months she'd moved to the fastest lane. Swam with you, didn't she, Sean?"

"She swam *behind* me. I led the lane."

Hal merely grunted, ignoring him. "Yeah, she was incredible. That body just ate up the water. Smoothest, longest stroke you've ever seen on a thirteen-year-old. Hell of a pair of lungs, too. You remember those underwater sets I'd throw at you guys?"

"You mean the ones where we'd all be seeing black spots?"

"Not all of you. Not Lily. Damn, that girl could go on and on. So, it's true she's back? Hadn't heard from her in awhile."

Hal kept all of Lily's postcards. The whole gamut, from gaudy beach bunnies to spectacular tropical vistas, lined his office walls.

"Yeah, she's back," Sean replied shortly.

"What do you think the likelihood is of her coming to a workout?"

"Real slim. You'd have better odds playing the lotto."

Damn it all, swim practice was the only chance he had to push his body until he was so physically spent, his exhaustion outweighed his sexual hunger. With Lily in the pool, he'd have to be dead not to want her.

"Ah, come on, Sean, be nice and invite her to a practice. Besides, I'm not sure our friendship can stand you blowing me out of the water for the duration of her stay." Dave's grin was pure evil.

"Yeah, Sean, it'd be like old times," Hal chimed in, way too enthusiastically. "Glory days."

Sean groaned loudly. "You haven't been listening to Springsteen again, have you, Hal?" he asked, shaking his head in despair. "I'll let you in on a secret: Some of us have actually accomplished something since the wonder years of high school."

"Let's see how cocky you feel after this sprint set, Mr. Mayor," Hal said.

He shrugged, sending ripples through the water. "Bring it on, Hal. Dave needs all the pumping up he can get. That way he might even see something the next time he flexes in front of his bathroom mirror."

"A low blow, McDermott. Just for that, I think I'll drop by the marina tomorrow and say hi to Lily and that photographer of hers. Might slip in a word or two about our swim team to her." He laughed as Sean's jaw went slack. "That'll teach you to try and drown your best buddy."

You're such a troll, John.

Karen would be eating her words if she could see me now, John thought. Maybe he should have brought her along, if only to show her how well he was treated in certain places. He'd have loved to see her expression when they walked into the Dolphin and he was greeted by name. But then again, she would doubtless have embarrassed him with one of her typically moronic questions, like, *Was the wine organic?*

John rolled his eyes in disgust, reached for a pretzel, and chewed reflectively. Besides, who cared what a ditz like Karen Masur thought? Not him, not when he had babes like Trish coming on to him. With a slight frown he raised his G and T to his lips. One look at Trish would have shut Karen's trap permanently.

"Hey, there, John," a familiar voice hailed.

John turned, his face clearing as Pete Ferrucci walked up and slapped a jovial hand on his shoulder. The older man pulled out the barstool next to him. "Good to see you again, John. Is Mike here treating you right?"

"Most excellently, Mr. Ferrucci." Mike, the bartender who was currently on duty, had not only known John's name, he'd been keeping an eye on John's glass, never letting it go empty. This place was definitely a trip and a half. John had never been in a restaurant where the staff went out of its way to remember the clientele's names. And Mike had been the one to wave Trish over so he could introduce her to John. The ultrafriendly Trish. She'd left a few minutes ago, but not before wringing a promise from John that he'd drop by her place and party with her later tonight. She'd written her address on a scrap of paper and shoved it down the front pocket of his trousers. She hadn't removed her hand until he had a dinosaur of a boner for her.

Yeah, who cared about Karen when there were babes like Trish ready to ball him blind?

"This is a really fantastic place you've got here, Mr. Ferrucci. The Dolphin rocks."

"It's Pete, remember, John? I'm glad you like it. I think the Dolphin's given Coral Beach a certain class. Someday soon, I'd like to open a few more places like this, really make the town into something. . . ."

"Well, if the Dolphin's anything to go by—" John began.

"Thanks. You can't imagine how damn hard it is. People around here—you know, the ones who've lived in this town forever, who hold the town in sway—these people have no vision. They can't see the possibilities, what this town *could* be. But enough of that," he said, as Mike set a glass down before him.

In silence, Ferrucci twirled the ice cubes of his drink with the red plastic swizzle stick until Mike reached the other end of the bar, out of earshot. "How's the study coming along? You went out today, right?"

"Yeah, it's a good-sized reef—there are a lot more specimens than I expected."

"Hmm." Ferrucci nodded absently. "Tell me, how do you and Banyon divide the work between you?"

"Well, I'm in charge of collecting water and algae samples, taking water temperature readings and core samples. Banyon positions the sediment traps, makes observations in her notebook on the different coral species. When we get to the lab, I give her my readings, and she logs all the data into the computer."

"That's interesting. Now what are these core samples all about? I don't remember Lesnesky mentioning them. They important?"

"Definitely," John said, nodding. "Core samples are another way to gauge the amount of sediment and pollution in an area. We take core samples by inserting a six-inch cylinder into the ocean floor. Then the lab technicians examine the strata trapped inside the tubes, test them for different kinds of bacteria, pollutants, nitrates, or metals. Core samples give a really good picture of what's settling over a certain area, and how heavily."

Ferrucci twirled the plastic stirrer between his fingers. "And these analyses, you conduct them at the lab here in town?"

"No." John shook his head. "This college lab doesn't come close to having the kind of equipment we need. We store the samples, then ship them in batches to the Marine Center. They analyze them, give us the results, and Lily enters all the data into the computer."

"Wow," Ferrucci replied, sounding impressed. "That's a helluva lot of sand to store. Must get kind of confusing, remembering what sample came from where?"

"Yeah, it's a lot of sand, lot of everything. But we do the labeling back at the college lab after each day's diving. That way, nothing gets mixed up. And we record everything in our notebooks, too, in case the computer crashes. . . . Banyon's a stickler for details like that." There was a grudging respect in John's voice.

A frown crossed Pete Ferrucci's face. "Hey, John, d'you remember those friends of mine I was talking about?" he said, switching topics abruptly. "They were very interested when I told them about this young hotshot biologist I'd met. You know, there are a lot of doors waiting to be opened by a guy like you." He helped himself to a pretzel. " 'Course, marine biology is a highly competitive field. In order to get ahead, sometimes you have to take a little initiative. . . ."

"I do my work, my dissertation's almost finished. I'm sure—"

"Yeah, maybe," Ferrucci interrupted, his tone was

skeptical. "I'm just worried that Banyon might prevent you from getting what you deserve. Damn, I've just got to get you together with these guys. I know you'd really like them, and it might give your career a boost." Ferrucci straightened abruptly on the stool. "Say, are you by any chance free tomorrow night?"

"Uh, I guess so." Realizing how weak-assed his response sounded, John cleared his throat. "Yes, I'm definitely free, Pete."

"Great. Give me a call at this number." He wrote down a number on the back of his business card. "I'll let you know if my friends can meet us." Ferrucci gave him a hearty slap on the back, then raised his glass. "Bottoms up, John." And he took a long, satisfied sip.

CHAPTER SEVENTEEN

The phone was ringing as Lily opened the door to the apartment, with her damp beach towel draped around her neck, her swim goggles dangling from her fingers. Kicking off her sandy flip-flops, Lily dashed across the living room before the incessant ringing could wake Karen.

"Hello?"

"Dr. Banyon? This is Evelyn Roemer. I'm sorry to disturb you at this hour, but I've gathered you like to set out for the reef quite early. I thought I'd try and catch you before you left."

Lily's eyebrows rose. She hadn't realized Coral Beach's town hall kept such extended hours. As Lily had walked from the beach back to the condominium, the morning sky had been only a faint, pale gray. "What can I do for you, Ms. Roemer?"

"Well, first of all, I wanted to find out how you're settling in. Do you have everything you require?"

"Actually, no." Lily cleared her throat. "I'd intended to call you later this morning. I was wondering if I could have a copy of Dr. Lesnesky's report. We'll be getting our first batch of tests results from the Marine Center early next week and it'd be helpful to have Dr. Lesnesky's data for comparison."

"Oh, yes, Sean already asked me to contact the university. Of course, I couldn't speak with Dr. Lesnesky himself—he's in New York until the end of his treatment— but I talked to his graduate assistant, who assured me he'd organize and photocopy Lesnesky's papers as quickly as possible. I gave him the Bay Towers address, knowing you'd be staying there."

"Oh. Thank you."

"You're welcome. I'm sorry we didn't have all the documents waiting for you when you arrived, but Dr. Lesnesky was somewhat disorganized in his presentations to the committee. We never received a formal written report. I presume he was waiting to finish the last part of the study before submitting it."

"That's possible." Lily's tone was carefully neutral. She didn't want to sound critical of a fellow scientist before she'd even read his work.

"And the apartments are to your liking?"

Lily glanced around. While mind-numbingly sterile, the condo was nonetheless more than adequate to their needs. She hadn't noticed a single cockroach scurrying for cover, which was too bad—it might have been fun to phone Pete Ferrucci and demand that he deal with something as repugnant as an infestation. "Yes, thank you, Ms. Roemer, we're very comfortable."

"Oh, good. The town is so grateful to the Marine Center for taking over the project. This reef study offers a marvelous opportunity to raise public awareness about the environment. Even though Coral Beach is a seaside community, most of us are appallingly ignorant about the ecological issues at stake."

"That's not very different from many places in the world, Ms. Roemer," Lily said, shifting restlessly. She was leaving a damp spot on the wall-to-wall carpet. She didn't particularly care about the state of the carpet, but it would be nice to strip out of her wet swimsuit and shower off the sand and salt water and perhaps get a little work done before leaving for the marina.

Unfortunately, Evelyn Roemer sounded as if she were ready for a nice chinwag.

"Educating the public is so vital, don't you agree, Dr. Banyon?"

"Yes, of course," she replied. "The Marine Center considers it a fundamental part of its mission."

"I'm absolutely delighted to hear that. Sean assured me we could count on you."

"Count on me?" she echoed, bewildered. "I don't understand—"

"It's only an hour, but the potential for positive impact on our community will be—"

"Excuse me," Lily interrupted. "What *exactly* will be just for an hour?"

"Coral Beach High's Career Day talk," Evelyn Roemer answered smoothly. "The principal, Hugh Feldron, was beyond enthusiastic when he heard you might be willing to address the school."

Lily's blood began to boil. "And it was Sean who volunteered my name to the principal?" *How dare he pull this kind of stunt?* she fumed silently.

"Why yes." There was the slightest pause before Evelyn Roemer asked, "Is there a problem, Dr. Banyon?"

"Where is he?" Lily demanded.

"At home, I imagine, though he'll be here shortly. Should I have him call you—"

"The address, Ms. Roemer, if you please."

"I don't think Sean—"

"The address, or I say no right now," Lily warned. "Your choice."

"Three sixty-nine Grove," came the immediate reply.

"A pleasure chatting with you, Ms. Roemer," Lily said, before hanging up the phone and running to grab a shirt and car keys.

Sean was sitting on the stoop of his bungalow, his cordless phone pressed to his ear, when Lily pulled up with a squeal of tires.

"Yeah, she's here already, Evelyn," he said. His eyes were trained on Lily as she slammed her door shut. "Must have driven at her usual leisurely pace. You might want to call Chip Reynolds, tell him to have his traffic cops keep their eyes peeled for a blue Ford Focus; it's like money in the bank. Sure, I'll fill you in when I get to the office. No, this won't take long." Sean clicked off the phone, his eyes taking in Lily's long, sandy legs as she stormed up his walkway, like some glorious Amazon goddess. His vision so acute, he could have counted the grains of sand clinging to her skin.

"Hello, Lily, what can I get you? Coffee, tea, a shower?"

"Ha! Very funny. I came here to tell you I'm not playing your games. *Any of them.*" Why in the world had she come here when she could have picked up the telephone and yelled at him from a safe distance—where she wouldn't have to look at him? Lily asked herself. He hadn't even finished dressing. His freshly laundered shirt, a deep cobalt blue, hung open, framing his tanned, muscled torso.

How could she argue while staring at that? Already she felt her heart kicking into overdrive.

Damn, but she was something else, Sean marveled silently. Lily's chest was heaving. With each indignant breath, her oversized denim work shirt inched up alabaster thighs, then dropped down in a mouth-watering peepshow.

Lust clawed him, sharp and relentless. He stood, the only way he could tear his eyes away from her naked legs. "Come on in," he offered over his shoulder, as he stepped onto his porch. "If you don't want a shower, maybe I can interest you in a pair of pants."

The bang of his screen door told her the decision was hers alone. Though Lily's brain screamed, *Run, fool,* her legs weren't listening. Wobbly, they followed him through the narrow arched entry hall that gave way to a large living room with dark, gleaming hardwood floors and walls painted a soothing off-white. There were prints on the wall, but Lily didn't get an opportunity to examine them closely, for Sean bypassed the living room's two matching gray twill sofas and continued on toward the back of the house.

He pushed the swinging door to the kitchen all the way open, until it caught, and flicked on the overhead lights. Lily stood uncertainly on the threshold of the small, tidy kitchen, watching as Sean went directly to the counter near the stove where a large gleaming espresso machine sat. He opened a canister and poured coffee beans into an automatic grinder.

"The cups are in the cabinet to your right," he informed her without turning around. He pressed a switch and a loud whirring noise filled the air, which was soon scented with the rich aroma of coffee.

Lily breathed deeply, as if the smell alone might fortify her, then moved in front of the blue wooden cabinet, opened it, and retrieved two white porcelain demitasses from the upper shelf. From behind she heard the sounds of Sean tinkering. There was a brush of air as he walked past her. "The cups go underneath the metal spouts. Back in a sec."

With impeccable timing, Sean returned just as the machine had finished expelling rich black coffee. He had a pair of jeans in his hand. "Here, put these on," he said, tossing them to her.

Lily caught them instinctively. "Don't be ridiculous," she said, thrusting them back at him. "I'm not going to wear your jeans. This shirt covers more of me than most skirts."

Sean's gaze dropped to her bare legs. And stayed there, until slowly, inch by inch, it traveled upward, leaving a trail of fire as it went. "If you want to talk, Lily, put them on. Of course, if you prefer to . . ." He let the sentence dangle as his mouth curved in a smile worthy of Lucifer.

"Fine," she snapped, painfully aware that he was toying with her, using her flustered embarrassment to his advantage. Defiantly, Lily kicked off her flip-flops and thrust one leg after the other into the jeans. *Thank God they fit,* she thought, as she pulled them over her hips. "There," she said, yanking up the zipper. "I hope you're satisfied."

He stifled a short, incredulous laugh. *Unbelievable.* He'd just suffered through a reverse striptease, was a heartbeat away from jumping her bones on the kitchen floor, and what did Lily do? Look him straight in the eye and ask if he was satisfied. There was a beautiful irony there somewhere, but Sean was damned if he could find it.

He picked up a cup and drained it, welcoming its scalding heat. "Fire at will, Dr. Banyon."

"I want answers, McDermott. What's the angle here with my giving this high school talk?"

"No angle," he replied with a careless shrug. "I simply saw a great opportunity for the kids and their parents to understand how important your job here is."

"Parents? What are parents doing at a career talk?" Lily demanded.

He smiled. He'd wondered whether she'd catch that one. "Hugh Feldron was so excited by the idea of your coming, he's decided to include parents; the local press will probably send a reporter, too. Great PR for your Marine Center."

"Very neat maneuvering, McDermott. Of course, you forgot to mention it's also great PR for town hall." Her eyes narrowed when he acknowledged her remark with another shrug. "Okay, let's try another question. How will a talk at the high school concerning my work and the reef study affect this development project for the marina?"

Sean had been leaning casually against the counter. He straightened slowly. "Where have you heard about a development project?"

"I have my sources." Remembering Sean and Ferrucci's exchange, she added silently, *And this information came straight from the horse's mouth.*

"Well whoever they are, your 'sources' are jumping the gun. There is no development project—"

"Not *yet*," Lily stressed.

Sean's jaw tightened, yet he continued as if Lily hadn't spoken. "South of the marina there's a large parcel of land that's been purchased by a group of private investors. They want to develop the area, double the marina's size and build some condominiums."

Lily's eyes widened. "That'd be a huge construction project," she said, envisioning the potential damage to the environment such a project could wreak.

Sean's brow lifted, as if he'd read her thoughts. "I dare say that's an understatement. It would be the most ambitious project undertaken in Coral Beach in decades. I've seen some preliminary plans for the development, but I've told them I won't bring the issue of the marina's expansion before the townspeople until the reef study is complete."

"So the town might vote the proposal down anyway. . . ."

Sean gave a brief smile at the hopeful note in her voice. "Doubtful. The town stands to make a huge amount of money if this project goes through, and there are a number of people who are very vocal about bringing Coral Beach into the twenty-first century."

"So what happens when my study is complete?"

"I'll have to make a decision whether or not to support the marina development."

"And if my data doesn't mesh with Dr. Lesnesky's? What if we disagree?"

"I don't foresee that happening. Lesnesky never reported anything to lead us to believe that Coral Beach's reef was threatened."

"Discrepancies *do* arise, however," she said pointedly, pressing him for an answer.

Sean crossed his arms and regarded her levelly. "You

want to know what I'd do if it came down to your study against Lesnesky's?"

Lily nodded, unconsciously holding her breath.

"That's easy. I would try to get the development shelved indefinitely, if not permanently."

Her shock must have been written all over her face.

"I trust your professional word, Lily." His hazel eyes bored into hers. "Now what if I ask the same of you, Dr. Banyon? Do you trust me?"

Sean's question hung in the air between them.

Lily's hesitation answered for her.

"Right," Sean replied, his brusque tone implying he'd expected nothing else. "Well, at least we've got our positions straight. So," he continued, "what should Evelyn tell Feldron? Yes or no for the Career Day?"

"When is it?" Lily asked, uncomfortably aware she was the cause of the sudden chill in the kitchen. But she also knew she'd been honest. She wasn't sure Sean could say the same.

"The talk's this coming Tuesday, at twelve P.M." Sean ignored her gasp. "Plenty of time to whip something into shape, Dr. Banyon."

God, she hated public speaking. But this might be her best chance to raise interest in the reef. She could give a talk at the high school that would at least make her audience pause and consider the impact such a huge coastal project might have on the marine environment. "I'll get to work on something."

"Thank you. I think you'll be surprised by how many people will attend—not just because of the work you're doing on the reef, but because it's you, Lily. This is your town, too. Like it or not."

She shook her head. "No, I never really felt like I belonged here."

"You know, if you gave this place a chance, you might find out how wrong you are."

"I'll be gone before that happens," Lily said.

Sean gave her a long look, then shook his head without saying more. *Maybe it was for the best,* he said to himself. She was too damned dangerous anyway. For in spite of everything—the pain of her patent distrust of him, of her refusal to acknowledge the ties that bound her to Coral Beach, he still wanted her so badly he was almost shaking from it.

And if she stayed here a minute longer, he would touch her. Do his damnedest to seduce her out of his Levi's. And the warring pain and pleasure of making love to Lily might destroy him. . . .

"Cheer up, Lily. Here's some good news: I won't be coming on any dives for a while. I'm snowed with work at the office." He made a show of glancing at his watch. "Speaking of which, I've got to head over there now."

"Oh, of course," Lily stammered. "I need to get back to the condo." She cleared her throat. "I'll drop the jeans off—"

"Keep 'em." He gave a cynical smile. "As a souvenir of your trip to Coral Beach."

Later that afternoon, May Ellen and Anne sat under the large market umbrella on May Ellen's patio, two worn and well-thumbed address books open before them. A stack of invitations was the centerpiece of the table. They were at the *H*s, talking as they addressed envelopes in their perfect flowing script.

"My, we played until late last night!" Anne remarked.

"Still, it was a nice evening, don't you think, May Ellen?"

"Mmm, yes," May Ellen said, affixing a stamp in the upper corner of the cream envelope. "Though why Alicia led hearts in that last hand is beyond me."

"Well, Alicia's never been the brightest bulb," Anne reminded May gently. She laid an invitation made out to Dolly Heffernan on top of the pile to her right and reached for another.

"True, but one would hope that after . . ." May paused, pen suspended in midair. "Dear me, after *fifty years* of playing bridge, you'd think she'd begin to get the hang of it."

"Well, if she's lucky, she'll have a few more years before her bulb dims completely." Anne shook her head and sighed. "I suppose I should do the right thing and call Alicia tomorrow and offer to play as her partner Monday night."

"Oh, no, Anne! That would be going too far!"

"It would? Oh, good," she said with evident relief. "I'm afraid I would do something terribly unladylike if she were to bungle a hand as badly as she did last night."

"I know exactly what you mean, dear. Sometimes when I play a rubber with a partner who seems intent on losing, I'm almost overcome with evil thoughts. It reminds me what a blessing it is to know how to play the game. Of course, if I were as hopeless at strategy as Alicia, I'd switch to golf. Any dodo can hit a ball," May pronounced with a sniff, and turned the page of her address book.

"Speaking of strategy, that reminds me," Anne said. "Did you reach Lily?"

"Yes, I did. Not the easiest task—that girl spends most

of her time underwater. Just imagine, Anne, they're diving *twice* today; I'm afraid we didn't take into account how hard she works."

"Young people these days." Anne pursed her lips. "Sean's the same—always rushing around, doing things— I hope you told Lily how unhealthy that is."

"Of course. Anyway, it's all arranged. Lily promised she'd come tomorrow, when she's finished at the lab."

"And you called Lloyd?"

"Mmm-hmm," May nodded, licking the back of an envelope. "I'll ring you the second I see her pulling up— she won't think twice about our chatting on the phone. Then you call Lloyd so he can drive right over."

"He'll remember what to say?"

"Why, I certainly hope so! Lloyd's years younger than we are. He has no excuse for memory loss."

"Good. We haven't made nearly as much progress as Lily has with her reef study."

"I don't suppose that lovely George Hunt could find another project for her, in Vero Beach maybe?" May said, half-jokingly.

"No, George has done his bit, just as he promised. Now it's up to us, May."

"And Sean, has he even tried to see her?"

Anne frowned. "I called Evelyn. He didn't go out on the boat with them again, the stubborn fool. But she mentioned something about his having arranged for Lily to talk at the high school. That's an encouraging sign—I think. He's coming to dinner tonight. I'll lay it on thick over pot roast and key lime pie," she said determinedly.

"That boy does love his key lime pie," May Ellen said

with a fond smile, as she turned to the *K*s in her address book.

"Yes," Anne agreed, chuckling. "Almost as much as he loves that granddaughter of yours."

CHAPTER EIGHTEEN

The lab was nearly silent. The banks of florescent lights gave off a muted hum, a white noise that reinforced the overall quiet. Eyes glued to her computer screen, Lily was mapping the areas where she and John had collected samples into the program. She was utterly absorbed in her task, satisfied, too. They'd made good progress, as exemplified by the advancing block of Xs and color-coded dots, demarcating where they'd taken the water and core samples, temperature and sediment readings from each transect.

At the loud, shrill ring, she started, looking around wildly. Then she saw the alarm clock, the Post-it notes, and remembered. Knowing her tendency to get lost in her work, she'd stuck the bright yellow squares everywhere— on her notebook, on the test tubes, on her computer, on the top of the clock itself—with *May Ellen!* scrawled in bold letters. She was due at her grandmother's in twenty minutes.

The blasted thing was still ringing. "Okay already!" she muttered in exasperation, as she grabbed it and turned it off. Silence descended once more.

"What's with the alarm clock?"

Lily spun around with a gasp, her hand to her throat. John was sitting at his station by the window, a row of test tubes aligned before him.

"God, you startled me!" She gave a shaky laugh. John had been working so quietly, she'd forgotten his existence. "You're still here?"

"Yeah. What's with that?" he asked with a nod at the clock in her hand.

Lily felt her cheeks warm. "I've got to go see my grandmother. I set it so I wouldn't be late," she admitted, then glanced at him curiously. "I'm, uh, surprised you're working this late."

A lot had been surprising about John these past couple of days. He'd been unusually cooperative aboard the *Tangiers*, his demeanor atypically inoffensive, as well.

"Yeah, I've got to finish putting the labels on these core samples. We're sending this batch off to the center tomorrow, right?"

"Yes." Lily nodded. "I'm sorry, I didn't notice you were still here. I'd have lent a hand."

"That's okay," he said with a shrug. "I'm almost done. It won't take too much longer."

She felt her jaw drop to the floor. John working late? Maybe the lecture Simone had delivered to him before their departure had done the trick. She would have to tell Simone about the new improved John Granger when she called her tomorrow. "Wow. This shows real dedication, John."

"Some of us have to take this project seriously."

"What do you mean by that? Oh," she said, as understanding dawned. "You're referring to Karen."

" 'Course I'm talking about Karen," John drawled sarcastically. "What does she think this job is? Some kind of Club Med vacation? She's supposed to be working! But what does she do instead? Drives off with Cullen to another dive site, twenty miles south of here."

John actually sounded more jealous than anything. Lily frowned, bewildered. "But John, didn't she ask you to go to the movies with her?" she pointed out reasonably. "You turned her down, said you already had plans. That was when Dave asked her whether she wanted to explore this site."

"Yeah, well, if I'd said yes, Karen would have dragged me to some boring chick flick," John said sulkily.

John Granger's new, improved character had just taken a nose-dive, Lily thought. She hoped he'd get over his fit of pique soon, because Dave Cullen gave all the signs of being quite taken with Karen. Cullen had dived with the research team both yesterday and today.

Unlike John, Lily had no problem with Karen and Dave's blossoming friendship. She much preferred having Dave aboard the *Tangiers* than dealing with Sean's unsettling presence . . . once she got past the sharp pang of regret. It was far easier to concentrate on the study without Sean there to muddle her mind. Really, the only reason she wanted to see Sean McDermott was to vent her frustration about this darned Career Day talk he'd managed to rope her into . . . which was probably why he was avoiding her so assiduously.

With a sigh, she directed her thoughts away from Sean and looked at the clock cradled in her hands. She had fifteen minutes to get to Granny May's. If she drove fast, she could make it to Laguna in seven minutes.

"Look, John," she said. "Why don't I give you a hand with these labels? As you said, you've got plans. If we work together, we'll be finished in ten minutes. Then we can lock up and call it a night."

John picked up his thin black marker. "That's all right," he said, and shook his head resolutely. "You go ahead and visit with your gran."

"Well, if you're sure."

Lily looked over her work area to verify that the samples she'd processed were neatly arranged. She slipped her notebook inside her shoulder bag and zipped her laptop into its carrying case. With a final glance around the small lab to ensure she hadn't forgotten anything, Lily picked up her bags.

"Thanks for locking up, John," she said, by way of reminder.

"No problemo. You can count on me."

"Right. Well, I'll see you in the morning, then."

"Don't forget to say hi to your gran for me," he said with a condescending smirk.

The smirk was classic Granger. Lily felt a rush of relief as she closed the door behind her. John was definitely reverting to type: one hundred percent obnoxious. Thank God for that—she didn't want to have to start liking him.

"Hello, Lily, darling. Come in. I'd just picked up the phone to call Anne when you rang the doorbell. I'd better do it now, otherwise I'll clean forget what it was I wanted to say to her," her grandmother confessed with a bright smile. "Just go on into the kitchen, dear. I have a lovely Pinot Grigio in the refrigerator. Or, if you want something a bit stronger . . ."

"No, wine would be perfect, Granny May."

"Good. Pour a glass for me, too. Why don't we sit out on the porch. The sun will be setting soon."

She had just placed two wineglasses on the wicker coffee table when May Ellen joined her. "Well, I'm glad I got that accomplished. Anne and I were double-checking the invitation list for the party we're throwing." She sat down on the chintz-upholstered settee and patted the cushion beside her. "Come sit by me. You can see the sky so much better." She reached for the wineglasses, holding one out to Lily. "*Mmm*, isn't that delicious?"

"Yes, absolutely," Lily agreed.

"Oh, look at that beautiful shade of pink! See, below the clouds there? It reminds me of raspberry sherbet." She gave Lily's hand a gentle squeeze. "I'm delighted you're here to share this time of day with me. Sometimes sunsets can be so lonely," May Ellen finished with a quiet sigh.

Lily glanced at her grandmother in surprise. Granny May was more socially active than most people half her age. But then she considered her grandmother's words, remembering the countless times she herself had sat on a beach at sunset, watching the last fiery rays dip beneath the silvered sea, and feeling an empty ache spread inside her that there was no one special with whom she could share the moment. "Yes, they can be," she agreed quietly. "I'm very happy to be here, too, Granny."

She reached out and laid her hand over her grandmother's.

Her grandmother's lined face lifted in a gentle smile. "How maudlin we must sound! Which is ridiculous, because I'm beside myself with joy that you're home—even if it's only for a short while. Your homecoming has brought so many memories of you as a young girl. You were such a lovely girl, Lily."

"Granny!" Lily cried in protest. "I was awful, and horrible-looking, too!"

"Nonsense, you just *felt* that way because you were miserable," May Ellen replied stoutly. "But that was your mother's fault . . . and mine too, for not stopping Kaye."

Lily swallowed the hard lump in her throat. "Granny, that's all in the past—"

"I could kick myself every time I think of it," May continued, as if Lily hadn't spoken. "Kaye was head-strong and spoiled, and so very unhappy—especially when she and your father split up. And because I was worried sick about her, I stupidly kept my own counsel. I'm sorry about that. I realized too late that you were hurting more than any of us. I have a feeling your mother has some deep regrets about the past."

"I don't—"

"I understand, you don't want to talk about it. But, Lily, I want you to know that Kaye's changed since she and Scott married. I think she's finally grown up. Scott's done wonders for her. You might be surprised when you see her next."

That wouldn't happen anytime soon, Lily thought. Over the years, she had come to realize that she and her mother got along best when they were about a thousand miles apart. She held her tongue, however, unwilling to spoil the evening.

Perhaps sensing her mood, her grandmother patted her knee and said, "Now, tell me how your reef study is coming along."

"So far, so good," Lily replied, grateful for the switch

in topic. "We've been collecting lots of samples. The corals that we've looked at show few signs of damage or disease. The reef seems to be quite healthy. We were out on zone three today. There were some good-sized schools of mackerel and jacks. I even spied a couple of barracuda."

"How thrilling. That's so good to hear. Your grandfather and I loved exploring that reef when we first married. Are you almost finished?"

"We covered the northern portion so far. There's still quite a bit of work ahead of us."

"Oh." May Ellen was silent for a moment. "Well, I hope the storm system that's coming this way won't cause too much delay."

Lily had forgotten May Ellen was a Weather Channel junkie. If the Weather Channel ever decided to hire grandmothers as forecasters, May Ellen would be a shoe-in for the job. "Storm system?" she parroted.

"Oh, yes. It's the season." Her grandmother nodded happily. "Should be a messy one, too. Heavy rain, with potential thunderstorms . . . pretty much a typical fall weather disturbance. Ryan Jeffries—I only tune into him, those others wouldn't know an occluded front from their derriere—" May Ellen pressed a hand to her lips and turned bright pink with embarrassment. Clearing her throat delicately, she continued, "Ryan says the rain should begin tomorrow or the next day, then sit on the coast. I already canceled my hair appointment—" She broke off at the sound of the doorbell chiming. "Oh! That must be Lloyd," she said, jumping to her feet. "I'd forgotten all about him."

"Lloyd?" Automatically, Lily rose as well.

"Lloyd Gans, my internist. He promised he'd drop by with the results of my exam."

"Your doctor makes house calls?" Lily asked incredulously, as she followed May Ellen.

"I used to baby-sit Lloyd. I can still remember how bad those poopy diapers smelled. Of course he'd make a house call for me! I find doctors' offices terribly depressing."

A doctor who made house calls? In the twenty-first century? Fascinated, Lily trailed after her grandmother.

This had to be the most unconventional doctor's visit in history. Dr. Lloyd Gans, comfortably ensconced on the sofa, was happily drinking his wine while he systematically devoured rounds of Brie and chutney on toast and mini mushroom quiches. Seated next to him, Lily studied him covertly, trying to match this hearty, silver-maned, sixty-year-old doctor with Granny May's description of him as a smelly-diapered toddler. It defied imagination. Giving up, Lily concentrated on her wine.

Dr. Gans's bedside manner was novel, too. Ignoring May Ellen, he focused exclusively on emptying the hors d'oeuvres tray and on quizzing Lily with questions about Coral Beach's reef study. Twenty minutes later, Lily knew Lloyd Gans was an avid scuba diver, was quite familiar with many of the sites Lily had researched, and that he'd even read her book on coral reef ecology.

On the topic of her grandmother's health, however, he remained surprisingly mute. It took May Ellen a number of prompts before he abandoned his description of a recent dive in Belize and addressed the issue of her health.

"You should be quite pleased with your lab tests, May Ellen. Your numbers are excellent for someone your age." With that, he rattled off May Ellen's blood pressure and cholesterol count, a proud smile on his face, as though this were a professional triumph.

Strangely enough, her grandmother seemed less than delighted at the news. Then, as if realizing how odd her reaction appeared, May Ellen added hurriedly, "That's such a relief, Lloyd. Because you know how worried I've been about the dizzy spells I keep having."

"Oh!" Dr. Gans's silver brows beetled together. "Oh, yes!" He cleared his throat importantly. "Your dizzy spells. I'm sure they're nothing serious, May Ellen, but I want you to stay away from that stepladder. And no heavy lifting."

"But, Lloyd, I was planning on moving these pictures this week!" May exclaimed, gesturing about her. The papered walls of the living room were almost hidden, covered with framed artwork, large and small.

"You were planning on moving all these, by yourself?" Lily asked. She set her wineglass down with a clink. Maybe she'd had too much to drink.

"Why, yes, I consulted an interior decorator, Angelo Barbieri. He's very successful. He told me it's a wonderful way to give a room a fresh look. I want to switch all the art in the dining room, the den, and the guest bedroom in time for this party. Did I mention Anne's wonderful idea, Lily? She suggested we make it a dual celebration, a combined homecoming and birthday party. Won't that be fun?"

"But, Granny, I don't need a home—"

"You most certainly do," May Ellen interrupted in a tone of voice that brooked no resistance. "There are countless people who are dying to see you, and I can't think of a better time to celebrate my seventieth birthday.

After all, you might be on the other side of the world when my actual birthday rolls around," she reminded Lily, making her feel about two inches tall. "I hope you'll come, Lloyd. We sent out the invitations today."

"I'd be delighted, May. Thank you. However, it's absolutely out of the question for you to move even one of these pictures by yourself."

A woeful expression settled over her grandmother's features. "It's so difficult to be old and alone," she said with a sigh. "You remember my grandsons, Mike and Ned, don't you, Lloyd? They've moved away and are busy with their lives. I don't want to be a burden, make them drop what they're doing and drive all this way, simply to spend an afternoon moving pictures for me. Kaye's still on her cruise—I can't recall when she's due back, but I'm *sure* it won't be in time to help me." With a visible effort, she brightened. "I suppose I can ask Sean, Anne's grandson. He's always been such a help."

And what am I, Lily wondered, *chopped liver?* Her grandmother had named her entire family as possible support, but not her. Bringing up Sean was the last straw.

"I'll do it for you, Granny May."

"Oh, no, Lily! I couldn't ask that of you. You've got the study to complete—though if this storm comes, I'm not sure how much work you'll be getting done. Have you listened to the forecast, Lloyd?" she inquired, but then continued before Lloyd Gans could reply. "No," she repeated with a decided shake of her head. "Sean can move them for me. I'll telephone him—"

"Really, Granny," Lily insisted. "I'm more than happy to hang your pictures." *All fifty of them.* But it could have been a hundred, and still she'd do it.

It bothered her profoundly that it was Sean to whom

her grandmother instinctively turned. *Maybe she has to, since you haven't bothered to come home,* an inner voice reminded her pointedly. Well, she was home now, and it was *she* who'd rehang every etching, print, and Homeresque watercolor in her grandmother's possession.

"Well, if you insist, Lily, dearest," May Ellen capitulated with a radiant smile. "Why don't you come the day after tomorrow?"

CHAPTER NINETEEN

What could make a horde of bored teenagers sit up and pay attention? Lily asked herself for the hundredth time. Ever since Sean had maneuvered her into speaking at their old high school, Lily had gone about her work with one part of her brain worrying over the question.

No solution satisfied her.

Inspiration came from an unexpected source.

In Lily's case, creative genius wore tie-dye and multiple body piercings.

It was later in the evening and Karen, unable to find anything sufficiently entertaining on TV, had asked Lily if she could use her computer to look at some pictures she'd posted on her Web site.

With a nod to her laptop, Lily said, "Go ahead," and returned to reading the proofs of an article she'd written on the current debate over artificial reefs. The article would be published in the upcoming issue of *Scientific American*.

Karen sat down beside her and booted up the computer. A few minutes later, a flash of vibrant colors had Lily glancing sideways, curious to see what Karen had pulled up. The corrections Lily was working on, indeed, her entire article, were forgotten as she gazed at the image of a moon jellyfish.

Round and nearly transparent, except for traces of blue and purple, the jellyfish floated in front of a large elkhorn coral. The branches of the coral were visible through the body of the jellyfish. The photo had the quality of a wonderful abstract painting, and yet, all the elements remained immediately identifiable.

Lily scooted her chair closer to Karen. "God, that's beautiful."

Karen grinned, her eyes fixed on the screen. "Thanks. You really like it?"

"It's incredible. How'd you manage to stay still for that shot?" The thread-thin lines delineating the jellyfish were incredibly sharp—no blur to betray the tremor of an unsteady lens.

"That was the trickiest part. I was super lucky. There was a patch of sand just in front of the elkhorn. I sat down cross-legged and held the camera tight against me. The hardest part was remembering to breathe."

Lily smiled in understanding. "I have that problem, too. Forty feet below and suddenly, you see something unimaginably spectacular. At that moment, drawing air into your lungs is the last thing on your mind. I wish these biogeneticists would forget about cloning and concentrate on figuring out how to give us gills."

Karen's shoulders rocked with mirth. "Come on, you're already as close to a mermaid as you can get. You want to abandon land completely?"

"It's tempting. But then maybe I'd take all this for granted," she said, pointing to the underwater world on the computer screen.

"Want to see my other pics?"

"Definitely. These are fantastic, Karen. I only wish more people could see what you've got here." She stilled as a thought occurred to her. George Hunt, the head of Lily's department at the Marine Center, had a favorite saying: "When you go to enlighten the public, use every resource at your disposal. Captivate your audience. Make them dream." Who better to emulate than the center's brilliant showman, the man who could transform iron-willed CEOs into misty-eyed donors?

And what better way to make an audience of hyper-critical adolescents dream than with images such as these?

"Karen, can you use a computer to splice images together?"

"Into a film format? Sure, that's a piece of cake. I did that with a bunch of photographs I took down in Mexico. They came out really well. I've got it on a CD in my room. I'll go get it."

A minute later, Karen had inserted the CD and was clicking the mouse in a series of rapid commands. "Wait until you see this. It's totally orgasmic."

The screen before them went black, dark as a night sky. Slowly, the large, striated mound of a brain coral, glowing greenish gray, came into focus. For a second that was all, the brain coral set against the eerie aquatic stillness. Then it happened. Across the coral's surface, countless tiny polyps opened, releasing a salmon-colored cloud.

The coral was spawning.

Before their eyes, the cloud broke up, separating into rosy, bead-sized bundles, thousands upon thousands of them. The bundles drifted across the screen just as in life they drifted along the ocean's current. It signaled the start of a journey of creation that might take months, until at last these tiny spawn settled on a propitious surface and began to divide and grow.

The scene over, Lily let out an unconscious sigh. There were few things as awesome as witnessing mass procreation, animal style. "Wow. Orgasmic indeed," she murmured, echoing Karen's description.

With a flash, a new image appeared on the screen. An angelfish approached, coming close, so close its mouth almost touched the lens of Karen's camera. Then, shying abruptly, the fish was gone in a vibrant streak of black, yellow, and royal blue.

"Karen, would you be willing to put together a short film with these pictures? I'd love to show them to the high school kids I'm talking to tomorrow."

Karen nodded, looking pleased. " 'Course you can. Let's go through them and you can pick out the ones you want."

Time flew as they pieced together a twenty-minute film.

"Know what'd be really cool, Lily?" Karen asked, her brown eyes glowing with excitement.

"No, tell me."

"If we burned some music and arranged it so that in between your narration, there'd be musical sequences."

"By *music*, I take it you don't mean Beethoven?"

"Are you kidding? And have the kids sawing *zzz*s? No, you need to give them something as wild as what they're looking at."

Lily patted Karen's T-shirt-clad shoulder. "Sorry. Though it kills me to admit it, I think I'm already too old to know what high school kids consider 'wild.' " She raised her hand as Karen opened her mouth, no doubt intending to inform Lily at length. "Nor do I particularly care," she added with a smile. "But if you think putting in a soundtrack will make the film better, go for it. Do whatever you want—just be sure there aren't any lyrics that are objectionable. We don't want to get the center in trouble."

"You're sure you don't want to vet it first?" Karen looked stunned.

Lily smiled and shook her head. "Nope. You have my complete trust." It was true. She'd gotten to know Karen pretty well since coming to Coral Beach and Lily's appreciation for her idiosyncratic and slightly offbeat roommate had grown immensely.

She stood and stretched, her muscles tight from sitting too long. Then she blinked in amazement. Her watch read two o'clock. She and Karen had been at the computer for nearly half the night. "Karen, do you realize what time it is?"

"Must be late. But if I don't do this now, I'll have tunes playing inside my head all night. I think I heard John come in a few minutes ago. I'll go knock on his door and see if he wants to help."

Lily ducked her head, smiling. Karen was not only quirky and fun, she was also truly kindhearted—and determined—as evidenced by the fact that she was still on her "be nice to John" kick. Lily wasn't sure if Karen's campaign of benevolence was having any effect on him, but that was none of her business.

"I'd stay and keep you company, but I have to get up extra early and e-mail a status report to Simone before we dive tomorrow. And if I have time, I'd like to sneak in a swim."

"You'll definitely need to go early for the swim. The weather's supposed to turn to crapola soon."

"So I heard," Lily replied, remembering her grand-mother's weather prediction.

"Go get some sleep. You have to be on your toes for an auditorium full of teens—and I bet there'll be a few other people in attendance, too."

"And you know this how?" Lily asked.

Karen smiled. "Well, when Dave and I drove to the site this afternoon, he asked me all about it. He's real excited about your talk."

"Then I'm even more grateful I'm going to have such stunning visual effects. But I think Dave will probably be far more impressed by your pictures than by my speech." *That wouldn't be hard,* Lily added silently, trying not to think about how much she hated public speaking. She knew that some people, like George Hunt, became posi-tively energized when they addressed an audience. It brought out the showman in them. Lily would consider herself lucky if she managed to remember her own name.

"Dave might like my pictures," Karen conceded. "But I figure if Dave's coming to the school tomorrow, chances are someone else will be, too. And I bet that certain per-son will be far more interested in *you*," she predicted confidently.

Lily felt her heart skip a beat.

Karen stood and brushed her braids back behind her shoulders. "I'm going to see if John feels like helping—he has fairly decent taste in music. Sleep tight, Lily."

"Good night, Karen," Lily replied distractedly, hardly noticing when Karen stepped out of the apartment to rap on John's door.

Her mind was awhirl.

She truly hadn't considered the possibility of Sean coming to her talk.

No, he wouldn't come, she reassured herself. Sean probably never wanted to lay eyes on her again, especially after their last conversation, when she'd made it clear she didn't believe he'd give up the development project to protect the reef. Which was for the best, she reminded herself hastily. She couldn't afford to get any more deeply enmeshed in the tangled threads of Coral Beach's politics. She'd do exactly as she had told Sean: conduct the reef study, present her findings to the committee, and then leave.

CHAPTER TWENTY

Sean checked his watch, grimaced, and lengthened his stride down the hallway. He'd make it to the high school—but only if he skirted around town instead of cutting through. It was 12:40 P.M. and the downtown streets would be clogged with motorists battling for lunch hour parking.

He was halfway down the granite steps when he spotted Dave and Evelyn standing beside his car in the lot reserved for official use. He raised an eyebrow at the twin smiles of angelic innocence on their faces. "What are you two doing, camped out here?"

"That should be obvious," his secretary replied. "You tipped your hand when you canceled your lunch with Ferrucci and the oh-so-friendly developers. So Dave and I decided we might as well share the ride. No point in taking separate cars when we can carpool."

He made a show of looking at his watch. "You want a lift to the deli for sandwiches? Fine, hop on in."

Evelyn made a clucking noise with her tongue. Her pink curls shook lightly. "Sean, we're your friends. If we're willing to admit to unholy curiosity, then you should, too."

Dave merely nodded in agreement, wisely holding his tongue. A good thing, too. These days, Sean's temper had a real short fuse, wired to explode. He didn't want to throttle his best friend in the town hall parking lot.

Sean had thought it would be easier not to see Lily, but he'd been wrong. Just knowing she was near had him craving even a glimpse of her. It was a gnawing hunger that nothing could appease . . . except her.

He didn't have the time to stall or bluff with these two. Shooting them an aggrieved look, he went around to the passenger side and unlocked the door for Evelyn.

His secretary took her own sweet time settling herself in the seat, adjusting her jacket just so, then resting her patent leather purse upon her lap. Finally satisfied, she smiled up at him. "Thank you, Sean."

Biting back a less than chivalrous growl, Sean shut the passenger door and ran around to the other side of the car. He slid behind the wheel and started the engine, thrusting the gearshift into reverse. Although the sky was heavy with ominous clouds and the air damp with the promise of rain, Sean, like a true Floridian, automatically reached forward to press the button on his car's dash that would lower the convertible's faded canvas top.

"Oh! Just a minute, Sean," Evelyn demanded. From the depths of her purse, she fished a silk scarf with porcine-looking flamingos parading across it. Deftly, she wrapped it over her curls, whose color nearly matched the flamingos'. "I did my hair last night. I'd hate to get it mussed." She patted her head to verify it was adequately protected. "You can go now."

Sean caught Dave's reflection in the rearview mirror. Cullen was grinning from ear to ear.

"Please remind me precisely why it is I put up with the two of you?" Sean asked before shifting into first gear and roaring out of the town hall parking lot.

The podium had been pushed front and center on the high school's stage so that it was positioned directly beneath the large medallion, which depicted Coral Beach High's insignia. Of carved and painted wood, the medallion represented a dolphin leaping over a wave-crested sea. A star-studded sky provided the backdrop for the dolphin's arched body. Embossed gold letters encircled the scene with the school's motto: *From the Sea We Learn.*

The auditorium was already filled with students, parents, and faculty and the buzz and squeak of restless murmurs and shifting bodies when Sean, Evelyn, and Dave entered. Finding three vacant seats near the back row, they sat down. Sean propped his elbows casually against the armrests of his seat, a genial expression stamped upon his face. His relaxed air was a sham. Inside, anticipation roiled, building steadily.

He wondered if Lily had the slightest inkling of the power she held. Sean wasn't thinking of how her reef study might influence the town's decision to vote on the multimillion-dollar development. No, it was the power she wielded over him, one which kept him enthralled, day and night.

And now, as well. From the sudden prickle of awareness, Sean knew she had arrived. As always, her presence made him feel as though a current were racing through him. Drawn by a magnetic attraction, his eyes fixed on Lily, his true north.

She'd come in by one of the side doors nearest the

stage. Hugh Feldron, the school's principal, was with her. Sean watched as she shed her dampened raincoat, shook it lightly, and then laid it over a front row seat.

Lily's head was turned toward Feldron, who, as usual, seemed to be talking away. Sean's hungry gaze fastened on her, noting everything—how the auditorium's track lights illuminated the raindrops that clung to her careless locks, crowning her head with the spark of diamonds. How her skin glowed like the palest ivory. A fantasy, fully formed, sprang to mind, of him feasting upon that rain-scented skin, of Lily's helpless moans as he pleasured her.

His erotic daydream came to a screeching halt when Evelyn leaned close and whispered, "There's a full house today. Your Dr. Banyon's quite a draw, Sean."

Your Dr. Banyon. Sean sat back against the velveteen-covered seat, stunned. There it was, voiced aloud, the crux of the problem that tormented him. He wanted Lily. Wanted her to be *his*.

That was another fantasy he'd indulged in, a thousand times over, free to do so because a fantasy was safe. Acknowledging his desire openly, showing Lily how much he wanted her, how much he cared, was anything but.

In the political arena, Sean suffered no lack of confidence, of courage. But he was damnably afraid when it came to Lily Banyon. Like his desire for her, he could admit this awful vulnerability, but only privately. For all of Sean's instincts screamed, *No!* at the thought of revealing them to her.

Because the thing Sean feared most of all was that Lily would toss his confession on the ground, then trample it with her high heels as she walked away from him.

* * *

When the assembled teens saw their principal mount the side steps and walk across the stage to the podium, the noise level altered, dropping to wary murmurs, silence descending by degrees. From Sean's previous experience talking to these same teenagers, he knew the momentary quiet was a short-lived prelude to a mass, vacuous state—far more unnerving to a speaker than the odd whisper or squeak of chair springs. He felt a sudden, uncomfortable pang of guilt that he'd cornered Lily into this.

Hugh Feldron fumbled with the microphone and cleared his throat. "Good afternoon, students, parents, faculty, and guests," he began. "Welcome to the inaugural lecture for this year's Career Day talk. I am especially pleased to introduce today's speaker, Dr. Lily Banyon, marine biologist. An alumna of this very school, Dr. Banyon is a senior researcher at the Marine Center in Gloucester, Massachusetts, and is currently involved in a project of immense importance to us in Coral Beach. She has been asked to supervise the final phase of our town's reef study. Please join me in welcoming Dr. Banyon back home."

Lily's leggy stride carried her across the stage to where the principal stood, and Sean's libido instantly kicked into overdrive. It was a reaction he instinctively knew was shared by every other male present, aged fifteen to sixty-five, as the welcoming applause turned from polite to enthusiastic. Dressed in a white tailored shirt, a short gray skirt, and black high heels, Lily shattered every stereotype of what a scientist was supposed to look like.

A broad smile on his face, Feldron stepped to the side of the podium as she approached. Lily shook his outstretched hand and murmured something that made him laugh out loud. With a nod, he quickly strode off the stage.

Lily took her place behind the podium. "Thank you," she said when the applause died down. "I don't usually receive such a warm reception at the conferences I attend," she confessed with a wry smile. "I also never imagined I'd have the honor of speaking at Coral Beach High's Career Day talk. Back in the Dark Ages, when I was a student here, the school didn't have such wonderful programs, so you'll have to forgive me if I deviate from the standard format of these talks.

"As Mr. Feldron already mentioned, I'm a marine biologist. It's a job that has given me the chance to travel around the world. It's also given me the chance to see incredible things and meet wonderful people. My area of specialty is studying coral reef ecosystems. Now at this point in your life, some of you may think *studying* is a four-letter word." Lily paused, a smile playing across her face as muffled laughter echoed throughout the auditorium. "But studying, learning more about coral reefs and the life they support, is not only fascinating, it's crucial."

She looked out over the audience in frank appraisal. "Let me ask you a question. Who can tell me what the largest structure ever built on Earth is?"

The auditorium became totally silent. The audience was doing its best to be invisible. Sean felt a clammy sense of panic on Lily's behalf, worried she might have lost her listeners by turning the focus on them.

"Come on, don't be shy," Lily cajoled with a grin. "Here, I'll give you a hint. This structure is so big it's identifiable from outer space. It covers a larger area than

the Great Wall of China but it's a whole lot more inviting, prettier, too. . . . Surely one of your teachers has
mentioned it."

A hand was raised timidly near the front.

"Yes?" Lily asked brightly.

"Is it the great barrier reef in Australia?" A girl answered in a halting voice.

"That's absolutely right. Excellent, you get an A-plus."
She gave the girl a quick wink.

Beside him, Evelyn chuckled. And Sean expelled a
breath of relief, his face relaxing into a smile. Lily was
going to be fine. More than fine.

"Coral reefs—like Australia's great barrier reef, like
our own here in Coral Beach—have existed for millions
of years," Lily told the audience. "They are a vital habitat for nearly a quarter of all marine life. When coral
reefs succumb to disease or are destroyed, the loss affects
not only marine life, but human life, too . . . in ways we
scientists are only just beginning to understand.

"Let me ask another question. How many of you have
gone scuba diving or snorkeling and explored a reef
habitat?"

About a third of the audience raised their hand. Lily
shook her head, the straight line of her mouth reflecting
her disappointment. "That's not nearly enough. I can see
we'll have to do something to rectify that," she said enig-
matically as her gaze swept back, to the very rear of the
auditorium.

And Sean realized that not only was Lily alert to his
presence, she also knew precisely where he was sitting.

Perhaps he wasn't the only one suffering the effects
of heightened awareness. The thought made his smile
widen. The auditorium's overhead lights must have been

angled just right, because Lily's eyes went suddenly wide
and a flustered expression stole over her.

Quickly averting her gaze from his, she reached for the
glass of water placed next to the podium. He watched
her take a long sip. Setting the glass back down, she continued. "As I was saying, I'd like for many more of you to
know firsthand the wonders that are right in your own
backyard, so to speak. With the remaining minutes I
have left, let me give you a preview of what lies on the
other side of the beach. Remember, though, this is only a
glimpse of what makes my job fascinating, exciting, and,
above all, incredibly rewarding.

"Marine biologists often work in a team, each person
bringing a different specialty or talent to it. The photographer on my current team, Karen Masur, captured the
sights you're about to see. Karen and my research assistant, John Granger, worked together on this film for you.
The three of us hope you'll enjoy it."

Lily raised her head slightly, focusing her attention to
the very rear of the auditorium. "John, if you'd please
dim the lights? Karen, when you're ready?"

Sean glanced to his left. John and Karen were behind
the booth that housed the controls for the lighting and
electronic system. At Lily's cue, the lights dimmed to soft
blackness. Simultaneously, a large screen descended behind Lily, stopping just above her head. The screen went
from white to a kaleidoscope of colors flooding the
screen.

And the audience descended into Lily's world.

As she began to describe the creatures before them,
Sean knew from the profound quiet that the students
were awed by the magical realm Lily was showing them.
She was the perfect guide. As the film played, she was

careful to allow them time to absorb the beauty of the image on their own before quietly telling them about the creature or plant they were seeing.

Now they were looking at a speckled maroon sea anemone. In impossibly slow revolutions, the anemone was somersaulting across what Lily identified as the rounded hump of a starlet coral. She explained how the surreal, rolling tumble of the anemone was its only mode of locomotion.

From the agonizingly slow, they went to the lightning quick. A few in the audience gasped in surprise when a moray eel darted from its hiding place, grabbing its un-suspecting prey in its teeth-lined, oversized maw.

On it went, a spectacular display. What they heard equally so. As the film progressed, Lily's commentary was punctuated by the pulsing beat of music. Its inclusion was a brilliant stroke to a masterful performance. The music provided a bridge between the kids' everyday world and the new, fantastic one that Lily was introducing.

The climax came with Jim Morrison singing about lighting the night on fire while the screen exploded with coral spawning, sexual fireworks in the night blackened sea. The audience exploded right along with the film, applauding loudly. Sean did the same, filled with pride for Lily.

Whatever conflicting emotions lay between them, Sean couldn't—wouldn't—hide his admiration. Lily had done a hell of a job. She'd gone beyond the Career Day talk's framework to give the audience a glimpse of why they all needed to care about what happened to the marine environment.

Sean had a sudden sense of déjà vu; the first time it had happened was aboard the *Tangiers*. He was seeing once again what a special, what a giving, what an utterly compelling woman Lily had become. This time the sensation was a thousand times more powerful, for he was on dry land, away from the exotic magic of the sun-dappled sea. Hope flared bright inside him. He wasn't chasing an illusion after all.

CHAPTER TWENTY-ONE

The students were still applauding. From the podium, Lily could see Sean's broad smile as he stood clapping—she'd have had to be blindfolded to miss it. That dazzling smile had her insides doing a funny kind of flip-flop. Her lips curled in self-conscious response. While admittedly relieved that the talk had gone well, it was Sean's obvious approval that made Lily feel as if she'd been awarded a prize.

When the auditorium finally quieted, Lily spoke. "Thank you very much, and thank you for inviting me to speak to you today. But the people who really deserve your applause are my assistants, Karen Masur and John Granger. Karen and John, if you'd please come down?"

As her assistants walked down the center aisle, Lily began to clap, and the audience joined in. Karen blushed with pleasure while John acknowledged the audience with a wave of his hand, like a rock star before a stadium filled with fans.

Lily waited until they were by her side to issue her challenge. For a second, she hesitated, uncertain whether to proceed with her plan. She suspected that as soon as Sean heard it, that warm smile would vanish.

But she needed to see what kind of man Sean was, what kind of mayor he was. The knowledge was suddenly of vital importance—to whom, she refused to admit.

"If you recall, I mentioned earlier that I hoped to encourage more of you to explore what is literally in your own backyard. Before my talk, when I was sitting in the front row, I looked up at the school motto." Lily pointed to the medallion above her head. " 'From the Sea We Learn,' " she recited. "Back when I was a student here, I didn't really grasp how fitting a motto this is for Coral Beach. Now, as a marine biologist, I can assure you that *all* of us need to learn and understand more about the sea and the riches it holds."

Lily's eyes skimmed over the audience, verifying she had its full attention. The time had come for Sean to take a turn in the hot seat. "During my talk earlier, I noticed that among the audience we have not only Mayor McDermott and his very capable assistant, Ms. Roemer, but also the director of Parks and Recreation, Mr. Dave Cullen." Lily gestured to where Sean, Evelyn, and Dave sat. Her arm extended, she raised it, inviting the three of them to rise.

They did so slowly while the rest of the audience stared openly.

Lily smiled. "In the interest of educating the citizens of Coral Beach, I'd like to propose to Mayor McDermott and Mr. Cullen that the town organize a weekend of scuba diving instruction for its residents."

At Lily's suggestion, excited murmurs swept through the auditorium.

Dave, covering his mouth with the back of his hand, whispered a rueful, "Damn. I had a hunch Lily would

find a way to retaliate after I suggested you could beat
her swimming. Looked like she wanted to pitch me off
the boat—and we weren't anywhere near the shore."

"Now you begin to understand Lily's no one to mess
with," Sean replied out of the corner of his mouth. "Can
the Parks Department handle an event like this?"

"Yeah, I think we can swing it. Actually it's a damn
fine idea."

"Good. Set a date ASAP and make sure Lily and the
Marine Center receive all the kudos in the publicity release. Uh-oh," he warned, "here comes Feldron."

The school principal had rushed up to the podium. He
beckoned Sean and Dave to the stage, as well. Resigned,
they advanced down the center aisle to join Lily and the
others.

The handshaking and polite formalities over, everyone
had drifted off the auditorium stage in cordial clumps,
still discussing Lily's proposal for a community scuba
diving weekend.

Somehow Lily found herself paired with Sean. In her
hand, she clutched an engraved paperweight with the
school's motto etched on its surface. The gift had been
presented to her by none other than her old zoology
teacher, Mr. Sneel. Amazingly, Mr. Sneel seemed to have
shed the curmudgeonly demeanor she remembered so
well and become a gray-haired sweetie pie. From his delighted smile one might have thought Lily had been his
very favorite student, which had definitely *not* been the
case—Mr. Sneel had been supremely democratic in his
dislike of *all* his students.

Lily wished she could pretend that the lightheadedness

she was feeling now was due to lingering shock over Mr. Sneel's effusive thanks or perhaps to postlecture adrenaline. Unfortunately, however, the source of her dizzy excitement started exactly where Sean had his hand wrapped around her elbow. With each step they took as he led her from the auditorium, a sizzling heat spread through her.

Lily knew Sean's gesture was purely chivalrous, one he doubtless performed unconsciously, thus wholly at odds with the melting warmth it engendered.

"That was a really nice thing you did back there, Lily," Sean said. "Karen looked ready to burst with pride when those kids started asking questions. Even Granger seemed happy."

Lily shrugged. The movement caused the back of Sean's hand to brush the curve of her waist. She forced herself to concentrate, to ignore the tingling fire he'd just ignited. "It was the least I could do," she replied, pleased her voice sounded fairly normal—the faint huskiness could be from her lecture, after all. "The two of them did a great job with the film. Karen got John to brainstorm with her on the music selection. They ended up pulling an all-nighter." She'd awakened at four-thirty this morning to find Karen and John sitting in front of her computer—though by that time they'd finished with Karen's film, and Karen was busy revamping John's Web site for him.

"Your talk was terrific," Sean continued. "I'd be willing to wager a lot of those kids are going to pay far closer attention in their biology classes from now on."

"Perhaps." She was careful not to shrug again.

"Matter of fact, your talk was such a success, I've decided to overlook the nasty trick you pulled."

Lily's gaze flew to his. *His hazel eyes are so beautiful,* she thought, and then swallowed.

"Tell me," he said. "What would you have done if I'd nixed the community scuba program?"

"I'd have been as disappointed as the rest of the assembly."

He pulled her to a stop in front of the display case, which lined the hall. Despite his relaxed expression, his eyes sparked with intensity. "So, you're not . . . disappointed."

She thought back to how Sean had stepped up to the podium and praised the community scuba diving initiative, announcing that the Parks Department would begin organizing the effort posthaste. As gifted a politician as Sean was, he could have easily side-stepped the idea and avoided committing himself and the town's resources. But he hadn't.

"No, I'm not disappointed," she said simply. "I'm grateful. The townspeople will be, too."

His smile was like staring into the sun.

Flustered, Lily turned her head and stared blindly at the contents of a display case, the image of Sean's brilliant smile still shining in her mind's eye.

"Looking for your old trophies?"

"What?" Lily asked distractedly.

"Swim team plaques. We passed the science awards two cases ago." Sean pointed. "Right here. Girls' record holders. There you are. Again and again, and—"

"You can stop now," Lily interrupted, feeling absurdly self-conscious. Yet her eyes strayed to the plaques nonetheless. Memories welled inside her. They were good memories. She'd loved breaking those records, hitting the electronic timing pad to stop the clock, then looking up into the stands to see her swim coach, Hal Storey, whooping ecstatically.

"Did you know that Hal's coaching a master's team these days?"

"I believe Dave mentioned something about it."

"The practices are at night," he continued. "People pick and choose according to their schedules. It's a big group." He paused. "You'd see a lot of familiar faces."

"That'd be almost as much fun as running into Stacy Malloy—" Lily could have bitten her foolish, jealous tongue.

Luckily, Sean didn't notice the slip. "Stacy won't be any-where near the pool. I doubt she could swim a hundred meters. No, I meant other people—you know, from school, from swimming. You'd be surprised how many of them ask me what you're up to."

"Why do they ask you about me?"

"Maybe because you've become a near-celebrity in your field, and have traveled to places and seen things that most of us only dream about."

"I didn't mean that." She brushed the idea of herself as particularly noteworthy aside. "Why do they ask *you* about me?"

Sean looked at Lily searchingly. She wasn't fishing, he realized. She didn't have a bag of flirtatious ploys like Stacy. No, Lily was honestly mystified.

She was so damned gorgeous.

"I suppose it's because everyone knows how close my mom and yours still are, how our grandmothers practi-cally live at each others' homes." Shutting his mouth before he added, *And probably because a number of them have guessed that I've been crazy about you forever and enjoy tormenting me with unending Lily Banyon questions.*

"Oh. That makes sense."

They continued walking. In the main lobby, Sean finally dropped his hand to sign out at the security desk and unpin his visitor badge from his light gray jacket, waiting as Lily did the same.

On the other side of the high school's double doors, rain was falling in solid sheets. Sean gripped the dull metal handle to push the door open for Lily. "So, are you going to come to a swim practice, put a smile on Hal's face?"

Lily shook her head. "No, I don't think so. I'll make time to visit Hal this week, but I prefer ocean swimming these days."

Sean looked out at the pouring rain. "In this muck?" His smile turned knowing. "Oh, right. I see."

"What? What are you talking about?"

"Why you don't want to come. It'd be embarrassing to swim with your old coach if you're no longer . . ." He let the sentence trail off.

"I'm just as fast as I used to be," she retorted.

"Hey, it's okay, really," he said in a soothing tone, one that he knew would infuriate her. He was, after all, blessed with a true talent when it came to pissing off Lily. "Lots of swimmers lose their edge—"

"What time's practice?" she demanded curtly.

The annoyed glint in her crystalline eyes told Sean all he needed. He had her. "Eight to ten, every night," he informed her easily. "So, you'll come?"

Lips pursed, refusing to give him the satisfaction of an

answer, Lily swept past him, regal as a queen under a drenching rain.

With a grin Sean called after her, "See you later tonight, Lily."

CHAPTER TWENTY-TWO

Lily's former coach spotted her from across the width of the fifty-meter pool. Hal Storey was kneeling with a wrench in his hand, tightening the ratchets on the lane lines. "Lily Banyon! Long time no see!" he bellowed, then springing to his feet, he rushed around the perimeter of the pool.

Hal enveloped her in a rib-crushing hug. When he finally released her, he stepped back and inspected her from head to toe.

"My, my, Lily Banyon, all grown up. You're looking good, really good," he pronounced, his face creased in pleasure. "It's good to see you."

Lily blinked away the sudden moisture in her eyes. "You, too, Hal," she said, in a voice thick with emotion. "I'd have recognized you anywhere. Still wearing the same old hat," she teased. It was true; she would have recognized Hal anywhere, even without the ragged Miami University baseball cap. There weren't that many friendly giants who dressed in Bermuda shorts and beat-up flip-flops, who wore stopwatches about their necks the way others did gold chains, who always had a clipboard at the ready, tucked under a hairy, muscular arm.

"You been doing much swimming, Lily?" he asked, in his typically direct manner.

"Some," she admitted. "Strictly open water, though. My flip turns are probably rusty."

"You used to nail 'em like an archer hitting a bull's-eye."

"I wanted to get them right for you, Coach."

Hal surprised her by blushing. "You always were a good kid, Lily. A real fighter." He rubbed his hand across a cheek covered with what looked like a five-day growth. "We need to celebrate your return, Lily. I'm going to dig up one of my vintage workouts, give you guys a blast from the past. You'll feel right at home, I promise," he said, winking. He broke off to look around the pool area.

Clustered in small groups, the other swimmers were chatting, others stretching. Nylon swim bags littered the pool deck.

"Hey guys, y'all remember Lily," Hal called in his booming voice. "Come on over and say hi." To Lily, he added, "Gotta run to the office for one of my old notebooks. Back in a sec."

Hal's words had the swimmers breaking apart and heading over to where Lily stood. She was soon surrounded. Sean hadn't been exaggerating this afternoon. She recognized many of the faces here—but unlike Stacy Malloy, they seemed genuinely happy to see her. Lily was barraged with questions about her job at the Marine Center, the reef study, how long she planned to be in the area, whether she'd be attending swim practices regularly.

Eric Sullivan, who'd sat behind Lily in calculus class, spoke up. "By the way, Lily, in case we're all too busy moaning and groaning at the end of practice, we have a long-standing tradition on this team. A bunch of us head over to the Rusted Keel for a couple beers and a round of darts. That is, if our arms aren't too tired to throw 'em. Even on the nights you're too busy to swim, drop by for a brew. It's always fun."

Lily smiled. "Thanks, Eric." Had Eric Sullivan ever said more than five words to her before?

Sean walked up to the group surrounding Lily in time to hear Eric say, "So, if you feel like some liquid calories after workout, join us. I can give you a lift."

Jesus, Sullivan was all but asking Lily out on a date, Sean fumed. He frowned, trying to remember whether Lily had ever liked Eric back in high school, and battling the jealousy spreading inside him. He was tempted to haul Sullivan over to the bleachers and explain a few basic facts. Number one being that Eric was welcome to any woman in the world but Lily.

Eric's voice floated past Lily, unheeded. Sean had arrived. He'd changed into wheat-colored khakis and a black polo shirt, his gear bag slung over his shoulder. A frown marred his face. *Was he annoyed that she'd decided to come to a practice?* Lily asked herself, filled with sudden uncertainty.

Her thoughts were diverted by Hal's shout of welcome. "Hey, Sean, hey, Dave, it's about time you two showed up." He waved a clipboard at them. "Get suited up and in the water, pronto. Special workout tonight—in honor of Dr. Lily Banyon."

Lily glanced at Sean again. His expression had become studiously blank. Catching her stare, he gave her a terse nod in place of *hello*, then he knelt and dug his mesh equipment bag from inside his larger nylon bag, tossed it by the edge of the pool, and headed toward the men's lockers.

Her eyes followed him, her uncertainty turning to misgiving. Sean obviously didn't want her here.

"All right, guys, let's get going. Hop in." Their coach's loud voice cut through the casual chatter around the pool. "We'll start with a nine-hundred meter warm-up. Four hundred swim freestyle, three hundred kick—with fins or not, your choice—followed by two hundred pull freestyle."

At once, the swimmers disbanded, heading off to their usual lanes. Lily quickly shucked off her cutoffs and T-shirt, stripping to her Speedo. She rummaged through her gear bag, pulled out her goggles, pull buoy, and fins, shoved her clothes inside, and rezipped the bag.

"I think I'll have you swim in lane eight, Lily," Hal said. "McDermott and Cullen usually have the lane to themselves. They need some fresh talent to keep them sharp."

Lily opened her mouth to protest, but Dave spoke first. "Hey, Lily. Glad you could make it, but I think you'll be keeping Sean company on your own tonight. My shoulder's been feeling a little tender, Hal." Dave rolled his tanned shoulder tentatively and winced, giving proof to his words. "I'm going to drop down a couple lanes and give it a rest. Wouldn't want to injure my rotator cuff."

Hal nodded, a frown furrowing his heavy brow. "Swim in lane four. You can put on your Zoomers and lead the group, but if that shoulder starts to hurt, get out," he cautioned. "And don't forget to ice it tonight."

"Sure thing. Have fun, Lily," Dave said with a wink, before grabbing his blue mesh bag and sauntering over to the pool's middle lane.

"You set for equipment, Lily?"

"Yeah, I've got everything, thanks."

"Then get going, kid," he ordered, as if Lily were thirteen again. "Sean's already in."

"I'm going, I'm going," she said, wishing she were a hundred miles away from Coral Beach's brightly lit natatorium.

She was dawdling, making a huge production of placing her fins by the foot of the starting block, aligning them just so, then positioning her pull buoy alongside the fins. She killed some more time as she fiddled with her goggles, adjusting and readjusting the thin rubber strap, which already was a perfect fit. Unfortunately, swimming was a minimalist sport. She was running out of ways to avoid the inevitable, when she'd have to jump into the water and share a lane with a nearly naked Sean McDermott.

What in the world had she gotten herself into?

Sean was already well into the warm-up. His freestyle was smoother than she remembered. She watched critically as his elbows emerged high above the water on his recovery, as his fingers and forearms, like a blade, sliced cleanly into it again, making hardly a splash. His powerful stroke ate up the fifty meters with an effortlessness that convinced her he could continue swimming like this for hours and hours.

His strength was unbearably sexy.

She watched Sean glide into the wall, reach up for his black fins, and pull them on. Not once did he look up, his concentration ferocious. Without pausing, he pushed off the wall, his fins adding extra force to his kicks. He swam submerged on his back.

While Sean was pulling on his fins, Lily had pretended

to be busy herself. She'd made a show of tugging on her goggles, just in case he happened to glance up, and saw her staring like an obsessed ninny. Through the tinted blue of her goggles, she watched him surface.

Oh my God. Her knees went weak, threatened to buckle.

Sean was doing a butterfly kick on his back.

Her eyes traveled down the length of his torso and stopped, transfixed. She swallowed convulsively. Yet she couldn't have torn her eyes away from the sight of Sean's narrow hips if someone had screamed, *Fire!* Encased in black Lycra, they moved in a suggestive rhythm, breaking the surface of the water, sinking, and then rising again, over and over. Unbearably erotic, an answering beat drummed deep inside Lily. Helplessly, she conjured endless hours of sex, Sean's body driving into her with the same relentless, unbroken rhythm, each flex of his hips thrusting to her very womb.

"Something wrong, Lily?" Hal's impatient voice demanded.

Lily nearly leaped out of her skin. She was the only one left on deck besides Hal. "No, nothing," she said hurriedly, hyperconscious that her voice was reedy thin. "Just about to jump in."

To clear her mind of the sexual fog that lay thick and heavy, she blinked rapidly—only to mutter a soft curse when she realized what had happened. Yanking her goggles off, she dropped to a kneel and swished them viciously in the water.

"What's the problem now?" Hal's patience was obviously wearing thin.

Embarrassed, resentful, and praying Hal wouldn't

guess the real reason why, Lily ground out her explanation. "My goggles fogged."

"They broken? I've got—"

"No, no . . . ," she interrupted tersely, and felt immediately guilty. It wasn't Hal's fault her goggles had literally
fogged from the heat of her aroused body. It was hers.
That's what she got from staring at Sean McDermott's
groin for too long: fogged mind, fogged goggles.

Determined to ignore the sight of Sean moving like a
bold lover through the water next to her, that incredible,
muscled body within touching distance, Lily gritted her
teeth and dove in.

It was torture, physical and sensual.

Sean should have known he was playing with fire.

Out of habit, as swimmers do when only two occupy
a lane, Sean and Lily split it, swimming side by side,
back and forth, in long, repeated sets. They'd hardly exchanged a word, which was for the best.

Sean wasn't sure he could form a coherent sentence at
this point.

His mind was filled to bursting with Lily, with her
body. She was a wet dream come true. Her silver-and-blue
Speedo clung like a second skin. When he saw the outline
of her nipples pressed against her suit, he groaned, a loud
underwater moan of frustration. He wanted to tear away
the fabric and cover those tight nipples with his mouth.

He wanted her.

Instead, he raced her.

It began slowly, and he was the one who instigated it,
out of self-preservation and desperate reasoning. If he
swam fast enough, he'd keep ahead of her, wouldn't have
to gaze at the luscious curves of her body as he was tak-

ing a breath, wouldn't screw up his timing like some novice swimmer and choke on a lungful of chlorinated pool water.

And if he swam fast, really fast, the blood would remain near his pumping heart rather than flowing straight to his cock. He'd never swum with a hard-on before and he didn't intend to tonight.

Lily had always been a true competitor, and with Sean, competition was second nature. Almost immediately, she sensed his intention to pull ahead of her at every send off, a mind game of intimidating raw power. Instinctively, Lily increased her pace, refusing to give way.

Their attitude was no different than when they'd tested each other as children, sprinting to touch the wall first. But now, they were adults, and no matter how gifted a swimmer Lily was, she couldn't out-swim Sean. A superb male specimen, he was stronger, bigger, and thus his stroke was more powerful. Moreover, Lily hadn't been subjecting her body to the kind of grueling interval workouts Hal Storey devised for his swimmers.

They'd come to the last segment of the night's workout. Hal had instructed them to do a set of five two-hundreds, "descending," meaning that each two hundred was to be swum at a slightly faster pace than the preceding one.

It was demanding to say the least, and by the time they had finished the third two-hundred, Lily's arms felt like spaghetti, her legs like blocks of cement. Nevertheless, she continued, pushing herself to the max. Her reward, the knowledge that at least she was making Sean work for each victory he clocked. They were both gasping for air as they watched the electronic timer for the next send-off, intense focus mirrored on their faces.

I should have known this wouldn't work, Sean thought. Lily had way too much grit and perseverance. As they waited for the sweep of the second hand to signal their send-off, he could see the telltale signs of fatigue laying claim to her: the trembling of her arms, the rapid rise and fall of her chest. Yet she was still swimming like a torpedo.

Maybe he should ease up on the pace with this last two hundred, give her a little rest.

The second hand hit the top of the clock and, as one, Lily and Sean pushed off the wall, their bodies perfectly streamlined. Rather than pulling ahead of Lily, this time Sean backed off, consciously setting a slower pace.

Within ten strokes, Lily had surged ahead of him by half a body length. For Sean, the next one hundred and seventy-odd meters seemed an eternity. He tortured himself, watching her through his goggles, the way her hips rotated toward him, as though offering herself on their watery bed.

With an outstretched hand, Lily slammed into the wall, finishing just before him. She tore off her goggles, her eyes glittering angrily as he pulled up alongside her.

"Nice set," he offered shortly.

"You creep," Lily growled the accusation. "You want to be some macho jerk and set a race pace for the entire workout, fine. But don't you *dare* toss a measly two hundred meters my way, like you're bestowing some present."

Guilty as charged. If the tables were turned, he'd be as furious as she was. Especially since she didn't know the real reason he was swimming like a man possessed. What was he supposed to do? Drag her flush against him so that she could have hard proof that she was turning him into a lust-driven madman? He wanted to howl in frustration. "You looked like you were struggling," he snapped defensively. "I was merely giving you a chance to recover. . . ."

"Yeah, whatever." Lily looked pointedly away from him.

Hal's voice had them both jerking their chins upward. "How are you feeling, Lily? You two been swimming up a storm. Nothing like some good friendly competition, that's what I always say—"

"What's next?" Sean interrupted, wanting nothing more than to get the practice the hell over with. Lily was staring fixedly ahead, refusing to look at him. *Shit,* he cursed silently. He wished he could take that last set back. He hated it when someone sandbagged—slacked off intentionally, and that's just what he had done.

Sean could have kissed Hal's unshaven cheek when he looked at the clock and said, "I think that'll be it for the night. That was a good workout, guys. Swim down easy. . . ."

She could hardly move, yet she continued swimming, fully aware she would hurt even more if she left the pool without a proper warm-down. Little by little, the pool had emptied, swimmers tiredly hoisting themselves out of the water. Gathering up their gear, they trooped off to the showers. Sean had abandoned the lane long ago, hardly bothering with a warm-down.

If there was a God, Lily hoped He'd make Sean suffer leg cramps and painfully tight shoulder muscles tomorrow.

Hal signaled to her from the side of the pool. She pulled up and treaded water. "Yeah, Hal?"

"I've got to duck into the office and make a call to a coach who's hosting an upcoming meet. You remember where the lights are?"

She nodded.

"Hit them when you're done."

"Okay."

"And Lily?"

"Yeah?"

"Don't drown."

"Very funny," she replied with an answering grin.

"You did good tonight, kid," Hal praised her gruffly. "You can join my masters' team anytime."

For the second time tonight, absurdly emotional tears pricked her eyes. "Thanks, Hal. If I ever stayed in one place long enough—"

"Who knows? After all these years of wandering, maybe it's time to settle down. You could do worse than your own hometown, Lily. Coral Beach needs people like you. Think about it." Hal grinned down at her. Then, with a wave of his hand, said, "Finish your warm-down, kid. I've got to call Lester before he hits the sack."

CHAPTER TWENTY-THREE

She was standing in the shallow end, against the pool's wall. Her arms were crossed on the deck for support, her slicked blond head was bowed over them: the picture of fatigue.

Sean had returned to the pool deck, looking for Hal so they could discuss entries for the upcoming meet. But Lily was alone. Seeing her like this, looking so exhausted, left him feeling lower than a snake's belly. He shouldn't have pushed her so hard. But he would only make it worse if he showed any sympathy; she'd only read it as pity.

He adopted his standard mocking approach. "Having trouble getting out of the pool, Lily? There's a ladder on the side there for the old ladies who come and do aqua aerobics."

Everything inside her stilled. *That condescending wretch.* She felt him come closer, and was careful not to stir an inch, not even a hair.

"You should get out of the pool and take a long hot shower. It'll make you feel better," he suggested, not ungently. His brow furrowed with worry.

She ignored the thread of concern in his voice and

concentrated on not moving too suddenly. Slowly, as if in unbearable agony, she lifted her head. He was dressed once more in his khakis and shirt; his sneakers were in one hand, his gear bag in the other. Good. She let her face crumble, her expression slip into wretchedness. Her lower lip trembled, a special added effect. "I—I'm not sure I can even make it to the ladder," she confessed haltingly. "My whole body's shot."

Damn, she must be hurting worse than he'd imagined. Trying not to stare at her lush lower lip quivering helplessly, Sean dropped his gear bag and sneakers and stepped forward. "Here," he said, leaning over, stretching out his hand. "Grab my hand. I'll pull you out."

She'd braced her feet against the wall of the pool, knowing she'd have to strike fast. They grasped hands. The second his tightened about her forearm, she jerked backward with all her strength.

Physics was on her side.

Caught off-balance, Sean somersaulted through the air, with only enough time to yell, "Shit!" before he landed with a cannonball-sized splash.

Lily braced her arms on the pool deck. She'd intended to jump out and make a mad dash for the ladies' locker room but her efforts were hampered by her convulsive laughter.

A surprised, *"Oof!"* flew from her lips. Sean's arm had snaked out and wrapped around her waist, dumping her backward into the water. She pushed to the surface to find Sean glowering menacingly.

He was sopping wet and just as furious. Lily's laughter redoubled, then died away when his hands took her by the shoulders and pulled her close. Mere inches separated their bodies.

"What are you doing?" Her voice came out an alarmed squeak. Her eyes flew to his. They sparkled with green and gold lights.

"Payback time, Lily. You've pushed me once too often. I had my cell phone in my pocket. I don't think it's waterproof. My leather wallet is in my rear pocket, crammed with pictures of my adorable niece and nephew. Basically, Banyon, you owe me. Big time." His tanned face, with drops of water still clinging to its chiseled planes, descended.

He was going to kiss her, she realized, panic-stricken at the thought. "Don't, Sean, don't!"

"I think I have to. It's been a long time coming. Oh, by the way, I like lots of tongue."

Indignant, her mouth opened, ready to skewer him.

But Sean was quicker. He shut Lily up the way he'd been dreaming of for so long. For years she'd driven him mad, made him crazed with desire. Now, by God, he was going to taste her. The passion and frustration inside him erupted. He seized her mouth, molding her lips to his own. Carnal fantasies gave way to a reality a thousand times sweeter. Starved for her, Sean's lips plundered, boldly claiming her as his.

Lily's resistance died on a ragged moan of pleasure.

He reveled in the sound, in the helpless tremors that racked her limbs, in the lips that parted, welcoming him. He wanted even more, wanted her tongue tangling wantonly, mating with his. His tongue swept inside, sampling her honeyed warmth. Triumph surged when Lily met him with an eagerness that matched his own. In the long-standing duel between him and Lily, this skirmish was the sweetest of battles.

Lily had never been kissed like this, with an ardor so

dangerous it sizzled and cracked, sending sparks shooting everywhere. Her fingers clutched his sodden shirt, needing to feel him pressed against her, to glory in his solid, muscular heat.

"Lily," he whispered, his warm breath fanning her lips. Slowly, Lily's eyes opened, stared dazedly back at him. Her eyes had never looked like this, like a summer sky painted in the softest of blues. Their loveliness shook him.

"This payback could take awhile—years even," he warned her huskily. "Let me taste you again," he whispered, his mouth already settling over hers.

When at last their lips parted, Sean's breath was ragged. Although his face was only inches away, to Lily the distance seemed vast. She drank in the sight of him— Sean, the headiest of wines—and it made her flush with pleasure, made her heart sing to see the blatant, masculine arousal stamped upon his features. To see his eyes gleam green and gold, fired by desire.

Her own need left her dazed, out of control. All she knew, all she craved was his touch, his taste . . . the feel of him. The urgency of it nearly painful, Lily gave a helpless cry. Sean's response was immediate: his arms tightened, drawing her flush against him, and his mouth swooped down to thrill her anew.

His hands roamed in long, sweeping strokes, greedily learning curves known only from stolen glances. Some part of him had always thought of Lily as an icily distant goddess. Wrapped in his embrace, she burned and fanned his own desire into brilliant flames that licked and spread, engulfing them both. She was all that was soft and giving. And Sean couldn't get enough of her. Somewhere in the back of his mind, he realized he would never get enough, that his desire for Lily was insatiable, endless.

He cupped her breasts and gave a ragged groan of pleasure at the feel of their generous softness, then watched Lily's face as his hands caressed her. Her lips, swollen from his kisses, were parted as she breathed in short, shallow gasps. Languorously, her eyes opened, meeting his, and Sean knew he'd never beheld such a beautiful sight as Lily in his arms.

Their gazes locked. Her arms reached upward, bracketing his head. Her fingers tangled in his damp hair, and she tugged, a wordless command. For a moment he resisted, wanting to memorize the piercing, haunting beauty of Lily's face gone soft and dreamy with desire. For him. He swept his thumbs arclike over the tight buds of her nipples, watching her face flush with passion.

"Do you know," he said huskily. "Sometimes I think I've been waiting all my life to touch you, to feel you like this."

Lily couldn't reply, could only moan as Sean's fingers stroked her in achingly tender ministration. Her moan became a ragged cry born deep inside her as his fingers closed over her breasts, caressing her boldly with a master's touch. Lightning heat flashed through her, making her tremble all over. Her back arched, taut like a bow, offering herself to him. From her lips tumbled soft, frantic whimpers.

The sound drove him wild. He captured her lower lip, biting down, absorbing her shudders. His hands traveled down, past her heaving rib cage, lower still, until they encircled the soft swell of her buttocks. He pulled her to him, letting her feel the rigid length of his erection through his wet clothing, holding her there.

With a tortured cry, her lips pressed against the flushed

column of his throat. And then it was his turn to feel the sharp bite of teeth.

Raw need roared through him.

He squeezed her bottom, his mouth hot against her ear as he whispered, "Wrap your legs around me, Lily."

Her head jerked, eyes meeting his, and Sean saw in them the same wild, reckless need. She was so close to the edge. "Do it, Lily. Open for me," he urged. His hands closed, kneading persuasively. "Let me see you fly."

Helpless to resist the erotic lure of Sean's heated words, desperate to have what only he could give her, Lily obeyed.

Sean's smile was her first reward. Then, holding her in a fiercely tender grip, he flexed his hips and thrust against her open cleft in a bold caress.

Lily's head fell back with her broken keen filling the air.

"Holy shit!" Hal came running flat out, Lily's cry still reverberating. He skidded to a halt on the slippery deck, his panicked rescue unfortunately bringing him quite near to where Sean and Lily were fused together. For a moment he stared, his mouth agape. As comprehension dawned, embarrassment colored his face a flaming pink blush.

Instinctively, Sean shoved Lily behind him, shielding her with his body. He could feel her tremble against him. *Were her tremors the aftermath of blazing passion, or were they from horrified mortification?* he wondered. He wished he could see her face.

"Sorry we gave you a scare, Hal. I, uh, fell into the water. Then somehow, Lily and I got caught up in a water fight to the death. Guess I forgot how ticklish she is." He coughed. It was a pathetic story, but the best he could do right now.

At his words, Hal looked up from his seemingly rapt examination of the deck's tiles. Although his face was still as pink as Evelyn Roemer's dyed hair, his lips parted in a smile of relief. "Oh, yeah," he nodded, more than willing to play along. "Everyone needs a good tickle now and again." He cleared his throat loudly and said, "Sorry to break up the fun, but you two have probably had enough water sports for one night." Hal's gaze moved past Sean. "You okay there, Lily?"

Behind Sean, Lily froze. What to say? That she'd been nanoseconds away from a soul-shattering orgasm when Hal came barreling poolside.

Bereft of Sean's intoxicating kisses to drug her senseless, Lily hardly recognized herself. Had she gone mad? Probably. She wondered whether she would ever recover from what was undoubtedly the most intensely erotic experience of her life.

Oh, God! Of all the people to have interrupted her and Sean in the pool! Hal Storey was as close to a father as Lily would ever have. He'd always supported her, believed in her. . . .

"Lily?"

"I'm fine, Hal. Just a bit achy." She cringed, sure Hal would guess that the parts of her that ached and throbbed had nothing to do with swimming. The memory of Sean's hands was imprinted on her body. And still her flesh cried for more. Drawing a deep, steadying breath, she abandoned the sheltering screen of Sean's body, waded over to the edge of the pool, and climbed out. She could feel both Sean's and Hal's eyes boring into her. Quickly, she went to her bag, yanked out her towel, and whipped it around her body, hiding behind a protective cocoon of thick cotton.

"Why don't you go take a shower," Hal suggested. "It, uh, might make you feel better. Just don't stay too long, 'kay? I've got to lock up the building soon."

She managed a strained, "Sure, Hal," before gathering up her belongings and fleeing to the locker room.

She didn't look at me even once, Sean thought, feeling an icy chill of disappointment, far colder than the pool water. Abruptly aware that he was still standing in the pool, fully dressed, looking like an idiot, he hauled himself out.

Hal's obvious concern had transmuted into narrow-eyed disapproval. Sean pretended not to notice. He was too preoccupied to deal with Hal right now, too busy trying to figure out what might be going on in Lily's head.

Damn it, why couldn't things ever be simple between Lily and him?

With a grimace, he emptied his dripping pockets, dumping his wallet and ruined cell phone onto the deck. He grabbed his sodden towel and made a halfhearted attempt to blot his dripping clothes. Thank God his drenched clothing hid the evidence of his arousal. Fierce need still clawed, its talons deep. If Sean hadn't been damned sure Hal would hurl himself in a flying tackle if he tried it, he would have marched right into the ladies' locker room and dragged Lily back where she belonged: into his arms. Arms that ached from the loss of her.

Monitoring Sean's success with the towel, Hal gave a grunt of disgust. "Come on. I have an extra towel you can use in the office. No way can you drive home like that—you'll ruin the car's interior. 'Sides, we need to talk," Hal added heavily. Turning on his heel, he headed back toward his office.

Sean followed with a decided lack of enthusiasm. They entered Hal's cramped cubicle of an office and Hal shut the door behind him. It closed with an ominous bang.

He took a towel hanging from the hook on the door and tossed it at Sean, who grabbed it one-handed.

"Thanks," he said, as he bent to pat his khakis dry.

"I hope you know what the hell you're doing." The warning tone in Hal's voice had Sean pausing to glance up at his friend. He straightened, towel forgotten.

"Hey, I didn't plan what you saw back there, Hal. It just happened."

"What'd she do? Pull you into the pool?" Whatever he saw in Sean's expression had Hal's face shifting into a lop-sided grin. "Thought so. Serves you right, McDermott. You were being a total SOB. You knew it, so did she. Christ, you would never pull that kind of stunt with Dave." He gave a snort of disgust. "I was watching the two of you the entire workout. Don't think I didn't see when you finally took pity on her. Any slower, and you'd have been doing a dog paddle. Real shitty of you, McDermott."

I know, Sean admitted silently. "Right. If she ever agrees to swim with me again, I'll let her swim her arms off. She got her revenge anyway."

"Good for her."

Sean's gaze narrowed. Sometimes Hal was a pain in the ass. "Gee, thanks, Coach."

Unfazed by Sean's sarcasm, Hal continued. "You know, I always suspected something would happen between you and Lily. Intense rivalry can't come without intense passion; I figured the attraction was there, just waiting for the right moment." He paused to glare at Sean, then said,

"But I would have hoped you'd have a hell of a lot more smarts than to try to seduce a beautiful woman in *my* pool! Anybody could have walked in on you!" His voice was at a near shout.

Sean winced inwardly. "I don't think that's anyone's business, Hal. Not even yours," he added defensively. A colossal mistake.

Hal's temper exploded. "What do you mean, not my business? Okay, McDermott, we'll skip over the political repercussions for you as mayor if someone other than me caught you and Lily. I guess the phrase *conflict of interest* doesn't ring a bell. To tell you the truth, I don't give a rat's ass about politics. I'll go straight to what I do care about: you breaking Lily's heart."

"What?!" Sean exclaimed.

"Yeah, I know. You're gonna tell me that what I interrupted a few minutes ago was just a casual romp in the pool. That's a load of crap, McDermott. You know as well as I that Lily's never been casual about anything in her life. *Especially not you.* 'Sides, what I witnessed back there was *not* casual. Shit, I'm surprised the water wasn't boiling with the heat you two were making."

"Christ, Hal." Sean spread his hands, his palms up. "Things kind of exploded between us. But Lily's not a girl anymore—"

"If you're stupid enough to believe that, then you don't understand dick about Lily—no matter how hard you were trying back in my pool!"

Sean opened his mouth, but Hal was in full rant. "I've known Lily since she was a lonely, awkward kid. Of all people, you, Sean, should remember what she was like, how it was for her."

"She ended up fine—"

"Yeah, she did. Because of her brains and her heart, she's accomplished everything she's dreamed of. But accomplished as she is, with all that beauty, she's as lonely, as vulnerable as she was at thirteen. She needs a home, McDermott. She needs to know she belongs. That there's a place for her to care about *above* sea level."

"Hal—"

"I'm warning you, Sean. I'll have your ass if you go and hurt Lily and make her run away. Now, get out of here before I get really pissed."

Hal was wrong, and his protective impulse was way overblown. *Thoroughly misguided, too,* Sean thought, as he slammed the office door behind him. It was he— not Lily—who was in need of protection. Sean had an awful feeling he'd lost his heart back there in the pool, and that when Lily discovered she had it, she'd toss it away.

The apartment was in shadows when Lily entered. She left the lights off and walked in darkness to the large picture windows. The rain had stopped and yet the glass panes blurred, dissolving into nothing. She blinked back the tears that brimmed, refusing to let them fall. She would lock up her tears, along with her heartache.

Stifling a moan of despair, she bit her lower lip, a lip still swollen from Sean's tender assault. *What had she done?* she asked herself wretchedly. She knew the answer: She had let Sean touch her. She'd never dreamed how devastating the result would be.

She'd never felt lonelier or more confused in her life.

The reef study would be finished soon. So far, the coral appeared uniformly healthy. If the remaining transects proved to be in equally good condition, her job would consist of simply tying up loose ends. Once she received Lesnesky's report, she'd compare her data with his and then present the results of the study as a whole to the reef committee.

And it would be over. She would be free to do what only days ago she'd been anticipating eagerly: purchase a ticket for the next flight to the Bahamas.

The thought of leaving had the tears sliding down her cheeks.

She swallowed painfully and dashed them with the back of her hand.

When she left, she wouldn't see Sean again. Hundreds of miles away, exploring the magic of the oceans' reefs, she would eventually forget him.

But Lily's aching heart told her differently, knew that she could travel to the ends of the earth, to the deepest depths of the sea, and still she'd yearn for Sean. She'd stayed away from Coral Beach for ten years. It would take far longer than that before she could forget how Sean had made her feel tonight. Perhaps a lifetime.

CHAPTER TWENTY-FOUR

Pete Ferrucci climbed out of his Mercedes. It was early, the sun only just above the horizon, its golden shafts of light piercing the banks of low-lying clouds.

No one was moving near where the *Tangiers* was moored, which suited him fine. He wanted his business concluded and his man in place before Banyon and the others arrived.

Ferrucci gave the windswept, gray-green ocean a cursory glance before turning his back to it and to the glory of the rising sun breaking through clouds.

He far preferred the view of the marina.

The marina was what McDermott and his crowd liked to call *picturesque*. Picturesque meant quaint, charming, colorful. . . . *Yeah, yeah,* Ferrucci thought scornfully. He had a different definition for picturesque: rinky-dink and dead. But once this reef study was over, the marina would be shiny, big, and new. Moreover, it would be hopping, twenty-four–seven.

Ferrucci looked out over the marina and in its place envisioned the full-scale model of the developer's blueprint brought to life.

There, he thought, *from that copse of trees on down.*

That's where the new section of the marina would be built. The parcel of land had enough coastline that they'd be able to carve out roughly double the existing marina's space. All they needed to do was to chop down the trees and start dredging, scooping out chunks of shoreline to the south. Then, to make sure the newly carved coast didn't wash away, they'd buttress the shore with steel-reinforced concrete pillars. Ferrucci had seen the kind they used before. They were huge, shaped like massive drums, not that he or his partners gave a shit what the blocks looked like—after all, they'd be underwater.

South of the new marina, Ferrucci planned to put up two fifteen-story condos, with the ground floors reserved for retail space, making it like a minigalleria. The people who bought the condos would be demanding a higher class of retail and services than what was currently offered in two-bit shacks like the Rusted Keel, Norma Jean's, or the stores selling marine supplies. Nuts, bolts, stays, and life vests . . . piddly shit-merchandise with a profit margin that was fucking laughable. Those mom-and-pop businesses would be closing shop for good, once the more upscale boutiques and cafés opened.

And Ferrucci would rake in a mountain of money.

Yeah, the place was going to look fabulous. He could picture it so easily, a whole new community where before there'd only been boring, empty space. His eyes swept over the wooded area and his lip curled in disdain. Hell, even the trees were boring. Puny. Gnarly. Boring.

His cell phone buzzed in his pocket. He pulled it out. "Yeah? Good, it's you. So, what else is new? Traffic's always a bitch. I'm at the marina. Get here fast."

A few minutes later a nondescript, late-model sedan pulled into the parking lot. He didn't recognize the car, but he could guess who it was. A man got out and looked around.

He was right. Ferrucci withdrew his hand from his trench coat pocket and waved. Spotting him, the man began walking his way. Ferrucci noted he hadn't changed much. He still carried himself with his bony shoulders rounded in a permanent slouch. He'd grown his hair longer, though, wearing it pulled back with a rubber band, à la Steven Seagal.

The only thing Ferrucci really cared about, though, was the man's eyes, and they looked as sharp and cunning as ever. They shook hands. Ferrucci took out a white envelope from inside his sports coat and handed it to him. "A thousand, as we agreed. You'll get a five hundred dollar bonus for every picture I buy. Here's the address where she's staying. I own the building, so if you need to, follow her right in. I've alerted the security guards. No one'll stop you. She also spends time at her grandmother's place. The name and address is in there as well."

"Grandmother?" Thin eyebrows shot up in disbelief.

Ferrucci shrugged. So what if grandmothers' homes weren't the usual territory. "Her and McDermott's families are close. I don't want you to miss an opportunity. When they get here, I'll go down and spend some time talking to her so you can identify her—not that she's easy to miss. She's tall, blond, and built. And pale as vanilla ice cream."

"Whooee!" the man exclaimed with a hungry smacking sound. "I got a real sweet tooth." He shoved the envelope Ferrucci had passed him inside his leather bomber jacket without bothering to count the money inside. "And the target, he's the mayor of this burg?"

"Yes." Ferrucci handed him a newspaper photo of Sean, taken at a committee meeting months ago. "But you're better off tailing the woman, Banyon. She's the honey pot. He'll dip his digit soon. Keep on the job until you've got something I can use. It shouldn't take too long."

It better not. Ferrucci wanted to get something on McDermott soon. His partners had been livid when McDermott canceled their lunch meeting yesterday. Ferrucci himself had exploded in rage when he discovered *why* McDermott had blown off the meeting—so he could go and look good in front of a bunch of high school kids.

What was even more infuriating to Ferrucci was that McDermott and Banyon had made the local headlines again, this time with their cutesy, do-gooder plan to offer a community-wide scuba diving program.

His associates were going to hit the roof once they saw the morning papers. If people started going out to the reef, becoming nature freaks, some grass-roots nut would kick up a fuss and protest the development project. Which was yet another reason why he definitely wanted Banyon and McDermott in the news—but with a very different kind of story attached to their names. One that would really make waves.

Ferrucci's pen and paper, telephoto-lens-toting friend here was going to ensure that happened.

He glanced at his watch. "They should be coming any moment. Go down and snap some pictures of the marina at dawn like a good tourist."

Karen slammed the car door behind her and walked back to the trunk, waiting for John to open it with the key. Careful to avoid looking at the distant waves, she kept her eyes trained on the calmer waters of the marina.

"Ugh," she groaned, and laid her forearm protectively over her stomach. "Now I really am going to heave."

"What? Your stomach again? We haven't even gotten on the boat yet," John said, inserting the key and opening the trunk. He hefted his gear bag from the trunk's interior.

"No, it's not the swell, it's the human garbage. Look over your shoulder," Karen said, pointing. Pete Ferrucci was down on the dock, beside the *Tangiers*'s lines, pumping Owen Rafern's hand. "*That's* what's making me gag."

John pivoted, glanced out at the marina and saw Ferrucci. "God, you are such a priss sometimes. It's a free country. We've had McDermott and Cullen hanging around, checking on our work. Why shouldn't Ferrucci?"

Karen looked at him and shook her head. "Maybe because he's a creep and they're not." She bent over the trunk, grabbed her gear and camera bags, and lowered them onto the pavement alongside John's.

"You're only sticking up for Cullen and McDermott 'cause they snow you with compliments," John said. "Ferrucci's not that bad, not when you get to know him—"

"Yes, he is," Karen retorted, then paused, eyeing him quizzically. "How come you think he's okay? We only met him that once, at the advisory meeting, and he was the king of jerks. . . ."

"Yeah, well—"

"Ms. Masur, Mr. Granger." Ferrucci must have seen them standing by the car. He approached them. "Nice to see you again," he said.

John straightened. "Hi, Mr. Ferrucci."

"I thought I'd drop by and check on how our research team is doing. Is Dr. Banyon here?"

"She's coming in the other car," John said.

With a scowl for Ferrucci, Karen turned to John. "Here, give me your bag, I'll go stow it on the *Tangiers*. We need to leave *really* soon."

"Gee, thanks for the news flash. Here," he said, giving her his gear bag.

Without sparing Ferrucci another glance, Karen shouldered the three bags. She hurried along the dock toward the *Tangiers*, the cumbersome bags bumping against her.

Ferrucci waited until he heard Karen call out a friendly, "Good morning, Owen," before speaking. "So, how's everything progressing?"

"Only three sections left," John replied.

Ferrucci brushed a tiny speck of lint off the sleeve of his trench coat. "And you're making sure the samples Banyon's sending back to the lab are nice, clean, and very unremarkable," he asked softly.

"I'm taking care of it."

"Good. That's very good." He gave a quick approving nod. "Look, there's a club I'm going to with some of my friends and a few ladies, Trish, too. Why don't you join us? My friends and I have something we'd like to discuss with you. A possible career opportunity. Trish knows the address—" Ferrucci broke off at the sound of car wheels rolling over gravel. "We'll talk more later, John. Get on the boat, and keep sending that lab in Gloucester the cleanest sand in Florida. Go on," he said, barely veiling his impatience. "I don't want her to connect you and me in her mind."

Ferrucci waited until John was almost at the *Tangiers*

before fixing a wide smile on his face. "Dr. Banyon!" he called.

Lily's eyebrows rose. Pete Ferrucci didn't seem the type to be so jovial this early in the morning. "Hello, Mr. Ferrucci."

"As I was just telling your assistant, I came by to see how the research team is doing." He pointed a thumb at John's retreating figure. "Mr. Granger said you're nearly finished with your study."

"That's right."

"Very impressive. It took the other scientist, Dr. Lesnesky, far longer."

"Perhaps that's because he was one man versus three?" she replied dryly.

"Hmm, well, yes. I suppose that could account for it. So only three sections remain?"

"That's correct."

"I noticed the water looked pretty rough out there."

"The conditions aren't the best right now," Lily said with a shrug. "But the wind's supposed to die down soon." She hoped it would. Karen tended to suffer in heavy chop. Lily, however, would rather walk over hot coals than admit to any problems concerning her team to Pete Ferrucci. "The chop might be unpleasant, but we've dived in worse."

"Such dedication."

Lily inclined her head. Over Ferrucci's shoulder she could see Owen Rafern already aboard the *Tangiers*. The engines were churning, their steady rumble filling the air. He, Karen, and John were waiting for her. Adjusting the webbed strap of her gear bag on her shoulder, she said, "Nice seeing you, again, Mr. Ferrucci."

"I was hoping that now the study's nearly complete,

you might take me up on our rain check. Lunch? Dinner perhaps? We can discuss the reef study, as well as this idea for a community scuba diving program. Your presence has certainly generated a lot of local interest, Dr. Banyon." He smiled. "I understand Mayor McDermott's been out diving with you, Dave Cullen as well. I'd like to have a chance to be as abreast of the study as they are."

Lily couldn't believe it. Ferrucci had actually dropped his gaze, letting his eyes linger on her chest as he spoke of remaining *abreast*. The bastard.

"I'm involved in a scientific project. Any member of the advisory committee is welcome to join us and observe our procedures. Even you, Mr. Ferrucci."

His eyes narrowed fractionally at her barbed comment. "Sadly, I'm not much of a water enthusiast."

"Too bad. Then you'll just have to wait for my report to the advisory panel next week." Her heavy bag brushed him none too gently as she passed.

Ferrucci stared after Lily's retreating figure. "I'll look forward to it immensely, Dr. Banyon."

Chapter Twenty-five

"Here, Lily, I've written a list with all the pictures numbered. And in this column, I've noted where I want the piece moved." May Ellen walked over to where a print hung on the wall. "Now, do you see the little red dot here?" She tapped the glass protecting the large print with an index finger. It depicted an Indian parade, complete with elephants, their riders perched behind their flapping ears. In the lower right-hand corner, a little red dot was affixed. Lily stepped forward to peer at it and made out the number 5 written in black pen.

"Anne and I numbered them all yesterday. There are thirty-eight in all," her grandmother said, handing Lily the stapled sheets of paper listing her artwork.

Thirty-eight! Lily flipped through the sheets. She was exhausted from spending a sleepless night tossing and turning, unable to stop thinking about Sean, the passion of his kisses, the way he made love with his mouth.

Then the dive this morning had been less than ideal. Lily had been taken aback by the poor visibility; the water had been surprisingly murky, even for an admittedly choppy sea. On top of that, she'd been worried about Karen. The heavy surge had left Karen feeling so woozy that they'd returned to shore as quickly as possible, when Lily would have far preferred to examine the corals in zone three more closely. Now she had thirty-eight pictures to rehang and the beginnings of a massive headache.

"Granny May, are you sure you want this done? Your rooms look lovely," she lied desperately. After all, some people liked the overdecorated, overupholstered look.

"Yes," May Ellen said with a firm nod. "My friends come here too often. They've no doubt memorized every print and painting. I want something *new* for our party. Look," she said, and pointed to her coffee table. "I bought everything we'll need."

Half of Home Depot was piled onto the mahogany coffee table. Hooks, wire, measuring tape, pliers, hammer, and a few other thingamajigs Lily couldn't identify. She bent and poked at the pile, wishing there were a way to get out of this.

"Do you want anything to drink or eat before we start, Lily?"

"No, thanks, Granny," she said, her smile weak. "Looks like we have some work ahead of us. Might as well get started." She picked up a hammer and a packet of hooks and tried to inject some enthusiasm into her voice. "Which one first?"

"Hmm, let's see. . . . Where's number one? It's a little oil sketch of a waterfall. I've always loved it, but it's completely hidden behind that palm. It'll look much better in the dining room."

Lily stifled a sigh and went over to the small painting, carefully removing it from the wall. May Ellen picked up the measuring tape and pencil. With a cheerful trill, she told Lily to come along—and to be sure not to bang the picture.

Once in the dining room, it became clear Granny May hadn't made up her mind on which wall the waterfall should go. Then there was the question of height, of position: too high, too low, to the left, no, to the right. . . . By the time the oil sketch was hung, the inside of Lily's cheek had gone numb from her teeth gnawing it.

If each picture took this long to hang, she'd be here until doomsday. Lily suppressed her impatience, however, for she could tell May Ellen was having a good time. Her grandmother drifted from room to room, giving Lily detailed histories of each precious knickknack, where and when it been acquired, and shared with her the plans for the upcoming party.

"It's really a party for you, Lily, but you know how much I love birthday cakes—it'll have to be a big one since I'm turning seventy. Lloyd Gans can say what he wants about my health," she said, sniffing dismissively. "Fact of the matter is, we old folks can go just like that." She snapped her fingers in emphasis. "When Lloyd reaches my age, he'll change his tune pretty fast," she predicted ghoulishly.

"Granny!" Lily exclaimed, her stomach clenching at her grandmother's words. Was there something her grandmother was keeping from her?

"So that's why I've decided to throw a lovely party when I can actually enjoy it." May Ellen gestured airily about her. "But you, Lily, are the real reason for the celebration. There are so many people who haven't laid eyes on you in years. I'd like them to have the opportunity to see you again, to get reacquainted."

"Granny, you don't have to go to all this trouble," Lily

said. "I'll be leaving Coral Beach as soon as the study's over. . . ." She struggled to mask her awkwardness and regret.

"Nonsense," May Ellen replied stoutly.

In alarm, Lily's gaze flew to her grandmother's face. Surely she hadn't misled May Ellen into believing she might remain in Coral Beach?

"It's absolutely necessary," May Ellen continued. "I want to show you off to my friends. It's my prerogative as a grandmother." Her blue-gray eyes twinkled. "Comes with the contract, don't you know?"

Lily's mouth quirked, her lips parting in a smile of exasperated affection. "Whatever makes you happy, Granny May."

May Ellen nodded with approval. "That's what I always think. Now, time to stop dawdling, young woman. I have an appointment with Ida and I can't be late." She patted her neat silver perm. "She wreaks the most awful revenge otherwise."

The rearranging went a little faster after that. Lily discovered ways to preempt agonizing moments of indecision. "This looks great, Granny May. I really like the way the light falls on it," or, "Wow, look at the way those colors glow beside the wallpaper," was usually sufficient to get the nail hammered, and the picture hung.

Lily was in the midst of rehanging a series of small seascapes done in watercolor. She'd already measured out the distance on the wall. Her lips were pursed around a bunch of nails. Hammering the first nail into the wall, she turned to Granny May for the picture. "Granny?" Lily prompted as intelligibly as she could with a mouthful of metal.

Her grandmother paid no attention. Her head was

cocked. "Why, whoever could that be?" she asked in response to a muffled voice calling out. "I'd better go see." May Ellen laid the watercolor on the sideboard, just beyond Lily's reach and hurried from the room.

Lily's lips tightened. Another interruption. At this rate, *she'd* be seventy before they finished.

"Look who's come to lend a hand, Lily!" Granny May said breathlessly.

Lily turned and froze.

"Hello, Lily," Sean said.

Time became fluid. Last night suddenly seemed long ago—an eternity—since she'd beheld his face, been held in his fiery embrace. And yet, looking at Sean now, it was as if only a moment had passed since their fevered interlude.

Dear Lord, the things Sean had done to her, the things they'd done to each other. . . . Heat flashed through Lily as she relived the passion they'd shared. The intensity in Sean's hazel eyes told her that he was remembering, too.

They stood and stared and the air grew thick, charged with emotion.

In the silence May Ellen's self-conscious laugh sounded shrill. "What a ninny I am! I just remembered my appointment with Ida was moved forward this week. I bet Anne's already waiting for me outside. I must fly, Lily, dear—the parking's terrible at this hour."

"Mmmph!" The forgotten nails flew out of Lily's mouth, landing on the area rug some distance away. "Granny, wait! You can't leave!"

"Sorry, Lily," May Ellen called. She was already past the dining room, heading toward her kitchen. Seconds later she reappeared, her purse and house keys in hand. "I'm sure you and Sean will do a great job. Lock the front door when you leave. Bye, bye."

May Ellen rushed out, in what was the closest she'd come to a flat-out sprint in forty years. Slamming the front door behind her, she dashed over to Anne's silver Park Avenue. "Hit the gas, Anne. Burn rubber," she said dramatically, as she shut the door and buckled her safety belt.

The car took off with a lurch, its tires spitting pebbles. "That bad?" Anne asked, gripping the steering wheel firmly.

"No, that *good*." May Ellen smiled, ecstatic. "I didn't want to spoil things by staying another second—Oh, no!" May Ellen groaned, pressing a hand to her mouth.

"What is it?" Anne asked.

"I was having such a good time with Lily, I forgot to tell her that Kaye's arriving today."

Anne was silent as she digested this bit of news. "May Ellen, I do believe this situation calls for evasive action. We'd better stay out shopping a few extra hours."

Sean had obviously come straight from town hall. He wore charcoal gray trousers and a white button-down shirt, the cuffs rolled up, exposing his tanned forearms. Remembering the strength of his arms when he'd held her made Lily's knees go weak. . . . She locked them, and then stiffened her spine for good measure. She didn't want Sean to think a few kisses had turned her to mush.

It would have helped her self-confidence if she were dressed in something a bit spiffier than ragged cutoffs and a rumpled T-shirt. And she couldn't help but feel a bit resentful by how easily he managed to make her heart slam against her ribs. All it took was that sexy grin playing about his lips. "Why are you grinning?" Lily demanded.

"I've never seen anyone actually spit nails before." His grin widened.

Lily shot him an aggrieved look.

Sean stepped into the room. She resisted the impulse to take a step in retreat. Besides, her back was practically to the wall.

"By the way, Lily, you've lost your touch."

"What?" she asked, perplexed.

"The nails," he clarified. "They didn't hit me. In the good old days, they'd be sticking out, probably from right about here." He lifted a long, blunt-tipped finger and touched the slight bump on his nose. "It's proof positive you're feeling much friendlier toward me."

"A momentary lapse, I assure you," she replied, staring at a point beyond his left ear. Inside her, guilt churned as she remembered how she'd hurt him with the volleyball.

"No, Lily, I think our relationship has entered a new stage, a much more satisfying one. But as you appear to have some lingering doubts. . . ."

Panicked, Lily's gaze flew to his. The intense gleam in his eye had her shoulder blades flat against the wall.

"Kissing you was like holding fire, Lily. Magic. I can still hear your cry when you came in my arms."

Her cheeks grew hot with embarrassment. "I didn't."

"Yeah, you did." He smiled. "That's all right, I love making you scream, almost as much as making you—"

"I didn't!" She yelled. "Hal came!" Embarrassment nearly choked her.

That stopped him. He stared wide-eyed, finally understanding her words. A slow, heart-melting smile spread over his face. "Ah, Lily, I'm real sorry about that. Let me make it up to you."

"No, thanks. I'll pass," she managed coolly enough. Her eyes narrowed when he ignored her, approaching nearer still. "Back off, McDermott. For that matter, buzz off. I have work to do." She picked up the scattered nails and turned back to the wall. Maybe if she ignored him, he'd go away.

"What a coincidence." His husky voice was a warm breeze on her sensitive skin. "That's what I'm here to do."

Lily whirled. Confusion, uncertainty, and desperate desire fused together into a pure, liberating anger. "I mean it, Sean," she hissed. "Granny's gone, so you can skip the Boy Scout routine. Go away, and leave me alone."

Boy scout? More like a lust-crazed twenty-nine-year-old. Sean couldn't believe it. But it was true. Lily was shooing him away as if she didn't want to buy a gallon drum of popcorn.

Well, he wasn't leaving. Provoked that she could remain aloof while he was tied up in knots of desire, he growled, "Listen, my grandmother called me at the office, practically in tears, pleading that I come and help May Ellen with her pictures. She's been fretting all week about how big a job it is—"

"That's ridiculous. I promised May Ellen days ago that I'd do it. She wrote a whole list of instructions. Go away, Sean," she repeated.

Instead, he picked up the sheet and looked at the walls. "Are you out of your mind? You can't hang these all by yourself."

Infuriating man. "Yes, I can," she insisted. She'd stay here till midnight if necessary. "She's *my* grandmother. Stop trying to butt in."

"I am not butting in!" he yelled back. "I'm helping an

old lady whom I happen to adore get her house ready for a party she's throwing to welcome home her mule-headed granddaughter!"

Lily blinked. Sean's eyes were brilliant, the emerald green and gold flecks in them arrow sharp. And they were only three inches away. Abruptly, Lily realized that she and Sean were nose-to-nose, shouting at each other. She blinked again and lurched backward. Her elbow banged against the wall with a loud thud. "Ow!" she said, wincing. "Damn it!"

"You okay?" he asked. His voice sounded oddly subdued, now that he wasn't attempting to out-shout her.

Lily prayed he wouldn't try and touch her, sure she'd fall apart completely if he did. "Yeah, I'm fine." She fingered the back of her elbow gingerly. "And I'm not mule-headed."

"Yeah, well, I'm not trying to steal your grandmother, either. I've got my own, thank you very much. But May Ellen's my grandmother's best friend. They're both excited to be organizing this party for you. If redecorating May Ellen's entire place is on the to-do list of preparations, that's what I'm going to help with. Give up, Lily. And hand over the hammer."

Lips pressed in a mutinous line, she eyed him silently. He was waiting, his broad hand open. With a loud sigh, she let it drop into his palm.

"Thanks," he said, and his mouth curved in a tender smile. Lily's heart squeezed in painful longing.

CHAPTER TWENTY-SIX

Lily and Sean worked steadily. In the aftermath of their blowup they were on their best behavior. The unspoken détente had a fragile delicacy that neither wanted to damage.

"How'd the diving go today?" Sean asked as he backed away from a large, gilt-framed painting he'd just put up.

"Not as well as I'd have liked. The waves were a bit rough and unfortunately Karen got a little queasy. We managed to get our samples, however. We only have zones one and two of the last transect to cover. If the weather cooperates, we should be finished tomorrow." Lily fell abruptly silent.

What she'd left unsaid hovered in the air like a bleak cloud. Once the lab tests were finished and Karen's slides developed, Lily would report to the reef committee, and then leave Coral Beach for her next project.

Don't think about that now, Lily told herself. "You know," she said, forcing a lighthearted note into her voice. "I've never worked on a study which received so much personal interest from its committee members. You dived with us, so has Dave, and today we had a visit from Pete Ferrucci. He was at the marina—at the crack of dawn. He seems very interested in knowing how the study is progressing."

Sean drove the next nail into the wall with a vicious rap. "Not surprising. He's probably already walking around the marina with dollar signs in his eyes."

Dollar signs? Lily repeated silently. "Do you ever plan to tell me what's really going on with this development project?"

"Why, Lily?" Sean turned and faced her. "Why do you want to know? Could this mean you might actually care what happens to your hometown after all?"

Her face warmed. She was definitely beginning to care . . . deeply. "Maybe."

He regarded her in silence, as though debating what to tell her. "Ferrucci doesn't want any restrictions placed on the reef . . . no matter what."

"I guessed as much during that first meeting. That's not exactly an uncommon stance, Sean. I run into it all the time. People hate what they perceive as governmental meddling, especially on environmental issues."

"Yeah, but in Ferrucci's case, there's a hell of a lot more involved.

"So where does he fit in?"

"I don't know yet. I've been trying to find out more about the backers behind this development deal, but so far I've come up with zilch to link Ferrucci directly." Frustration laced his voice. "But I'm convinced he's connected somehow—that he's more than just their very willing lobbyist. Ferrucci's a canny bastard. I only became suspicious about his involvement when he went ballistic over continuing with the reef study after Lesnesky had fallen ill."

"I remember how 'vocal' his objections were at that first advisory meeting," Lily said.

"That was Ferrucci at his most restrained. He wants the reef issue dead in the water so he can ram the development project down the town's throat. I know how he operates, though. This is just one of his many plans. After he gets the development project accepted, Ferrucci will go to work on burying me alive."

"What do you mean by that?" she asked in surprise.

Sean gave a mirthless laugh. "I almost hate to disillusion you, Lily, but I ran on a pro-conservation ticket. I beat Ferrucci by a nose. Coral Beach isn't that large a town; the reef study is the biggest environmental concern to date in my tenure as mayor. Ferrucci would love to make it look like I've done nothing but waste the tax payers' money on some idiotic liberal cause. He'll use the reef study to show that the environmental platform I ran on was a *nonissue*. A damned effective way to destroy voter confidence. One he'll definitely use in the next election," he predicted.

Lily frowned as she considered Sean's words. "But if the reef study shows no need for restrictions, then the development can go up."

Sean's fingers raked his short hair. "True, but the more I think about developing the area around the marina, the less I like it." He broke off abruptly. "Come here," he said, taking her hand and leading her to a small, rather pretty oil painting. "Look at this. Does it seem familiar?"

She stared at the scene of a crescent-shaped bay. "Yes, vaguely."

"It's probably difficult to recognize since you normally see this view from about sixty feet above ground, from the windows of the apartment complex where you're staying." His index finger lightly touched the glass protecting the painting, indicating the spot where the condo stood. "It was pretty before, wasn't it?"

Lily nodded.

"Well, if the development goes through, Coral Beach will have two new buildings towering over the marina, changing the coastline forever."

For a minute, they stared at the painting. Then Sean spoke. "You know, Lily, when Lesnesky fell ill, I wondered whether he'd perhaps missed certain areas or overlooked signs that the reef was deteriorating. He was kind of weird toward the end—just before his cancer was diagnosed. I realize now a part of me was hoping that you'd come up with something that would scuttle the plans. But I've seen how systematically you and your team have covered the reef. Since the reef is healthy, I don't think there's any way to stop the development from happening."

"Sean." Lily's voice was quiet. "I'm sorry—not about the reef—but because I doubted you. I was sure you intended to use the study to push the development through."

The corner of Sean's mouth lifted in a half smile. "I forgive you," he said. "As a marine biologist, you're probably conditioned to distrust politicians on sight."

Lily gave a soft laugh. "Some politicians are better than others."

"Thanks. It doesn't mean I'll give up, Lily. I've decided to vote against the development. And I won't let Ferrucci win without a fight."

"I can't believe Pete Ferrucci is any match for Sean McDermott."

"Damn, I hope not. If he becomes mayor, the marina development will be just the beginning. He'll destroy

Coral Beach in the name of progress." Sean grimaced. "Jesus. How did this conversation become so depressing? I need a beer. Want one, *Bella*?"

Alone, Lily tried the endearment hesitantly, wonderingly. *Bella*? Sean didn't even seem to have noticed that he'd called her beautiful. Did he really think her so?

Lily's thoughts spun wildly as she collected the pictures May Ellen had earmarked for her guest room in the back of the house. Lily had left this group for last, stalling, nervous about being in a bedroom alone with Sean. Now, though, thoughts competed chaotically, distracting her. Gnawing her lip as she moved about the bedroom, her mind went back to the conversation she'd had with Simone at the Marine Center. She remembered how she'd begged Simone to send someone else to Coral Beach, arguing that as a native of Coral Beach, her findings in the study might be viewed as partisan.

At the time, Lily hadn't believed a word she was saying. Because she hadn't believed she could care what happened to this small Florida town.

Her work here was almost finished. She'd examined nearly the entirety of the patch reef and had found nothing to alarm her as a marine biologist. As Sean had said just now, that was good news. And yet, despite the fact that the reef appeared healthy, Lily was filled with a strange sense of melancholy.

For the first time in her career Lily wasn't thinking with her usual scientific objectivity.

There was no use pretending any longer that she was indifferent to what happened to Coral Beach. And like a mask splitting apart, her professed disinterest gave way to what had been hidden for these many years. Her mind accepted what her heart had always perceived. She loved Coral Beach and the people who lived here.

Who was responsible for awakening these long-dormant feelings? Lily couldn't deny the truth anymore. From the very beginning, Sean had loomed larger than life for her. He'd been her childhood enemy, her wily foe. But here, too, her understanding had undergone an irrevocable transformation.

A deal like the marina development would bring in huge revenues for Coral Beach. When she'd first returned home, Lily had been so prejudiced against Sean that she'd immediately assumed he would be the type of leader to take credit for the money that would pour into the community, then manipulate the surrounding publicity to bolster his political career.

She knew better now.

She had a new insight into Sean. And the more she looked, the more she yearned. For the man she'd come to know was intelligent, decent, and caring. A man of integrity . . . a man Lily could love.

Sean pushed against the kitchen door, his fingers wrapped around three long-necked beers, the brand May Ellen kept stocked especially for him. Three because he'd already downed half of one and didn't feel like going back immediately to the kitchen for a second one. He wanted to be near Lily.

For some reason, he kept hearing Hal Storey's irate voice inside his head. Hal was yelling again, telling him how Lily needed to feel a sense of belonging to something other than her all-consuming career as a marine biologist.

Perhaps Hal's wish was coming true. Sean was sure the

concern he'd read in Lily's blue eyes was genuine. Or had he been fooling himself, desperate to believe that she cared? That she might stick around long enough for him to show her how much *he* cared about her . . .

Sean frowned. The living room was empty. He'd just passed through the dining room. It, too, had been vacant. Where was she?

"Lily?" Nothing. His scowl deepened. "Lily?" he called louder, and cocked his head. A tapping noise was coming from the other end of the house. He followed it.

She had her back to him, her arms raised as she tried to hang a painting that was approximately two and a half feet wide. The painting's dimensions were too big for her to sneak her arm underneath and lift the wire so it could rest upon the hook. Her middle name *Stubborn*, Lily was trying anyway, standing on tiptoes, muttering her aggravation.

She'd kicked off her sneakers. His eyes devoured her, starting with the supple arch of her feet, moving upward . . . up, up the length of her smooth, pale legs. Legs sexy enough to cause a riot.

Nevermind about Lily belonging to a community, Sean decided. *She belonged to him.*

The desire that exploded inside him was, impossibly, more feverishly urgent than ever. Because now Sean knew what it was like to hold Lily in his arms, to taste her, to stroke her.

This time he was determined to sample every inch of that incredible body. Placing the bottles carefully on the carpet, ensuring they didn't betray his presence with a clink of glass, Sean approached silently.

Lily jumped at Sean's touch. Despite the clothing separating them, she could feel his heat, sense his awesome hunger. An answering need burst free. The painting slipped, leaving a faint scratch on the floral wallpaper.

"Careful." His breath, sultry and moist against her ear, sent shivers down her spine. "No, don't move or you'll drop it." He moved closer, his body brushing hers. "Stay. I want to touch you like this."

"No, Sean," she moaned. "Don't . . . I *can't*."

The trembling had started already. She could hardly stand.

"Yes, you can. I'll hold you." And his strong, muscled arms wrapped about her, drew her even closer to his solid heat. Fingers splayed against her stomach, he caressed her with slow, tantalizing strokes, grazing the lush curves of her breasts, skimming the waistline of her shorts. His mouth rained kisses along her jaw, the nape of her neck. Unerring he found the exquisitely sensitive spot behind her ear. His tongue tormented, lathing it slowly, then drying it with the warmth of his breath. Insatiable, he continued on, lightly raking the tender column of her neck, his tongue soothing where teeth had scored.

As his mouth traced the hollows of her collarbone, Sean breathed deeply, inhaling the perfumed scent of Lily's warm skin. Delirious with pleasure, his mouth closed about her, claiming her, marking her as his.

With a soft cry, she dropped the painting. It fell, landed unheeded. "Please . . . kiss me," she cried desperately.

His hands guided, turning her until she faced him. At the sight of Sean's cheeks stained with dark flags of desire, pleasure streaked through Lily, pooling hot and sweet in her center. She arched against him, her fingers reaching, threading through his silky hair. "Sean," she breathed, pulling his mouth to where she craved it most.

Their mouths met in a kiss of blind passion. Mouths slanted, their tongues mated, fanning the riotous flames. Hands gripped, clasping and stroking greedily. Urgent now, Sean's fingers found and deftly unclasped the front of her bra. He dragged at the satin fabric, replacing it with his hands. His hands closed about her and he groaned. "Nothing has ever felt like this, Lily. I ache to touch you everywhere, to taste you."

Lily's body answered for her. She pressed against him, heated flesh melding. He shuddered in ecstasy at the bounty of her offering, and his hand dropped to her waist. He released the first metal button of her shorts, then the second. Boldly, his fingers slipped past the narrow elastic of her panties. The dampness of her curls had his cock throbbing, straining to be inside her.

As Sean's fingers parted her to stroke with wicked expertise, Lily began trembling wildly, uncontrollably, the pleasure coursing through her electrifying. Her head bumped against his. At the pain her eyes opened to stare blankly at the papered walls, at the canopied bed. And she remembered where she was.

Aghast, she tried to free herself, but Sean's fingers were inside her shorts, inside her. *"Argh!"* she cried helplessly. "Let go!"

Lost in a haze of passion, his fingers circling her slick nub, Sean merely tightened his hold.

Lightning flashed in her very core. Lily's breath caught, then rushed out in a convulsive gasp. "No, Sean! We're at my *grandmother's*! She could . . . no, stop! I can't—" Her desperate plea was interrupted by a loud call of, "Mother!" from the other end of the house.

The word triggered horror, pure horror.

"Mother!" The voice sounded again, closer this time.

And though its presence was totally incomprehensible, Lily could recognize that irritated tone anywhere.

She tore herself away from Sean's hold, hysteria threatening. "Oh, my God," she cried. "That's *my mother*!"

CHAPTER TWENTY-SEVEN

"Hello? Mother? Where are you? Mother, are you here?" And Kaye Alcott, a vision in red silk, burst into May Ellen's guest room. The heels of her taupe slingbacks slipped on the thick pile carpet. For a second she teetered in wide-eyed astonishment. "*Lily?*" she gaped. "What on earth are you two doing here? And where's Mother?"

"Uh, hi, Mother," Lily said, crossing her arms defensively, hiding her breasts as best she could. She hadn't had time to check that her bra was hooked properly, and could only thank her stars that her T-shirt was long enough to cover the waistband of her shorts. The buttons were still undone. Her hands had been shaking too badly to deal with them. If her mother noticed, Lily planned to pretend her new fashion guru was Britney Spears—no, her mother would never fall for that one. Lily would have given anything to be a thousand miles away from here, so she could button her shorts, fix her bra, and try and remember how to breathe—without her mother watching.

Her mother, of course, looked stunning. Whatever cruise she and her husband, Scott Alcott, had taken boasted an excellent spa. Kaye's golden hair was artfully swept back, her face tanned yet wrinkle free. Kaye Alcott appeared far too young to have been married four times. She looked young enough to be Lily's sister—Lily's very chic, very sophisticated sister.

Her mother's eyes swept over the room, a careful inspection that missed nothing, neither the forgotten beers, the painting lying facedown on the carpet, nor what Lily knew must be her own very disheveled appearance.

"What in the world are you doing here, Lily?" Her mother repeated the question.

Fighting the urge to escape out the door, Lily hugged her folded arms tighter still. "I'm hanging pictures."

Kaye's perfectly plucked brows arched in disbelief. "You're in Coral Beach to hang pictures?"

"Oh!" Feeling like an idiot, Lily shook her head violently. "No, I'm doing a reef study."

"You're supposed to be in the Bahamas."

"Well, yes—"

"And what have you done to your hair?"

Lily froze. What had she done to her hair? More pertinently, what had *Sean* done to her hair?

"Lily's here because the town needed a marine biologist to replace the one we'd hired for our reef study."

For the first time since she struggled free of Sean's intimate embrace, Lily hazarded a glance in his direction. Her breath caught in her throat. Sean's eyes gleamed with a dangerous, unsettling light. The angled planes of his face were carved in harsh relief by skin stretched taut. His entire being screamed of stormy passion held in ruthless check.

Kaye's wide, china blue eyes focused on Sean. Lily was sure her mother was piecing the scenario together, adding it all up. Amazingly, her mother's lips curled in what looked very much like a satisfied smile. "Well, that clears up one thing. And you're here, Sean, because?" she asked, her tone arch.

Well, Kaye, I'm here because of your daughter. As a matter of fact, I was just about to make love to Lily when you showed up. And goddamnit, I'm so hard I might crack, he added mentally along with a string of vicious curses.

If Sean had been slightly less disciplined, he'd have drawn the sheer curtains in May Ellen's guest room and tossed Lily's mother out the window. It wouldn't hurt. This was a ranch; she'd land in the shrubbery. His fingers twitched. They were coated with the haunting essence of Lily. With Kaye gone, he could pull Lily into his arms again and rekindle the lush-scented heat of her desire. He cast a longing glance toward the curtained window. A flicker of movement outside distracted him for a moment. *What was that?* he wondered.

"Yes, Sean?" Kaye prompted ever so sweetly.

Sean realized he hadn't gotten around to answering Kaye. "I'm here to give Lily a hand." He'd be giving her his body if Kaye hadn't waltzed in. "And I think Lily's hair looks great this way. Sexy as hell."

"Yes, it is rather. It's just so different." Her mother's gaze sharpened and an expression of horror crossed her features. "Lily, have you been out in the sun without any block? You *know* what happens to your skin. . . . Is that a rash on your neck?"

Have I ever liked Kaye? Sean asked himself. Forget tossing her out a window, he could strangle her instead. "Leave Lily alone, Kaye," he said, determined to stop the maternal tirade before Kaye could gather steam. "Hanging pictures is hot work. We were about to break for a beer." Sean scooped the beers off the floor and strode to where Lily was standing. He took her hand and pressed a beer into it. She wore a shell-shocked expression, as if she were caught in the middle of an adolescent nightmare with Kaye reprising her favorite role: the hypercritical mom.

He leaned close to whisper in her ear. "Relax and take a long swig of beer. It'll help." His voice dropped lower still. "If you want me to, I'll gladly chuck her out the window."

Lily choked back appalled mirth. "Thanks." Then did as Sean suggested, chugging down several gulps of lukewarm beer.

"Thatta girl," Sean murmured in approval, and took a long sip himself. "Would you like one?" he asked Kaye belatedly, holding the remaining beer out in invitation.

"Why not?" Kaye shrugged.

Startled, Lily stared. Her mother wasn't exactly the beer swilling type.

"But would you mind terribly fetching me a glass, please?"

Sean's eyes narrowed. He didn't want to leave Lily alone to the mercy of Kaye. Perhaps he should take Kaye into the kitchen and give her a Hal Storey special, a little lecture on what her daughter needed.

"And Sean?" Kaye smiled prettily. "While you're in the kitchen, you might want to call your mother. I'm sure Dana is searching all over town for you."

Nice try, Kaye, Sean thought, and gave her a cool smile. "My mother has enough tact to leave me alone," he said pointedly.

* * *

Without Sean's presence to act as a buffer, Lily bore the brunt of her mother's scrutiny. She downed the rest of her beer. Sean was right. It did help. It was only too bad she didn't have a keg. She set the empty bottle aside and picked up the fallen painting from the carpet. She prayed it wasn't damaged, and felt herself color at the thought of explaining to Granny May exactly how her painting had gotten that way.

She cleared her throat and, injecting a cheery note into her voice, said, "Well, I guess it's time to get back to work."

"Lily?"

Warily, she turned to face her mother.

"I'm . . . " Kay hesitated fractionally, then continued, "I'm sorry if I made things awkward for you just now."

Lily felt her jaw come unhinged. Her mother had never uttered the word *sorry* to her before. Never. Ever.

Her astonishment must have been as plain as the love bites on her neck, for Kaye gave a wry smile. "I really wasn't thinking too clearly when I walked into the room. Rattled, I guess. I'd been calling for Mother when I thought I heard a noise coming from this room. I immediately assumed she'd fallen and injured herself."

"No, she's fine. She went off with Mrs. Prentiss to have her hair done."

Kaye's eyebrows drew together. "How odd. I called her yesterday to tell her I was arriving. We agreed I'd drive her to Ida's tomorrow."

Lily shrugged. "I'm pretty sure that's where Granny May said she was going."

"And when we talked, she didn't even mention you were in town—that's totally unlike her, too."

"Perhaps the party plans have made her distracted." Although May Ellen hadn't struck Lily as being either distracted or forgetful.

"Party? What party?"

"It's this Saturday . . . ," Lily replied vaguely. She didn't want to go into *why* May Ellen felt the need to throw a party. Instead she gestured about her. "She decided to give the rooms a new look by changing the art on the walls."

"And so you're hanging pictures for her?" Kaye asked carefully. Her frown deepened.

Lily nodded. "Sounds pretty strange, doesn't it? But her doctor advised against any heavy lifting and she was bound and determined to redecorate." She gave a short laugh. "So here I am."

"She hasn't redecorated in twenty years," her mother said firmly. "Lloyd Gans told her not to lift things?"

"Yeah." She nodded again. "Granny May's been having dizzy spells."

"Dizzy spells?" Kaye's blue eyes grew round as saucers. "Mother's having dizzy spells?"

"Yup, Dr. Gans made a house call one evening. I was there," Lily informed her. God, this was weird, a real *Twilight Zone* moment. Here she was, a source of inside knowledge, briefing her mother.

Her mother, too, seemed to recognize the bizarreness of the situation. She shook her blond head slowly back and forth, her lips curved in a perplexed smile. "I'm going to have to give Lloyd Gans a call, find out what's going on," she said. "But I'm glad you've been here, Lily, to look after Mother. Especially with her acting this peculiarly."

"Granny hasn't acted all that peculiarly," Lily said, feeling the need to defend May Ellen. "We've had some nice talks together."

Kaye inclined her head. "Is that so? I'm glad to hear that." Then she gave Lily a smile, a warm smile, and while Lily stood paralyzed with confusion, she kicked off her high heels. Picking up a painting, Kaye asked, "Now, where does this one go?"

Sean was careful to hide his surprise at the unprecedented sight of Kaye and Lily working side by side. He was relieved, too, that he wouldn't have to toss Kaye out the window—at least not yet. But that meant he had to figure out another way to get Lily alone.

"That needs to go up a bit on the left, Lily," Kaye said. "There, that's perfect."

"Here's your beer, Kaye."

"Oh, lovely." She smiled her thanks. "Just set it over there, Sean." Kaye waved to the end table near a blue-and-gold-striped chaise longue.

"Uh, do you mind if I borrow Lily for a moment, Kaye? Something's come up about the reef study I need to discuss."

"Of course not," Kaye replied cheerfully. "I need a break. You're right, Sean, this is hot work." Kaye settled herself on the chaise and took a dainty sip of beer.

At any other moment, Sean would have stuck around to savor the incongruous sight of Kaye Alcott drinking beer in her stockinged feet. Instead, he grabbed Lily's hand and with an, "If you'll excuse us, Kaye," practically dragged her out of the room and down the hallway. Then, before Lily could begin asking him what in the world he was doing, he had her pinned against the wall, his mouth moving hungrily over hers.

"I think I'm addicted," he murmured huskily, when his lips at last released hers. "You've got me craving you, Lily," he confessed as his teeth worried her lower lip. "But damnit all, I've got to leave. I just checked in with Evelyn. All hell's breaking loose. We've been threatened with a lawsuit over the accident at the Bellemer Bridge, and someone's leaked a story to the press about a certain development project that would bring in piles of money and countless jobs for the town if only the mayor would back the proposal. And the only thing I can think about is when I'll be able to have you to myself." His mouth slanted, covering hers, kissing her deeply. "When, Lily? When can I see you?" he demanded in an urgent whisper.

"I . . ." The sentence degenerated into a moan. Sean's fingertips were tracing the shell of her ear. How was it possible that he knew exactly where to touch her? *Would it always be like this?* she wondered dazedly. A touch, and she was robbed of coherent speech. Valiantly, she tried again. "I have to go back to the lab."

His eyes were mesmerizing in the soft light of the hallway. "Tonight then? Tell me tonight, Lily."

"I don't know—" She hardly recognized her own voice, breathless and quavery.

"I do." His hands began to knead the nape of her neck, and Lily's limbs turned to jelly. "You and I have unfinished business. By my count, I owe you two orgasms." His words ignited a fire within her. "That's just for starters," he murmured with a smile that turned the fire into a blaze. "I want to give you as many as you can take, Lily." The flames raced, licking her everywhere. "A good politician doesn't welch on his promises. Tonight is ours.

I promise, Lily." With a devastating smile, he sealed the promise with a last, lingering kiss. "Until later, *cara*."

Lily managed to hold on until she heard the front door slam. Boneless, she slid to the floor.

CHAPTER TWENTY-EIGHT

Lily stepped out of the condominium's elevator and began walking down the carpeted corridor. Busy thinking about a long, steamy shower and massive amounts of food and which she'd rather indulge in first, she didn't immediately notice the object lying on the carpet.

Her feet slowed unconsciously as she tried to identify whatever it was half-obscured by the gloom. All she could tell from here was that the thing was brown and large, and was resting against her and Karen's door.

Was it perhaps a really big, dead rat? she wondered, then gave a mental shake. She must be even more tired than she realized; she was beginning to have walking nightmares.

Nevertheless, she approached cautiously until she saw that it wasn't an animal, dead or alive, but a box . . . or, rather, the remains of one. Its corners squashed, its edges ripped, and the cardboard stained and scuffed, the box looked like it had been used as a soccer ball in a match played by very competitive gorillas.

Lily bent down and peered at the label. Though smudged to the point of illegibility, she made out the words *University of Miami* in the upper left-hand corner.

It must be Dr. Lesnesky's papers. But if this was the graduate assistant's handwriting, he needed to go back to first grade for a refresher course.

But who was she to criticize another scientist's assistant? She had just spent an hour at the lab, labeling all the samples from today's dive by herself. John had been supposed to join her there, but he hadn't bothered to put in an appearance. Right now, sloppy handwriting seemed a minor deficiency compared to an assistant who didn't show up for work.

She dug the key from her bag, unlocked the door, and opened it without calling out, "Hello." Karen had said she was going to try to sleep off her bout of seasickness. With a tired sigh, Lily tugged the heavy carton across the threshold and into the apartment.

An hour later the living room looked like it had been hit by a snowstorm. White papers covered every surface. Lily stood in the center, surveying the disaster around her, and wanted to howl with frustration. She closed her eyes, wishing the papers back in the box. Wishing she'd never opened it. She still couldn't believe the state of Lesnesky's so-called report. The papers seemed to have been dumped inside, with everything randomly mixed together, dates and dive locations completely jumbled.

She'd begun the arduous task of sorting through them. By Lily's calculation, it would take several more hours before the papers were in some semblance of order. What was far more troubling, however, was the lurking suspicion that Lesnesky's notes themselves would be equally disorganized and incoherent.

Her worries were interrupted by a loud rap on the door. Could it be Sean? She hurried to open it.

Disappointment mixed with annoyance had her frowning at John Granger. "Where have you been?" she demanded, rounding on him as he sauntered into the apartment.

"What do you mean?" John countered. His eyes lit on the damaged box and the piles of paper, but he studiously kept his face blank, as if Lesnesky's papers held no interest—which wasn't far from the truth. Pete Ferrucci had paid him three thousand bucks to go through every damned sheet and make sure none of Lesnesky's data showed numbers that might indicate elevated levels of pollutants. Hell of a boring job—but the cash sure was sweet.

He pulled out a stool by the kitchen's breakfast bar, sat down, and gave her a guileless smile. "I went to the lab. You weren't there. Then I started poking around and saw you'd labeled all the samples. What happened? Did your granny nod off?"

"No," Lily enunciated through clenched teeth. "John, I told you to meet me at the lab at four P.M. Where were—"

"No, you told me five." John tapped the face of his watch. "I remember specifically. Even set my alarm. You said five, Lily. That's when I showed up."

Lily stared at him in disbelief as she tried to remember their conversation. She was sure she'd said four o'clock. Was it possible she'd gotten confused? What a stupid question. She'd been so distracted by Sean, by his intoxicating kisses, it was a wonder she'd even remembered that she was supposed to meet John, let alone get the hour right. Wearily she rubbed her forehead. "I'm sorry John. My mistake. I guess I got mixed up."

"Yeah, whatever," he said, and rolled his eyes.

John had a right to be surly, Lily thought. She was the one who'd screwed up. As the head scientist, she was in charge, responsible for everything running smoothly. Instead, her thoughts revolved endlessly around Sean. The condition terrified her, for she wasn't certain of Sean's feelings for her—beyond an obviously intense physical attraction. She knew he'd be generous with his passion, but was that all Sean would willingly give of himself? She tried to calm her fears with the thought that she'd see him tonight, that they'd talk, that she could trust him with her heart.

"Hello!"

Lily started. John was waving a hand in front of her face. "Hello," he repeated. "Earth to Banyon,"

"Oh, sorry, John. What were you saying?"

"Where's Karen?"

"She's still asleep. I guess she must have been feeling pretty lousy."

John gave a disgusted shake of his head. "Which means she didn't add any new stuff to my Web site like she said she would."

Lily felt her patience snap. She opened her mouth to tell him that Karen had already spent hours revamping his site, when the phone rang. It pealed shrilly on the counter beside John's elbow. "Excuse me," she said coolly, and picked it up. "Hello? Michelle! Thanks for calling back. Yes, I was wondering whether you'd be willing to take a look at this film a photographer friend of mine made. Yes, she works at the center too. No, it's a short piece, about twenty minutes long." Lily paused, listening, then said, "Her name is Karen Masur," and spelled Karen's name aloud. "Terrific, I'll tell her to mention that in her cover letter. Yes, I've got your address at the *Geographic.* Thanks a million, Michelle. Talk to you soon."

She hung up and turned back to John. "Is something the matter?" she asked.

"Why should something be the matter?" he replied.

Lily certainly didn't know. But John's eyes had narrowed to angry slits. She shrugged. "No reason."

Jesus Christ, thought John, seething with resentment. It was just like Ferrucci had predicted. Banyon was more than willing to help her dyke girlfriends get ahead, but she wouldn't do shit for him. He couldn't fucking believe it. Goody-two-shoes Karen Masur was going to get to play documentary filmmaker. One telephone call from Banyon, and Karen was sending her dumbass movie to *National Geographic.* It was funny. John had actually suffered a moment of guilty indecision before agreeing to help Ferrucci with his little problem. He sure as hell didn't have any qualms now, though. Banyon deserved whatever she got. Her reputation was way overblown anyway—she wasn't even smart enough to figure out what was going on. And he'd take Pete Ferrucci as a friend over Banyon any day. Thanks to Pete, John was making a shitload of easy money.

"Well, I'm outta here," he announced. He wasn't going to waste his time hanging around here. He'd go have a few drinks at the Dolphin before picking Trish up at her place.

"Why don't you wait?" Lily suggested. "Karen's bound to wake up soon. Maybe she'll be able to work on your site."

Right. *Like I want to sit around this dump and hold hands with Karen,* he scoffed silently. "Tell her maybe I'll drop by later this evening."

And there went the ever-charming John Granger, Lily thought, shaking her head, as the door slammed loudly behind him.

Miso soup. Her life was reduced to making miso soup. Lily stirred the pot's contents glumly, watching bean curd bob to the surface like broken bits of Styrofoam floating in a backwater.

Sean hadn't called and hadn't come by.

John hadn't returned, either. Lily was beginning to think men were as lousy as bean curd.

With nothing to do but wait for Sean, she had picked up Lesnesky's papers and stacked them on the table. Then Karen had tottered in, looking like death warmed over, and Lily had abandoned the papers for the contents of the refrigerator. She was too tired to deal with Lesnesky's report, and Karen needed something in her system.

A braided ball of misery, Karen was presently curled up on the sofa with a blanket wrapped around her. She'd turned the TV on. From the kitchen, Lily could hear some sitcom dishing out canned laughter every three minutes.

The soup looked ready—but really, how could she tell? What was there to check? It was clear to Lily she wouldn't last twenty-four hours as a vegan. She yanked open drawer after drawer, searching for something she might use as a ladle, and ended up with a large plastic spoon. Grabbing a dish towel, she tipped the hot soup into two bowls, then added spoonfuls of seaweed, diced scallion, and cubed bean curd to the steaming broth.

"I heated up some pita bread," she said, as she carried

the first bowl over to Karen. "Think your stomach can handle anything else?"

"No, this is great, though." Karen smiled wanly. "Thanks, Lily." She took a slow, cautious sip of the soup.

"I watched the news while you were asleep," Lily told her. "The local forecast says it's supposed to be much calmer tomorrow. But as we only have two transects left, I was thinking that we could wait until the afternoon, give your stomach a chance to settle. It won't matter if we finish a day later—I can still get the results from the lab—"

"No." Karen shook her head. "I'm sure my stomach will be fine by tomorrow morning. And it's stupid to delay when we're this close to the end."

"Yeah, I guess it is." Lily fell silent, staring blindly at the TV.

When the doorbell rang, she jumped. "No, I'll get it, Karen," she said, hastily putting aside her miso soup. She strode to the door, excitement flowing through her veins. *Sean*. He'd said he'd find her later. It must have been total chaos at town hall. Perhaps he'd tell her about it after they had made love. How many orgasms *could* she take? Lily's breath quickened. She'd never had a lover who was interested in finding out, but she knew with delicious certainty that Sean would conduct a very thorough, very rigorous study. She opened the door.

Her smile faltered, died, becoming an *Oh* of ill-concealed disappointment. "Uh, hi, Mother," Lily said belatedly.

"Hello, Lily."

Her mother twice in one day. Could she stand it? Then, remembering some semblance of manners, she stepped back and said, "Please, come in."

"Thank you."

Karen was looking a bit livelier, interest animating her face. "Hi," she said to Kaye.

"Mother, this is my roommate, Karen Masur. She's a photographer at the Marine Center. Karen, this is my mother, Kaye Alcott. Uh, can I offer you something to drink, Mother?"

"No, thank you. Actually, Lily, I came by to see whether I might invite you to dinner. There's a lovely Italian restaurant Dana and I have grown quite fond of."

Lily's stomach rumbled at the thought of a real meal, with real food. But accepting meant sharing a meal with her mother and perhaps missing Sean. "I'm sorry, Mother. I'm going to stay in tonight. Karen—"

"Oh, that's all right, Lily," Karen said. "Don't worry about me. I'm feeling loads better now that I've had something to eat. Lily made some miso to settle my stomach, Mrs. Alcott," she explained.

"Miso?"

"Karen's a vegan," Lily said to her mother.

"Oh. How nice," Kaye said politely.

Lily was pretty sure her mother had no idea what the term meant. *Klingon* would have as much resonance. So when her mother turned to her with a pleading light in her eyes, and said, "Please, Lily. I'd really like to have a chance to talk with you privately," she relented.

"I'll need a few minutes to change."

"Take your time. Karen and I will sit and chat."

As Lily left the room, she heard her mother ask, "Uh, how does one cook miso?"

Chapter Twenty-nine

The restaurant was packed, but the maître d' recognized Kaye the second she entered.

"Signora Alcott!" he welcomed her jovially. "What a pleasure to see you again!"

"Thank you, Marco. It's good to be back. I've been on a cruise. The food was delicious, but it couldn't compare with yours."

"You're too kind," he beamed. He looked past Kaye to Lily. "A table for two?"

"Please. Marco, this is my daughter, Lily."

Marco was good, Lily thought. He let loose a torrent of Italian. While she couldn't translate every word, she understood the general gist: Such divine beauty in a mother and a daughter was a blessing of the gods. Very nice.

Lily was far more impressed when, at the snap of his fingers, a waiter instantly materialized, then hurried off just as quickly, intent on carrying out Marco's rapid-fire instructions.

Marco led Lily and her mother through the crowded restaurant to a corner table. He held their chairs for them and when they were seated at the red-and-white-checked table, he lit the candle that was stuck into a ratafia and wax-encrusted Chianti bottle.

To Lily, Marco became divinity incarnate when he placed a basketful of gently steaming bread and a bottle of deep green olive oil on the table. She realized she was starving.

With a flourish, he produced the menu.

"Oh, no, Marco," Kaye said, waving it away. "You always choose so well. Please pick out something extra special for my daughter and me."

"With pleasure, *Signora*."

Aghast, Lily bit her lip. She'd break down and sob if she had to eat spinach and polenta. When Marco suggested that *la bella signorina* might enjoy the bistecca alla fiorentina, Lily mumbled a prayer of thanks. *Steak*.

"Lovely," she said, smiling brilliantly.

Lily and her mother had finished their first courses. The salmon carpaccio had been delicious, disappearing quickly in mouth melting bites. Shortly afterward, the waiter returned and set a large, glorious steak in front of her. As soon as her mother had her saltimbocca, Lily picked up her knife and fork. Her first bite had her eyes closing in sybaritic pleasure.

"This is wonderful," Lily pronounced happily. She was feeling increasingly mellow from the food and wine.

"Yes, the food's divine." Her mother reached for her red wine and sipped. "Marco's fabulous. If I didn't love Scott to distraction, I'd throw myself at the man."

"From the looks of it, he'd be very happy to catch you." A reaction shared by most men when her mother smiled.

Kaye pinkened becomingly and shook her head. "No,

I love Scott. He's the one. It took me years to find a man like him. I'm not about to give him up." She took a small bite of her saltimbocca. "I called Scott earlier. He said to send you his love. He wishes he could be here now, but he can't leave his patients so soon after returning from our cruise."

Scott Alcott, her mother's most recent husband, was a psychiatrist. Lily had met him once. He seemed nice enough. But she'd learned not to get too involved with her mother's spouses. There were too many exes through them. "So he's doing well?" Lily inquired politely.

"Oh, yes. He's just so busy. Everyone knows what the top profession in Florida is: plastic surgery. And, of course, personal training is a great way to make a killing financially. But what people don't realize is how much in demand good psychiatrists are. Fascinating, isn't it?" Kaye asked.

Lily stared in amazement at the laughter twinkling in Kaye's eyes. Her mother was actually joking with her.

"The majority of Scott's patients feel lost without him." She paused to trace the wax covering the Chianti bottle with her fingertip. At last she looked up and met Lily's eyes across the candlelight. "Actually, Lily, Scott has been talking to me a lot . . . about mother-daughter relationships. He thinks you and I need to clear the air. I do too."

Something inside Lily went perfectly still.

At Lily's lack of response, her mother sighed and plunged ahead. "I really don't like discussing certain aspects of my life; they're difficult for me. But there are things that have been weighing on my mind that I need to explain to you. Things I should have talked about years ago," she admitted. She broke off a piece of her bread and began to toy with it. "When I married your father, I was very young, not so much in years but in maturity. But Niels was so handsome—tall, strong, and with your extraordinary blue eyes. Whenever I look at you, Lily, I see Niels. Anyway, it only took one look, and I fell head over heels in love with him." She smiled faintly. "Mother and Father did everything they could to talk me out of marriage, but I wouldn't listen. When I think about it, I don't believe Niels really wanted to marry me. But I wanted him, and I've always been good at getting my way, which I've learned is one of my biggest problems. . . . However, that's not want I wanted to talk to you about." Kaye raised her wineglass to her lips and took a long sip. "Our marriage wasn't bad, Lily. But it wasn't very good, either. Things fell apart completely when Niels was offered a job in Norway. His mother's family was still there and he'd always reminisced about his childhood summers there. Anyway, Niels accepted the job, Lily, without even consulting me. You were just a newborn. I didn't know any Norwegian . . . not any Norwegian I could use outside the bedroom, that is," she clarified candidly. "And, well, I'm a *Florida* girl, one hundred percent. Norway's dark for at least half the year. I begged, I screamed, I threw every tantrum in my repertoire. I did everything I could to make him reconsider, but he wouldn't. And I wouldn't go with him. . . ." Kaye's voice faltered and she lowered her eyes, fixing them on her half-finished veal. "This is the hard part," she admitted softly. "My marriage failed and instead of blaming myself, instead of hating your father for walking away, I took everything out on you. I told myself that if I hadn't had a baby, maybe I'd have gone with him. A stupid lie, but a really easy one to swallow. I resented you so deeply, Lily. Unfortunately, that was only the beginning. It got worse. Because you grew up, were no longer this passive baby, but a person, an individual. And frankly Lily, I didn't know what the hell to do with you."

As her mother had begun talking, Lily had slipped her hands under the table, out of sight. By this point, her short nails had gouged deep into her palms. The pain so intense, not even Lily's mask of stony indifference could hide it.

Her mother looked at her, and her beautiful face crumpled. "Oh, Lily, you've got to listen to me! Please, please listen."

"Yes, of course, I'm listening, Mother." Lily's lips moved stiffly, frozen from the inside out. "You were at the point where you didn't know what to do with me. No—what the 'hell' to do with me."

"Oh, God!" Kaye wailed. "That sounds awful. And I was awful. But you were completely foreign to me—maybe even more foreign than Norway. All those horrid, smelly experiments you were always conducting in the basement, those science textbooks you closeted yourself with. And you never cared what you looked like!"

"Yes, Mother, I can see why you wouldn't have liked that." Lily laid her napkin on the table. The steak wasn't worth finishing. Besides, she felt quite ill. She made to push back her chair.

Kaye's hand shot across the table, detaining her. "No, you've got to hear me out." There was a note of desperation in her voice. "Let's reverse roles: You be the young mother, I, the child. Try to imagine giving birth to *me*, a girl who only wanted to play with Barbie dolls, have tea parties, and try out new hairstyles. What would you have done?"

Lily stared through her.

"Yes, I know the answer, too." Kaye's shoulders drooped in defeat. "You'd have played tea party with me until you went stark-raving mad. And I *should* have read those damned textbooks, at least asked you what was in them. But I didn't—and that's something I'll regret for the rest of my days. But Lily, you know what? In the end it doesn't matter that I was a lousy mother for you." She leaned across the table, tears making her eyes shimmer brightly. "Look at yourself. You're strong, talented, successful. Beautiful." The tears began to stream down her cheeks. "I am so very proud of you." Pressing her clenched hand against her mouth, Kaye wept brokenly.

For a while, Lily watched her with a kind of frozen detachment, cynically wondering how long the performance would last. Slowly she began to realize that her mother's anguish was genuine, the tears ugly and raw and endless. "Mother." Lily's voice heavy, filled with unwanted emotions. "Mother, stop . . ."

"I can't," she sobbed. "I'm sorry, so sorry."

As Kaye wept, Lily recalled the evening she'd spent with May Ellen. Granny May had told her that Kaye had really changed since marrying Scott Alcott.

At the moment she couldn't decide if she considered this a change for the better.

Lily had always instinctively shied away from analyzing the motives behind her mother's constant criticisms, probably because of the pain involved in probing those memories. But one thing was clear from her mother's tearful confession. Kaye had been a desperately unhappy woman. And flawed though it was, Lily's childhood was behind her, in the past. She was grown up now and was, as Kaye had remarked, a strong woman.

Lily realized she had a choice. Either she could use her strength to punish her mother for past wrongs, or she could use it to try and lift the burden of her mother's regrets. What was the point in making her mother suffer? Any satisfaction would be cold, empty.

She reached out and shook her mother's arm gently. "Mother, listen to me. Some of the things you did as a parent were fine. After all, if you'd really been dead set against my setting up a lab and doing chemistry and biology experiments in the basement, you'd have chucked the stuff. And my swimming—you were convinced that I'd end up with the shoulders of an East German weightlifter, but still you let me continue."

Kaye lifted watery eyes and sniffed loudly. "Your shoulders are great, like the rest of you. Thank God I had the sense to let Hal Storey into your life. He always understood you, Lily, let you be, knowing you'd achieve your goals. You know, he used to call me and tell me everything was going to be fine, what a great kid I had." Using the corner of her napkin, Kaye mopped her eyes and managed a shaky smile. "But even if I had tried to make you give up those things, your science, your swimming, you'd have figured out a way to get around me. You were . . . are so darned stubborn."

"I know. I inherited that from you, Mother."

"Kaye," her mother corrected Lily. Drawing a breath, she said, "Scott and I think you should call me *Kaye*, and not *Mother* anymore."

Lily blinked, nonplussed.

"You see," she explained, "I was so terrible as a mother to you, calling me that only makes us remember the hurt. . . . We can't get beyond the past. So Scott suggested we start over, and I could be *Kaye* to you. Maybe we could be friends. I think I could be a damned good friend, one that wouldn't let you down. I know it may take years, but please say you'll give me a chance. Please, Lily," she whispered.

Lily stared at her mother, at a woman she really didn't know. Did she even want this person to be her friend? But she'd learned an invaluable lesson since coming back to Coral Beach. Everyone deserved a second chance. "Yes, I'd like that . . . Kaye."

Marco seemed too elegant a man to rush, but rush he did. "Signora Alcott, is something wrong?" Horrified, he looked at Kaye, who sat with tears streaming down her face. "Was the saltimbocca not to your liking? *Signora!*" he cried.

Kaye collected herself. "I beg your pardon, Marco," she said, giving him a tremulous smile. "My daughter and I have just made a very special pact. What can you bring us to celebrate the occasion?"

"Ahh!" He nodded indulgently, a smile of relief lighting his face. "But of course! I have a lovely Prosecco I keep for special moments only. To go with it, perhaps a tiramisu?"

A knock sounded on Sean's office door. Dave ducked his head inside, his brows raised in silent inquiry. The phone pressed to his ear, Sean motioned for him to come in.

"Hello, is that you, Karen? It's Sean. Could I speak to Lily? She's not? Oh, I see. When did they leave? Do you know where? No, of course not. Well, listen, could you tell her I called, that I'll call again in an hour? Thanks." Sean made to hang up, but Dave grabbed the phone from him.

"Karen, you there?" he asked. "Yeah, it's me. . . ."

Sean looked out the window, tuning out Dave's conversation with Karen, trying not to feel envious of his friend. He'd been anticipating Lily's voice over the phone, hoping she'd answer with breathless anticipation so he'd know she felt the same as he did.

But Lily was gone, out with Kaye somewhere. And Karen had no idea when she'd be back. She hadn't left a message for him. Sean checked his watch. *Damn it*, he should have called her earlier, but he and Evelyn had been swamped, with one crisis after the next rolling in, as relentless as the ocean. Poor Evelyn had been weaving with exhaustion when he'd sent her home, ten minutes ago.

Sean was beat, too. He'd go home and take a shower, then wait for Lily to return from dinner. But first Cullen had to get off his phone. *He and Karen sure are chatty,* Sean thought. He caught Dave's eye, scowled, and made a slicing gesture in front of his throat.

Dave smiled, gave him the finger, and continued talking. "Listen," he said, "I'll bring something over to cheer you up. Yeah. See you in ten minutes." He hung up the receiver and sat back, oozing satisfaction.

"So, Dave, you have anything else to say or are you all talked out?"

"Hey, don't be a sourpuss just because your girl stepped out." Dave's grin widened as Sean's scowl deepened. "I came by to see whether you were heading over to practice tonight."

"No—"

"Me neither. See you, McDermott." Sean's office door shut behind Dave with a depressing thud.

Sean was shrugging into his jacket when the door

opened again. Assuming it was Dave coming back to
pester him some more, he didn't bother to look up.

"Hi, Sean. I'm so glad I caught you alone." Stacy Malloy smiled.

The plate of tiramisu, placed in the center of the table
so that Kaye and Lily could share, was half-finished. Her
stomach deliciously full, Lily sat back in her chair and
raised the glass of Prosecco to her lips. The champagne-
like wine was exquisitely chilled. She breathed in its delicate fragrance and closed her eyes, savoring it as she
drank. Opening them again, Lily couldn't believe what
she saw. She blinked to clear her vision. Instead, a red
mist of anger descended.

"Lily, what's wrong; what's the matter?" Kaye asked.

Lily spoke with glacial calmness. "Nothing. I was
merely thinking about how much I detest politicians."

Kaye relaxed. "Oh, well, we all do," she said, and
laughed lightly. She straightened as Lily's words registered. "What? What politician? Surely you don't mean—"
She made to turn her head.

"No! Don't turn around," Lily hissed frantically. But
she was too late. Stacy Malloy had spotted them. She
must have been scanning the dining room, on the look-
out for familiar faces. A brilliant, ultrasatisfied smile lit
her face as she zigzagged her way past the tables, towing
Sean behind her.

Sean was just giving their order to the bartender when
Stacy began dragging him by the sleeve. He looked back
over his shoulder, wanting to make sure the bartender
got him that double whiskey straight up. He deserved
one, needed one after being cornered in his office by
Stacy Malloy—undoubtedly one of the scarier moments

of his life. Spooked by the possibility that she might try some idiotic seduction ploy, like stripping naked in his office, he'd hustled her out of there with the promise that he'd take her out for a drink. After all, what could she do in public? And Marco's was as public you could find.

The place was jumping, waiters bustling to and fro. Sean assumed Stacy was leading him to some corner table where they could discuss balloon colors, crepe paper, and Christ only knew what else. Glancing about, Sean didn't see an empty table anywhere. All he saw was . . . that he was fucked.

The pain of seeing Sean and Stacy together here at Marco's enveloped Lily, surrounded her like a frenzied swarm of bees attacking. There was nowhere she could run and hide. The hurt intensified a hundredfold when Stacy stopped before their table.

"Hi, Mrs. Alcott. Hi, Lily. How sweet, you're having a mother-daughter night out. Don't you just adore this restaurant? It's so romantic! Sean *insisted* we come here tonight." She preened, a gloating expression on her face as she smiled down at Lily and Kaye. "He always picks the perfect place for us."

Despite being dulled with shock, Lily's brain nonetheless registered certain details, such as the fact that Stacy was dressed to the nines—the plunging vee of her dress practically down to her bellybutton, and that she kept turning toward Sean and brushing her bared flesh against him.

Unable to bear the pain any longer, she somehow managed to rise and made to brush past the happy couple. Dimly, she was aware of Kaye standing, too.

"Lily—" Sean's voice stopped her in her tracks.

She refused to look at him, knowing she'd fall apart if she did.

"Don't—" he said.

She clenched her teeth, biting back a scream of betrayal. "Why don't you drop dead, McDermott?" she suggested, and walked away.

She hadn't uttered another word, even now that she and Kaye were in May Ellen's Cadillac, driving back toward the condo. But Lily hardly needed to speak; her mother was talking enough for two.

"I never did like that girl, Stacy Malloy," she said. "Very pushy. And she dresses atrociously. Dana tells me she's been absolutely insufferable ever since she got picked as president of the Junior League. She's convinced Stacy only ran so she could be involved in this campaign party for Sean. Stacy seems to believe Sean is her personal property." Braking for a red light, she glanced over at Lily. "I do wish you'd let Sean speak to you, Lily. It's always a big mistake to let someone like Stacy think she's won the battle."

Lily's temples pounded. "There is no battle. Stacy can have him."

"Oh, no she can't!" Kaye contradicted vehemently. "Dana having to deal with a daughter-in-law like that? Besides, Sean doesn't want her, he wants—"

"I don't care what Sean McDermott wants," Lily said, cutting her off.

For a moment Kaye was blessedly silent. Then, "Mother and I were discussing the party on Saturday."

Lily sagged with relief at the switch of topics.

"I think it's lovely that Mother wants to throw a party

for you. We were wondering whether we might buy you something to wear for it, something really smashing."

"I really don't—"

"A wonderful friend of mine has this boutique she's opened. Fiona's got great taste, buys from only the best designers."

"I'm incredibly busy right now, wrapping up the reef study."

"I'd love to see you in something dazzling, something that does credit to your beauty," Kaye continued as if she hadn't spoken. "So many people will be at the party. Oh, no!" she exclaimed, as if a thought had just occurred to her. "I hope Sean's not planning to bring Stacy! But that's right—you don't care what Sean and that tramp do."

Lily flinched, anguished as she pictured Sean and Stacy arriving arm in arm at her grandmother's party. "I don't see how buying a dress will accomplish anything."

"You leave that to me," Kaye said confidently as she made a left-hand turn, easing the Cadillac into the circular drive in front of the condominium complex. "We'll work around your schedule—I'm totally flexible. I've nothing planned except running errands for Mother. Just call. I promise I won't bully you into buying anything you don't like."

"Nothing in pink or green?" Lily asked, still leery of the whole idea.

"You're Lily Banyon, not Lilly Pulitzer. Quite a different look," Kaye laughed. "Trust me, Fiona will find you something Sean McDermott will never forget."

"That would be a major triumph," Lily replied bitterly under her breath. Sean obviously found her all too forgettable.

* * *

At first glance, it looked as if Karen hadn't budged from her spot on the sofa. She was still wrapped in her blanket, staring at the TV. It wasn't until Lily stepped into the apartment that she realized she was mistaken. She sniffed the air. *Popcorn.* Karen must have microwaved herself a batch.

"Hi, Lily." Karen looked up. She lifted the bowl that was nestled in her lap in offering as Lily sank down on the sofa beside her. Lily shook her head in refusal.

"Sean just called . . . for the third time," Karen informed her. "He seems really anxious to talk to you."

"Appearances can be deceiving." Lily's voice was flat. "Especially where Sean McDermott is concerned." How could he have held her in his arms, kissed and touched her until she moaned with desire for him? How could he have made those heated promises, then turn around and escort Stacy to a romantic, candlelit restaurant?

She couldn't bear the idea that Sean had so easily replaced her. She hated knowing that at this very moment Stacy was doing her utmost to keep Sean "entertained."

She'd call Sean when hell froze over. No, make that when politicians started keeping their promises . . . that would never happen.

Resolving to put Sean out of her mind as easily as he'd forgotten her, she turned to Karen. "You must be feeling better," she said, consciously injecting an upbeat note in her voice. "I see you made popcorn."

"No, Dave popped it for me."

"Dave? Dave Cullen?"

"Yeah." Karen nodded. "Dave must have been with Sean when he called the first time. He stopped by with a movie." She gestured toward the screen. Something greenish black was roaring as it writhed and flailed.

"What is this?"

"*Godzilla versus the Sea Monster*. It's a classic." Karen shoved a mouthful of popcorn in her mouth, chewed, and added, "Dave's so sweet. He watched it with me for a while, but then he had to leave. He's got a breakfast meeting with his staff—they're working out the logistics for the scuba weekend."

"That was thoughtful of him to bring you a movie." Dave was an okay guy. It was his friend, McDermott, who was a jerk. "So John didn't come back?"

"No." The blanket around Karen's shoulders moved in a shrug. "No great loss there."

"What? I thought you were still on a 'Redeem John Granger' crusade."

"I've decided it's not worth it." She scowled as Godzilla grappled with a slime-covered creature that was a dead ringer for the Loch Ness monster, then glanced back at Lily. "Remember this morning?"

Morning was eons ago. "Refresh my memory."

"Okay. Remember how we took two cars, and John and I arrived at the marina first? Ferrucci was already there when we pulled into the parking lot. I pointed him out to John and said something about what a sleazoid creep Ferrucci was. Know what John said in reply? That Ferrucci wasn't so bad . . . not once you got to know him. I think John's become pals with Ferrucci. If so, he's a total loser himself."

John Granger friends with Pete Ferrucci?

And what would being friends with Pete Ferrucci entail? she wondered. Hanging out in Ferrucci's bar and making passes at any woman who happened to walk by was the obvious answer. The second one that insinuated itself in Lily's mind was too absurd to credit.

Lily didn't like John, hadn't ever liked John. But personal antipathy didn't give her license to contemplate—even in passing—that John might do anything to compromise the reef study. John was an ass-grabbing boor, but that didn't mean he was corrupt. For Pete's sake, he was a marine biologist, or would be, once he'd finished his dissertation.

Besides, there wasn't anything to be suspicious about. Lily had gone over almost all of the patch reef and found no evidence of disease thus far.

"I don't know what John does in his free time," Lily admitted wearily. "I agree Ferrucci's scum, but I find it difficult to believe John and he are very well acquainted. I've passed by Ferrucci's place, the Blue Dolphin. All those neon lights and wall-to-wall mirrors probably lured John inside. Who knows, maybe they have a great ladies' night or something. Think about it, Karen. What could John and Ferrucci possibly have in common?"

"Other than being creeps? Yeah, I guess you're right," she concluded glumly. "It's just depressing. I really thought John was getting more *normal*."

"Character improvement is a lifelong endeavor. Most people fail miserably. But I think you've had a good influence on him, he's been much more . . . cooperative on this trip. I wrote as much to Simone in the update I e-mailed her."

"Yeah? Thanks, Lily. So, aren't you going to call Sean? He's going to be disappointed."

"I doubt it." Lily dropped her head against the back of the sofa and closed her eyes.

"What happened? I kind of got the impression that you two might have a thing going."

"No. Not one that would work anyway. We're too different. Our lives are too different. We don't care about the same things." *He doesn't care about me.*

"I don't buy that." At Karen's censorious tone, Lily opened her eyes. Karen was shaking her head as if deeply disapproving. "You and Sean are both dynamic people who care about the world you live in. You're both incredibly brave, too. And you're both obviously attracted to each other—no, don't try to deny it."

"I'm not denying it," Lily said, feeling miserable. "But that's all it is. Physical attraction." *At least on Sean's part,* Lily thought.

Karen snorted. "Show me a relationship that doesn't start that way."

She had a point there, Lily conceded, but only silently.

"So it would be pure cowardice and darned stupid, too," Karen continued, "if you were to walk away from what you and Sean could have together without even giving it a chance." At that, Karen put the bowl of popcorn on the coffee table and stood, the blanket draped over her shoulders. Then, with the blanket billowing like a sail behind her, Karen left Lily alone with her bleak thoughts and Godzilla.

CHAPTER THIRTY

"Sean," Evelyn Roemer said in surprise. "What are you doing here this early?"

Sean looked up from his computer. "Morning, Evelyn. I'm putting the finishing touches on my press statement."

His secretary walked over to the espresso machine, saw that he'd used it already, and frowned. "Did you get any sleep at all?"

"Not much." He shrugged. "Could you make it a double? My first cup tasted like sludge." He hadn't slept at all. But the reason, contrary to what Evelyn believed, had nothing to do with his mayoral duties and everything to do with a beautiful blond scientist. His initial chagrin at running into Lily and Kaye with Stacy draped all over him—and then having Stacy babble about candlelight and romance and how her and Sean's meeting might take half the night—had eventually undergone a metamorphosis, turning into righteous indignation.

After prying himself free of Stacy, he'd tried telephoning Lily a dozen times. All he got was a busy signal. It took him a while to figure out that she'd taken the phone off the hook. He knew from experience what banging on her door would get him: a flattened face. Infuriated that she wouldn't even listen to his explanation, he'd barely shut his eyes last night, frustrated, remorseful, furious . . . and missing her so damn much.

He had to find Lily and convince her he was blameless in the debacle of last night. He had a freshly laundered handkerchief in his pocket. He'd use it as a gag if he had to. Then, after he'd humbly apologized for having inadvertently ruined a night he'd dreamed of for years, he'd remove it and kiss her senseless.

But first he had to get through this morning. A morning that promised to be rotten, with the potential for a slippery slide into hell itself.

Evelyn placed a fresh espresso in front of him.

"You're a lifesaver," he said gratefully. "I'd appreciate it if you'd read over the statement I've prepared, Evelyn, and give me some feedback. The basic message is this: Yes, Coral Beach has been approached by a group interested in developing the land south of the marina. But at this point, no specific plans have been discussed. As I've gone on record repeatedly, I refuse to make any decisions about land use along the southern coast until the final report to the reef committee has been submitted. To do otherwise would not only be premature, but irresponsible. The tone should be firm, but not defensive. Got it?"

"Got it." Evelyn nodded. "I'll bring your faxes and phone messages." She went into the adjoining office and returned, messages in hand.

"Thanks."

"You've got your first appointment at nine."

Sean's expression hardened. "And what better way to start the day than with a lawsuit? By the way, Mike Coehlo's going to arrive a few minutes early." Mike Coehlo was Coral Beach's legal counsel.

"I'll get the copies of the police report," Evelyn said.

"Good. I want to go over it one more time before Mike gets here. Christ," he muttered, shaking his head, "I still can't understand why Mrs. Ritter decided to do such an idiotic thing."

"Ambulance chasers." His secretary's answer came with a disdainful sniff. "They lurk everywhere. One of them probably convinced her she'd be able to buy a mansion in Hawaii with the money she won."

"She'll get nothing but a mountain of legal fees if she decides to go through with the suit," Sean said flatly.

"Looks like it's going to be another long day."

"That's right. The life of a politician's just nonstop fun."

"It'll be even jollier once your reelection campaign begins," Evelyn said.

Sean's smile died. "That reminds me, Evelyn. If Stacy Malloy telephones, drops by, attempts to contact me in *any* way, I am unavailable. Let's make that a standing order."

"Oh, Sean! You mean you won't have time to consult Ms. Malloy about where to put the microphone on the podium?" She struggled to hide her grin and failed miserably.

"Don't push it, Evelyn," he growled. "Or I'll let *you* tell her where to put the microphone."

"I don't think Ms. Malloy would care for my suggestion."

"Mr. Coehlo is here, Sean," Evelyn announced a short time later.

"Thank you." Sean stood and walked around his desk to greet the lawyer.

"Mike, good to see you again," he said, shaking the town counsel's hand. "How are Patty and the kids?"

"Doing great, although Patty's going through a period of adjustment. She's having a hard time getting used to the fact that our youngest, Jamie, is a freshman in high school. Speaking of which, Jamie came home and announced she wants us to sign her up for this scuba program the Department of Parks and Recreation is organizing." Mike's grin widened. "Plus, she's decided to go to summer school and take an environmental science course. Says she's thinking about a career in marine science, like this Dr. Banyon who gave a talk at the high school."

"Good for Jamie." Sean laughed, feeling better for the first time today. He couldn't wait to tell Lily that her talk at the high school was already affecting lives. "Have a seat, Mike. Can I offer you some coffee?"

"No, thanks, I'm trying to cut back." He sat in the chair facing Sean's desk, laid his brown leather briefcase across his knees, and pressed the locks with his thumbs. They opened with a snap. He drew out a sheaf of papers, closed the briefcase, and set it against the legs of the chair. "I'm sorry I couldn't meet with you yesterday afternoon—"

"No need to apologize, Mike. Mrs. Ritter's lawyer will be here shortly," Sean said. "This is a copy of the police report; take a look." He leaned forward and handed it to him. "I made an asterisk next to a paragraph I thought might interest you." As the lawyer's eyes skimmed the report, Sean continued, "No one pressed charges, but when they interviewed the other driver, the woman claimed she'd seen Mrs. Ritter with a cell phone pressed to her ear. Yeah, that's the relevant paragraph." He was silent while Coehlo read the passage.

Mike Coehlo raised his head and looked at Sean. A smile split his freckled face. "*Oops.* Looks like this slimeball didn't do his homework. Thanks, Sean," he said. "I may actually get to play that round of golf after lunch."

"My pleasure."

The intercom buzzed. Sean checked his watch. "I believe our slimeball has arrived. Should we make him wait?"

"Definitely." Mike grinned. "So, what have you been up to lately, Sean?"

When Evelyn finally ushered Joseph Anders, the lawyer representing Mrs. Ritter, into Sean's office, no coffee was offered, no pleasantries wasted, either.

Anders settled himself in the only remaining chair, adjusted his tie, and with his chin thrust out pugnaciously in Sean's direction, said, "As I informed you on the phone yesterday, Mayor McDermott, my client, Mrs. Susan Ritter, intends to file a suit against the town of Coral Beach for failing to make necessary safety improvements to the Bellemer Bridge and the Bellemer Road that leads to it. The town's gross neglect caused my client and her young children extensive injuries. We feel five million dollars—"

"Excuse me, Mr. Anders," Sean said. "This is a copy of the investigation report by the police." He picked up the photocopy and then let it drop onto the desk. He gave the lawyer a smile. "Have you read it by any chance?"

"Naturally," the lawyer replied.

Anders was bluffing. Sean could see the tiniest flicker of worry in his eyes. In a poker game, Sean would take him to the cleaners. He exchanged a look with Mike, leaned back in his chair, and let Mike have his turn.

Coehlo picked up the copy of the police report and offered it to Anders. "Perhaps you should review page three, paragraph four, Mr. Anders. Then we'll discuss whether your client really wants to file this lawsuit."

Sean watched a grimace of embarrassment steal over the lawyer's face. He doubted Anders was even aware of the odd little noises he was making. Whoever worked as Anders's paralegal was about to be out of a job. Sean let him sweat a little before nodding to Coehlo.

"I assume you understand that Mrs. Ritter's suit will go nowhere, Mr. Anders," Mike said. "I suggest you get in touch with your client immediately. And when you do, you might mention that based upon this police report, the town has a solid defense of contributory negligence. Holding a cell phone to your ear while negotiating a curve is a pretty dumb idea. Especially when your kids are in the backseat," he finished flatly.

Sean took over. "If you don't have the good sense to dissuade Mrs. Ritter, I will ask Mr. Coehlo to contact the county prosecutor, who may very well choose to bring Mrs. Ritter to trial for reckless endangerment. Have a nice day, Mr. Anders," Sean said. "Oh, yes, one other thing. You can give your client a bit of practical advice from me. That curve leading to the bridge? It's a piece of cake with both hands on the wheel. She should try it sometime."

"Thanks for coming, Mike," Sean said, as Mike Coehlo replaced the papers inside his briefcase and stood up. Sean walked him to the door.

They shook hands. "God, I loved the look on Anders's

face when he realized just how deep that shit hole was. I haven't had this much fun all week." He laughed and gave Sean a hearty slap on the shoulder. "Let's do it again sometime."

"No thanks, Mike, I'd rather not. What I would like to do, however, is find out who put Anders on the Ritters' doorstep. I saw Mrs. Ritter at the hospital after the accident. She didn't strike me as the type of person who'd get involved in this sort of thing."

"Any names pop up?"

Sean shrugged. "Gehring, Ferrucci . . . hell, maybe I'm becoming paranoid."

"Tell you what, I'll make a few discreet inquiries. I have some friends at the DOT, too."

"Don't let it interfere with your golf game."

"God, no." Mike grinned. "I've got my priorities. I'll give you a buzz if I unearth anything."

"I'd appreciate it, Mike. Give my love to Patty and tell Jamie to have fun scuba diving."

Sean shut the door after Mike and turned to Evelyn. "Think you can work your magic on the espresso machine again for me? I've got a few minutes before I have to go ten rounds with a roomful of journalists."

"Be happy to." Evelyn made to rise from her chair, when the phone rang. Sitting back down, she answered it. "Mayor McDermott's office, Evelyn Roemer speaking." She paused, listening. "Just a minute, please," she replied, and clamped a hand over the mouthpiece. "Sean, it's the governor for you."

Lily, Karen, and John slid into a vacant booth. A waitress wearing a faded shirt with glittery letters spelling *Norma Jean's* emblazoned on its front brought them their menus, asked whether they would like coffee right away, and disappeared.

"Nice place you're treating us to, Lily." John leaned back, resting his arms along the back of the vinyl-covered booth. His sunglasses reflected the noonday sun as he surveyed the other patrons eating lunch, the lunch board with the handwritten specials all but obscured by grime. "Yes, indeed. Real swank. Definitely pulling out all the stops for us."

Lily smiled tightly. "Pulling out all the stops?" she repeated. "I think clogging all the arteries is a better way to describe a meal at Norma Jean's. And for you, John, only the finest grease in Coral Beach will do." She was too tired to put up with John's sarcasm. She'd spent the night staring at the dead phone, trying to convince herself that this was for the best. Yet as the clock ticked off the minutes creeping by, she kept hearing Karen's voice saying the word *coward* over and over again. Perhaps Karen was right. Perhaps she was a coward, but at least she'd be leaving Coral Beach next week with her heart merely bruised and battered—not lost forever.

When the waitress returned to take their orders, Lily said, without bothering to consult the menu, "I'll have the Jimmy Buffet. Hold the beer, please."

"What's a Jimmy Buffet?" John asked her.

" 'Cheeseburger and Paradise,' " Lily quoted.

"So what do they call it if you want a cheeseburger with bacon?"

Lily pretended to think about it. "That would be a bacon cheeseburger."

"Jesus." John tossed aside the menu. "Bacon cheeseburger for me."

"I'll have the salad, please." Karen said. "Oh, and some Jell-O."

Despite the air of neglect that permeated the place, Norma Jean's was fast and efficient. Their orders arrived before they'd finished talking about the morning's dive.

"I got to admit, this is pretty good," John said around a mouthful of burger.

Lily nodded. "Yeah, these are the best burgers in Florida. I figured our last lunch should be a memorable one."

"Oh, I'll definitely remember this trip," John said with a laugh. Demolishing his burger in short order, he left to use the rest room.

Karen had merely picked over her salad, muttering about wilted iceberg. With a sigh, she pushed it aside, picked up a spoon, and pulled the bowl of green Jell-O closer.

Lily signaled the waitress to bring them their check, doing her best not to look while Karen poked tentatively at the green globs.

"Maybe this wasn't such a good idea," Karen said, watching with sick fascination as it jiggled wildly.

"You certainly wouldn't catch me eating that stuff," Lily said.

"Mind if I join you?" Sean slid into the space vacated by John.

"Hey, Sean," Karen said, smiling brightly for the first time today. "Want some Jell-O? I haven't taken a bite."

"I'll pass. Thanks though, Karen." Sean paused and gave Lily a long look. "Hello, Lily."

She maintained a stony silence.

"Here's your check," the waitress said, and placed the

slip in the middle of the Formica-topped booth. "You want something to eat, Mayor McDermott?"

"No, thanks, Sue."

"A cup of joe?" she asked.

For a second, Sean's gaze released Lily to look up and shake his head at the waitress. Lily's hands flew to her wallet. Opening it, she riffled through the bills. Damn, they were all twenties. She'd have to wait for change.

"Lily, we need to talk."

"That won't be possible, Mr. Mayor. We're just leaving."

"I thought I'd come on the dive this afternoon—"

"No!"

The vehemence of Lily's response made Karen start. "Gosh, I really need to pee before we set out," she exclaimed, scooting out from the vinyl booth.

Like Lily, Sean ignored Karen, paid no attention to her hasty departure. "What do you mean no?" he asked softly. "You're not barring me from this expedition, are you, Lily?"

"You bet I am," she hissed angrily to hide her hurt. "This is already our second dive of the day. We have only one last transect to cover and the study will be finished. We've been working our butts off on this project. My team is exhausted. *I'm* exhausted. The last thing we need is you, Mr. Mayor, breathing down our necks—"

"Listen, I'm sorry about last night! I couldn't get rid of Stacy—not with the bloody fund-raiser coming up. I'll make it up to you, I promise—" The word hung in the air between them. Sean stopped, as conscious as she of an earlier promise made, then broken.

Lily paled. "Your promises are worthless, Sean. Go utter those sweet nothings to Stacy Malloy. I'm not interested in listening to a two-faced liar." Her eyes raked over him contemptuously. "I only wonder how many other lies you've told."

She made to scramble out of the booth, but Sean's hand shot out, grabbing her arm.

"Wait a goddamned minute!" he demanded, his anger matching hers.

She wrenched her arm free. "Don't you dare touch me." Her tone was glacial. "Stay away from me—I'm sick of being harassed by the likes of you, Mayor McDermott." Lips pressed together, Lily rushed out of the diner. Karen followed hurriedly, casting worried looks over her shoulder at Sean.

"Banyon giving you a rough time, McDermott?" John drawled, shaking his head at Lily's retreating figure. "Take it from me, Banyon's the bitch of the millennium. You'll never get her to open wide."

Like a shot, Sean was up, his face inches from Granger's. His voice low and vicious, he said, "For two cents, I'd beat the shit out of you, Granger. Keep your mouth shut until you leave this town, or I'll shut it for you."

"Yeah, fuck you, too, McDermott," John snarled, shoving past him.

The waitress scooped up the check and money Lily had thrown on the table. The 80 percent tip put a smile on her face, so when she stopped at the adjacent booth, glass coffee pot in hand, her voice was extra perky and cheerful. "Need another refill?" she asked, holding the pot over the empty, chipped porcelain cup.

"No, thanks." The man didn't bother to look up, busy scribbling in his notebook. Yet when the waitress continued to hover, he cocked his head, glancing up at her sideways, and saw that her eyes were trained on the pad of paper. Casually, he closed the cover and pushed the wire-bound notebook off to the side. "Sorry, honey, I don't let anyone read my work till it's published."

"Oh! You a writer?" the waitress asked eagerly. "What you working on? A novel?"

"That's right. The story's a real pot-boiler."

"Ooh, good. I love those."

CHAPTER THIRTY-ONE

Alone on the stern of the *Tangiers*, Lily stared at the shoreline. The wind whipped about her, drying her tears. But nothing could stop the sorrow that engulfed her.

She'd been a fool, a jealous fool. Furious with Sean, with herself, she'd hurled those bitter, angry words at him and then had run. Coward that she was, she'd run, hoping with every fleeing step that Sean would run faster, catch her, and never let her go.

Idiot, she scolded herself. *As if Sean would follow after the things you said to him.* He had his pride. He wouldn't chase after her when she'd behaved like a jealous shrew.

She had to apologize. As soon as they got back from the dive, she'd go to him. It was time she faced her love with courage.

Squaring her shoulders, she swiped at the lingering wetness on her cheeks. With this last section of the reef complete, she'd be close to one end. Her fervent wish, though, was that she be given the chance to start anew with Sean.

Lily's fins hit the water with a slap. Bobbing to the surface, she treaded water, looking up through the tempered glass of her mask at the *Tangiers*'s stern for John and Karen to make their entries. Two splashes later, their scuba-clad bodies were beside hers. The three of them kicked over to the ladder and Owen passed down the equipment. At Lily's signal, and John's and Karen's answering thumbs up, the team began its descent.

This was it, the last section of the reef.

A little over two weeks ago, they'd begun their study at zone one's northernmost tip. It had taken them more than twenty dives to examine the patch reef section by section. They'd become familiar with it—with the corals, the fish—as familiar as one might be of a garden lovingly tended and watched over.

Just as there had been a sense of excitement, of thrilling anticipation on Lily's first exploratory dive, there was a correlative sadness that pervaded this last dive of the study. More and more often, when Lily conducted a reef study and then returned to visit the site a few years later, she would find the once colorful exotic valleys, ridges, and caves that she'd explored earlier had become diminished, lifeless, like underwater ghost towns. Here faster, there more slowly, the decline of coral reefs could be seen the world over.

Coral was a home and life source, the foundation of a vast, complex ecosystem. When coral sickened and died, its inhabitants too were affected, no longer able to feed, grow, or to use it as shelter.

Many of the dangers that threatened coral reefs were invisible to the naked eye—which was why so many samples were collected, and then subjected to a barrage of chemical and bacterial analyses. Some diseases, however, were all too easy to spot, and were becoming a sadly common sight. There was *bleaching*, when the vibrant tissue of the coral turned white and brittle, the discoloration spreading inexorably over the entire organism until it died. Another was black band disease, an algal infestation that grew in an ominous black ring, like a malevolent bull's-eye, killing the coral polyps as it spread. Macro algae bloom attacked coral with a suffocating blanket of brownish-green fuzz. Unfortunately, these were just a few of the countless diseases that ravaged and destroyed the extraordinary marine life forms.

Perhaps it was because Lily had seen no evidence of these dangerous diseases, no warning signs on the rest of the patch reef, that she had begun to think that perhaps Coral Beach was just plain lucky.

Nothing in Abe Lesnesky's report had led her to suspect trouble. In the mixed-up mess of papers, graphs, and charts, she hadn't found a single number or reading to question the vitality of the reef.

That was why, when Lily swam over the flat relief of zone one and came upon a colony of stag coral, her breath rushed out in a stream of dismay. Stag coral, in its natural state, was usually white or tan, with a delicate triangular fringe decorating its hornlike branches. The one in front of her was an especially large specimen.

Had the stag coral been healthy, it would have been a thing of beauty, a large and wonderful sculpture that had taken millennia to create. Thus to see suddenly the multiple, thick, black bands encircling its branches was devastating. The disease had already spread, taken over. One glance told Lily the coral wasn't merely unhealthy, it was dying.

She flutter-kicked slowly, circling it, mourning what she saw. Her eyes traveled downward, to the coral's base. A hillock of sediment surrounded it. She took a test tube from her case and carefully scooped up a sample. Stopping it, she replaced the tube and swam over to John and Karen, who were examining several small sponges.

For the next hour, Lily and John took core samples of the ocean floor. They collected sediment and algae samples that coated dying coral. When they had accomplished that, they began filling their underwater notebooks with observations, noting down the different types of disease.

With her cameras, Karen photographed sea fans, sponges, brain coral, elkhorn coral, too many of which showed evidence of algal infestation and massive bleaching.

It took over an hour to inspect the disease-ridden transect, but less than a minute for Lily to realize that this last transect was a *hot spot*, the term used by marine biologists to describe an area in which one or more types of disease had spread, destroying coral species.

As she worked, Lily felt a sympathetic condition take over, as though she too were being attacked by some invidious germ. She was sickened by what she saw.

Why was this happening, and so quickly, too? The question repeated itself with each sample she took, each notation she made. The onslaught of algae and disease must have been extremely aggressive. Otherwise, Abe Lesnesky would have reported it in the updates he gave to the committee.

When the team surfaced five yards from where the *Tangiers* was anchored, there was none of the excited, ebullient chatter that usually flowed between them, once their mouths were free of their regulators' bulky mouthpieces. They gathered around the foot of the aluminum ladder in cheerless silence. Wearily, they handed their equipment up to Owen, tugged off their fins and, one after the other, climbed the short ladder.

Owen Rafern picked up on the mood quickly. "Something the matter, Dr. Banyon?" he asked, helping Lily off with her scuba tank.

She unsnapped her weight belt, lowered it to the deck, and then shrugged out of her buoyancy control vest. "There were some troubling signs in this area. Some of the coral and sponges are diseased," she said. It was all right to divulge basic information. The fact that this section of the patch reef was threatened would be public knowledge as soon as she made her report next week.

But it was yet another reason to berate herself for her foolish tantrum with Sean at Norma Jean's. If he had accompanied them on the dive today, he would have observed firsthand the signs of rampant disease.

"Can you tell what's causing the disease?"

Lily shook her head tiredly. "No, I can't say for certain yet." She reached for the zipper of her wet suit and tugged it down, freeing herself from the neoprene's constricting fit. "Let's weigh anchor, Owen. I need to get back to shore quickly."

Owen nodded. "Happy to oblige, Dr. Banyon, especially as the wind's picking up again. More rain on the way," he predicted.

Only then did Lily notice the heavy roll of the *Tangiers* beneath her bare feet. She immediately looked over at Karen, knowing her photographer's intolerance for rough seas.

She was right to be concerned. Karen's face had taken on a sickly gray-green cast. Still in her wet suit, she sat slumped against the side of the pilothouse with her knees drawn up.

"Hold on a sec, Karen, and I'll help you out of your wet suit," Lily offered. "Just let me stow the tanks first. John, give me a hand here. Let's get going, Owen. Karen's sure to feel better once we're moving."

"I'm fine," Karen said just before she vomited.

"Really Karen, there's no need to be embarrassed," Lily said when at last she and John joined her by the rental cars. "You know Owen washes down the deck every day."

Lily and John had been making trips back and forth between the *Tangiers* and the marina parking lot, carting the boxes full of samples, the bags with their gear, as well as Karen's belongings. Karen had sat guard over them, too sick to stand, let alone help. Though her stomach seemed to have quieted, she remained the portrait of despondency, wretched and green.

What else could go wrong this afternoon? Lily wondered tiredly. The reef was sick, Karen was sick, it was about to start raining, and there remained a ton of work to do before she could go find Sean.

"All right, let's figure out how to do this," she said, thinking aloud. "Two things require immediate attention—Karen and the samples. Karen, you need to go back to the apartment and lie down. I'll drop you off and meet John at the lab."

"I can't go back to the condo yet," she protested weakly. "I've got to FedEx my film to Duggal—"

"What, and puke all over the FedEx counter, too?" John interrupted. "They'll really love that." He gave an aggrieved sigh. "You take Karen to the condo, Lily. *I'll* drop the film off at the FedEx. Then we'll deal with the samples."

Karen turned huge, glazed eyes on John. "You'd do that for me, John?"

He shook his head. "Christ, it's not like you need an advanced degree to FedEx a bunch of film. After all, you manage to do it. Write down the address, Masur. I'll get the friggin' film rolls shipped."

"Remember to insure them, too, okay?" Karen said.

Lily passed her the camera bag, which Karen pulled onto her lap. One after the other, she took out her cameras and rewound the film inside them. Opening the backs of the cameras, she removed the rolls of film and inserted them into protective metal canisters. She stood weaving as she placed the silver canisters in John's open hand. "Thanks a million, John."

Lily fished a pen out of her bag, and in block letters wrote the photo lab's New York address as Karen dictated. She handed the slip to John. "John, you're really saving the day here. Thank you. You can meet me at the lab when you're done at the FedEx." She bent over to pick up one of the boxes containing the core samples.

"Why don't I take the samples in my car?" John suggested. "The FedEx won't take long. I can start the labeling as soon as I get to the lab." With a sheepish grin, he added, "I was kind of hoping you could stop at the deli on your way to the lab and pick me up a couple of roast beef sandwiches and a Coke. Seems like we ate those burgers a hell of a long time ago."

Lily gave John a warm smile. "It's a deal. I'll be over as quick as I can."

John got into the rental car with the samples and the film and a smile on his face. He started the motor and eased out of the parking lot just in case Lily and Karen were watching. His hand reached into his sweatshirt pocket to pull out his cell phone.

Ferrucci answered on the second ring. "Yes?"

"Pete, this is—"

"Yeah, I know. Hold on a sec." There was a pause, and John knew he was checking that no one overheard the conversation. Ferrucci came on the line again. "What's up?"

"I've got something to show you in the trunk of my car. Something real valuable. I think we should talk about it. I'm heading toward town now."

"Stop at the Amoco for gas. Then wait for me."

Lily's tires squealed as she turned into a parking space in front of town hall. Thankfully rush hour was waning, so the traffic had been lighter. She'd raced here from the laboratory where she and John had labeled and packed all the core, water, and algal samples into special shipping crates, compelled by her pressing need to see Sean, to make things right between them.

The sky had deepened to a dull, dark gray as she ran up the wide marble steps in front of the town hall. Entering the high-ceilinged hall, she came to an abrupt halt. She had no idea where Sean's office was. Her sneakers squeaked slightly as she walked down the long empty hall, checking nameplates as she passed. Then, at the far end of the hallway, a door opened, and a bright pink head appeared.

Lily smiled in relief.

"Ms. Roemer," she called, her voice raised slightly to catch the secretary's attention.

Evelyn Roemer glanced up from the papers she was reading. Her eyes widened as they took in Lily's grubby field attire, topped by hair dried in short, salty, punklike spikes. "Dr. Banyon! May I help you?"

"Yes, I was looking for Sean."

Evelyn Roemer looked even more surprised. "I'm sorry," she said. "You've just missed him. He left for the airport to catch a flight to Tallahassee. The governor called him this morning. Sean had planned to take the first flight tomorrow, but then he changed his mind." With a puzzled frown, she added, "I'm surprised he didn't mention anything about it when he saw you earlier."

Disappointment rocked Lily. "No, I'm afraid he didn't get a chance." She hadn't given him one.

CHAPTER THIRTY-TWO

Lily rang Simone at dawn the next morning. "Simone? It's me."

"Lily. Hi."

"I didn't wake you up?"

"No," Simone reassured her. "I've even had my morning coffee."

"How are things? How's George?"

"Fine and great. He's in the shower, has to catch the shuttle to New York. There's a fund-raiser this weekend. Want to talk to him?"

"No, that's okay. Tell him best of luck, though."

"Will do. How's everything down in Coral Beach? You finished the dives yet?"

Where to begin? Lily asked herself. So much had happened since her last update—and all of it lousy. "Well, first of all, I finally received Lesnesky's report—if that's what you want to call it. I'm still wading through it. Simone, this guy has the sloppiest methodology I've ever seen. As far as I can tell, he never looked at a single tide chart or consulted any data on the outflow from the Intracostal Waterway."

"Maybe since the reef overall is in such good condition—"

"That's just it," Lily interrupted. "There's a hot spot."

"What?"

Lily began circling the living room as she talked. "Yeah, you heard me right. If I had to give a rough estimate, I'd say over sixty percent of the species in the last transect we looked at are affected. John and I finished labeling and packing all the samples yesterday. Simone, I'm going to need these last transect samples analyzed immediately and the results faxed to me. I've sent you an e-mail with all the transect numbers. A few earlier sites had significantly decreased visibility. Now that I know about the hot spot, I wonder if the problem hasn't begun to spread."

"If the shipment arrives by this afternoon, I can get the results to you by Monday."

Lily calculated quickly. "That'll work. I'm supposed to give my report to the committee next Thursday. If I'm going to be bearing bad news, I better have the data to back me up. Especially since this is the first they'll have heard of the hot spot."

"Karen photographed the area completely?"

"Yes. The rolls of film are on their way to Duggal."

"What's your hypothesis, Lily?"

Lily stopped her pacing to stare through the window at the sea below. "I've got to assume it's a local impact which is affecting the coral. The hot spot's located in the southern extremity of zone one, closest to the inlet," she explained. "This morning I'm going to download water patterns for the area. It's possible the outflow from the Intracoastal Waterway could be drifting right to the spot and dumping a ton of crap."

"Check the tide charts for the area, too," Simone suggested.

"Okay." Lily gnawed absently at the tip of her thumb. Then voicing her frustration, she added, "What really stumps me, Simone, is why Lesnesky didn't notice any earlier signs of the disease."

"Yeah, for an area that large, there should have been some early indicators long before this. Well, the reef samples will give us some answers."

"Answers I'm not sure many people on this reef committee want to hear," Lily said worriedly.

"As long as they don't shoot the messenger delivering the bad news."

Lily gave a weak laugh. "Maybe I'll ask Sean to have them do a security check at the door."

"Sean? Who's Sean?"

Her cheeks grew warm. "Sean McDermott, mayor of Coral Beach, chairman of the reef committee. I've known him all my life."

"This the first good news I've heard yet," Simone said. "You'll need a friend in your corner if this thing gets dicey."

Lily was uncertain if her relationship with Sean could be classified as a "friendship"—but she didn't correct her boss.

"So, there's a *Sean*, " Simone mused. "Is he single?"

Lily rolled her eyes. Simone loved playing matchmaker. "Yes."

"And cute?"

God, no. Sean was gorgeous, mouth-wateringly handsome, but definitely not cute.

Her silence had Simone laughing. "I'll take that as a

'yes.' " Abruptly switching topics, she asked, "How are Karen and John doing?"

"Karen is sleeping off a nasty case of seasickness. Once we got back onboard after the final dive yesterday, she was so sick she could barely stand. But John really came through. He was terrific. Sent off Karen's film for her, and then helped with all the labeling—we had a lot of extra samples because of the hot spot."

"I'm pleased—and relieved—to hear that about John. He hasn't always demonstrated the best work ethic. . . ."

"Yeah, I know what you mean, but he seems to be coming around."

"Great. Let Karen sleep the whole day if she wants. I'm worried about you, too, sweetie. You sound totally stressed. Listen, after you check the tide charts and read over Lesnesky's report, I want the three of you to take a little R-and-R. You've been working really hard, and I won't have any concrete information until Monday. Just forget about the study over the weekend, 'kay? Maybe you and this Sean can go out. . . ."

"I'm worried our plan has backfired horribly, May Ellen. Dana said that Kaye and Lily were eating dinner at Marco's and—"

"I know," May Ellen replied. In her agitation she stirred her ice tea vigorously, making the spoon clink loudly against the glass. "Kaye told me about it, too."

May Ellen Farrady and Anne Prentiss were at their tennis club. Though neither woman played anymore and they both abhorred golf, they needed a place where they could talk without their daughters dropping by unexpectedly.

Anne took a sip of her decaffeinated iced coffee, dabbed her lip with a napkin, and said, "I am so mad at that governor for calling yesterday! What does he need a task force for? And what will we do if Sean doesn't make it back in time for your party? I watched Ryan Jeffries this morning. There's another weather system brewing—"

May Ellen's eyes widened in alarm. "No, Anne," she said, shaking her head. "We just won't go down that road. But you're right. Everything does seem to be falling apart—Lily hasn't been by since she rehung all those pictures for me. Maybe that wasn't such a good idea, Anne . . . and so terribly confusing, too. I hardly know where I am when I walk into a room!"

"You could call her up and tell her she needs to move them all back, that you're feeling very disoriented." Anne suggested, her lips quivering.

"Anne!"

"Just a thought."

"*Humph!*" May Ellen pronounced. "Why don't we have *you* be disoriented?"

Anne smiled sunnily. "No one would believe it."

"Anne," May Ellen said warningly.

"All right, no disorientation for either of us. But we do need to get serious. So has Kaye started to patch things up with Lily?"

"Yes. She seemed very happy after their dinner. Said they had a 'really good talk.' "

"That's lovely. And concrete progress, isn't it, dear? Did you mention to Kaye that you wanted to buy Lily a dress for the party?"

"Yes, but I don't believe Kaye got very far with that one."

Anne thought for a moment, then nodded decisively. "Call Lily, May. And get her to that dress shop!"

*　　*　　*

Beside Lily's laptop a small mountain of data had formed. The pile consisted of every chart and report Lily had been able to get her hands on. She had maps detailing the tide and current patterns around Coral Beach. She had engineering reports for the Intracoastal Waterway, to check if any recent construction might have altered the ICW's outflow. If there had been any recent dredging or building, it was possible that the changes to the flow patterns had allowed harmful pollutants or bacteria to be carried to the southern section of zone one.

Still dissatisfied, Lily had continued with her marine detective work. After downloading the charts and reports, she had packed up her scuba gear and driven over to the marina. Donning her wet suit and tanks, she'd dived amidst the moored boats and flotsam, taking additional water samples, then plunging her test tubes into the murky bottom of the marina. She'd even scraped algae off the submerged piers. Lily had then packed up the samples from the marina and shipped them to the Marine Center. With luck, she'd get the results back within a day or two of the samples she and John had taken from the reef itself.

She was confident that once all the sample analyses were in front of her, it would be a matter of comparing the compositional breakdown of the locations and seeing whether she could find a common culprit.

But now that she'd accomplished all the data gathering, there was really nothing more she could do. Unfortunately, Lily had never been good at "hang time," as John called it.

He, however, had leaped at the chance to take the weekend off.

"That's great. I have this, uh, 'friend' whose friends own a boat. They were talking about cruising down to Miami, spending the weekend there." He scratched his unshaven chin. "I'm pretty sure they said they're leaving this morning."

With a smile, Lily said, "Go now if you want, John. Of the three of us, you definitely deserve time off, especially after yesterday's marathon session. Have fun."

"Oh, yeah, I will. This one-horse town is getting lame."

Karen, who was still sleeping off the effects of her sea-sickness, made an appearance a short while later.

When she wandered into the living room, Lily was once again at her computer, mapping the southern transects' coral species. Closing the program, Lily told Karen about her telephone conversation with Simone and John's decision to cruise down to Miami.

"Sounds like fun," Karen said with a sleepy smile. "I think I'll hang here, though. Dave mentioned that he wanted to do something this weekend. It's too bad John's gone. He might have joined us. He's really okay once you give him a chance. So what are you going to do, Lily?"

Think about Sean and how much I miss him, her inner voice replied. She didn't even know when he was due to return from Tallahassee. She'd been so disappointed by the news that he'd left that she'd forgotten to ask Evelyn Roemer. Would he call her when he did return?

Other than moon over Sean's absence, Lily had no definite plans. Perhaps that was why she couldn't manu-facture a decent excuse when her grandmother phoned a few minutes later, to remind Lily that Kaye wanted to take her shopping for a dress for the party.

"Granny, that's really nice of you, but I have plenty of clothes already—"

"Lily, this party is my chance to show you off to my friends, and I want to treat you to something. Please say yes, and make an old woman happy."

"I . . ." Lily sighed. "Yes, I'm free today."

"Good. Kaye has such lovely taste, she'll find just the thing. By the way, Lily, I noticed your hair was looking a little dry and lifeless. No point dressing up if your hair's a disaster. I'm going to make you an appointment at the spa."

"Granny May, I don't need to go to a spa!"

Her grandmother must have missed Lily's reply, for she said, "Oh, wait, I have an idea! I'll make the appointment for two, and you and your friend, the photographer, can go together. My treat. Dear me, someone's at the door. Bye, Lily."

Lily stood, staring at the receiver in bemusement.

"Who was that, Lily?" Karen asked.

"My grandmother. Hey, Karen, have you ever been to a day spa?"

Lily was reading an article on endangered sea grasses when her mother arrived.

"Hi, Karen. Hi, Lily."

"Hello, M . . . Kaye," Lily managed to remember.

"*Definitely* Kaye." Her mother nodded encouragingly. "We're going to have fun this afternoon." Kaye turned and smiled at Karen. "My mother made the appointment at the spa for three P.M., Karen. It's on the corner of Palmetto and Locust. Why don't you meet Lily there?"

"Sure thing, Mrs. Alcott. Have a great time with Lily."

"Thank you, Karen. I'm so excited," Kaye confided to

Lily as she hustled her out the door. "Fiona's just going to flip when she sees you."

Fiona Gray was so elegant, she made Kaye look like a dowdy frump. Dressed in a navy serge tailored suit, she moved with the sensual confidence of a 1940s matinee idol. Right now, Fiona was circling Lily. Slowly. A three hundred and sixty degree, X-ray-eyed inspection of every physical imperfection Lily possessed. Acutely self-conscious, Lily tucked in her stomach and tried not to fidget. *How,* she asked herself, *had she gotten bulldozed into this shopping expedition?*

The inspection was performed in total silence. Fiona had hung a closed sign in the window the second Lily and Kaye walked in, barring other customers from entering. At last Fiona came to a stop next to Kaye. Arms crossed, her slender finger tapped meditatively as she continued to evaluate Lily.

Just as Lily's eyes were beginning to cross—it was only a dress, for Pete's sake—Fiona nodded as though arriving at a decision. Lily breathed a sigh of relief. *It was almost over,* she thought.

"Thank you, Kaye. At last I have a real woman to work with," she said. "You mentioned a party?"

"Yes. Mother is celebrating Lily's return home. Everyone's attention will be focused on her."

"Gee, now I'm really looking forward to Saturday night, Kaye," Lily muttered, unnerved by Kaye's prediction.

"Oh, you will, Lily . . . once you see the dress I have in mind for you," Fiona said, smiling confidently. "Why don't you go into the dressing room and remove your clothes. The brassiere, too."

*   *   *

"My God, Karen, is that you?" Lily gaped three hours later.

Karen raised a hand to her head. The braids and beads she'd been wearing for the past two months had disappeared, to be replaced by shoulder-length, light brown hair, which fell in soft waves about her face.

"Do you like it?" she asked uncertainly. "My head feels so weird. And silent! But the stylist freaked when she heard how long my braids had been in. Said my hair would become royally damaged if I didn't take them out. Then she forced me to sit with this really goopy conditioner on my head."

"Well, whatever they used, it looks fantastic. To tell you the truth, I'd forgotten what your hair looks like. It's lovely."

There were mirrors aplenty in the salon to verify this. Karen tugged the belt around her black polyester smock tighter, then walked up to the nearest mirror and stared. The stylist had let Karen's hair hang naturally, without twisting it into any kind of sophisticated hairdo. Like threads of gold, the sun-kissed streaks in her hair glimmered in the light.

Karen inspected herself critically, a pleased smile growing on her face. "Yeah, I think I'll keep it this way— the braids were getting kind of itchy," she admitted. Her eyes met Lily's. "You got a nice cut, too, Lily."

"Thanks. It's not quite as dramatic a transformation as yours, but they put some of that goop on my head, too. I may have hated it, but my hair thinks differently."

"They do any other weird stuff to you? The woman who gave me a pedicure went at my feet with a boulder."

"Yeah." Lily nodded. The movement made the ends of her newly cut hair brush featherlike against her cheekbones. "They plastered my face with seaweed," she said with a laugh. "I didn't know how to tell them that I'm up close and personal with seaweed three hundred and sixty-five days of the year. Then they rubbed my body with salt—at least, that's what I think it was. Again, I didn't have the heart to tell them I get plenty of sea salt, too." She shrugged, grimacing as she did so. "I think some of my hair must have gotten under this smock because it's all prickly. I'm starving, too. Though I'm probably going to have to *eat* seaweed from now until the party if I want to wear the dress my mother and Fiona Gray picked out for me. What do you say we change and get out of here?"

"Definitely." Karen allowed herself one last happy glance at the mirror before turning away. "But Lily?"

"Yeah?"

"I had a blast. Thanks."

Lily grinned back at Karen. "We can both thank Granny May. This was her brainchild."

Later that evening, Lily went to swim practice. The combined effect of her shopping expedition with Kaye at Fiona Gray's boutique and her so called makeover at the day spa had made Lily extremely aware of her body. And thanks to Kaye and Fiona's choice of evening dress, everyone at Granny May's party was going to be, too. She hoped she didn't give her grandmother a heart attack when she walked through her front door.

Swimming a few miles might make all those bulges she was sure she'd seen in the dressing room mirror disappear miraculously.

But Lily had another reason, far more important, to go to the swim practice. Sean might be there.

Her spirits plummeted when Sean wasn't anywhere on the pool deck, but they recovered somewhat when Hal gave her one of his rib-breaking hugs of welcome.

"Lily." Hal grinned. "I hoped you'd come. So Sean passed along my message?"

Her heart thudded heavily at the mere mention of Sean's name. "Sean? No, I haven't seen him."

Hal scowled darkly. "Guess I'll have to beat him up again."

"You beat Sean up?" she asked.

"Broke him down might be a better way to describe it. Came by yesterday afternoon in a really bad mood, cruising for a fight."

Lily swallowed. That must have been just after he'd seen her at Norma Jean's. "Anyway," Hal continued, "I gave him a workout he won't forget. He was one hurtin' puppy by the time he left."

"I didn't know you had this sadistic streak in you, Hal."

"Sean didn't, either," he chuckled. "Good thing he thrives on challenges. That's why he likes us so damn much—"

"I'm not sure he likes me very much at the moment," she said with a sad smile.

"Sean likes you fine," Hal said firmly. "You're one of the few people strong enough to stand up to him. And keep on doing it, Lily—it's what he needs. Go hop in the lane with Dave. He's a nice guy, just don't let him talk you out of swimming hard."

"Dr. Lily Banyon, welcome to lane eight!" Dave said, as she dropped her fins and pull buoy beside him. "I was getting lonely with Sean gone."

Me, too. "Hi, Dave. When's he due back?" She tried to keep her voice casual.

"Saturday . . . I think that's what he said."

Lily pinned a smile to her face. "Then it's just you and me. By the way, I should warn you, Hal suspects you're not putting your 'all' into his workouts."

"He's right. If I did, I wouldn't have strength left to lift a beer bottle to my lips, which is the only reason to swim."

"To lift beer bottles?"

"No, to drink what's *inside* them. And tonight's not the night to start taking Storey's workouts too seriously. I'm picking Karen up after practice. We're going to the Rusted Keel. Want to join us? There'll be others from the team."

"Thanks, I'd like that. And since you've been kind enough to invite me to tag along, would you like to come to my grandmother's seventieth birthday?" She struggled not to laugh at the appalled look on Dave's face. "In addition to a house full of silver-haired grandparents, Karen might come—she's still undecided."

"I love old folks, but let me swim on this. Whoops, here comes Hal." Dave's voice dropped to a conspiratorial whisper. "Buy you a beer, Dr. Banyon, if you slack off a wee bit on the workout."

"Sorry, Dave. I have to fit into my party dress."

The phone was ringing as she opened the apartment door, Karen a step behind. Quickly walking over to it, she picked it up. "Hello?"

"Don't hang up."

The sound of Sean's voice triggered an explosion of

happiness within her. Lily spun around from the knowing grin on Karen's face, who was mouthing, "I told you so!"

"Lily, are you there?"

"Yes," she answered breathlessly. Her hand clenched the phone, pressing it closer to her ear, wanting him close. "Yes, I'm here. Sean, I'm sorry—I didn't mean any of the things I said—"

"Ahh, Lily, I'm the one who's sorry. I really screwed up the other night." His voice deepened. "I haven't stopped thinking about you once. I just sat through twelve hours of meetings, and I can't remember a single word that was said. I'm in serious trouble here, Lily," the admission a husky caress.

Lily shut her eyes, giddy with happiness. "Me, too," she said softly. "I miss you."

"Hot damn," he whispered in an awed voice.

Laughter tumbled from her lips. "Were you this eloquent at the meetings, Mr. Mayor?"

"Not nearly. So, can I see you tomorrow?"

"Before or after Granny May's party?"

"Christ, I'd forgotten all about that. I was hoping for a more private reunion. How about before, during, and after? I'll pick you up. Think of me until then. Sweet dreams, Lily."

CHAPTER THIRTY-THREE

"Bye, Karen, have a good time tonight. Say hi to Dave for me," Lily called, loud enough to be heard through the closed door.

Karen's door opened a crack and her nose peeked through. "Wait!" she said, sticking her wet head out further. "Let me see. Ooh, Lily, that's pure dynamite. I almost wish Dave and I were going."

Lily gave a nervous laugh. "No, believe me, a double feature of *The Invasion of the Body Snatchers* and *It Came from Outer Space* will be a lot more entertaining."

"It *will* be cool." Karen nodded enthusiastically. "It's so great the community college is running this series. These old films hardly ever get shown on big screens anymore."

"Well, enjoy yourself. Uh, I'm not sure when I'll get back."

Karen's eyes twinkled. "Me neither. Dave said there's this blues bar . . ."

"And who knows where that will lead?"

It was Karen's turn to blush. "Dave's nice."

"Yes. I agree. And you've got him wrapped around your finger." Lily smiled, recalling the dazed expression

on Dave's face last night when he got his first glimpse
of Karen's new look. She didn't think Dave would be
watching much of the double feature, as he couldn't
seem to keep his eyes off Karen. "Have fun tonight."

"You, too, Lily, though I'd say in that dress it's guaranteed. Sean won't know what hit him."

"I think that was Kaye's and Fiona's intention. I only
hope I can pull it off."

"I wouldn't worry on that account."

May Ellen's party was to begin with cocktails at six P.M.,
followed by a dinner, which was being catered and served
by the staff from Marco's. Ordinarily, Lily would be
drooling with anticipation at the thought of sampling
Marco's delicious creations again. In the dress she was
wearing tonight, however, she doubted she would dare
accept so much as a carrot stick.

She pulled her dark gray raincoat from her closet, but-
toned it, then knotted the belt firmly about her waist.
The leering doormen loitering in the lobby weren't going
to get a single peep. She glanced around, certain she was
forgetting something, shaking her head when she saw the
beaded black clutch. *The things a woman has to keep
track of,* she thought. Drawing a deep breath to steady
her nerves, she glanced at the clock for the thousandth
time. There were five minutes left before Sean said he'd
pick her up. But she was too nervous to wait in the apartment. She'd go downstairs, she decided. Pulling the front
door open, she gave a soft gasp of surprise.

Sinfully handsome in an impeccably tailored black
tux, Sean stood in her doorway. "Hello, Lily." He raised
his hand and held out a single white rose.

Fingers trembling, they brushed his as she accepted his offering. Throat too constricted with emotion to do more than whisper her thanks, she brought the rose to her face and inhaled its delicate perfume.

Sean stared at the woman who haunted him night and day, mesmerized by her loveliness. During his trip, he'd thought of her constantly, drawing on the myriad memories he possessed. Tonight she seemed different somehow. Something about her subtly altered, which made her features even more alluring.

His eyes swept over that face he knew, yet didn't, only slowly realizing what had changed.

Lily was wearing makeup.

Not heavy, dulling layers of the stuff, just a touch to accentuate her natural beauty—black mascara framed the dazzling clarity of her eyes, a sweep of shimmery blush accentuated her high, slanting cheekbones, a lick of gloss applied to her lips made her mouth temptingly moist.

When Lily's eyes lifted slowly, meeting his, Sean saw what was the greatest transformation of all. Her eyes no longer held that touch of cool reserve. Tonight they glowed with a warm joy. His heart pounded in his chest.

"You look exquisite," he said quietly. "I don't dare kiss you, as I frankly don't think I could stop. But after this party, Lily . . ." He let the sentence trail off.

And Lily understood that its ending was hers to finish. "Yes," she replied, her voice equally quiet. "Yes, after the party." A sudden fit of nerves assailed her. She reached for the belt of her raincoat and gave it another firm tug.

Sean noticed the raincoat for the first time. He shook

his head. "Your grandmother's in luck. The weather's held; it's a beautiful evening." He gestured to the functional overcoat, totally incongruous with the black evening gown that showed beneath its hem. "You don't really need to wear that—"

Lily's soft laugh answered him and a secret smile played over her lips. "Oh, yes, I do."

Sean didn't fully comprehend the significance of Lily's enigmatic smile or her cryptic comment until they stood in May Ellen's entry hall.

"Let me take your coat," he offered, moving behind her, his fingers ready to pluck it from her shoulders.

Slowly Lily unknotted the belt and dealt with the buttons. Sean saw her shoulders lift as she took a long, indrawn breath. *No doubt she was steeling herself for a party dominated by nosy seventy-year-olds,* he thought.

Then Lily stepped out of the coat.

And he stood transfixed. His breath caught, trapped in his throat.

Lily in a black evening dress. A black dress—that should have been something he could handle. But this one, it was black and sparkled as though sewn with a thousand diamonds. Black, sparkling, it was also sheer, a tantalizing veil. Nearly transparent, the evening dress clung to Lily's elegant, womanly body like the caress of a loving hand. Her back to him, Sean's eyes traced curves molded by shimmering darkness.

When she turned, his breath escaped in a low hiss— eyes seeing what his besieged brain had failed to grasp.

The dress hung from Lily's shoulders by the slenderest of straps. That the dress was diabolically designed, sewn with an extra layer of sheer fabric, cleverly concealing the lush outline of her breasts, didn't stop the truth from exploding in his mind, nearly destroying him.

Lily was braless, braless in that sinful gown, and he knew that all evening long that thought would pound in his fevered mind.

Lily saw Sean's stunned expression and how his eyes flared, burning bright. She saw his struggle to control his rampant desire and the monumental effort that exacted. What she saw made her heart skip and then race madly, and she offered silent thanks to Kaye and to her grandmother. The dress was a wondrous gift, one that gave Lily the courage to conquer and claim her love.

"Lily, my dear, don't you look spectacular!"

Lily smiled and kissed her grandmother's cheek. "Thank you, Granny May, I wasn't quite sure until a moment ago," she said, glancing sideways at Sean.

"Really? Let me take a look." May Ellen, regal in a long-sleeved, lavender gown and a rope of cultured pearls wrapped about her neck, stepped back and inspected her granddaughter from head to toe. "Why ever not? Kaye was right. It's perfect for you. She has impeccable taste. She would never choose anything remotely unbecoming. And what do you think, Sean?"

Sean's jaw tightened. The dress was bewitching. A perfect foil for Lily's incomparable beauty. "I'd say Kaye knew exactly what she was doing."

"Just so." May Ellen nodded approvingly. "Not every woman could wear this. Such a lovely figure you have, my dear. Come, let me show you off."

"Wait, Granny May." Lily opened her clutch and withdrew a slender, square box. "Happy early birthday," she said, and pressed her lips to May Ellen's soft, lined cheek.

"Lily! You shouldn't have! May I open it?" May Ellen's hands were already tugging at the simple ratafia bow.

"I hope you like it. I found it in the Seychelles."

"Oh! It's lovely!" May Ellen carefully lifted the sea horse into the palm of her hand. It was perfectly preserved, from the elongated, square snout, to the fanned ridges of its dorsal, to the tip of its delicately swirled tail. "Thank you, Lily. Besides your being here tonight, this is the nicest present I could imagine, because it will always remind me of you." Linking her arm through Lily's, she said, "Come along, Sean, and help me introduce Lily. She may not remember everyone."

Lily was soon separated from Sean, brought into the fold of this group or that. But she never lost the sensation of Sean's eyes watching her with a feral intensity. At dinner, she and Sean were placed next to each other and the tension that sizzled between them became almost unbearable. Though Lily gave every appearance of following the animated conversation around their table, every cell of her being was tuned to the dark, thrilling danger emanating from him.

By midmeal she was dying to leave. Dessert and champagne passed in a haze of toasts, clapping, and smiles, none of which registered. Then her grandmother stood up from her place. And suddenly, as endless as the dinner party had seemed, it was over. Lily glanced across the room where Kaye was seated. Kaye's smile was knowing as she nodded, and then gave Lily a quick wink.

The message was clear: Lily was free. Kaye would say the necessary politeness when she disappeared.

She rose wordlessly, knowing Sean would follow.

*   *   *

She breathed in the night air, hoping it would clear his head, cool the blood that sizzled as it coursed through him. He walked with his eyes trained on the sensual sway of her hips encased in moon glittery black. His fingers dragged at the bow tie of his tux, loosened it, and pulled it off. Shirt studs and cufflinks dropped onto grass, onto sand, as Lily led him down to the beach. His jacket landed at the foot of a palm tree.

He watched as she bent down to remove her high-heeled sandals. For a moment she was caught in a moon-beam of silvery white, a nymph of pagan beauty.

"Hi," she said softly as she straightened.

"Hello." Sean thrust his hands deep into his trouser pockets. They were balled in tight fists to prevent him reaching out and pulling her into his arms. As fiercely aroused as he was, his mood was mercurial. Some primal part of his being resented her ability to bring him to this flashpoint of need so effortlessly.

"That was kind of fun tonight, don't you think?" Though her voice was low, it carried over the sounds of the gentle surf.

He shrugged, his shoulders shifting beneath his tuxedo shirt.

Lily appeared not to notice his obstinate silence. Letting her sandals drop to the sand, she spoke again, her voice musing. "It's so beautiful here at night. I'd forgotten how quiet it is. Just the sea and the palm trees stirring. I guess when we were kids we were too loud to notice the quiet."

She had strayed to the edge of the water, her pale hair a silvered halo about her face. Sean stared, unable to look away, his heart hammering inside his chest. Her lips shimmered faintly as they parted in a smile. "I love the water on nights like this." As though proving her words, she raised the hem of her dress, exposing the delicate points of bone and sinew of her ankles, and stepped into the gently lapping water.

He swallowed. "What are you doing?"

"Testing the water. It's cool. Delicious. Like that champagne we were drinking earlier."

"And how much have you drunk?"

She laughed, a musical note that teased lightly. Balancing on one leg, she raised the other until only the toe of her arched foot trailed through the surf. "Sean, you know exactly how much I've drunk. You've watched me all night, watched me swallow, seen the way I forced each sip past my throat. Little tiny sips, droplets really, because everything inside me is wound tight from wanting you."

She stepped back onto the sand and approached him unhurriedly. Her eyes were fixed on his face as she drew near, loving how the moon cast his handsome features in savage relief. Loving him. "You've watched me as I watched you." She stopped a short distance from him. Her hands grasped the fabric of her dress and began gathering it, slowly lifting it higher and higher. "The water's perfect, Sean. Perfect for a night swim. Come in with me. Come and swim in the night."

Lily's invitation had Sean tearing off his shirt. For a second, it floated, parachute-like, before drifting to the sand. In the moonlight, his chest, with its smooth, sculpted planes, heaved with each labored breath. With the same rough speed, his hands moved to the fastening of his trousers, but then Sean stilled.

"Undress for me, Lily," he commanded softly. "Show me what I've dreamed of."

She smiled, the simple curve of her lips conveying everything she felt for him. Her dress rose.

Scan dropped to his knees before her.

They came together in the sea. Fierce and elemental, wrapped in each other's arms, he moved, surged inside her in counterpoint to the waves breaking against them, to the water sweeping around them. A gentle, generous plundering, he took everything she gave him. Offering all he had in return. She melted, pouring herself over him, and her cry of joy pierced the night sky. Thrusting deep into her core, he took her with him. As one, they plunged to a fathomless love.

Her limbs still trembling, her body replete, he carried her in his arms, up the silent, deserted beach to the shelter of the palms, where he eased her down upon the soft sand. Lily lay, languorous from his passion, gleaming from the sea. Sean knelt, his arms braced over her, drinking in the sight of her, with a thirst that was unquenchable. Lowering his mouth to her, he tasted ocean warmed by silken flesh. His lips traveled, catching drops of salt, savoring the sweet tang of desire. Dipping his tongue into the shallow indentation of her navel, he pressed a smile against her quivering flesh, at the throaty moan of pleasure he'd wrung from her, and continued his erotic journey.

She felt like liquid, flowing wherever he touched. And Sean touched her everywhere as he loved her with his mouth, as he worshipped her with his hands. When the wet warmth of his tongue probed her core, sampling her essence, she came in a flowing rush of ecstasy, her back arching as the pleasure went on and on, as she wept his name to the stars.

Smooth and fluid he moved over her, his mouth seeking hers. Entwined, their bodies pressed against each other, the contact triggering their desperate wanting anew.

Lily's hands slid greedily over taut muscle and burning flesh, guiding him to her own slick heat. His gaze, bright with emotion, locked with hers. In one strong thrust, Sean entered her, sheathing himself, filling her, completing them both.

She rested with her back nestled against Sean's naked torso. Cradled between his muscular thighs, with his arms wrapped about her, the incredible heat from Sean's body kept her warm, warding off the chill of the witching hour. His slow, even breath fanned the shell of her ear, a lazy tickle that had her smiling softly, snuggling deeper in the cocoon of his embrace. Never had she felt this secure, this satiated, this . . . loved. She gave a soft murmur of happiness.

"Hmm, what?" His voice was as lazy as his hands, which were stroking her with slow, drugging caresses. When he traced circles over her breasts, she arched against him, her eyes drifting shut at the sensation.

She gave a moan of pleasure before saying, "I was thinking of a night on the beach long ago, the first time I realized I wanted to be held like this in your arms."

"What night was this?" he asked, pressing his mouth to the hollow behind her ear. Lily shivered, feeling the moist heat travel all the way down to the base of her spine.

"It was years ago, eleventh grade," she told him. "There was a beach party. I was sitting across the fire from you. For the first time, I looked at you and really saw you. It hit me like a bolt of lightning, how much I wanted you. . . ." She paused. Then shook her head lightly. "No," she said, correcting herself. "*Longed* for you is a better way to describe what I felt at seventeen."

"I'm not sure I remember—"

"You went off with Stacy Malloy into the trees and the next day I broke your nose. I'm sorry, Sean," she whispered. "I didn't mean to, I was so jealous of her. I hate that I hurt you."

His arms tightened, rocking her. "Shh," he said, laying a kiss against her temple. "If I was stupid enough to go off with Stacy Malloy, I *deserved* to have my nose broken. Just for the record, Lily, there's never been anything between Stacy and me—except whatever awkward fumblings occurred that night." His hands drifted upward to trace the delicate wings of her collarbone. "And I always thought you despised me," he said, his tone marveling.

"I mostly did," she admitted ruefully. And her laughter mingled with his. "You were so perfect, Sean. You had everything—looks, friends, a wonderful family— everything. I envied you those things, that it all came so easily to you."

"Not everything," he contradicted her. "For instance, I had three years of 'longing' for you, starting way back in eighth grade. I'd say by eleventh grade, I was pretty much in a state of physical agony whenever you came near. *You* were what I wanted most."

"No! That's impossible," Lily said with patent disbelief.

" 'Fraid so." His arms hugged her close. "And if I'd

had a volleyball handy, I'd have torpedoed it straight at your boyfriend's head in Rome."

Lily straightened slightly. "Boyfriend?" she echoed in confusion. "What boyfriend? What are you talking about?"

"The guy you were with when I came to pick you up at the *pensione*," Sean explained. "He came up behind you and stood smirking at me, 'cause he, the lucky bastard, was with you—"

"Oh, my God!" she cried, feeling both appalled and saddened. "Sean, that wasn't *my* boyfriend! He was a guy who'd hooked up with Petra, my college roommate."

Sean turned Lily around by her shoulders so that she faced him. His eyes searched her expression. "You're kidding me," he said, then cursed as she shook her head silently. "What a bloody fool I was."

"No more than I," Lily reminded him softly. "I was convinced Kaye had forced you to come. I was so mortified, I wouldn't let you into the room."

"Ahh, Lily," Sean said. His voice was filled with regret. His fingers stroked her, gently caressing. Then he spoke again. "Maybe it was meant to be, that you and I were at cross-purposes all those years. You see, Lily, I've dreamed of you, dreamed of holding you in my arms just like this. And the reality turns my wildest dreams to the palest of shadows. So perhaps it's for the best that we had to wait until now. If we'd gotten together too soon, I might not have understood—let alone appreciated— what I know now." When Sean paused, Lily turned her head to gaze at him, and her heart swelled at the tenderness of his smile. "I wouldn't have known," he said, "that I will never love another woman the way I love you, Lily." His mouth found hers in a melting kiss. "Let me take you home," he whispered. "Let me make you mine."

CHAPTER THIRTY-FOUR

Sean scooped Lily out of his convertible before she had a chance to walk, then he refused to set her down, laughingly insisting they'd go much faster this way; the swing of her hips when she moved was too damned distracting.

With her head resting against his broad shoulder, she asked, "Are you rushing because you're afraid you'll drop me, McDermott?"

"What are you talking about?" He hefted her in his arms as he unlocked the door to his bungalow. "You're nothing but a puny girl."

"I am not puny!" she retorted, grabbing a lock of his hair and yanking hard.

"Ow! Okay, you're right." With a grunt, Sean kicked the door shut behind him. "Thank God we're nearly there. My arms are giving out." Then suddenly, he loosened his grip, laughing when she squealed and clutched his neck.

Sean's bedroom was dominated by a king-size bed. Directly above it, a wide-blade ceiling fan rotated slowly. He'd left the lamp on the bedside table burning and its light cast a honeyed glow over the room. Lily had assumed Sean would stop here, perhaps toss her onto the gigantic bed in retaliation for her teasing.

He didn't. He continued on, carrying her into the adjoining bathroom. Only then did he slowly let her down, gently setting her on her feet as if she were a priceless work of art.

She stared about at the marbled splendor of his bathroom. "Wow."

"Amazing, huh? The guy I bought this place from had a serious bathroom fetish. There's another, smaller version by the second bedroom."

"It's, uh, very impressive," Lily said.

"Let me get you out of this dress and I'll show you impressive." With a wicked grin he slipped his fingers beneath the thin shoulder straps of her gown. He seemed to derive special delight in peeling the dress slowly down her body, in blowing teasing breezes at the specks of golden sand, which clung to her alabaster skin. His skilled hands tormented, touching, tracing her breasts lightly until she shivered, her nipples tight and aching. "Sean," she whispered, arching toward him in supplication.

"No, Lily, you've got to hold still. This is a most delicate of operations, this first stage of sand removal. I don't want a single grain to abrade your skin."

At last, Lily stood before him, with only the tiniest scrap of black silk covering her hips. Reverentially Sean removed this last remaining barrier.

He rocked back on his heels, his eyes drinking in the beauty of Lily's body.

She was pale and downy soft.

His hand trembled as he reached out to brush the nest of light gold curls. He looked up, meeting her gaze with a somber expression. "I'm undone. You terrify me, Lily.

That you can be this exquisite, all dazzling beauty and a brilliant brain—"

"A brain," she interrupted in a shaky voice, "which will be fried if you don't undress and make love to me *right now*. I mean it, McDermott. Consider this your duty—in the interest of science."

He sighed, rising to his full height. "No doubt, just one among many sacrifices I'm destined to make, in the interest of science, in the interest of mankind," Sean said, his shirt already hitting the tile by their feet. "Turn on the water, Dr. Banyon."

Much later in the night, Lily woke briefly to the sound of rain beating against glass. Sean lay facing her, his leg and arm draped over her possessively, holding her captive. She didn't want to go anywhere. She cuddled closer to his solid warmth, and placed a palm over the steady thudding of his heart. With a soft, dreamy smile, she listened to him breathe and drifted back to sleep.

"Good morning, Doctor, how's the brain?"

Lily opened her eyes and blinked. Sean looked wonderful, dressed in just a pair of jeans and a lazy masculine smile. Lord, what would it be like to be treated to a smile like that every morning?

She stretched, saw how his eyes zeroed in on the vee of her legs, and felt a secret thrill of womanly satisfaction. "The brain's fine. No permanent damage," she murmured, her voice husky with sleep and awakening desire.

"That's a relief." Sean sat down on the bed, his blue-jeaned hip next to her waist. The weight of his body had her rolling toward him. He leaned over so his mouth could nuzzle the hollow of her throat.

"*Mmm,*" she purred. "What's that I smell? It's divine."

"Me, perhaps?"

She shook her head against the pillow. "No, better." And had to bite her lip when he glowered at her.

With an exaggerated sigh, he said, "It must be my coffee then. I made you breakfast. I figure, maybe if I feed you, you'll realize what a wonderful guy I am."

Dear Lord, she was only too aware just how wonderful Sean was. Looping her arms about his neck she drew his face down to her. "I think I might have figured that out." She paused and frowned with sudden confusion. "But the reasons why are a little hazy now."

He dropped a kiss on her nose and grinned. "Then I guess it's time for a refresher course."

He shifted, settling himself over her, and the feel of his erection prodding the juncture of her thighs had Lily's toes curling in anticipation. Her legs slid against the sheets, opening for him. He didn't need to be prompted twice. His hips dropped in an erotic grind of denim against flesh. It was like a spark that touched off a wildfire. Lily was consumed by desire.

In silent demand, she pushed against his naked shoulders. Ever obliging, Sean rolled onto his back. She followed and straddled his hips, and her body tightened with anticipation.

He looked at her, naked and open above him, and growled low in his throat. His hips jerked instinctively, seeking her damp heat.

Lily's gaze held his. She smiled, shaking her head slowly in teasing denial. Then, lowering herself over him so her nipples grazed his chest, her smile grew wicked at the sound of Sean's breath whistling through clenched teeth. Mouth open, Lily began pressing wet, lingering kisses along the fine arrow of dark brown hair that led to the waistband of his jeans. The kisses continued as her fingers went to work, tugging at the metal buttons. Sean's harsh groans filled the air. Lily pulled the denim wide, and Sean's cock sprang free. Momentarily tearing her eyes from the awesome sight, Lily gazed into the scorching heat in Sean's eyes. Knowing just what would drive him wild, and feeling an answering wildness deep inside, she licked her lips. "Behold a very eager student."

Lily stirred languidly beneath the lazy petting of Sean's hands. As her head shifted against the pillows, she cast a glance at the rain-spattered window. The dark, overcast day made it impossible to judge the hour. "What time is it?" she wondered, hardly aware she'd spoken aloud.

Sean lifted his arm from her waist and checked his watch. "Twelve."

"Oh, my God!" She made to swing her legs out of bed, but Sean's arm snaked about her waist, holding her back.

"Whoa, there." Laughter threaded his voice. "What's the rush?"

"Karen! She'll be worried—"

"Ever heard of a telephone, Banyon?" he asked, as his other hand reached up to stroke her naked shoulder. "I called the apartment earlier. Told Karen you were with me. Didn't seem terribly surprised or concerned. She said hi, by the way."

"Oh," she muttered, and sank back onto the pillows.

Sean leaned over and kissed the slight furrow on her brow. She had an adorably disgruntled look on her face. For some reason, that filled Sean with a ridiculous, irrational happiness. Lord, he loved her madly. She was grumpy and he was charmed.

"Relax, Lily," he said, his mouth quirked in a smile. "It's a perfect day."

"It's pouring outside, Sean."

"Yup. Nothing but rain in the forecast—the paper even said a big storm may be heading our way."

"And that's perfect?"

"Damn straight. It's Sunday, there's food in the fridge. The newspaper's in the kitchen. I've got you, you've got me. . . . Who could ask for anything more?"

Her stomach had begun rumbling at the mention of food. "How about breakfast in bed?"

"Sure thing, Dr. Banyon." He leaned over and captured her lips in a long, honeyed kiss. His voice had a now-familiar huskiness when he spoke again. "Then, if you're extra nice to me, I'll make love to you until you never want to leave."

He was too late, Lily thought, as she watched him roll out of bed and pull on his jeans. The very idea of being apart from Sean wrenched her heart. But as she lay in the bed, she found herself staring pensively out the window, unable to shake the feeling that the world outside threatened all she held dear.

The empty breakfast tray was on the floor. Newspaper sections lay scattered across the floor. Once again, Lily was floating in a state of lazy contentment, her previous worries banished by the magic of Sean's lovemaking. Her eyes were closed, the better to feel Sean's hands moving over her body.

It felt almost decadent, this surfeit of happiness. She loved how he touched her, how he knew precisely where to touch her, so that she cried and flew apart in a thousand tiny pieces. She loved how he knew to hold her gently, making her whole once more.

Lily felt Sean shift beside her. Her heavy lids lifted to find him propped on an elbow, his hazel eyes lit with a warmly possessive gleam.

"So our study's finished?" she heard him ask. They'd been having a conversation of sorts; stray comments interrupted by tantalizing caresses and soft, whispered moans.

"Study?" she said blankly. Her mind conjuring only the fascinating discoveries Sean had made studying her body, learning all her erogenous zones. *Please don't let him stop.*

"Study," he repeated. Amusement thread his voice. "As in reef. You remember the reef, Lily. . . ."

She sat up with a gasp.

Sean laughed softly, his grin wide. "You should see your face. You've got this look like you've come to school having forgotten your homework."

She dropped her head into her hands. "I was distracted."

"Ahh, Dr. Banyon, you are incredibly good for my ego. A few more compliments like that . . ."

Her head lifted and she shot him an exasperated look. "Can it, Sean. This is really serious. I can't believe I forgot. That last reef dive we made? There's a hot spot."

"What?" Sean said, his jaw slack with astonishment.

"The southernmost section of zone one has a hot spot," she clarified. "A hot spot is—"

"Yes. I know what a hot spot is. I've read your book and your articles, too. A hot spot is a localized area in a reef which has succumbed to some kind of disease, right?" When Lily nodded, he asked, "But what's it doing there?"

"I don't know. I should get the results from the center's lab tomorrow. I've already started collecting data on current and tide charts for the area. And I took some additional samples at the marina. Once I get the breakdown of all the samples, I should have a better idea of what could be attacking the coral."

Sean was silent, his brow knitted in thought. "So how bad's the problem?" he asked. "Is this hot spot very big?"

She nodded glumly. "Big enough to be alarmed. I noted an unusual amount of coral bleaching. Both the hard and soft coral in the area are affected. And there were a number of dead sponges, too."

"From the types of diseases you saw down there, can you guess what the cause is?"

"No." Lily shook her head. "I can't, not at this point. It could be anything—heavy metals, fertilizers, fecal matter, petroleum by-products, even paint scrapings from the hulls of boats—the possibilities are just too numerous."

"But whatever it is, it must be pretty lethal, though, to affect the area so quickly. Do diseases typically spread so rapidly?"

"Well, sometimes there are flukes, random outbreaks that are like an epidemic. . . ."

"But you don't think that's what is happening here?"

"No, I don't." Lily's somber tone matched his. "Which means there's another problem." She fell silent for a moment, absently tracing her finger along the seam of the bed sheet. "Sean, I've been going through Lesnesky's notes. In the three studies he made of the reef system, there isn't a single reading or observation that points to a problem."

"And you couldn't have missed something? No, forget that, stupid question." He leaned back against the pillows, lost in thought. "So basically," he said slowly, "what this means is that your study is going to contradict Lesnesky's in a major way."

"Yes," she agreed quietly. "That sums it up very neatly. But I'll have a body of evidence to support my findings—a full analysis of the water and sediment compositions, as well as Karen's slides showing the diseased specimens."

He took her hand in his and kissed her knuckles lightly. "I believe you, Lily," he said. "And if Ferrucci starts screaming town hall down, we can shove a regulator in his mouth and take him on an underwater tour of the hot spot. Better yet, let's forget the regulator."

CHAPTER THIRTY-FIVE

Lily and Sean spent the rest of Sunday cloistered in the house, talking, laughing, and making love. Absorbed in the marvel of their newfound feelings, they were unwilling to leave their private refuge. Monday morning and the demands of the real world intruded far too soon.

Sean drove Lily back to the condo. He felt both vindicated and shaken by the news of the hot spot. He wanted to get to the office early, so he and Evelyn could begin working on a strategy. The presence of a hot spot on the reef would surely thwart the plans to develop the marina. But he had to be ready for a brutal fight.

The car's wipers were on high. They whined in protest as they swiped ineffectually at the rain sheeting across the windshield. Chilled by the damp penetrating the old car, Lily burrowed deeper in the bucket seat, grateful she was wearing something warmer than her evening dress. She'd borrowed yet another pair of Sean's jeans and a white, button-down shirt, which hung to midthigh. He'd given her one of his raincoats, too, as she'd left her own at May Ellen's.

Sean pulled up near the front entrance of the condo and ran around to her side to open the door. In the time it took for her to climb out, Sean's hair was plastered to his head. He didn't seem to care. He stood, holding the lapels of the coat he'd lent her, gazing into her face. Even though her heart ached, already missing him, Lily managed a smile as she leaned forward and placed a soft kiss on his lips. "Thanks for the clothes."

"Any time," he said graciously. "My clothes look damn fine on you. If you move in with me, Dr. Banyon, I'll let you share my closet."

Sudden tears sprang to her eyes. Her heart felt as though it would burst. "Sean—" she began shakily.

"Shh," he said. With a smile, he laid a finger to her lips while his other hand brushed her cheek lightly, smoothing the tears away. "I've rushed you, I know. I'm sorry. I'd told myself to take it slow and let you get used to the idea. We'll talk later, sort out what you want to do." His hands cradled the sides of her face and he gazed deeply into her eyes. "I love you, Lily. We can make this work." Holding her gaze, he lowered his mouth to hers, and kissed her. A kiss that turned ravenous in the pouring rain.

"Go on up, before you're soaked through," he murmured when at last he released her. "Get some sleep, too. I've plans for us tonight," he said, grinning. With a last, lingering kiss, he jumped back in his car and sped off.

Lily walked through the lobby in a daze, and was hardly even aware when the elevator doors closed behind her. All she saw was Sean's face in the rain, telling her he loved her, that he wanted to be with her. When Sean had gently brushed away her tears, he'd assumed they were caused by confusion and uncertainty. He was wrong.

Lily had never wanted anything so badly in her life.

Indeed, it was the intensity of her desire that terrified

her. Her happiness surreal, she wondered whether she was dreaming, whether she'd awaken to find Sean's words in the rain a figment of her imagination.

It was early, so Lily took care to shut the door quietly. She unbuttoned Sean's coat and hung it in the bathroom to dry. The apartment was totally silent apart from the angry drumming of the rain. The rain hadn't stopped once since yesterday. The morning's paper warned that the present system might possibly develop into a tropical storm.

May Ellen would love that, Lily thought with a smile. She would call her grandmother later, at a respectable hour, and thank her and Kaye again for all they'd done . . . for the party, for the dress. Kaye might not have been the perfect mother when Lily was a child, but she was turning out to be a pretty good friend—and one who had dynamite taste in clothes.

A sudden gust of wind howled outside, rattling the windows. The noise made her vastly relieved that she and John had finished collecting the reef samples, that Karen's photos were taken. No one should be diving under these conditions.

Her fingers raked her wet hair back from her forehead and she gave a sleepy yawn. Exhaustion hit her, settling over her like a heavy blanket. She found she could hardly keep her eyes open. Little wonder, she'd had precious few hours of sleep and prolonged bouts of intense physical activity.

She'd do as Sean had advised, she thought, yawning again. She'd crawl under the covers and sleep for an hour or so. Lily padded toward the bedroom with a smile on her face, knowing she'd dream of Sean.

* * *

She awoke to the sound of banging.

"Lily, are you in there?" It was Karen's voice. The urgency in it had Lily sitting up, rubbing her eyes.

"Yes," she managed groggily. "Just coming." Rolling off the bed, she stumbled toward the door.

"I'm really sorry to wake you, Lily, but I'm a little freaked out, and I don't know what to do."

Karen certainly looked panicked. Her brown eyes were enormous in her drawn face and she was pacing the apartment, wringing her hands nervously.

"What's happened?" Lily asked as she sat down on the sofa.

"I've just talked with Baldev—the guy at Duggal Photo Lab. I'd tried to call the lab a few times on Friday morning, but I kept getting a busy signal. Then, when I telephoned again Friday afternoon, there was this message saying the lab had closed for the weekend. So I made sure I was up by ten this morning, when I knew they opened. Lily, you won't believe what Baldev told me: *They don't have my rolls of film.*"

Lily stared, trying to absorb what Karen had said. "John dropped them off Wednesday afternoon," she reasoned slowly, "which means that even if they missed the afternoon shipment, the film would have gone out on Thursday. That—"

"Would have given the package plenty of time to arrive by today—I know!" Karen cried. She had the hem of her purple sweatshirt in her hands and was knotting it as she wore a path in the carpet. "But Baldev insists they haven't received anything from me."

"Where's the FedEx receipt? We'll call FedEx, ask them to track the shipment—"

Again, Karen cut her off. "John has it. I forgot to get it

from him 'cause I was feeling so sick. And then he took off for Miami."

"Where is John? He's back, right?" But Lily knew the answer just by looking at Karen's distraught face. "Why don't you go pound on his door? It's possible he got back and is racked out," Lily said with an optimism she was far from feeling. "I'll try him on his cell phone."

Pete Ferrucci pulled into the condominium's parking lot and killed the car's engine. Although it was broad daylight, he'd decided this was a safe spot to meet. The rain was coming down so hard it was practically impossible to see one's hand in front of one's face. Anyone who did recognize his Mercedes would assume Ferrucci had business in the management office.

He lit a cigar and waited.

It was all coming together, he thought, puffing with satisfaction. Banyon's reef study was down the drain—literally. That slob Granger's chest had been bloated with self-importance when he'd opened his car trunk and shown him the samples and film. The hot spot changed things, Granger had told him. He could sure use a little extra cash in his bank account—to tide him over until he started that job Ferrucci had lined up for him in Key West.

What a fuckin' moron, Ferrucci thought. He'd paid Lesnesky twenty times the chump change he handed over to Granger. 'Course, it was pretty clear that Granger was a stupid shit—he really believed he had a plum job waiting for him in Key West. There truly was a sucker born every minute.

At the sharp rap on the window, Ferrucci turned his head. He stubbed his cigar out in the ashtray and depressed the lock release. The man climbed inside.

"Shut the door quick. It's a monsoon out there," Ferrucci said impatiently. "Show me what you've got."

"Ain't much, I'm afraid. Oh, they're at it hot and heavy, all right, but your guy McDermott is one lucky SOB—and boy, do I mean lucky. The first time, the fucking curtains at the grandmother's house were drawn. The second, it was goddamn black as pitch. I'd have needed studio lights to catch 'em. This is best shot I've got so far."

Ferrucci thumbed through the glossies on his lap. "Christ," he said in disgust. "Is this the best you can do? I can hardly tell it's them!"

"That's not my fault. I'm tailing these two around the clock. You don't like the work, pay me my money and I'll head back to—"

"Hey, hey, calm down," Ferrucci said hastily. "I didn't mean it to sound like that. Only I want McDermott's ass real bad."

"I understand, Mr. Ferrucci. I do have something you may find useful. It's not a photograph, though. Which means we'll have to negotiate a mutually agreeable price. It's part of a conversation I happened to overhear between a certain scientist and the mayor. I know a newspaper or two that might be *very* interested in picking up the story."

Ferrucci smiled.

One hour later, Lily was ready to admit that she was as "freaked" as Karen. An awful sense of dread consumed her. She had tried reaching John on his cell phone, only to hear the same message repeated over and over again: The cell phone customer she was calling was unavailable at this time. Meanwhile, increasingly lurid imaginings had wormed their way into her mind—of John lying dead in an alleyway behind some Miami nightclub, of his car smashed and mangled in an accident, the police unable to ID John or contact her.

Between calls to John's nonoperational cell, she'd also made one to FedEx, nearly babbling with relief when she was connected to a real live human being. The FedEx rep assured Lily that they could put a trace on the package. The computer would find either Karen's name or Duggal Photo Lab's in their shipping log. They'd call her as soon as they had any information.

When the phone rang, both she and Karen jumped. Lily, her hands wrapped around a fortifying mug of coffee, cursed as hot liquid sloshed over the back of her hand.

"Hello?" Karen spoke anxiously into the receiver. "Oh, hi, Simone," she replied, her shoulders slumping with disappointment. "Yes, she's here. Just a sec."

Lily went to the sink and quickly ran cold water over the reddened skin where the coffee had splattered. When she couldn't find a dish towel, she patted her hand gingerly with her shirttail.

Karen passed her the phone. Lily took a deep, calming breath. "Simone? It's me."

"Was the phone off the hook? I thought I'd never get through. Listen, I have the results of the samples you sent last week—of the hot spot in zone one."

Something in Simone's voice made Lily clutch the phone in a death grip. "What'd you find?"

"The most pristine core samples you could wish for outside the Garden of Eden."

Lily sat down heavily on the stool. "What did you just say, Simone?"

"The sediment samples we tested from zone one had

only trace amounts of heavy metals and petroleum by-products."

"What about bacteria or fertilizer? E-coli?" Lily asked desperately.

"No, no, and no," Simone replied. "The amounts of harmful materials and bacteria we found in the core and water samples are negligible. On a blind test, I'd have guessed samples this pristine came from the Galápagos rather than half a mile off Florida's coast. What's going on, Lily?" Simone asked, the concern plain in her voice.

Lily closed her eyes and tried to breathe.

"Lily? Lily? Are you there?"

"Simone, this is bad. Really bad."

Fifteen minutes later, Lily hung up the phone, or tried to. Her hands shook so much, the simple act became a noisy clattering of plastic against plastic.

"Shit!" she cried furiously, as she finally slammed it down. Jumping off the stool, she stalked across the living room, her hands clenched at her sides. She came to a standstill before the picture windows.

"John screwed us, didn't he?" Karen said flatly. She, too, stared down at the storm-tossed waves crashing against one another. "He took the reef samples, dumped them, replaced them with God-knows-what, and shipped them off with a fake, phony smile on his face. He *stole* my rolls of film. Two rolls, thirty-six exposures, that makes seventy-two photographs that he ripped off. And I let him because I was a trusting, naive fool. I could kill that son of a bitch!" she seethed. "What are we going to do, Lily? We can't let him get away with this."

"He won't," Lily said with steely determination. "We're going to find him. It's a waste of time to search his apartment—he'll have cleared it out."

"Then where? He could be in Miami or Timbuktu for all we know."

"No, I don't think so." Lily shook her head. "He's the kind of guy who likes to gloat." She turned to Karen. "Let's go down to the Blue Dolphin."

"Ferrucci's place?"

"Yeah. I think that's an excellent place to look for scum."

Lily and Karen drove into town. The wind had picked up. The strong gusts buffeted the tiny rental car and sent rain pounding from all directions. Although it was almost noon, the downtown streets were empty, people preferring to remain indoors and dry. Lily pulled into a parking space directly beneath the bright blue neon sign.

Entering the Blue Dolphin, Lily realized it was nearly as deserted as the streets. She quickly glanced around the interior and felt a bitter disappointment that John wasn't among the patrons seated at the glossily varnished tables. She touched the sleeve of Karen's wet slicker and nodded toward the bar.

The bartender who was wiping down the zinc bar with a soft cloth glanced up at their approach.

"Hi." He was young, dark haired, and sported what looked like a carefully maintained three-day beard. His eyes were frankly appraising as he smiled at her and Karen. "What can I get you?"

"Some help," Lily said lightly, giving him an easy, friendly smile. "We need to find a guy named John Granger. Perhaps you've seen him around. He's blond with cropped hair, medium build, in his midtwenties."

Something flickered in the bartender's eyes and he

straightened. "Lady, this is Florida. You just described half the population that walks through these doors."

He knew something, Lily was sure of it. She leaned over the bar, holding her elbows close to her side, intentionally enhancing her cleavage. She knew a cold satisfaction when the bartender's eyes dropped and his Adam's apple bobbed.

Karen caught on immediately. She, too, leaned closer. "Aw, come on," she said, warmly cajoling. "I'm sure you've noticed him. He's not as cute as you are, but he thinks he's a real Romeo. He's been coming here lots."

The bartender glanced between them. Lily upped the wattage on her smile. "Yeah, I think I've seen this dude around. He's been hanging with a girl named Trish who's a regular here."

Karen traced an idle pattern on the shiny metal surface of the bar, the tip of her finger inches away from the bartender's arm. "Do you know Trish's address by any chance?"

"Yeah. It's at the edge of town. Four seventy-nine Sunset. But I wouldn't bother going there. Trish usually comes in about now—she likes to keep tabs on the lunch crowd, see whether anyone catches her eye. Stick around, why don't you? By the way, I get off work at three. . . ."

"That's good to know," Lily said. And bit the inside of her cheek.

"We'll definitely keep that in mind," Karen agreed solemnly.

Shoving back from the bar, Lily said, "I'll have a frozen vodka at that table over there." She looked inquiringly at Karen.

"Make that two." Karen smiled. "And thanks loads for the help."

* * *

The mirrors in Ferrucci's restaurant definitely came in handy. Lily didn't have to turn around when John walked in behind a brunette wearing a miniskirt and a shrink-wrapped tank top. John's hand was resting on the woman's rear as he hailed the bartender loudly, then guided—no, herded—the woman to a table. They were just taking their seats when the woman giggled something to John and tripped off in her platform heels toward the back of the restaurant, where the rest rooms were located.

Lily waited until John was seated, fury mounting inside her. With a terse nod to Karen, the two of them rose in unison.

John started as he saw them approach. His face went pale, then all splotchy. "Hey, Lily. I, uh, just got back from Mi—"

Lily kept her temper under tight rein. Nothing would be more satisfying than wringing John's neck, but right now she wanted answers. "Skip the play-acting, John. We know what you did."

The flush on John's face darkened to an unbecoming red. "What are you talking about?" he blustered.

"Oh, *please*." Karen's tone was contemptuous.

"We're talking about the samples. Karen's film. Why, John? Why'd you do it? Did you really think we wouldn't figure it out?"

"Like I said before, I don't know what the hell you're talking about." His eyes narrowed as he smiled. "But I'm guessing from Masur's pitiful expression that something must have happened to her film. Did it get lost?" He shook his head. "Ahh, that's a real shame."

He wasn't going to admit a thing, the bastard. Lily

leaned forward over the table, her anger an icy blast that had John recoiling instinctively. "You stole Karen's film and switched the samples. *You saw the hot spot, John.* And still you went and tampered with the samples."

"Screw you, Banyon," John snarled. "You can't prove a damn thing you're saying, so it looks like it's your ass on the line. Serves you right, too. You blew this study off, running around with McDermott, visiting your granny, your old high school, like you were some fucking homecoming queen. It's gonna be funny as hell watching you get covered in shit when it hits the fan. I'll be laughing my head off."

Sickened, she stared at him. "You mean you deliberately ruined a research project just to get back at me? Why, John? Because I didn't like having my ass grabbed by you?" She saw the truth in the petulant look that crossed his face. "Jesus, you really are stupid. But what about Karen? What did she ever do to you, besides try and be your friend?"

"Yeah, you slimy creep. What did you do with my film?"

John looked at Karen and shrugged. "Gosh, I just don't know how they could have got lost. You could always go out there and reshoot. Oh, but that's right!" John exclaimed, then sniggered like a delinquent school boy. "Your little tummy gets upset in big, bad waves—" Before he could finish, Karen's hand whipped out and slapped him across the face.

"You bitch!" Enraged, Granger leaped out of his chair, lunging for her.

"Don't even think about it," Lily warned, quickly planting herself in front of Karen. "You try it and I'll break your arm."

John froze.

Without taking her eyes off him, Lily said, "Let's get out of here, Karen. By the way, Granger, you're out of a job."

"Oooh, like that's a big fucking deal. I was going to quit this lousy research position anyway. I've already got a better job lined up."

"Not one in marine biology, you don't. You think I'm a ball-busting bitch, don't you?" She smiled. "You ain't seen nothing yet. You can kiss your Ph.D. good-bye. No university will take you after I spread the word about what you did. I'm going to make it my personal mission to ensure you never work in this field again. By the time I'm finished, John, you'll be lucky to land a job cleaning out the fish tank in a Chinese restaurant."

"I wish I'd slapped him harder." Karen's voice shook as she dashed away the tears that ran down her cheeks.

Lily shut the apartment door and turned to her. "I know," she replied tiredly. "I'm as furious as you are, Karen."

Shrugging off Sean's raincoat, she went over to the coffee table and picked up the remote control. She turned on the TV and flicked through the stations until she reached the Weather Channel. A map of the East Coast filled the screen. Masses of dark green obscured the southern half of Florida. Just off the coast, there were the ominous, grayish-black swirls of a storm system.

Lily stood, staring grimly at the television, while in her head, John Granger's damning accusations resounded. His words were like a corrosive acid, all the more destructive because Lily believed them. John had been right when he'd accused her of blowing off the study, of spending more time thinking about Sean and May Ellen than about the reef. If she had been wholly focused on the study, she'd have noticed far sooner that something was amiss.

She had been distracted by the emotional tug-of-war she'd experienced upon returning home, torn by her desire to spend time with her grandmother and her reluctance to reacquaint herself with her hometown.

But of all her conflicting emotions, none were as complex, as overwhelming as her feelings for Sean.

It was as if her heart had been buried under icy layers of distrust and uncertainty. Little by little, as she'd come to understand the man Sean really was, those cold, hard layers had finally melted away and she was able to see what had been in her heart these many years. *Sean*.

Nothing came without a price, though. Discovering the truth of her love for Sean had been at the cost of one of the things Lily cared about deeply: preserving the wonders of the sea.

"I still can't believe John did this to us." Karen's voice tore Lily from her black thoughts.

She hit the power button on the remote control and tossed the remote onto the table. "We're not the only ones who've been betrayed," she said. "What John did affects all of Coral Beach. The people of this town are going to be deciding on some major issues based upon the information in my report."

"So what are we going to do? Are you going to inform the reef committee about what's happened?"

Lily shook her head. "No. We don't have any actual proof against John, and pointing the finger at him isn't going to change the only thing that really matters—the study's been compromised. We have to salvage what we can. Or else the entire reef may be jeopardized."

"But what can we possibly salvage? Everything's been destroyed or stolen!"

"That's why I'm going out to the reef," Lily said, staring out the window at the waves crashing wildly below.

"What?" Karen cried. "Lily, look what it's like out there!"

"I don't have a choice, Karen. This isn't dumb heroics on my part, I assure you. John or whoever put him up to sabotaging our research couldn't have timed it better."

"What do you mean, timed it better? Because of the committee meeting this week? Surely you can postpone the meeting and get the samples when this blows over!"

"Oh, I'm counting on being able to postpone the coral reef meeting—I'll need those extra days for the center to analyze the new samples I collect. But I *have* to get those samples today. You saw the weather forecast just now, didn't you?"

"Yeah, and the conditions are dangerous—"

"The rain and wind we're getting now might get a whole lot worse," she interrupted. "This system could whip itself into a tropical storm, possibly even a hurricane. Now do you understand why I need to go out today?"

Karen's eyes widened. "My God. You mean if the storm worsens, the waves will start smashing the reef."

"Exactly. A strong enough storm could destroy a lot of the coral. With the coral destroyed, the evidence that the coral is diseased will be gone, too. But that won't mean the reef will be rid of whatever agent is attacking the coral. Storms are a natural phenomenon. Given time, reefs can recover from the damage inflicted by them—

but not if they're already weakened by disease. But I need solid proof that there are *other* agents hurting the reef, otherwise no one's going to believe me."

"But surely—"

"No." Lily shook her head grimly. "My word alone won't be enough to halt the plans to develop the coastal area, because Lesnesky's study never gave any indication of a problem. And the longer I wait here, the more likely it is that the coral will be smashed to pieces before I get to it."

Her words spurring her on, Lily dashed across the room. She picked up the phone and dialed rapidly. "Hello, Ms. Roemer? This is Lily Banyon. Could I speak with Sean? He's in a meeting? Is it possible to interrupt him? Oh, I see. Well, could you give him this message? Tell him he has to postpone the reef meeting and reschedule it for later next week. No, I can't explain now. No, I don't know when he'll be able to reach me. I'm sorry, I've got to go."

Lily hung up the phone, then rushed to retrieve her scuba gear from the bathroom where it was drying. She pulled her wet suit and her buoyancy control vest from the shower rod and shoved them into her bag with the rest of her scuba gear.

When she returned to the living room, Karen was waiting, her rain slicker zipped over her jeans and sweatshirt.

"Can I borrow one of your cameras, Karen?" Lily asked, as she dropped her gear bag on the floor. "The committee members will be much more inclined to believe me if I can show them pictures of diseased specimens."

"I've got my cameras, but I'll be the one taking the pictures. My bags are already by the door."

"What! You can't go out in this. You get seasick in

weather only a fraction this bad. It's too dangerous, anyhow. I'm the head scientist—"

Karen held up her hand, stopping her. "Don't try and talk me out of this, Lily. I know it's rough out there, but I'm not going to let you go down and do *my* job for me—not that you could anyway—there's no way you'd get even one clear, readable image. I know which corals can be photographed most successfully under these conditions. It'll cut the amount of dive time dramatically—so we can get the heck out of there. Let's quit arguing and find someone willing to go out in this crap."

CHAPTER THIRTY-SIX

Lily had Karen drop her off at the marina. While Karen was at the dive shop, filling their scuba tanks with air, Lily was going to look for Owen Rafern. She was hoping that in spite of the foul weather, he'd be somewhere around the marina.

She found him drinking a beer at the Rusted Keel. He was sitting at the bar, his baseball cap tilted far back on his head, allowing him an unobstructed view of the TV. The station had been switched from ESPN to the Weather Channel.

"Hell, Charlie," Lily heard Owen complain to the bartender as she approached, "if this storm hangs around much longer, I'm gonna lose a lot of customers. Who wants to go out in this crap?"

"I do, Owen," she said.

"Jesus H. Christ!" he exclaimed as he turned his head. The abrupt movement made his cap fall off. He grabbed it, shoved it back on his head, and said, "What are you doing here, Dr. Banyon?"

She sat down on the stool beside him. "Hoping to find you. I need you to take me out to the first reef."

"You kidding? In this weather? Listen, I was only griping to Charlie here 'cause it bores the hell out of me to sit on my butt all day. You don't—"

"I need to get out there, Owen," Lily interrupted. "And I need to do it fast. We need to collect another batch of samples from that dive site we were at the other day."

"*More* samples? You guys never stop. Granger especially, he went out a couple of extra times, too, complaining that the samples weren't good enough. . . ."

So that was how John had obtained different samples without my noticing, Lily thought, seething with fury.

"Listen, Owen, Karen and I *have* to get out there. It's vital to the study. Can you take us? I'll pay you double."

"Naw, keep your money. You'll need it if your insurance company ever hears about it," he said, grinning. "Sure, why not? I'll take you. I never could resist women with a sense of adventure. Just make sure that little girl Karen has a bucket handy. So long, Charlie, my man. I'm off to battle the elements."

A severe-storm warning had been announced for the county.

Sean, Dave Cullen, the chief of police, Chip Reynolds, and Tom O'Shea of the Coral Beach Fire Department were gathered around a map of the town, which was tacked to the wall. Sean had called them together for an emergency meeting to ensure they were prepared for any contingency.

"Most likely, this storm will only dump a lot of rain and cause some flooding. But as it's hurricane season, I want to play it safe," Sean said. "First of all, let's close the beaches." He looked at Dave. "You and your staff ready to post the notices?"

Dave nodded. "We'll get right on it."

"Good." Sean turned his attention to Chip Reynolds. "Chip, tell your men not to hesitate to ticket any fool swimmer or surfer who disregards those signs."

"What about the marina, Sean?" Dave asked.

"There's already a small craft advisory," Sean replied. "But I'd like you to swing by there after you've posted the beach closings."

"Will do."

"Tom, how's the flooding so far?"

"The storm drains are holding up and we've got men out, keeping them clear. But if the rain intensifies . . ." The fire chief shrugged his shoulders.

"We've notified the high school that we may need the gym as an emergency shelter," Sean said. "But let's hope this storm dies out before it hits us. Keep your radios open, guys."

The men filed out of the meeting room, Chief Reynolds and Fire Chief O'Shea heading back to their stations, Sean and Dave walking in the opposite direction, toward their own offices.

Evelyn was just opening the door as Sean and Dave approached. "I was going to pick up some sandwiches for lunch. Do you want something, Dave?"

"No, thanks. I've got to round up my staff and post beach closing signs."

"Sean, you've got a bunch of messages on your desk. And Dr. Banyon telephoned."

"Yeah? She leave a message?" Sean felt a smile spread over his face. Just hearing the words *Dr. Banyon* made him happier.

"Yes." Evelyn nodded. "She needs you to push back

the reef advisory meeting until next week. Said she'll explain later."

Sean's brows drew together. "I'd better call her and find out what's going on. In the meantime, Evelyn, don't reschedule anything. I don't want Ferrucci or anyone else on the committee to suspect that there's something wrong."

Dave looked at him in surprise. "Is something wrong?"

"Lily found a hot spot on the southern portion of the shoreward reef. She says a lot of the coral there is diseased."

"Oh, man." Dave gave a long, low whistle. "Looks like things are going to turn nasty in this town."

"No, May Ellen," Sean said into the phone twenty minutes later. "I don't know where she is. That's why I'm calling. Did Kaye speak to her by any chance? No, don't fret, May. I'll find her. She and her assistants probably ran an errand somewhere. Yes, I promise I'll call as soon as I find her. No," Sean laughed. "No, I don't think she went for a swim. That's one thing you needn't worry about. Besides, we've closed the beaches. Talk to you soon, May."

"Where the hell are you, Lily?" Sean asked aloud as he hung up the phone.

The ride out to zone one of the reef took twice as long this afternoon as it did under normal conditions. Lily and Karen had suited up as soon as they'd climbed aboard the *Tangiers*. Lily wanted to be ready to dive the minute they reached the reef. They stood beside Owen in the shelter of the pilothouse, gripping the railing with both hands for balance.

Lily cast another worried glance at Karen, whose face, usually so animated, was drawn and leached of color. She placed her hand over Karen's, drawing her attention. "The swell will be rough underwater," she shouted over the combined roar of the engines and wind. "But it'll be even worse when we're at the surface. Remember, stay calm and don't panic. Keep your regulator in your mouth until the very end, when you reach the ladder." Her fingers tightened in a reassuring squeeze. "I'll be with you the entire time."

Karen nodded, her lips pressed in a straight, hard line. Lily turned to Owen. "Will you be able to drop anchor with the waves this strong?"

"Should be able to," Owen yelled, nodding vigorously. "But she'll probably drift. I'm going to position her just southwest of where you'll be diving. That way, when you surface, you won't be swimming against the waves to reach the boat."

"Good. The dive should take twenty minutes—half an hour, tops."

"You got it, Dr. Banyon."

If the ride to the reef was choppy, it was nothing compared to the pitch and roll of the *Tangiers* once Owen cut the engines.

Telling Karen to wait in the shelter of the pilothouse, Lily followed Owen out to help with the anchors. Unable to keep her balance on the seesawing deck, Lily stumbled. Once she was jostled so hard, her hip slammed into the side of the pilothouse. She grimaced at the shooting pain.

By the time she made her way back to the pilothouse, her hair was matted to her skull, rivulets of water streaming down her cheeks. Wiping the rain off her face, she stepped inside.

Karen was sitting on the captain's chair with her camera and light strobe in her lap, doing a final check of the equipment.

"Everything okay?" Unable to resist, she added, "Karen, you really don't have to do this."

"Yes, I do," Karen replied. "I'd never forgive myself otherwise."

"All right then, let's do it."

While Owen secured the ladder, Lily and Karen donned their remaining scuba gear—their buoyancy control devices, weight belts, masks and snorkels. Owen came and helped them both with their scuba tanks. Karen picked up her camera, held it close, and gave Lily a tense nod.

Fins in hand, her mesh bag with her sample case in the other, Lily led the way out.

This is not good, was Lily's first thought. *This is scary as hell,* her second, when she and Karen hit the storm-tossed waters and began bobbing violently in the waves. Lily was an experienced ocean swimmer; she knew how to angle her body so the surf's impact was lessened. But she could see that Karen was having a hard time. Reaching out, she grabbed Karen's arm. Together they began their descent.

The segment of the reef where they were diving was in the shallowest water, the depth only twenty to twenty-five feet. As she and Karen descended, the impact of the waves lessened, but only fractionally. The force of the surge was like being rammed by a truck. Lily's worry escalated. She wasn't scared for herself, but for Karen. Twenty minutes in conditions such as these would seem like an hour.

What would happen if Karen became overwhelmed by fatigue and she panicked?

The reef was transformed by the storm. Where before, all had been serene yet vibrant, now anemone and soft coral waved frantically. Fish darted nervously as if searching in vain for shelter. Constantly rocked by the force of the stormy ocean, Lily and Karen swam awkwardly among them. Lily held her sample case as she swam. Her head swiveled back and forth, trying to spot the locations where she and John had taken core samples previously. Though it was impossible to conduct as careful and systematic a sampling, Lily was going to try her utmost in the short time she'd allowed for the dive.

With every cylinder she dug into the sandy bottom, she cast a quick watchful look at her photographer.

Camera out, Karen was photographing the hard coral—brain coral, star coral, stag coral, and the like. Lily realized she'd chosen to concentrate on this type of species because their brittle structure made them easier to photograph. The soft coral that grew in zone one, the sea fans, lettuce coral, and sea plumes, were out of the question. They were whipping and swaying like saplings in a gale. Not even a gifted photographer like Karen would be able to get a decent shot of them—photographing the hard coral was damned difficult enough.

Lily soon realized Karen had figured out a way to combat the underwater surge while she photographed. Hovering over the coral she was photographing, she would steady her body by folding her arms tight against her ribs, and then depress the camera shutter. While Lily hurriedly filled test tube after test tube, Karen would drop, lie, and shoot. Then, exchanging thumbs-up signals, the two of them would swim over to the next specimen.

As they were diving under extreme conditions, Lily was careful to monitor the air pressure in her tank and was making Karen check hers frequently, too. After Karen had finished photographing an elkhorn coral covered in thick algal growth, Lily motioned to her. Spreading her fingers wide, she gestured emphatically, to signal that they had five minutes left. Karen nodded, signaling, *Okay* back to her.

Lily checked the compass strapped to her wrist. They would need to swim south for a few hundred yards before they began their controlled ascent. She gave a fervent prayer that the *Tangiers* hadn't drifted too far off.

Inserting her last water sample into the carrying case, she shoved the case into the bottom of her mesh bag, checked that the bag was attached to her buoyancy control vest, and then touched Karen's arm, pointing in the direction they needed to swim.

Owen had been smart to suggest we swim with the incoming waves, Lily thought. She could already feel the adrenaline rush leaving her as she kicked. Both her mind and body were suddenly tired, sluggish.

Not much farther now, she thought, rallying herself. Concerned that Karen might be severely fatigued, she looked over at her photographer and exhaled in relief. Karen seemed to be doing fine.

Lily's fins kicked steadily over the hard bottom terrain of the reef, then past the reef's southernmost boundary. She slowed to check her wrist compass once more. There, at that patch of sea grass, that's where they'd begin their ascent, Lily decided.

As they neared the wispy, tufted grass, something about it caught her attention, teasing her memory. Instinctively, she touched Karen's arm. Karen's mask turned toward Lily's, her eyes wide and questioning behind the tempered glass. Lily gestured to the patch of grass waving in the water. She curled her index finger, imitating someone taking a photograph. Karen immediately unhooked her camera and swam with Lily toward the bed of sea grass.

Lily watched her raise the camera to her mask, keeping her body as still as possible. When Karen moved, Lily knew she must have taken her shot. But instead, Karen looked over her shoulder and shook her head vehemently, obviously dissatisfied about something.

In response, Lily tapped her air gauge and waved to her. Karen held up one finger insistently. One shot.

Okay, Lily jerked her thumb up, giving Karen the go-ahead. One more shot and they'd begin their ascent, and get the hell out of the water.

Lily's body drifted with the current as she waited. Karen repositioned herself, sinking down until she floated a couple of feet above the sea grass. Lily saw her press her finger to the shutter, then lower her camera.

Lily started swimming toward her. Simultaneously, Karen lowered her legs so she could push off of the sandy bottom beneath her. Lily saw Karen's long scuba fins sweep the ocean floor, stirring the sand. All of a sudden a cloud whooshed upward.

A cloud of sand and something else, too—dark gray wings beating in ominous flight.

I have to help Karen, was her only thought. With one great kick, she propelled herself forward.

And put herself directly in the path of the stingray.

The stingray, with its capelike wings, enveloped her in a terrifying embrace. Panicked, Lily struggled and felt the knife-sharp pain, the white-hot burn as the ray's spiked, venomous tail whipped her once, twice, and yet again, cutting deep, before she was freed.

Her body jerked, convulsed with pain, and a single name was torn from her throat.

"Sean!"

As the stingray's poison spread, the pain took over Lily's body, becoming excruciating. Her breath was coming in harsh, rapid pants. *Too fast!* Her mind screamed futilely. Yet she couldn't slow down her breathing or her panicked ascent, despite Karen's attempts to hold her back. Lily could feel her arms about her, clutching her, trying to keep Lily from reaching the surface too quickly.

They broke through the water to more water. Angry white caps rolled over them from every direction. Lily felt herself go under. Then something was tugging at her vest. Dimly she realized Karen must be inflating it. Her head lolled, as useless as the rest of her, and the gray mist of pain that shrouded her mind darkened to a black night. Lily's mouth went slack.

CHAPTER THIRTY-SEVEN

Sean's face was etched in harsh lines as he sped away from the Bay Towers. The doorman on duty at the condo thought that, Yeah, maybe he'd seen Lily and her assistant leave some time during the late morning. Must have, the guy added with an indifferent shrug. If they weren't answering the buzzer, it must mean they weren't there.

Succumbing to a nagging worry, Sean had left the office half an hour ago. He knew that until he found her, he wouldn't be able to get a lick of work done. He'd left instructions with Evelyn, telling her to call him the second she heard from Lily. Then he'd gotten in his car and begun his search . . . his fruitless search for Lily.

The windshield wipers were fighting a losing battle with the rain. They dragged across the windshield, leaving wide, watery streaks. Sean steered with his hands locked tight around the wheel while the car sloughed and skidded along the rain-filled streets. He drove automatically, his mind centered on one thought. *Where was she?*

At a red light, he pulled his cell phone from his pocket and looked at the miniature screen, hoping perhaps he'd missed a call. The screen was aggravatingly blank. Though tempted, Sean knew he couldn't ring Lily's grandmother.

May Ellen was already beside herself with worry. He tossed the cell onto the passenger seat in disgust.

His unease became mixed with the first wrenchings of angry frustration. What could she be thinking, haring off somewhere without letting anyone know where to find her? Why hadn't she called? Where in hell could she be?

On a whim, Sean headed back toward the marina—although he'd already been by Norma Jean's once before. He'd found the diner deserted, the lone waitress thumbing through this week's edition of *TV Guide*. *No,* she'd replied, no tall blonde had come in to eat.

Might as well try again, he decided. Perhaps he and Lily had crossed paths. Or maybe she and Karen were holed up at the Keel, drinking beer and throwing darts because there was little else to do on such a lousy day.

He turned into the marina parking lot.

A sudden dread gripped him. In the distance, the lights of an ambulance flashed, a violent red-and-white pulse in the gray of the driving rain. His heart pounding, Sean hit the accelerator, then brought the car to a screeching halt a few yards away.

The ambulance was stationed by the gated entrance to the docks. Its back doors were open in readiness and two blue-jacketed attendants stood in the square of light emanating from the interior.

A crowd had gathered. Yellow slickers, oilskins, and baseball caps covered bodies and heads, and kept away the rain, but did nothing to banish the ghoulish, macabre air that permeated the scene. Sean threaded his way through the curious throng, anxiously scanning the faces he passed.

As he neared the paramedics, he looked at the tall man beside them and did a double-take. Dave—it was Dave Cullen.

"Cullen!" he yelled loudly, catching his attention. "What's going on? What's happened?"

"Sean!" Dave waved him over. "Christ, I'm glad to see you!" he said when Sean reached him. "I only arrived a few minutes ago myself. The stationmaster at the marina just received a radio distress call. A diver's been seriously injured. They're coming in now. Sean, the call came from the *Tangiers*."

Sean's unblinking gaze was riveted on the mouth of the inlet. At first he thought what he saw was a mirage, an illusion born of desperation. But then, against the backdrop of the fast-darkening sky, the faint gleam of green-and-red running lights emerged and grew steadily clearer. He gave a hoarse cry and ran down the dock, Dave by his side.

The *Tangiers* carefully navigated the choppy waters of the inlet, the throb of its engines uneerily loud in the tense atmosphere. From behind came the sound of hurrying feet. It was the paramedics with the stretcher. A sudden burst of light flooded the area, and somewhere in Sean's mind, he registered the presence of a TV crew.

But all that was pushed aside. The *Tangiers*'s engines had slowed to a low rumble and the trawler was easing into the slip.

Sean caught the rope an ashen-faced Owen threw to him. "It's Dr. Banyon, Sean." Owen's voice was raw with strain. "She got hurt bad . . . real bad."

"Sweet Lord, no," he whispered, petrified.

Sean was jostled as one of the paramedics jumped aboard. Shaking off his paralyzing fear, he helped lift the stretcher onto the boat, and then followed Owen as the captain led them to Lily.

Sean's heart clenched when he saw Lily lying on the cabin's bench, a thick blanket covering her. Her face was a chalky white, beads of perspiration dotting her brow, her lips an ominous blue. He fell to his knees beside her. With a shaking hand, he reached out to stroke her damp brow, his terror escalating when he felt her icy skin.

The paramedics crouched next to him. Immediately they set to work, one taking her vital signs, while his partner relayed the stats by radio to the emergency staff.

"Sean!" At the cry, Sean reluctantly looked away from Lily's ghostly pale face. Karen was standing to the side. Tears were streaming down her face. Dave's arm was about her, holding her close.

His throat tight with fear, Sean swallowed forcibly. "What happened, Karen?" he managed to say at last.

"It was a stingray. It was hidden under some sand near where I was shooting. I guess I startled it, and when Lily tried to reach me, it got her instead. The ray stung and cut her three times," she wailed, unable to continue as the tears started afresh.

"We've got to get the patient out of here," one of the paramedics announced. "You should come too, Miss, so we can check and make sure you're okay."

The medics carefully lifted Lily onto the stretcher, and then carried her off the *Tangiers*. Dazed, as if he were caught in a nightmare, Sean followed. His eyes remained fixed on the stretcher, his lips mumbling a prayer with each step he took.

They were nearly at the ambulance when Sean's path was blocked by a man. Sean stopped, blinking in the harsh glare of lights.

The man stuck a microphone in his face. "Mayor Mc-Dermott, we've just learned that you've been accused of

serious charges of misconduct by a member of this research team, Dr. Lily Banyon. According to our source,
Dr. Banyon has accused you of harassment. Can you give
us your response, Mayor McDermott?" The reporter
thrust the mike closer.

Fury erupted inside Sean. "Get the hell out of my way,"
he snarled menacingly, and shoved the reporter hard.

May Ellen and Kaye were in the hospital's waiting
lounge when Sean arrived. Catching sight of him, May
Ellen burst into tears.

He hugged her, patting her trembling shoulders as
she wept.

"Will she be all right, Sean?" Kaye asked. Her face
was haggard with worry.

"I don't know." The words choked him. "We have to
hope, and wait for the doctors to do what they can for
her."

"Come, sit down, Mother," Kaye gently urged a still-
weeping May. "Sean's right, of course. We have to wait
and let the doctors take care of her." She and Sean guided
her to a chair.

And so the vigil began.

Sean was sitting with his head bowed, his elbows resting on his knees, his fingers knotted together in a tight
ball. The sound of footsteps made him raise his head. It
was Karen and Dave. He jumped to his feet.

"Are you okay, Karen?" he asked, reaching them in
three strides. She looked wan, her eyes huge and shadowed. Dave must have given her his sweatshirt. Enormous on her, it hung to her knees.

"I'm fine," she said, brushing his question aside.

Sean's eyes met Dave's over the top of her tangled head of hair. Dave gave a grim nod of confirmation.

Sean felt his shoulders sag. This was the first good news they'd received. *Please God, don't let it be the last,* he whispered silently.

"Sean," Karen said. "I need to tell you why we were out at the reef."

"Why don't we go sit down by Lily's mother and grandmother?" Dave suggested. "You're about ready to fall on your face from exhaustion, Karen, and her family's going to want to hear every word you say."

Karen had just finished her story, which the others had listened to in appalled silence.

Sean was shaking his head in angry disbelief. "You mean to tell me that Granger tampered with the samples to get back at Lily?" he asked Karen.

Karen nodded. "He must have really hated her after the 'lobster threat,' " she said. "Do you remember when I told you about it, Sean, on the first day of our study?"

"Yeah, I remember. I wanted to pummel the son of a bitch. Now I want to kill him." His rage was such that Sean thought he probably could, too. "But I just can't believe Granger would do this out of petty revenge, Karen. He's too goddamned lazy. No," he said with growing conviction. "Somebody put him up to it—someone with a hell of a lot more initiative than Granger."

May Ellen pressed a crumpled handkerchief to her eyes. "Poor Lily. I never imagined she would be risking her life by coming back and finishing the study. How I wish that Dr. Lesnesky hadn't gotten sick—"

"My God!" Sean breathed. "That's it! *Lesnesky.* His

report didn't show any evidence of disease, which, in light of recent events, is just too damn hard to believe. I'm willing to bet his study was fixed from the very start—" Sean stopped in midsentence. A white-coated doctor was coming toward them. He sprang to his feet.

The anxious group had gathered around the attending physician, Dr. Paul Shumacher. Kaye had introduced herself and then asked the doctor if he could give them any news.

"At the moment, Mrs. Alcott, your daughter is still unconscious. We've administered an antivenom shot, but it will take some time for the antidote to take effect." He paused, his expression grave. "Dr. Banyon's system has been severely weakened. You see, in addition to having to fight the venom from the stingray, Dr. Banyon also ingested a significant amount of water when she lost consciousness—any more, and, frankly, her chances would have been slim indeed."

Kaye blanched. Blindly, she reached for Sean's arm, clutching it for support.

"The next twenty-four hours will tell us a lot," the doctor informed them. "We'll have to monitor her carefully, in case she develops an infection or, worse still, pneumonia. I must tell you, Mrs. Alcott, your daughter's a very lucky woman. She's extremely athletic, I assume?"

Kaye nodded mutely.

"That fact may very well have saved her life. Her heart rate is unusually slow. Which means the stingray's venom didn't circulate as quickly as it might have in another, less fit, individual. She's lucky in another respect, too." Dr. Shumacher looked at Karen and smiled. "The doctor who examined you in the emergency room told me that you attempted to restrain Dr. Banyon on your ascent. If not for your clear-headedness, she probably would have suffered an embolism."

Karen's lips trembled. "Thank you, Doctor." Overcome by emotion, she turned her head into Dave's shoulder.

"What would you say Lily's chances are, Dr. Shumacher?" Sean asked, and knew he'd never been so scared of an answer in his life.

"I'm guardedly optimistic. If the antivenom works quickly enough, her body should be strong enough to stave off an infection. In that case, I see no reason for her not to make a complete recovery."

Sean's knees went rubbery with relief. "When can we see her?"

The doctor checked his watch. "They should be bringing her up to her room now. I expect you'll be able to see her shortly. I'll have a nurse come down when they're ready."

Despite the doctor's prognosis that Lily would be all right, Sean's anger flared each time he thought of how badly she had been hurt. How close he'd come to losing her.

Restless with impatience to see Lily, and to exact vengeance on her behalf, he began to pace. "I'm not going to let whoever is behind this thing get away with hurting Lily. Karen, you said she managed to get new samples when you were out on the reef?"

From her seat beside Dave, Karen nodded. "And I got pictures, too."

Sean's mind raced. "Okay, this is what I need you and Dave to do. Dave, you've got to make sure Owen Rafern doesn't breathe a word about what happened today on the *Tangiers*—I don't want anyone else to know that Lily actually succeeded in collecting new evidence."

"Sure thing, Sean," Dave replied.

His mind racing, Sean continued, "Karen, can you telephone Simone Devaux and tell her what's happened?"

"Yeah, I bet she's worried—she and Lily spoke earlier today, so she already knows something's screwy."

"That's putting it mildly. Tell her we need her to analyze the new samples immediately. Come to think of it, I want to talk to her, too. Let's call her from here. Then, tomorrow morning you and Dave are going to pack up the samples and ship them express to the center." He broke off and his feet slowed. "I know all this is a lot to ask, after what you've been through—"

"Stop right there, Sean. We'll get the samples shipped."

He smiled at her. "Thanks, Karen. The fewer people involved, the better. The only way we can win this is to lull whoever is behind the scheme into a false sense of security. The word is bound to get out that there was an accident on the reef, but most people will assume the conditions were too rough to collect samples or to take photos."

"Should I send my film when I ship the samples?" Karen asked.

"The lab you use is in New York?"

"That's right. Duggal Photo, in Chelsea. Best lab in the country."

"If you'll trust me with it, I'd like to hand deliver your film. And while I'm in New York, I'll go pay a visit to someone I need to have a little talk with."

Dave regarded him assessingly. "So Lesnesky's still at Sloan-Kettering?"

"That's right." Sean's expression hardened. "I'll let him confess before he goes to hell."

"What can Mother and I do to help, Sean?" Kaye asked.

"The most important job of all. You're going to take care of Lily. As soon as the doctors say she can leave, I want you to bring her home to May's, and keep her there. I won't leave for New York until I'm sure she's out of danger, but that means I may still be gone when she's released. It'll be a big load off my mind if I know she's safe with you. But Kaye, don't you or May Ellen let her know where I've gone, or why."

May Ellen frowned. "Why ever not, Sean?"

"Because I have no idea how Lesnesky will react when I accuse him of having manipulated the reef study. He could very well deny everything," Sean explained. "I don't want to give Lily false hope. She's been through enough. Karen, can you help move her belongings out of Ferrucci's?"

"I'll be delighted. That place was giving me the creeps."

"You can pack your own things while you're at it," Dave said, taking her hand in his. "I'm not letting you out of my sight."

CHAPTER THIRTY-EIGHT

A single light illuminated the hospital room. Sean sat in the chair he'd pulled close to Lily's bed and stroked her outstretched arm, taking care to avoid the thin plastic IV tube taped to her forearm. The skin he lightly caressed was warm again. Her color, too, had improved. The signs gave Sean hope, and he clung to them.

He hadn't moved for the last hour since the others had left. Kaye would return first thing in the morning. Sean had shamelessly used his clout as mayor to stay past regular visiting hours. He couldn't bear the thought of Lily being alone while she was unconscious.

His voice was sandpaper-rough from exhaustion. He'd been talking, trying to reach Lily and lead her out of the night inside her. Rambling, he'd talked of everything, how much he loved her, how brave she was, how he dreamed of their future together.

When his voice gave out, he clasped her hand in his, entwining their fingers. He lowered his head to kiss the curve of her shoulder. Too tired to move, he let it rest there, and succumbed to sleep.

He awoke later, his hand still holding hers. He

stretched to ease the stiffness in his back, and his arm jarred hers a fraction.

Lily's eyelids fluttered.

Elation flooded him. Bending closer, Sean touched his trembling lips to the corner of her mouth. "Wake up, Lily. Wake up and let me see your beautiful eyes."

Though her lids quivered, they remained shut as if weighted down, a burden too heavy to lift. But when Sean felt her fingers tighten ever so slightly around his, he wanted to dance, to shout with triumph. "I'm here, Lily. Everything will be okay," he whispered. "Sleep, my love. You'll see me in the morning."

Lily's dreams were hazy. She thought that she dreamed of Sean, but he was far, far away. She heard only his voice, yet it was as elusive as he. Though she tried, she didn't have the strength to reach him. She gave a silent cry.

Then a soft breath stole over her, lulling and soothing. *Sleep, my love.*

The sound of the nurse entering the room with a steel trolley in tow woke Sean. He sat back in the chair groggily while she bustled about the room, her white crepe-soled shoes making little squeaking noises on the linoleum.

"Good morning," she said cheerfully. "And how's our patient?" she asked, replacing Lily's IV drip with lightning-fast efficiency.

"Good morning," Sean replied, and spared her a brief smile before fixing his attention on Lily. He gave the hand he'd been holding all night a gentle squeeze. "Lily, it's morning. Open your eyes for me. I know you can do it. Look at me, Lily. Lily, I need you so—"

"Sean?" The word was scarcely a whisper.

Thank God. "That's right, sweetheart. It's me, Sean."
His voice shook.

Turning her head toward the sound of his voice, Lily
slowly opened her eyes. She blinked, her blue eyes cloudy
and disoriented, and . . . so wonderfully alive. His own
eyes blurred then, with hot tears of joy that she was alive,
breathing, and staring up at him.

"What happened?" she croaked weakly. Her eyes widened in sudden alarm. "The ray . . . Karen—"

"Shh, love, don't worry. Everything's fine. You're going to be fine. The stingray stung you. But you're going
to be all right. You are incredibly brave and strong."

"Karen . . ."

"Karen's fine," he reassured her. "She'll be here later.
You're in the hospital. This nice nurse," he paused, and
glanced at the name tag pinned to the older woman's uni-
form, "Nurse Peters wants to take a look at you."

"Don't—"

"No, I won't leave you, Lily."

Lily's hospital room became a hive of activity. With
her return to consciousness, nurses and doctors filed in
and out, each taking a turn at examining her and checking this or that. A short time later, Kaye swept in with an
enormous bouquet of flowers. Seeing an exhausted but
awake Lily, Kaye all but melted in a cascade of tears.
When at last she'd calmed, she told Lily that her half
brothers, Ned and Mike, had arrived this morning and
were eager to see her. Scott Alcott would be by later, too,
with May Ellen.

Kaye's announcement gave Sean a bittersweet pang.
On the one hand, he was happy that Lily would soon
have her entire family caring for her. He knew, too, that
her friends were literally flying to her side. Simone De-

vaux, Lily's boss at the Marine Center, would be coming in from Boston as soon as she had the results from the water and core samples. Yet on the other hand, the arrival of these others told Sean that the time had come for him to go.

He hated the thought of being apart from her, but Sean told himself that the best way for him to help Lily right now was to fly to New York and confront Abe Lesnesky. He would wait, though, for Kaye to return. She'd gone down to the cafeteria to buy Sean and herself some much-needed coffee.

Her strength already taxed, Lily was drifting in and out of sleep, her eyes closing for longer and longer periods. When Sean's cell buzzed in his jacket pocket, she barely stirred.

"Yes," he answered, his voice pitched low so as not to disturb her.

"Sean, it's me."

"Hi, Evelyn, I was just about to call you."

"How's Dr. Banyon?"

Sean smiled at Lily's pale sleeping face. "Alert and on the mend. Though she's dozing now."

"That's wonderful. Please give her my best. I'll come by later this afternoon." Evelyn paused. The silence stretched long enough that he knew that whatever she was about to say, it was bad. "Sean, have you seen the morning paper?"

" 'Fraid not. I haven't left the hospital since I got here."

"The TV news?"

"No." Wearily he rubbed his unshaven cheek. "What's up?"

"Well, you're the lead story everywhere."

"I don't suppose they're talking about how I successfully renegotiated the contract with the sanitation workers' union?"

"A little more dramatic. The front page of the newspaper has a photograph of you and Dr. Banyon, as well as a rather damning article. The TV's picked them both up and has added a twist of its own—a five-second clip of a reporter asking you about a harassment charge, and you shoving him to the ground. I've seen it four times already this morning. The best spin I can put on it is that you are extremely photogenic. . . ."

"What in hell are they talking about? Who's accusing me of harassment?"

"The newspaper has a quote from Dr. Banyon."

He cursed, abruptly realizing what this was all about. Someone must have heard their fight at Norma Jean's and run to the press with the story. He ground the heel of his hand against his eye.

"Sean, are you there?"

"Yeah, I'm here."

"What do you want to do about the press?" Evelyn asked.

"Not a damn thing," he replied at last. Rising from the chair, he walked to the window and stared blindly at the still-empty parking lot. "I've got better things to worry about right now. Lily's been hurt and I'm responsible—"

"Sean, you can't—"

"No, listen to me, Evelyn," he said quietly, distinctly. "Lily nearly died out on that reef, doing a job for this town. Whoever set her up is going to pay. That's a hell of a lot more important to me than whatever the press is saying."

Over the line Sean heard her sigh of acquiescence.

"Hey, cheer up," he said. "Maybe Coral Beach's next mayor won't bug you to make espresso every other minute."

The joke fell flat, without a single chuckle from Evelyn. "Okay, here's what I need you to do. First, get me on the next flight to New York. Then call Simone Devaux at the Marine Center. Give her my arrival time so she can let George Hunt know. Give her my cell number, too. I'll drop Karen's film off then head uptown to the hospital where Lesnesky's being treated. I want Hunt there when I talk to Lesnesky."

"You think Hunt will convince him to admit that he fixed the study?"

"Yeah. I'm hoping that he can appeal to whatever dregs of professional integrity remain in Lesnesky."

"And what do you want me to say to the reporters? This is serious, Sean. They smell blood."

"Stonewall them. And don't tell anyone where I've gone. Call me back when you've got the flight information."

Sean hung up just as Kaye entered the room, two steaming coffees in hand, a newspaper tucked under her arm, and a stricken look on her face.

Sean eyed the folded paper. "That bad, huh?"

Kaye nodded tightly, her lips pursed with worry. "I was so distracted last night. And then this morning, I was trying to find a florist that opened early—Sean, have you seen it?" she asked, setting the coffee on Lily's bedside tray. Checking that Lily was still asleep, she handed him the paper. "Here, look for yourself."

Sean opened the folded newspaper. The photograph was front and center, positioned just below a headline, which screamed, *Mayor Accused of Harassment!* Though grainy, Lily's wheat blond hair was instantly recognizable.

The photographer must have taken the shot yesterday, Sean fumed, when he'd dropped Lily off at the condominium. His arms were about her, their mouths fused in a kiss that in no way could be described as platonic.

The edges of the newspaper crumpled as his hands tightened into fists. He wished only that his hands were around the neck of the bastard paparazzi who'd spied on him and Lily with a telephoto lens. It sickened and infuriated him to think some creep had been sneaking around watching his and Lily's every move . . . their lovemaking.

"How could they do this?" Kaye cried. "I thought the *Courier* was a responsible newspaper! There's an article, too. Sean—"

"I've seen enough," he ground out, handing the paper back. "Get rid of this thing, Kaye. I don't want Lily to know about this—it'll only hurt her more. And keep the TV off, too. They're apparently running a clip about us on the local news."

"Sean, you can't keep this from her forever," Kaye said.

Sean's gaze went to Lily lying in the hospital bed. Dark violet circles shadowed her closed eyes. "I know, but we can keep it under wraps at least until she feels better. I'll deal with the press when I get back from New York."

Lips pursed, Kaye shook her head but gave him no argument.

"Thanks, Kaye, and take good care of her." Sean went to the side of Lily's bed and kneeled so his face was inches from hers. He reached forward and cupped the side of her face. "Lily," he whispered gently.

Her eyes opened and slowly focused.

He smiled sadly, wishing he didn't have to leave her. "Lily, I've got to go. An emergency meeting's been called.

But I'll be back very soon. You rest and get better, love," he said, brushing her forehead with his lips.

Too weak to protest, too weak to follow, Lily watched Sean depart, her eyes swimming with silent tears.

The procession marking Lily's release from the hospital three days later was led by Lily's stepfather, Scott Alcott. He walked slowly, struggling to see past the overflowing mass of flowers he held in his arms, which had transformed Lily's sterile hospital room into a sweetly scented hothouse. The majority of the bouquets had come with a card signed, *Sean.*

More slowly still came Lily and her grandmother. May Ellen's hand was under Lily's elbow, offering support. Lily's teeth were clamped tight, her nostrils flaring in sync with each laborious step she took.

She hated this debilitating weakness. After five minutes of walking, her legs were wobbling like a drunken sailor's, the muscles in them having turned to jelly back at the reception desk in the middle of the lobby. At this point, pride alone was keeping her moving . . . and the fear that if she fell, Granny May would come tumbling down with her.

Kaye had parked the car by the hospital's front entrance. She rushed forward as they approached.

"Careful, Lily, watch the curb," May Ellen warned. "Let's get the poor girl home, Kaye."

"She looks all done in, doesn't she, Scott? I knew we should have asked for a wheelchair."

Lily tried to smile. She only hoped that very, very soon she'd be able to laugh about this conversation.

Scott helped Lily into the backseat, then opened the door on the other side and slid in next to her. "I bet you're happy to be out of there," he said, as Kaye pulled away from the curb.

"I never want to go to a hospital again in my life."

Scott nodded in understanding. "Sometimes I feel that way when I'm making my rounds. But I just can't seem to stop."

"It's a little different when you get to wear the white coat," Lily observed.

"Yeah, those hospital gowns look terrible on me," he said, and heaved a loud sigh.

A giggle escaped her lips as she pictured Scott with his rumpled, teddy bear looks, visiting his patients in a hospital gown.

"See, you're feeling better already," Scott pronounced happily.

"The Alcott charm. Works every time," Kaye said, and shared a smile with her husband in the rearview mirror.

When they reached May Ellen's house, it was Scott who led Lily up the walkway as Kaye and Granny May hurried ahead with Lily's flowers and the small bag containing Lily's toiletries that Karen had brought her from Ferrucci's apartment.

Her heart was thudding loudly by the time she made it to the front hall. It almost stopped when Scott led her into May's living room and a half a dozen people leaped out from behind chairs, sofas, and potted palms with a loud cry of, "Welcome home, Lily!"

Karen, Dave, her half brothers, Mike and Ned, Hal Storey, Anne Prentiss and—the biggest surprise of all— Simone Devaux grinned and laughed as Lily stared open-mouthed. Even after a round of teary hugs and hellos, Lily was still shaking her head in wonder.

"Surprised you, didn't we?" beamed Hal.

"You better believe it. My God, Simone! What are you doing here?"

Simone's expression turned outraged. "I'd have been here a lot sooner, kiddo, but I was waiting for the core and water samples to be analyzed."

"I'm so happy to see you," Lily told her.

"I'm darned happy to see *you*, Lily." Simone hugged her again, hard.

Lily turned to her half brothers. "And you! I thought you guys left yesterday."

Ned shrugged. "Plans change. Granny May wanted us to hang some pictures."

"A ton of them," Mike added in a stage whisper.

Lily's gaze swept around the living room. The pictures were exactly as they had been—before May Ellen had Lily and Sean rehang them. She shot her grandmother an accusing look. "Granny, how could you?"

"I'm sorry, Lily." May Ellen's expression was sheepish. "I decided I liked them arranged the old way better."

"I know!" Anne Prentiss exclaimed brightly. "Let's celebrate Lily's homecoming with a round of mimosas!"

The idea was met with near-unanimous enthusiasm.

"I think a glass of milk might be better for me," Lily said. "I'm afraid I'll fall flat on my face if I have anything stronger."

"What you need, Lily, is a protein shake," Hal told her. "You were looking a little peaked when I visited yesterday, so I brought along the mixings. Do you have a blender, Mrs. Farrady?"

"Of course. Follow me, Hal."

A sudden group migration toward the kitchen in search of drinks left the living room nearly empty.

Lily turned to Simone. "You said you have the sample analyses?"

"The printouts are in my brief—"

"And?"

Simone grinned. "I'd say you and Karen did a terrific job. I'll get the stats in a minute. But first, tell me how you're feeling."

"Loads better, now that you've assured me I didn't get zapped by that stingray for nothing."

"And the puncture wounds are healing?"

"They're fine," Lily assured her. "Just three tiny bandages. My lungs are clear, too. The doctor told me I can go back in the water in a couple of days. Though I'll probably sink," Lily confessed with a grimace. "The worst thing is how darned weak I feel."

Simone frowned. "I hope Hal's shake works as well as he claims. From the sound of things, this reef meeting is going to be more like an armed confrontation. I called Mayor McDermott's secretary, Evelyn Roemer. She told me they'd only managed to push the meeting back to this week. It's scheduled for the day after tomorrow. Two o'clock."

Lily sat down heavily in the wingback chair. "I'd assumed we'd have a little more time to prepare." She quailed at the thought of how much there was to do in so short a time. "Will Sean even be back from his trip by then?" she wondered aloud.

Since he'd left, Sean had called her every day but as Lily's room seemed perpetually filled with well-wishers, their conversations had been disappointingly brief . . . and distressingly stilted. As Lily's strength returned, she'd sensed something strange in Sean's tone. His cheerfulness sounded forced.

She wished she could see him, look in his eyes, and feel the warmth of his smile.

"Sean told me he'll be returning the same day as the meeting," Dave said to her as he crossed the living room, champagne mimosas balanced in his hands. Offering one to Simone and Karen, Dave took a healthy sip of his own. "Mmm, nothing like a mimosa for lunch."

Like a dog with a bone, Lily was still worrying the issue of the upcoming reef meeting. "Will your film be ready in time?" she asked Karen.

"Sean—" Karen's champagne spilled over the back of her hand when Dave accidentally bumped her with his elbow. "Oops!" she said with an embarrassed cough, then quickly licked her hand. "Yeah, I should be getting them tomorrow . . . uh, Baldev called."

"And I'll be here to help you organize the reef report," Simone chimed in. "George told me to call if we need any advice. Unfortunately, he has to root for you from the sidelines. He's been temporarily delayed in New York."

Lily smiled. "Busy twisting peoples' arms for money," she guessed.

"Something like that," Simone murmured, and raised her champagne flute to her lips.

"Simone," Lily said, her voice subdued. "I just wanted to say how sorry I am that I messed up—"

Simone frowned. "What are you talking about?"

"The reef." She shrugged miserably. "I got so distracted coming back home—you were right, Simone, when you said all those things about roots and family. I'd been ignoring my feelings and my ties to this place for too long. But I ended up neglecting the study. I let you down, as well as Karen, Sean, and the rest of Coral Beach."

Simone glanced at Karen. "Is this John's special brand of poison?"

"Yeah," Karen replied. "Easy to recognize, huh?"

"Damn. I should have guessed you'd be beating yourself up about this. This wasn't your fault, Lily. John is a thieving liar and I rue the day he stepped into my office. But he'll get his due."

"He certainly will." Dave Cullen's voice was cold and harsh. "He's going to find out how far the arm of Justice reaches."

Lily tried to summon a smile for her friends. Inside, the thought, *I wish Sean were here,* echoed in what had become a silent litany. Lily knew that all her fears would disappear the instant she saw him again, the moment he wrapped his arms about her and said, *I love you.*

Hal came into the living room, holding a tall glass before him. He presented it to Lily with all the pomp and ceremony reserved for a magic elixir.

With an effort, Lily set aside her yearning for Sean. But she couldn't help eyeing the thick orange shake somewhat dubiously.

"Uh, thanks, Hal," she said, before taking a tentative sip. "Hey!" She looked up. "This is . . . pretty good."

Hal glowed with pleasure as she took another sip, and then another.

"Well," Lily said after she'd gulped down half the shake, "if we've only got thirty-six hours to get this report in shape, we'd better get cracking."

CHAPTER THIRTY-NINE

Ferrucci sat in the back office of the Blue Dolphin, the morning's newspaper spread before him.

Now this is more like it, he thought. Mayor McDermott, pure as fuckin' Galahad, was covered in shit. The press was going to town over his alleged harassment of Lily Banyon. Their ire stoked by McDermott's bald refusal to comment.

Everything was working out beautifully.

Ferrucci had set it up so that the reef study was waiting to go off like a bomb in Banyon's and McDermott's faces. Perhaps sensing the catastrophe looming, McDermott was already running scared—literally. No one knew where in hell he was hiding, except maybe that pink gargoyle, Roemer. The second Ferrucci was elected mayor, she'd be out on her skinny ass.

McDermott's absence was making things even easier, Ferrucci thought. Because every day he stayed away from the news-starved press was another nail in his coffin. And Ferrucci knew how to hammer but good.

He'd drive the last nail into the coffin today, at the coral reef meeting, and bury McDermott alive. Then things would really start going his way.

*   *   *

Sean pushed Abe Lesnesky's wheelchair up the cement path that led to Fred Sneel's house. George Hunt walked alongside them. Sneel was waiting for them, holding the door to his home open.

Sean's words were hurried as he addressed Fred Sneel. "Thanks again for agreeing to help us—"

"I'm delighted to help Lily in any way I can," Sneel replied. "Just tell me what to do, Sean."

"There's an entrance on the side of the building which is wheelchair accessible. Try to arrive early if you can. The place will be mobbed with press and anyone else who's been following the story. I don't want to run the risk of Dr. Lesnesky being recognized."

"I understand." Sneel nodded. "Where do I take Dr. Lesnesky and Dr. Hunt once we're there?"

"I'll telephone Ms. Roemer once we're en route," George told him. "She'll have someone meet us."

Sean's gaze dropped to Lesnesky, who was looking skeletal thin in his wheelchair. His eyes were sunken, like deep-shadowed caverns, his skin gray and parchment brittle. "We're grateful that you've decided to do this, Dr. Lesnesky. We'll find an office where you can wait as comfortably as possible."

Lesnesky gave a mirthless laugh. "You can stick me in a broom closet—I'm beyond feeling comfortable. I just want to clear my conscience before I meet my Maker."

Sean nodded. "I understand," he said quietly.

His anger toward Lesnesky had dissipated over the last few days. It hadn't been too hard to convince him to come and testify—Lesnesky's guilt over sabotaging the reef study consumed him as much as the cancer laying waste to his body. The doctors gave him only a few weeks to live.

What had clinched Lesnesky's decision was when Sean and George Hunt told him about Lily's accident. He'd been horror-stricken that a fellow scientist's life had been endangered because of him. Lesnesky realized that this was his only chance to make amends for what he'd done—that he'd chosen to admit his crimes publicly conferred upon him a tragic dignity.

After exchanging good-byes, Sean got in his car and headed for town hall. Weary bitterness filled him as he thought of Lesnesky and how the reef study had become a sordid mess of corruption and lies. One that had tainted so much and so many.

What grieved Sean most was that it had hurt Lily—physically as well as professionally. He had to do what he could to restore Lily's image as a scientist whose reputation was beyond reproach.

Of course, his own career was in free-fall, Sean reflected with a kind of cynical detachment. Even if everything went according to Sean's carefully laid plans, it wouldn't stop his political enemies from accusing him of professional and ethical misconduct in harassing the head scientist of the research team.

He was fully aware that his adamant refusal to subject Lily to the cruel glare of the media was destroying his chances for reelection. Indeed, with each damning article, the cry that he should step aside so another candidate could run grew louder.

How ironic that a few short hours after the reef advisory meeting today, Sean would have to attend the gala fund-raiser that was supposed to be the kickoff for his reelection campaign.

Sickened and disgusted by the smear tactics being used against him, a part of him was sorely tempted to toss in the towel. He could march up to the podium tonight, thank the assembled guests for coming to support him, then inform them that he would not be seeking a second term as mayor. *Good night, folks, enjoy the champagne without me.*

But to quit would mean to leave the town where he'd been born and bred, the town that he loved, vulnerable to the avaricious machinations of more schemers like Pete Ferrucci. And that was unacceptable. So Sean would stand and fight, and pray that he could also protect Lily and their newfound love from being destroyed.

"What are all these TV crews doing here outside town hall?" Lily asked, stunned.

Karen was sitting beside her in the passenger seat. Her lips tightened as she stared at the throng of people milling about. "Dave said the media would probably be covering the reef meeting, what with your accident on the reef and all." She coughed to clear her throat. "He suggested we use the back entrance on Water Street."

Without another word, Lily bypassed the town hall parking lot and drove around the corner, leaving the camera crews in her rearview mirror. Her palms left a film of sweat upon the steering wheel as it slid between her hands.

She was more nervous than she'd ever been in her life.

She and Simone had spent a marathon session holed up in May Ellen's den, working on Lily's reef report for the committee, with Kaye and May Ellen providing fortifying meals and glasses filled to the brim with Hal's special protein shakes. Whenever Lily felt too drained to continue, she'd stumble over to the sofa, sleep for an hour, and return to work.

Yesterday, Karen's slides had been delivered. While Karen still mourned the loss of her stolen film, the pictures she'd taken during the storm showed very clearly the diseases that were attacking the coral.

Lily's final report was solid, buttressed by photographic documentation, by the data she'd compiled of both core and water samples, and by the charts showing tide and current patterns. But although her assessment contained all the necessary evidence to stop the development plan, Lily knew it could nonetheless fail to convince the committee members. Never before had it been so important to her that a committee accept and concur with her findings.

It seemed as though years had passed rather than a few short weeks since Lily had walked down the hall that led to the conference room. She'd been nervous before, filled with dread at having to confront Sean McDermott. She was a hundred times more anxious now. And Sean's was the only face she longed to see.

At the threshold, she hesitated, her eyes widening with shock. The conference room was packed. She couldn't even make out the U-shaped table at the front, where the committee members would sit. Karen stood rigidly beside her, equally unwilling to enter the crowded room.

Sean must have been watching for her. For suddenly he was wending his way toward them, his eyes fixed on Lily. By the time he reached them, Lily felt the first prick of tears.

Sean took her hand in his, for all appearances shaking it. But no simple handshake ever felt so electrifying. Lily blinked, thinking the tears of joy in her eyes were making her see stars, then realized that flashbulbs were popping around the room, aimed at Sean and her.

Her hand still in his, Sean stepped further back into the hall. Then, in a voice pitched low, for her ears alone, he said, "Are you okay? Are you sure you're up to this?"

Lily felt his concerned gaze sweep over her face. She'd spent extra time on her appearance today, using her makeup to conceal the fatigue still shadowing her features.

Sean looked wearied, too. There were lines of strain etched around the corners of his mouth. Her heart aching for him, she smiled reassuringly.

"I'm fine. I just have a pretty bad case of stage fright," she admitted with a shaky laugh. "But I can do it."

"I know you can. You're incredible, Lily," Sean said with solemn conviction. He squeezed her fingers gently. "Listen, don't worry if things get ugly really fast today. Above all, don't let Ferrucci rile you—"

"Sean." It was Evelyn Roemer. "Everyone's here."

"Right." The lines in Sean's face deepened. With a final, reassuring squeeze, he let go of Lily's hand. "Let's get the meeting started."

McDermott had reintroduced Banyon to the committee with stiff formality—*as if everyone in the room hadn't figured out the two of them were screwing like rabbits,* Ferrucci thought, choking back laughter. No, he couldn't laugh, much as he wanted to. That would be hardly appropriate behavior for the future mayor of Coral Beach.

Ferrucci didn't try to hide his smirk, however, as Banyon rose from her seat and walked over to the lectern. He leaned back in his chair and twirled his silver fountain pen between his fingers. He was going to bide his time and wait for the perfect moment to strike.

Lily had succeeded in conquering her attack of nerves by pretending that she and Sean were alone in the room. Her laptop was already set up, resting on the lectern, humming quietly. With a quick glance over her shoulder to check that she wasn't blocking the projection screen, Lily began her report to the coral reef advisory committee.

In a voice that grew increasingly confident, she explained what the team had found during their weeks of research. Using the computer's three-dimensional rendering of the patch reef to orient the committee members, she pointed out different sections of the reef and the condition of the coral that grew there.

But when the moment came for her to discuss the southern section of zone one, where the hot spot was located, Lily paused, her mouth suddenly as dry as cotton. Reaching for her glass of water, she stole a glance at Sean.

Although his expression was utterly impassive, his eyes were fixed on her. They gleamed, golden and intense. *You're incredible, Lily.* Sean's words came to her again.

She cleared her throat. "While a good portion of the town's reef does seem to be thriving, there is a very serious development that I and my team discovered in the course of our study. We found that the southernmost section of zone one has been attacked by disease."

As Lily clicked the mouse of her computer, she was

aware that the noise level in the conference room had altered. A buzz of surprise had started. "Ladies and gentlemen," she said, raising her voice slightly so that it cut through the noise. "If you would please direct your attention to the graph behind me. This graph shows the compositional breakdown of the sediment samples taken from the hot spot. Please note the high concentration of heavy metals and petroleum by-products."

Lily paused, giving the committee members time to read the graph and understand the numbers, and drew a deep steadying breath. "I realize that what I'm showing you here—the high levels of pollutants in this section of the reef—comes as a great surprise to you all. More disturbing still, however, is that these contaminants have affected the health of the coral and other marine life forms. Allow me to show you slides of the hot spot taken by my photographer, Karen Masur. They reveal only too well the destruction caused by these diseases. Diseases," she repeated heavily, "that will spread to other areas of the reef if preventive measures are not taken."

What the hell was going on? Ferrucci wondered, shifting angrily in his chair. Had Granger fucked up or had Banyon and her pea-brained photographer managed to collect samples and take the photographs in that damned storm? He'd gone and questioned Owen Rafern himself, who'd done nothing but blubber about how badly hurt Banyon had been.

How the fuck had they gotten samples and photographs?

Ferrucci could feel the concern spreading among the other committee members as they listened to Banyon describe the different types of disease afflicting the coral.

According to Banyon, they were all diseases that previous research had shown could be linked to man-made pollutants. Ferrucci's anger grew with each slide she presented.

"Members of the reef committee," she said, after showing them a picture of a brain coral covered with thick algal growth, "upon discovering the hot spot, I went to the marina and collected samples of the water and sediment there. Please take a look now at a comparison of core samples from the marina and from zone one."

The photograph of the brain coral was replaced by two charts that appeared side by side on the projection screen. Underlined in red were two pollutants common to both the marina and the hot spot: petroleum and traces of a type of heavy metal that was used in the waterproof paint on the hulls of boats.

"After studying these sediment analyses, it is my considered opinion that the outflow from the Intracoastal Waterway has carried these hazardous elements from the marina and deposited them over this section of the reef. I have—"

I have to stop her, Ferrucci thought, enraged. If she kept talking, his plans for the marina would be ruined. Nobody would vote to double the marina's size if it was thought that the source of the problem causing the damned coral to die came from there.

Ferrucci lurched to his feet. "Excuse me, Dr. Banyon," he said loudly, ignoring the collective murmur of surprise circulating the room.

As startled as the others, Lily immediately looked over to Sean. As chairman, it was his decision whether or not to reprimand Ferrucci for interrupting the speaker.

Their eyes met and he gave the slightest shake of his head. Lily then recalled the advice he'd given her before the meeting, not to allow Ferrucci to rattle her. Obviously the "ugly" part of the meeting had begun. "I believe you had something to say, Mr. Ferrucci?" she said stiffly.

"Yes, I do. I'd like you to tell us why we should give any credence to what you're saying. Those samples, those photographs, they could have come from anywhere."

She gave a gasp of shock as Ferrucci's words registered. Though she'd been expecting some sort of objection from him, Lily felt herself pale at his blatant accusation. "I assure you, Mr. Ferrucci, that these samples came from zone one of Coral Beach's patch reef. I collected them myself."

"Gosh, I know you'd like me to believe that," he replied with a condescending drawl. "But I can't. Not when I and everyone else in this room know how *involved* you and Mayor McDermott are."

Lily's eyes narrowed dangerously. "What are you implying—"

"I don't think I need to spell that out, Dr. Banyon." He smirked as he glanced about the room. "Let's just say I refuse to give any weight to this nonsense you've been telling us—nor should anyone else in this room—not after we've had a scientist carefully monitoring the reef for the greater part of a year. . . ." Ferrucci's voice died away, suddenly aware of a commotion at the back of the room. The other committee members, Banyon, too, were no longer listening.

He looked over to where their attention was directed. Fear stopped his heart, and then sent it racing madly.

"Why, Mr. Ferrucci, you look like you've seen a

ghost." Sean's voice, though quiet, reached the far corners of the conference room. "Please continue, Mr. Ferrucci. I believe you were talking about Dr. Lesnesky. You know, I had a feeling you might mention his study today, so I arranged for him to come and address the committee himself."

Lily was glad she was holding on to the lectern. Her legs were none too steady. What was George Hunt doing here? And how did he come to be here with this frail man in the wheelchair—this obviously desperately ill man, whom Sean had identified as none other than Abe Lesnesky. And the biggest mystery of all, when and how had Sean arranged to bring Dr. Lesnesky to the coral reef meeting? *What was going on?* she wondered wildly.

"Dr. Banyon," Sean said, penetrating her confused thoughts.

With an effort she collected herself. "Yes, Mayor McDermott?" answered Lily, pleased that her voice betrayed none of her confusion.

"If you'll be generous enough to excuse a second interruption, I believe Dr. Lesnesky would like to tell the members of this committee and the townspeople exactly why his study didn't reveal any indication of disease in the southern section of zone one."

"Of course," she replied with equal formality.

"Thank you." Sean inclined his head. "And on behalf of this entire committee, let me add that you have the town of Coral Beach's sincere gratitude for having conducted such a thorough and systematic study. Most of us here are aware that you and your team took extraordinary measures to obtain the samples and photographs we saw today. Your commitment to this project and to protecting the environment is exemplary." Around the room, applause started, and Sean joined in.

Lily pressed her trembling lips together and nodded in acknowledgment before walking over to her seat next to Karen.

Karen was struggling to hide a grin of triumph. Lily leaned close to her and whispered heatedly, "What's going on here?"

"You'll see. Sean went to New York while you were in the hospital. He did—" Karen cut her reply short.

Sean had just motioned for George and Lesnesky to approach.

"By the way, Mr. Ferrucci," he said, as George pushed Lesnesky to the very front of the room. "It might interest you to know that Police Chief Reynolds has already had a long talk with Dr. Lesnesky."

Lily saw Ferrucci's face turn ashen with fear.

Her gaze flew to Sean. He gave a quick nod, confirming her suspicions. She pressed her hand to her mouth, muffling her gasp of astonished outrage as the pieces of the puzzle fell into place.

But as she sat and listened to Abe Lesnesky's halting speech, Lily felt tears prick the back of her eyes. Although she was overwhelmed with relief that the fraud had been exposed and her own study vindicated, she was also horribly saddened by this dying man's heartbreaking confession.

When Lesnesky finished, the conference room erupted in pandemonium. Reporters rushed forward, trying to reach Lily, Sean, and Lesnesky. Two uniformed officers were already escorting Pete Ferrucci from the room.

Sean reached her before the reporters did. "Come on,

Lily," he said, grabbing her hand. "Don't worry about Lesnesky. George and Evelyn will take care of him."

In a mad dash, Sean led her through a maze of halls and doors. She was breathless by the time they finally reached the rear entrance.

A smile lit his handsome face as he turned to her. "God, you were fantastic, Lily. How are you feeling?"

Before she could reply, before she could catch her breath, Sean's mouth was covering hers.

Instinctively she pressed closer, her lips parting in eager welcome. His answering groan had her smiling against his lips.

His expression was achingly tender as he raised his head to smile back at her.

"Let's get you home, away from this zoo," he murmured. His fingers caressed her face. "You're still a little too pale for my peace of mind."

"I *am* a little woozy, but that's probably from shock," she said. "Sean, will you tell me what's been going on? How did you manage to get Lesnesky to confess to manipulating the study? It was so sad listening to him, the poor man. I nearly cried when he said that he wanted to donate the money Ferrucci had paid him to the town. And what was George doing—" She stopped in midsentence. Sean had uttered a string of curses. "What's the matter?" she asked, alarmed.

"More reporters," he said. "They're heading this way. I don't think we can avoid them. Listen, Lily, just follow my lead. You don't have to say a word to them."

It was intensely intimidating being surrounded this way. She and Sean had nearly reached the car when the group of reporters descended upon them, bringing her and Sean to a reluctant halt.

They were shouting questions and snapping pictures. Lily saw video cameras aimed directly at her, like hostile eyes. The questions were coming so fast and furious Lily didn't catch half of them.

Then one reporter out-shouted the others. "Dr. Banyon, can you give us a statement about whether you intend to press charges against Mayor McDermott?"

"What?" she gasped, stunned.

Impossibly, the shouting got louder, a relentless roar in her ears. Everything around her began to move in a strange slow-motion. She watched Sean step forward, placing himself between her and the reporters.

"Dr. Banyon has no comment on this issue, nor will she ever." His voice sliced through the noise, the anger in it forceful enough to part the pack of reporters. Sean took advantage of their momentary reprieve to rush Lily toward the car.

Removing the keys from her nerveless fingers, he opened the door for her. Numbly, she slid behind the wheel.

He leaned over as he closed the door. "Go home, Lily," he instructed, his tone harried. "I'm sorry, I can't come with you now—they'd only follow us. I'll do what I can to keep the press from hounding you."

Lily walked into May Ellen's kitchen. Her grandmother and Anne Prentiss were watching TV. They'd turned on the local newscast. As soon as she saw Lily, though, May Ellen reached for the remote. Lily stopped her.

"No," she said, her voice flat and lifeless. "Let me see it, Granny."

The TV crews at town hall must have been filming live, she thought absently as she sank into the chair, her eyes glued to the screen. It was funny how something appeared on the other side of the TV, on the other side of a camera lens. She looked pale and frightened as the reporter thrust the mike toward her, demanding to know if she intended to press charges; Sean looked as if he were about to explode with rage.

The clip ended with her driving away and Sean storming back toward the building. The newscaster took up the story. "While Dr. Banyon refuses to comment on the accusation of harassment and intimidation that she made against Mayor McDermott last week, the scandal has already begun to affect the Mayor's political standing. Our sources inform us that these charges could force the mayor to bow out of the upcoming mayoral race. We'll have more news for you after the break." The face of the news anchor was replaced by a commercial for laundry detergent.

Lily laid her head on her grandmother's kitchen table and wept.

May Ellen looked at Lily, whose shoulders were shaking with the force of her sobs, and her own eyes brimmed with tears. May Ellen stood, and, from a cupboard, took down three highball glasses. Anne rose, too, and fetched the whiskey bottle from the liquor cabinet.

Laying a hand on Lily's shoulder, May Ellen shook it gently but insistently. "Lily, sit up."

Anne set a glass of whiskey before her. "Drink this, Lily. You need it." Then added dryly, "We all need it."

The whiskey had definite restorative qualities. By the time Lily had swallowed half of it, she was able to look Anne Prentiss in the eye. "I can't begin to tell you how terrible I feel, Anne. I didn't mean any of those things I said." She cringed as she recalled the words she'd hurled at Sean. "I was consumed with jealousy, angry because I'd seen him with Stacy Malloy."

But Lily knew that was no excuse at all, and berated herself for her stupidity. Sean was an elected official, and she'd accused him in a public place of harassment.

"I only wish I'd known about this earlier," she whispered brokenly, hanging her head. "I would have tried to stop it."

"Sean wouldn't let us tell you what was happening," May Ellen told her. "He was so worried about you when you got hurt during the storm."

"The entire situation has caused a terrible mess," Anne said fretfully. "How I wish there wasn't this silly fundraiser tonight. You know politics, my dear. No one's going to contribute to Sean's campaign financially if they think their candidate won't make it out of the starting gate."

"The gala's tonight?" She'd had no idea. Of course, when Stacy Malloy had mentioned the date, it hadn't really registered. Lily had assumed she'd already be long gone, working on her reef regeneration project in Lucaya.

She guessed immediately why neither Sean nor anyone else had mentioned the gala to her until now. Sean had wanted to protect her from the media's feeding frenzy. And there was bound to be lots of reporters covering tonight's fund-raiser.

Her breath caught as a seed of hope unfurled inside her. "Are there speeches scheduled for the fund-raiser?"

"Why, yes." Anne nodded. "There are still *some* people who want to talk about the good Sean's done for this town!"

Lily jumped to her feet. "I've got to call Evelyn Roemer right away. Granny, where's Kaye?"

"Why, she's over at Dana's, of course. Probably watching the news."

"Can you call her on your phone and ask her to meet me at Fiona Gray's? I'm going to need her and Fiona's killer instincts." She turned to Anne. "I am so sorry for the hurt I've caused. You have a wonderful grandson and I'm desperately in love with him. I hope you don't mind if I shout it from the rooftops."

Her hazel eyes misting, Anne hugged Lily. "Of course not. You go right ahead, Lily." She pulled back to smile at her. "And you know he loves you just as deeply."

"Yes," Lily replied, thinking of all Sean had done for her. "Yes, I do know."

May Ellen was beaming with happiness. "It just took you both a while to understand what some of us have known all along. Once we get this nasty business sorted out, Anne and I will begin planning a lovely wedding for the two of you—"

"Of course, we'll have to let Dana and Kaye think they're the ones organizing it," Anne said with a sigh.

Lily grinned, not fooled for a second. "You know, I'm beginning to realize that the two of you have a great deal of talent when it comes to gently guiding people so they do exactly what you want."

"Why, Lily, whatever gave you that idea? True, we might have rung that lovely George Hunt a few times," May Ellen admitted with a girlish laugh.

"But we had to!" Anne chimed in. "We just couldn't wait much longer to be great-grandmothers."

"I'll pass that on to Sean," Lily promised solemnly.

"There's a good girl."

CHAPTER FORTY

The enormous double doors to the hotel's ballroom were shut. Lily paused in front them and drew a breath to quiet the million butterflies fluttering in her stomach. She turned and gave a quick hug to Kaye and Simone. "Wish me luck. I've never done anything quite like this before."

"Think of it as a new role, Madame Mayor," Simone suggested with a teasing grin.

"You'll knock their socks off, Lily," Kaye predicted.

"That's because you and Fiona are geniuses. Thanks for everything you've done, Kaye. I'm glad to have you as a friend." Lily smiled.

"Go on with you," Kaye laughed shakily, "before we all ruin our mascara."

Lily opened the door and slipped inside.

Large round tables filled the ballroom with elegantly dressed people clustered around them. The guests were clapping in a round of polite applause for the last speaker.

Lily swallowed nervously, smoothed her hands against the cool crepe de chine fabric, and began winding her way toward the podium, her head held high. As she passed by, excited whispers flew from table to table. The guests had recognized her. From the far side of the room, bulbs began flashing. Deliberately, Lily made her smile extra warm and looked straight at the camera lenses trained on her.

Seated at the center table, his back to the doors, Sean felt a sudden jolt of awareness course through him—that was as shocking as it was familiar. In stunned disbelief, he turned around in his chair.

Dressed like a goddess in a delicate shade of ivory that set her skin aglow and turned her hair into a halo of light, Lily was a vision of enchanting loveliness. Sean could only stare as his heart beat loudly, calling out to her.

Her eyes sought his as she came ever nearer. She held his gaze as her smile went from warm to radiant. Then, to Sean's astonishment, she continued past his table and stepped up to the podium.

"Good evening, ladies and gentlemen," she said in a voice that rang with confidence. "My name is Lily Banyon, and as anyone who has read the papers this past week can tell you, I have a lot to say about Sean McDermott." She paused, a mischievous smile playing about her lips as she let her dry words sink in. Her smile grew as she heard a scattering of startled laughs from the listeners.

"What you wouldn't know from either the papers or the TV, is that Sean and I are very close. Knowing Sean as well as I do, I could talk about him all night. I could tell you how committed he is to keeping this town a wonderful, beautiful place to live and to raise families. But you've already heard that tonight, in speech after speech. I could also tell you how brilliant Sean is, but I know tomorrow's papers are going to be filled with articles recounting how Sean exposed an attempt to destroy scientific evidence by one of the members of the coral reef committee. So that brings me to the real reason I am here before you tonight."

Lily paused to send a quick prayer heavenward that her gambit would work. So very much was riding on it.

"Ladies and gentlemen, I stand before you tonight because Sean McDermott can be positively infuriating. Sometimes he actually believes he can tell me what to do!" Lily exclaimed, infusing mock outrage into her voice. "Oh, yes, it's true," she said and nodded vigorously. "I've been trying to break him of this annoying habit all our lives. Haven't I, Sean?"

She looked at him with an angelic smile.

Sean's grin split his face. "Yes, dear, whatever you say," he replied with just the right touch of meekness to his tone.

"That's very good, Sean," Lily said approvingly. The assembled guests whooped with mirth.

When the laughter had subsided, Lily spoke again, and now her tone was earnest, simple and direct. "Last week, Sean and I were having one of these very silly disagreements. Unfortunately, someone overheard us. And that person used my words to hurt Sean's career. Those words, ladies and gentlemen, were spoken in private and were *never* intended to reflect on Sean's public role as mayor of Coral Beach," Lily said, letting her gaze travel to the farthest reaches of the ballroom. "Now, you all know what a fine and principled man Sean is. I'm sure you're equally aware that he is someone who's fiercely protective of the people and things he loves. That's why he is such an outstanding mayor. So you won't be surprised to learn that Sean decided to protect me from the very scandal I had unintentionally caused. His desire to shield me from public scrutiny came at a great cost to himself—too great. Tonight I hope you've realized what a fine man Sean McDermott is, and how much this town needs him. And I hope, too, that tonight this other unpleasantness has been laid to rest. Forever." Here, Lily stopped, allowing her words to settle over the room, then bestowed upon the guests her most dazzling smile as their hearty applause answered her words.

As the clapping echoed throughout the vast room, Sean felt as if his heart might burst. He couldn't believe what Lily had done for him. She'd single-handedly defused the scandal with a stellar mix of candid charm and clever wit. He wanted to rush up to her and take her in his arms. But he waited. This was her show, and from that special gleam in her eye Sean knew the finale would be worth hearing.

Lily raised her hand to quiet the applause. "Thank you. Ladies and gentlemen, I have just one more thing to say about the candidate tonight. He's a man who keeps his promises." She paused to look directly at Sean, and her heart began to hammer as he returned her look and gave her a smile—that was for her alone. It was the smile his face wore when he was deep inside her and she was trembling all around him. When Lily spoke again, her voice was husky, filled with desire for this wonderful man. "Now I have a promise I'd like to make in return. It is this . . . that I love Sean McDermott, and will continue to love him for the rest of my life. But he has to marry me—our grandmothers said so!" Lily's words came tumbling in a rush as Sean raced toward her to claim her in a passionate embrace.

* * *

The guests were still on their feet, cheering good-naturedly, when the strains of "I've Got You Under My Skin," floated into the room. Hand in hand, Sean led Lily to the dance floor.

"You are the most extraordinary woman in the world," he whispered. "By the way, I accept your proposal of marriage, Dr. Banyon," he said, capturing her lips again as their bodies began to move as one across the dance floor. "Though I'm somewhat annoyed you beat me to it." He grinned at her look of surprise. Then, his right hand releasing her waist, Sean pulled out a slender, velvet box from his pocket. Their feet stilled as he opened it for her. Nestled inside was a marquis diamond. It flashed, reflecting the lights shining from above. Lily's hand trembled beneath his as he slipped the ring onto her finger.

"I was working out the kinks in my plan to abduct you," he told her. "I was going to hold you hostage until you agreed to my every demand."

"And they are?"

"To love me forever."

"You're so easy, McDermott," she teased. "How about we abduct each other? I know this lovely cottage in the Bahamas we can rent for a couple weeks."

"This sounds very tempting." His fingers splayed across her lower back, pressing her against him. "We could work on your project—"

"That's right. And start on another one—one I think you'll be quite enthusiastic about." Smiling, she leaned closer to whisper in his ear. Pulling back slightly, she thrilled at the naked hunger stamped on his face. "It seems the grandmothers would like to be 'great,' " she added with a grin.

"Well, then, we'd better get to work right away."

"I have some other projects in mind, too." Lily said. "There's a certain town in Florida which is crying out for a study on reef regeneration. My boss wants me to start working on a book."

"Are you sure, Lily?" he asked, looking deep into her eyes. "Are you sure this is what you want?"

"I've never wanted anything more in my life. I love you so much, Sean," she said, sealing her words with the sweetness of her kiss. Then, her smile turned mischievous as she warned, "But I hope you realize I'll make a terrible politician's wife."

"No. You'll be perfect, because you're perfect for me." His arms tightened about her. "I love you, Lily."

Lily smiled, basking in the light that shone in his eyes. "You know, Sean, it's a beautiful night. And the storm is past. It's an absolutely perfect night for night swimming."

Subscribe to the new Pillow Talk e-newsletter—and receive all these fabulous online features directly in your e-mail inbox:

♥ Exclusive essays and other features by major romance writers like Linda Howard, Kristin Hannah, Julie Garwood, and Suzanne Brockmann

♥ Exciting behind-the-scenes news from our romance editors

♥ Special offers, including contests to win signed romance books and other prizes

♥ Author tour information, and monthly announcements about the newest books on sale

♥ A Pillow Talk readers forum, featuring feedback from romance fans...like you!

Two easy ways to subscribe:
Go to **www.ballantinebooks.com/PillowTalk**
or send a blank e-mail to
join-PillowTalk@list.randomhouse.com.

Pillow Talk—
the romance e-newsletter brought to you by
Ballantine Books